Damnation

CARRIE LEIGHTON

sourcebooks
casablanca

Copyright © 2023, 2025 by Carrie Leighton
Cover and internal design © 2025 by Sourcebooks, Inc.
Cover design by Elsie Lyons
Cover images © Miguel Sobreira/Arcangel

Sourcebooks and the colophon are registered trademarks of Sourcebooks.

All rights reserved. No part of this book may be reproduced in any form or by any electronic or mechanical means including information storage and retrieval systems—except in the case of brief quotations embodied in critical articles or reviews—without permission in writing from its publisher, Sourcebooks.

No part of this book may be used or reproduced in any manner for the purpose of training artificial intelligence technologies or systems.

Originally published as *Better. Dannazione* © 2023 Adriano Salani Editore s.u.r.l. Milano, Gruppo Editoriale Mauri Spagnol. Translated from Italian by Nicole M. Taylor.

This book was translated thanks to a grant awarded by the Italian Ministry of Foreign Affairs and International Cooperation.

Excerpt of *Collision* has been translated with the contribution of the Center for Books and Reading of the Italian Ministry of Culture, © 2025. All rights reserved.

The characters and events portrayed in this book are fictitious or are used fictitiously. Any similarity to real persons, living or dead, is purely coincidental and not intended by the author.

All brand names and product names used in this book are trademarks, registered trademarks, or trade names of their respective holders. Sourcebooks is not associated with any product or vendor in this book.

Published by Sourcebooks Casablanca, an imprint of Sourcebooks
1935 Brookdale RD, Naperville, IL 60563-2773
(630) 961-3900
sourcebooks.com

Originally published as *Better. Dannazione* in 2023 in Italy by Adriano Salani Editore s.u.r.l. Milano, an imprint of Gruppo Editoriale Mauri Spagnol.

Cataloging-in-Publication Data is on file with the Library of Congress.

Printed and bound in Canada.
MBP 10 9 8 7 6 5 4 3 2 1

*For those who, after a thousand falls, still
have the courage to try again.*

For those who have discovered within their weakness the strength to fight back.

For those who have fought for love and found it wasn't enough.

For those who are constantly at war with their demons.

*And for those who were broken by those demons,
losing a part of themselves forever.*

*Remember, there is a ray of sunlight waiting to shine on you.
All you have to do is look skywards and let it light you up.*

Prologue

I HAVE A CLEAR MEMORY of my seventh birthday.

We had a party at our house for all of my school friends. While the other children were playing in the yard, I hung back. Alex smeared dirt on my nose, trying to make me laugh, but he didn't succeed. The sun was setting and Mom called us in to blow out the candles; that's when I started to protest. The guests were ready for cake, the living room was all set up for the highlight of the party.

But I wanted my father.

I didn't care that Mom was there. And my grandparents. And all my classmates and my friends from the neighborhood. I wanted him.

He had promised me that he would be there, and he always kept his promises.

I remember asking Mom where he was, and she told me that a last-minute accident had him stuck at work, but he was on his way.

Then, that very moment, as if by magic, I heard the doorknob click, and my father's shape appeared in the doorway.

My eyes lit up with joy, and then, with a toothy grin, I ran to him and jumped into his arms. The long curls that fell down my back swayed, and my father's perfectly groomed beard rubbed my cheek as he peppered me with kisses, making me laugh out loud.

I was happy.

Dad hung his coat up on the rack in the entranceway and greeted

Mom with a kiss on the cheek and the rest of the guests with a warm smile as I played with his dark curls. I loved them so much. Then he made me get down and brought me over to the table. Only then did I allow my mother to bring out the cake—strictly pistachio flavored—and light the candles. I puffed out my cheeks and blew as hard as I could. And, with my eyes closed, I made a wish: that everything would stay just as it was.

The next day, my mother kept me out of the house all afternoon, distracting me with a trip to the playground, a candy binge, and a long nature walk. It was April, blue-sky'd and mild. When we got home, I saw that Dad was already waiting there for us. He picked me up and told me he had a surprise for me. I squealed with delight and inundated him with questions. He laughed; he laughed *loudly*. My inability to stifle my curiosity amused him. Mom watched us, looking a little bored as always.

Dad started climbing the stairs—my surprise was waiting for us in my room. He stopped in front of my closed door and set me down on the floor. He was shaking and his eyes were wet, so I wiped his tears away and reassured him, just like he did me whenever I was upset. He kissed me on the forehead and told me to count to three.

One…
Two…
Three…

He opened the door, and I was astounded. It was like a dream. I went in and walked around slowly, thinking that this couldn't possibly be my room. My room had always been bare; I didn't even have curtains. All I had was my wrought-iron bed and the wardrobe we got secondhand. The paint was peeling off the walls from moisture, and I had only plastic laundry baskets to serve as toy boxes.

The room before my eyes, however, looked like something out of a magazine. Walls the color of wisteria blossoms with clean white baseboards, a huge wardrobe, and a bed with a canopy, covered in soft toys. And there on the wall across from the door was a large bookcase.

I felt like a princess in her castle; I was so happy, I burst into tears.

Thanks to a recent promotion at work, my dad had been able to renovate my room and turn it into a masterpiece. He knelt down until he was eye to eye with me and asked if I liked my surprise. I nodded and hugged him so tightly. That evening, after eating dinner and playing with some of the birthday presents I had received, I ran upstairs to my window—my favorite place. I pulled aside my new curtain and let my mind wander as I watched the starry sky.

I loved looking out that window. I did it every evening when Dad came home from work and every morning when he left. I could see his car pulling into the driveway, and he knew I was already there, waiting for him. Every time, he raised his head and smiled up at me.

It became our private ritual, a ritual that should have lasted forever.

Instead, eight years later, I watched him walk down that driveway for the last time, two heavy suitcases in tow. He looked up at me, but he wasn't smiling anymore.

It was the day he had decided to leave us.

To leave Mom.

To leave the house.

And to leave me.

Then he was gone.

Forever.

PART ONE

PART ONE

One

HERE I REMAIN, WITH TEARS in my eyes and dead leaves stuck to the soles of my shoes. I stare at the empty place in front of me, where, up until a few minutes ago, Thomas was.

He's gone.

Unable to process what just happened, I drag myself up on to the porch, slide my bag off my shoulder, and dump it on the step before sitting down and closing my eyes for a moment. But even then, all I see is him.

His look of disappointment, resentment, and guilt. It was my own guilt I saw reflected in him. Guilt for not listening to him, for not believing him. For always being so naive and needing to be *good*. A warm, moist wind ruffles my hair, sending unruly black locks all around my face. I start to gather my hair into a ponytail before I realize that I no longer have a hair tie on my wrist. Great, I must have lost it somewhere.

My God, how stupid can I be?

How did I end up in this situation? How could I let this happen to me?

I rub my temples; I can feel a migraine coming on as I try to piece together the scattered fragments of the last few hours. Everything seems so confused and nonsensical. I remember confessing to Logan that I had feelings for Thomas and then storming indignantly to the door after the nasty things Logan said about him. But I also remember being coaxed into staying. He didn't want to be alone, he told me. And I let myself be swayed by his pleading tone. So we started watching TV, and then... it's a total blank...

A flash of lightning illuminates the sky, tearing the darkness into pieces. The thunder that follows makes the porch railing vibrate. I lift my face to watch the rain pour down. Where is Thomas going? Possible answers to that question terrify me. A small part of me is afraid that I already know exactly what he'll do.

Another, more powerful roll of thunder makes me jolt. It's as though the sky is agreeing with my silent, heartbreaking assumption. With my brain reeling from all sorts of repugnant imaginings and my soul in an uproar, I pull out my cell phone and try to call Thomas. But after just two rings, it goes to voicemail, which only reminds me how much I hate communicating via phone. I sigh and squeeze my eyes shut in frustration before I start mangling my fingernails. *Calm down, Vanessa. Relax. He's not Travis. He's not going to go hop into someone else's bed while I'm alone here. He won't do it.*

Right?

I pick up my phone again, but this time I try to contact the one person who can give me the answers I need. Or at least I hope so.

"Nessy?" Tiffany answers after just a few rings, sounding alarmed. How can I blame her? I'd be worried too if I got a call from her in the middle of the night. In the background on her end, however, I hear a cacophony of music and indistinct voices. As I figured, she's at the party Thomas mentioned earlier.

"Hey, Tiff, do you have a minute?"

"Sure. Are you okay? What's up?"

For a moment, I'm tempted to tell her everything, but upon thinking about it, I restrict myself to the bare minimum. I'll be able to explain more fully tomorrow.

"Nothing you need to worry about. Actually, I just wanted to know..." I sniffle and try to calm myself down. "Y-you're at a party, right?"

"Yeah, Carol threw a movie party. It was supposed to be a quiet night in, but it quickly turned into a zoo," she complains, moving away from the noise. "But why do you ask?"

"Well, I...I wanted to know if, by any chance, Thomas was around?"

"Around?" is her bewildered reply. "Why on earth would he be here without you knowing about it?" She pauses thoughtfully, then exclaims: "Wait a minute... Don't tell me he's being an idiot again. That's it, isn't it? God, if I see him, he's dead. I swear, I'm gonna grab him by that Danny Zuko hair of his and make him wish he'd never—"

I break in, hesitant. "It was me. I'm the one being an idiot this time."

"What?"

"I did something stupid. Really, really stupid," I admit. "He got mad and just took me home without saying another word. I haven't been able to contact him since." I rest a hand over my eyes and, heartbroken, hang my head. "He was completely beside himself when he left, and now he's not answering my calls, and you know how he is... You know what happens when he gets angry. He can't think straight, and he winds up doing stupid things. I'm afraid he might..." The mere idea of Thomas sleeping with someone else makes the words wither in my mouth. I take a deep breath, forcing myself to shove that nightmare scenario aside.

"It's okay; I get it," Tiffany says, sensing my fears. "Listen, Thomas wasn't here when I got here, but he showed up just before eleven thirty. He only stayed a couple of hours and then left. He seemed tense, honestly, and I haven't seen him since."

I should be relieved that he's not at Carol's party, but instead I'm even more anxious than before. If he's not there, then where is he? I reject out of hand the idea that he might have gone home; he was too angry to hide inside the four walls of his room.

"Do you know where else he might have gone? I mean, it's Monday; I'm guessing there aren't that many other parties going on tonight, right?"

"Maybe at the frat house? I heard Finn was doing something for his birthday."

This is going from bad to worse. If Finn was throwing a party, Thomas surely would have gone, and he's not the only one. An awful idea pops into my head.

"Tiff, do you happen to know if Shana is there?" I ask, biting the inside of my cheek in embarrassment.

"Shana? No, I haven't seen her here. But you know we don't exactly run in the same circles." And that's the moment my heart stops. She's not there. He's not there. *Please, God, just let it be a horrible coincidence.*

"Are you still there?" Tiffany asks me after a prolonged silence.

"Yeah," I answer, taking a deep breath.

"Hey, don't panic. Everything will work out, you'll see." Tiff tries to cheer me up as best she can, but it's useless and she knows that too. I tell her goodbye and end the call while the maelstrom of my thoughts overwhelms me, driving me crazy. Did he go to her? Are they together right now? I shouldn't be surprised if he did; Shana spelled it out for me just a few hours ago: He always comes back to her. And the worst part is, this time, I'm the one who sent him.

My teeth are digging into my lip, my fingers are trembling, and my eyes are burning as I try to call him again, refusing to believe the worst. But he doesn't answer.

Shortly thereafter, the porch light turns on, and the front door opens, my mother peering out from behind it. "Vanessa, what are you doing out there? It's two thirty in the morning and you're all wet; get in the house." Her voice is thick with sleep.

"No, I'm fine out here," I say shortly, not even turning around. I have no intention of pretending that things are okay between us, because they aren't, at all. I'm still hurt about our argument and the insane threats she made, ordering me to cut Thomas out of my life. I'm sure she would be thrilled if she knew about my current situation with him.

"With this cold weather, you're going to get sick," she insists, sitting down next to me and wrapping her fleece robe around herself. I ignore her and try to call Thomas for the umpteenth time. An endless series of rings, one after another, until his voicemail picks up, and I am overwhelmed by a new wave of despondency.

"Listen, Vanessa..." my mother begins. "I know we've been at odds lately. You didn't give me a chance this morning to explain how things are between Victor and me, and I'm very sorry you heard about him moving in from him and not from me. I just want you to understand—"

I turn and interrupt her with a miserable laugh. "'At odds,' you say? Think about it: without considering me in the slightest, you've decided to permanently move a man into our house. A man you've known for, what? A few months? And at the same time, you're backing me into a corner, threatening to take everything away from me just because you don't approve of the boy I'm seeing?" *Or was seeing, anyway*, I point out to myself.

"Must we go over that again?" she retorts, her face hardening.

"Would it do any good? Of course not, because you've already decided that Thomas is no good for me, and nothing's going to change your mind, is it?"

"I guess I wasn't entirely wrong about the boy, if I'm finding my daughter out here crying in the middle of the night, refusing to go inside the house," she informs me contemptuously, talking to me as though I were still a little girl.

I snort loudly. "You think you know everything, don't you?" I ask, glaring at her. "But it's not true. You don't know anything about me, and you don't know anything about him!"

"I don't know anything about you? Don't make me laugh. You are my daughter; no one knows you better than me. Do you think Victor didn't tell me about last night's little visit?" she snaps, giving me a reproachful look. She shuts her eyes and pinches the bridge of her nose while taking a deep breath, as if trying to remain calm. Then, she continues. "Warnings and advice notwithstanding, I am trying to be understanding with you, but it doesn't work this way. You can't just do as you please. This is my house, and the rules I set must be respected, otherwise..."

"Otherwise what?" I provoke her, tired of this constant prevarication.

"Are you going to take away my cell phone? Ban me from watching TV? I'm an adult, and I wish you would start treating me like one."

"'An adult'?" she mimics me sarcastically. "Believe me, you're proving yourself to be anything but adult right now!"

"Just because I'm not bending to your will?"

"No, because you still can't tell right from wrong!"

"And you can? You, who are letting a man I've met *once* move into our house and forcing me to share space with him? You are taking a huge step with someone you know very little about. Does that make you wiser or more *adult* than me?"

"If I didn't trust Victor one hundred percent, I would never have let him into our home. He is a good person."

"So you can say that about him, but I can't say the same about Thomas? Is my judgment of character completely irrelevant?"

"It's not irrelevant, but I am the parent, so what I say goes." She raises her chin with authority, firm in her convictions.

I shake my head, feeling anger burn my cheeks. "And like always, I'm the one who has to give up what I want because someone else says so, right?"

Her silence is answer enough.

"If you cared even a little about me, you would never put me in this position...my God," I say with an exasperated sigh. "I am your daughter; you're supposed to support me, have my back, be happy for me, and love me. Why is that so hard for you to do?"

Mom presses her hands to her chest with a pained expression on her face. "I want what's best for you, but you're too close to the situation to understand that it is not him. I'm sorry, but I'm not going to change my mind about that boy nor about what I expect from you!" Her overbearing tone as she says it is the straw that breaks the camel's back.

I suck in a breath through my nose, teeth gritted. "If you're trying to make me hate you, then congratulations, you're succeeding. But that's nothing new, because apparently making people hate you is what you do best. Just look at Dad: He got so fed up with you, with your tyranny, with your uncontrollable need to micromanage other people's lives as well as your own, that he ran away the moment he had the opportunity! He made a new life for himself. A life that you are not in. And—imagine that—he's happy! Far away from you, everyone is happy. That should tell you something, that you ruin everything you touch!" The words tumble uncontrollably from my mouth with a cruelty I would not have expected from myself.

Then, a fraction of a second later and just as unexpected, I receive a slap so hard that I can feel my cheek burning. My mouth drops open in shock just as my mother's does the same; apparently she's even surprised herself.

"Where is all this...*evil* coming from?" she asks, her voice shaking and her eyes furious. "I didn't think it was possible, but somehow the older you get, the more like him you become..." She studies me with disdain for what seems like an endless moment. Then she averts her eyes, adjusting her fleecy robe against her chest. Wiping a tear away with the back of her hand, she declares, "So you want to be an adult? Fine. Let's see how long you last. I want you out of this house by tomorrow, so you can finally be happy. You've got a job; you've got money; you can make it on your own."

With one hand still pressed to my searing cheekbone, I watch her get up and leave, slamming the door behind her as she goes.

I can't believe she really said that...

I know that I exaggerated. I know that I vented all my anger without thinking. I know my mother saw the end of her marriage as a failure. I watched her lock herself inside the house, humiliated at having been cheated on while my father doted on his new family, showing them all the care and attention that he'd once dedicated to us. All the care and attention that he had then ripped away from us. I know very well that he is the villain in this story. And if she is so cynical and I am so insecure, that's his fault as well. I know all of this because I suffered just as much as she did, and I'm still suffering. But her continued insistence on controlling my life made me lose all control. It's not fair of her to back me into a corner. I was so angry, part of me wanted to hurt her.

And because of that, for the first time, I think that perhaps Thomas and I aren't so different after all.

When the porch light turns off, I feel a stab of pain in my stomach. I squeeze my eyes shut, realizing that in less than an hour, I have managed to make Thomas leave me and goad my mother into kicking me out of my house. I have lost everything in just one evening... I feel the world collapsing in on me.

Exhausted and unable to do anything else, I go to the sofa near the front door and curl up on it in the fetal position. With my cheek resting on the pillow, I try to hold back the sobs that wrack my body, but I fail miserably.

It's all my fault.

It's always my fault...

Two

I HAVE NO IDEA HOW much time has passed when I feel my shoulder being shaken gently. The rain has stopped, leaving the unmistakable smell of petrichor in the air. The breeze has turned into a rather biting wind, but the sky is still dark. Slowly, I open my eyes, which are still burning, and a blurry image materializes in front of me. I frown, and in the nighttime darkness, illuminated only by the streetlamp, there are two soulful eyes staring worriedly back at me. A tattooed hand rests on my hip, which has been covered with a heavy black leather jacket.

"Thomas?" I murmur confusedly, sitting up. "W-what are you doing here?"

"You're shivering," he notes with a frown. He kneels down and rubs his hands over my arms to warm me up. "What are you doing out here?"

"I fell asleep," I say, still a little out of it. I look at him, trying to decipher his mental state. He doesn't seem angry anymore, just tired and worried.

"Out here?" he answers in dismay as he tucks his jacket around my shoulders. Now that he's so close to me, the scent of beer and smoke fills my nostrils. Did he go out drinking? That's a bad sign.

"I needed some air," I lie. I don't want to tell him about what happened. I just want to know where he was and what he did. I am about to ask him when I notice the way his forehead creases as he rests his gaze on my right cheek. He clenches his jaw and runs a knuckle over my cheekbone; I feel a twinge of pain. It's not hard to conclude that I must have a mark there from the slap I took. So I guess too much time couldn't have passed since the argument with my mother. I check the time on my phone next to me and see that it is well after three.

"Who did this?" he asks severely.

"My mother." He raises his eyebrows in surprise, but before he can ask me anything else, I go on the offensive. "Where have you been? I called you over and over, and you never answered…" I say, unable to hide the fear in my voice.

He bows his head, running a thumb over his left eyebrow before lifting his face again. "I had business to take care of."

I swallow hard and nestle deeper into his jacket to protect myself from the piercing cold. "What business?"

"Trust me, you don't want to know."

My heart pounds so loudly in my chest that I can feel it vibrating in my throat as a feeling of dread spreads throughout my body. He did it. He was with another girl. I'm sure of it. I can tell from the way he won't look at me, from his tense face, and from that mortified expression he wears, like someone who has made a huge mistake but doesn't know how to come clean.

"But I do want to know. After what happened with Travis, nothing scares me anymore," I say brusquely, taking his jacket off.

"What?" he asks, perplexed.

"Come on, Thomas, just say it."

"Say what?"

"Look, you left here furious, I didn't hear from you all night, and now you come back with your clothes smelling like alcohol, refusing to tell me what you did… And that's fine. I mean, you don't owe me anything. No justification or explanations, because we aren't actually together, but I've been through this before. I know how these things go and if you"—I feel my stomach clenching like a vise—"if you've gone back to her, I would like to know."

Silence permeates the space around us for several seconds, during which Thomas continues to look confused. Then he squeezes his eyes shut. "Hold on a minute. What do you *think* happened?"

I look down and don't answer him. I can't say it.

Then he lifts my chin gently, forcing me to look him in the eye. "Did you think I was with someone else?"

"Was I right?"

"Christ, no!"

"So...you weren't at Finn's party?"

He shakes his head.

"And you weren't with anyone else?" I whisper. It seems to me that he hesitates for a brief moment—during which I feel short of breath—but then he denies it again. I look into his eyes, scrutinizing them intensely, but all I see there is the truth.

"I thought I was being clear when I said I wouldn't do that."

"You say a lot of things, Thomas."

"I would never do anything like that to you."

"Then why didn't you answer your phone? Why won't you tell me where you've been or what you've been doing all this time?"

"Because there's things you should stay out of, for your own good."

By now, I should be used to him constantly pushing me away and shutting me out. Yet every time he does it, my heart crumbles into thousands of pieces. As if he can read my mind, Thomas takes my face in his hands, rubbing my cheeks with his thumbs and burying his other fingers in my hair before pulling me closer to him. I close my eyes as I feel tears beginning to prickle behind my eyelids. Like I haven't cried enough yet today.

"I was out of my mind when I left, that's true. But I want you to get one thing straight in your head: No matter how pissed off I am, no matter how much you piss me off...you are always my first priority." He stares intensely at me, resting his forehead against mine while I struggle mightily to contain my emotions.

Our mouths brush against one another, and our heartbeats quicken faster and faster until Thomas presses his lips to mine, a kiss of mingled sweetness and determination. And if, in the past, I struggled to understand and accept his insistence on keeping me out of certain situations, I am now starting to understand his motivations a little more clearly. He wants to protect me. I take his hands in mine, intertwining our fingers, and pull them from my face to rest on my thighs. He watches me with his head tilted to one side, trying to work out my intentions.

"I can wait..."

"'Wait'?" he repeats slowly.

"For you to let me in here," I say, placing a hand on his chest, right over his heart.

"Ness..."

"No." I silence him with an index finger against his lips because I don't want to hear what he has to say. Right now, he's going to be the one listening. "I can wait, Thomas. Whether it takes a day or a lifetime, I will wait. And when you're ready, when you finally let me in, I promise that I will be so quiet, so delicate with you. I will look and not touch, and learn to accept all the things that I can't understand." I lower my head for a moment before lifting it again, noting the bewildered expression on his face. "I don't expect you to do it now. I just want you to know that, when you're ready, I'll be ready with you. I want you to know that you don't have to afraid to bring me into your world, because you won't ruin me. You can't. You fix me, over and over again."

He doesn't say anything. He just stares at me with those magnetic eyes, which always intimidate me, and I get the feeling that he wants to tell me something, but he's holding himself back. Then, in one sudden motion, he pulls me to him and holds me tight. I rest my head against his chest, right there where the heartbeats echo against his ribs with shocking strength. I press myself closer to him and let myself be enveloped by his warmth, because God only knows how much I need it right now.

"I'm sorry about today," I tell him softly.

"Don't worry about it."

But it's impossible not to; the way Logan talked about Thomas still haunts me, lingering confusedly inside my head:

"Sketchy…"

"Out of his mind…"

"A disgusting coward…"

"You are just one more poor victim who has fallen into his trap…"

I break away from our embrace. "No, I was wrong. I shouldn't have gone to his room, and I shouldn't have stayed until I lost track of time. I was being reckless. But I swear to you that nothing happened between Logan and me; please believe me. I should have listened to you, but instead I just made you worried and angry—"

"Enough, Ness. Forget it. The important thing is that you are okay." He tucks my hair behind my ear with a slow movement while his eyes scrutinize me apprehensively. "Tell me why you're out here."

I tense up and feel my stomach drop. I can't tell him that my mother kicked me out over him. He would blame himself and wind up pushing me away. "Talk to me. What's going on?" he continues abruptly.

I straighten my spine and heave a deep sigh. "I got into a fight with my mother about her new boyfriend, Victor, who is coming to live with us. I don't agree with her decision, but she doesn't care. I said some ugly stuff—really ugly—and she…she made it clear that I'm no longer welcome in her house." It's not the whole truth, but it is *a* truth.

Thomas turns his face away slightly. "Are you kidding me?"

I shake my head. "No, but it doesn't matter anymore."

He presses his lips into a hard line. "How can it not?"

I shrug, not sure what to say. Of course it matters, but what's done is done, and talking about it now won't change things. Because I don't intend to give up on Thomas any more than my mother intends to rethink her beliefs about him. So I pull my knees up to my chest, rest my chin on them, and shutter myself inside a painful silence.

Realizing that he's not going to get any more of an explanation on this matter, Thomas runs a frustrated hand through his hair, stands up, and grabs a pack of Marlboros out of his jeans pocket. He sticks a cigarette in his mouth and lights it, inhaling deeply before sitting back down next to me, legs slightly spread. All of this he does without taking his eyes off of me. "What are you gonna do now?"

I shrug. "Nothing."

"Nothing?"

I raise my head to glare at him. "I don't have anywhere else to go. If I had a father in my life and that father lived in Corvallis, I would have another option, I suppose. But he's not here. He's busy being a dad to his son somewhere else, and there's no room in his life for me. My income from the Marsy is barely enough to pay rent on a run-down one-bedroom on the outskirts of town, not to mention the fact that I have no idea how I'll pay for school expenses now. So yeah, I don't intend to do anything. I'm just going to sit here and do absolutely nothing." I put my chin back on my knees again, exhausted by the whole situation.

Thomas lets me vent without saying anything, and after finishing his cigarette in total silence, he stands up, holds out his hand, and tells me, "C'mon, I'll take you somewhere."

I give him a bewildered look. "Now?"

He nods. "Right now. Night's still young, and it doesn't make any sense to stay here."

I peer uncertainly at his extended hand, and for a moment, I feel a sense of déjà vu. I remember that evening almost two months ago when he invited me to the frat house with him. I had only known him for a week, yet it had taken me less than five seconds to accept. And clearly nothing has changed between then and now, because, despite everything, I would still follow him wherever he wanted to lead me.

"Okay," I say with a faint smile. "Where are you taking me?"

He smiles in that familiar arrogant way that makes him so irresistible. "You'll find out."

Then he takes me by the hand, grabs my bag from off the ground, and walks me to his motorcycle.

We hurtle down the dark, wet streets of Corvallis, my arms wrapped around Thomas's waist, before arriving on campus. Thomas turns off the engine, kicks out the stand, and, with one foot on the ground, peers around as though looking for someone. Who does he think he's going to find on campus at this time, other than a security guard?

I slacken my arms around his middle. After we take off our helmets, he asks me to grab his phone out of the pocket of the leather jacket I'm still wearing. I hand it to him and watch him type out a text. We get off the motorcycle, and Thomas puts the phone back in his jeans pocket. Before I can ask him what we're doing here, I see he's rolled up the sleeve of his sweatshirt far enough to expose his wrist. He unties the black bandanna he always wears there and hands it to me. "Put it on."

I stare at him, dumbfounded. "I'm sorry, what's this for?"

"Blindfold," he answers decisively, smirking at me.

I cock an eyebrow. "What the heck are you up to, Collins?"

He gives me an amused grin before a whistle draws our attention, making us turn around. A tall blond boy with a lean athletic frame emerges from the men's dorm. "I've gotta get something; then you'll see," Thomas explains, before heading for the other guy.

At first, I don't recognize him, but after getting a closer look at him, I think he's the same guy I've seen with Thomas in the cafeteria a few times. They give each other shoulder bumps, and I can see them laughing together. Eventually, his friend looks over at me and gives me a very telling smile. I can practically hear the "*Niiiice*" from here. I cross my arms over my chest and watch as the stranger hands Thomas a key. They exchange a few more jokes before saying goodbye. I can't restrain my curiosity when he gets back to me. "What was that?" I ask cautiously, unrolling the bandanna.

"He plays on the hockey team."

"And why did he give you that key?"

Thomas sighs theatrically as he loops the two helmets over his right forearm and grabs the key out of bike's ignition. "You ask too many questions, Ness. Too many questions. Just tie that bandanna over your eyes and trust me."

I snort loudly, unable to hold back a grin. "Hey, you're not taking me to some freaky playroom now, are you? Because, if that is the case,

I should let you know that I don't do S and M, and I am not letting you smack me with a riding crop," I say as I blindfold myself.

He bursts into laughter so spontaneously that it makes my chest vibrate, and I forget all about the crap that happened last night. He wraps his arms around my waist and brings his mouth to my ear. His warm breath tickles my skin. "Fuck, guess I'll have to stick to the Italian kiss." I feel him laugh into my neck and then immediately give it a nip.

"The fact that I have no idea what this 'Italian kiss' is makes me kind of a loser, huh?"

"But you do know what it is. You know it very well." I can feel him grinning again.

"Oh…" I fall silent, embarrassment heating my cheeks.

"But don't worry, I don't want to do any of that right now."

"So what do you want to do, Thomas?" I ask him in a playful singsong tone.

I feel his lips touch mine and his warm, raspy voicing whispering to me, "I just want to make you happy." While my heart is caught up in a whirlwind of emotions, he puts his hands on my shoulders and pushes me forward, ready to guide me.

"Hold on, be quiet," he says. "Now, let's go right. No, the other right. Be careful, you're going to hit the wall."

"Hey, you're the one guiding me; you should be the one making sure I don't hit the wall," I retort, trying to survive his dismal orienteering skills.

"You don't listen to my directions."

"You don't know how to give directions," I say with conviction. "Need I remind you that, just a minute ago, you guided me into a glass door that you 'forgot' to warn me about, despite it being right in front of me?"

"I told you it was there; you're the one with the reflexes of a sloth."

"You told me when it was an inch away from my nose! And don't snort," I scold him jokingly, lightly elbowing his stomach. "I can hear you."

A feel a puff of air against my neck, which tells me he is smiling again.

"Okay, now lift your right foot; there's a step."

I do as he instructs, and we walk a few more feet until he stops me. "Are we here?" I ask, unable to stifle my excitement.

He doesn't answer.

He lifts his hand from my shoulder, and the next moment, I hear the sound of a door opening. A burst of cold air hits me.

Why is it so cold all of a sudden?

Thomas makes me advance until he grabs my hands and puts them on what feels like a balustrade.

"Okay, I think we're ready now?" The little undertone of sweetness in his voice as he asks me makes me melt. That's new.

"Surprise me," I urge him.

He pauses for just a moment before taking off my bandanna. In front of me is an immense ice skating rink, completely deserted and illuminated only by one overhead light. I am enchanted. It's beautiful, and instantly, childhood memories bubble to the surface, brief glimpses of perfect moments shared with the one man I thought would never abandon me. My father's laughter echoes in my head. His large calloused hands holding mine, supporting me so I don't fall. His encouraging words: *"Come on now, baby. I'm going to let go now so you can do it by yourself. You can do it. I know you can."* His fingers slipping out of mine, his proud smile bolstering me... I feel my eyes well up as I stare in wonder at the rink before me.

"You remembered?" My voice trembles with feeling. The night Thomas slept over at my house, I told him about how my father used to take me skating and how much I missed it.

Thomas steps up beside me and brushes my hair away from my face, tucking it tenderly behind my ear. With his thumb, he wipes away a tear I haven't even realized I shed.

"I can't give you a solution to your problems, but I can give you a little distraction that might help you forget about that reality for a while. I thought that this"—he looks out at the ice rink in front of us—"might be just the thing."

I lean into him and give him a tight hug, as strong as the gratitude I feel. Thomas seems surprised, as though he wasn't expecting this, but then he reciprocates, gathering me into his arms, and I take refuge there.

"You wanna get out there?" he asks, his voice muffled by my hair as he strokes the back of my neck.

I pull away and look at him uncertainly. "Can I?"

He looks around, shrugging. "Who's gonna tell you no?"

"The security guard, for example. We aren't supposed to be here," I point out, lowering my voice as though someone might hear us at any moment.

"The guard's probably sleeping at this time of night. We're alone here. So if you wanna skate, you can skate."

I bite my lip and rock back and forth on my feet, staring uncertainly out at the ice rink. "I want to do it."

This seems to satisfy him.

"Come on, let's go get your skates," he says, pointing to the skate rental behind him. "First, though, promise me you won't improvise a hoop jump or whatever the fuck it is; I don't want that on my conscience," he teases me, recalling the "minor" skating injury I told him about.

"Loop jump," I correct him, exploding into laughter. Then, putting on my most angelic face, I add, "I'll be good, I promise."

Before I can walk past him, Thomas grabs my hips and pulls me back into him. "You're good, right? I mean, other than your mother, you're...are you okay?" he asks, suddenly serious and even worried. I feel his arms around my torso, and his body heat warms me instantly.

"I think so," I answer automatically. "I mean, I'm still pretty shaken up, and I have a really bad headache but...I guess I'm okay." His cryptic gaze is fixed on me, as though my answer doesn't have him entirely convinced.

"Hey…" I touch his face with all the sweetness I can muster, ready to ask him what is going on in his head, but he doesn't let me.

He moves closer, and in the next instant, his mouth is pressed against mine. Hot, tender, delicate. I open my lips easily, as though my body has been waiting just for this, while his hands tighten on my hips. A shiver of desire runs down my spine. Because that is what happens every time he touches me, looks at me, or kisses me: shivers. My legs, my hands, even my heart feel like they're trembling.

When we pull back from one another, I get lost in those deep eyes, as green and brilliant as emeralds. They make me feel so protected, impervious to any danger. And even though I know that the greatest danger of all is standing right here in front of me, I can't help but look at him as though he's the only thing that matters in this world. Suddenly, I no longer care about my mother's demands, about not having a roof over my head; I'm not even worried about fending for myself, not if Thomas is here with me. I don't need anything else.

"Thank you for doing this, for bringing me here."

He shakes his head, frowning almost imperceptibly, as though I have nothing to be thankful for. As though taking me here is completely normal, just something anyone would have done. But it's not.

"Anyone" wouldn't take me skating in the middle of the might. But Thomas did. *He* did. And that is when I'm overwhelmed by a stunning realization, a truth that I've been trying to ignore for too long but can no longer suppress. If I admit it to myself, I'll never be able to go back to the way I was before. I'll never be able to pretend that it isn't the case. It will be the end—my end. But trying to deny it no longer makes any sense.

He smiles at me, unaware of my dangerous thoughts. Then, he steps back and gestures for me to go to the skate rental. I head for it with my mind in turmoil and my heart feeling like it's about to beat right out of my chest.

Oh my God…

I am in love with Thomas Collins.

The cold pierces my throat. The blades of my skates glide along the sheet of ice, scoring it. After a little bit of a run-up, I launch myself into a spin. I raise my arms high and take a deep breath of the freezing air that whips past my face. I am twirling so rapidly that it almost feels like I'm being sucked into a vortex. This is the third spin I've managed to complete without falling. The first four attempts were embarrassing failures. Every time I got enough momentum going, I would end up with my ass on the ice. Thomas, naturally, took every opportunity to make fun of me. Sitting in the empty bleachers, which are arranged in an oval around the rink, Thomas laughed and took pictures of all my falls. The asshole.

After a few more turns around the rink, I'm starting to feel the wear of my sleepless night, and from the slight redness of his eyes, I'm betting the same goes for Thomas. Still, he doesn't say anything and just sits there, silently watching me skate, waiting for me to put an end to our long night. I glide over to him, grabbing the railing and catching his eye, "Hey, do you want to leave?"

"You don't want to skate anymore?" he asks, getting to his feet.

"No, I'm tired, and it'll be morning soon, and campus is going to fill up."

"Okay, let's go, then."

I take off my skates and return them to the rental area, making sure to put them back exactly where I found them so I don't arouse any suspicion. Then, I return to Thomas, and we walk together through the deserted corridors of Oregon State University. I sport a shy smile as I cannot help but think about how good I've felt in the last hour. Skating once again after so many years was magical. He made it magical. And I know this sense of complete peace is only a temporary state of being and that, when the euphoria has passed, I'm going to get sucked right back into that vortex of misery. But for a brief and wonderful moment, Thomas has managed to make the pain tearing me up just a little more bearable.

We walk silently the whole way back, each of us lost in our own thoughts, and it's only when we get close to the exit that I feel my stomach clench so tightly that it leaves me breathless. Because I am realizing that I have nowhere to go when I leave here. I certainly can't go home.

"What's wrong?" Thomas's voice, deep and rasping, punctures the silence around us.

"Nothing."

He stops, ducks his face down to look at me as I tilt mine up. "Come on, Ness. You can't bullshit me. You should know that by now."

"I just don't understand how it all happened."

He frowns. "What?"

"All of it...my mother, who kicked me out, my father, who just stopped caring about me. I mean...I'm alone, and I have no idea how I got that way." My eyes are wet. My God, all I can ever do is cry; it's so frustrating.

Thomas pulls me close to him, resting his chin on top of my head. "You're not alone."

"I am, though." I grasp the fabric of his sweatshirt tightly in my fists while my throat constricts on a sob. I'm doing everything I can to hold back tears. "It feels like I've got no one left," I confess in a weak murmur.

Thomas takes my face in his hands and locks his eyes on mine as he says three simple words that mean more to me than anything else: "You have me."

Three

"YOU HAVE ME."

These are the words that follow me for the rest of the night—or at least for the few remaining hours between us and the dawn. They generate butterflies in my stomach and make me fall asleep with a smile on my face. *I have him.* I don't know if he really believes it, or if it was just a way to calm me down, but just hearing him say it was all I needed.

Bolstered by that confession, I asked Thomas if I could stay with him, reassuring him that I would figure out another solution tomorrow. His response was brusque and immediate: "I wouldn't take you back to your mother's house if you got on your knees and begged."

So we went back to his dorm room, I took a shower, put on one of his giant T-shirts, and we got into bed. We entwined ourselves with one another in what seems to have become our perfect fit: his arms wrapped around my waist, my back pressed against his chest, and his leg thrown over mine. It felt so good, but the little voice in my head warned me not to get too used to this, because his pity for me is going to run out, and then Thomas will go back to being surly and unmanageable. Needled by this fear, I tried to move away from him a little, but he didn't let me. He pulled me back against him, and we were lulled by the silence until we closed our eyes and fell asleep, just as the first rays of sunrise began to illuminate the darkness.

When I wake up, I'm alone in the bed. Various fragments of

memories overlap in my mind: Logan begging me, the box with the still-intact pizza inside, Thomas's fists on the door... For a moment, it feels like it was all a strange dream, but my exhaustion and puffy eyes confirm it really did happen. It feels like I've been sleeping for an eternity, and in fact, a glance at my phone confirms it's almost four in the afternoon. I also see a text from Alex asking me where I went last night and why I didn't show up for class.

Had a fight with my mother. Long story, tell you later. PS: I'm gonna need your notes, I answer.

I put my phone away and waste a few seconds staring at the ceiling. From the next room, I can hear Thomas's low voice talking to his roommate, Larry. Actually, it seems like more than talking; I dare say they are arguing. They probably think I'm still asleep and can't hear them. Well, they're wrong.

"Is this going to become a habit now?" I hear Larry ask. "Am I gonna start seeing her stuff appearing around the dorm all the time? We agreed, no girls here. You have the frat house for that kind of thing."

"What I do is none of your business, so get off my ass," Thomas silences him, exasperated.

"It absolutely is my business. This isn't just your apartment; it's mine too. I have just as much right to express my opinion on the matter. And may I also remind you that she is a squatter? She can't stay here."

"It's not going to become a habit. But now you listen to me: If you dare say anything to her, if you even look at her wrong or make her feel in any way uncomfortable, I swear I'll rip out your tongue and punch it down your throat. This is a shit situation for her too, don't you think?"

They're arguing because of me. Larry doesn't want me here. He probably sees me as an interloper preparing to invade his space, even if I have no intention of doing that. And he's not completely wrong; I *am* a squatter. If anyone found out they were letting me stay here, he and Thomas would be in big trouble. I sigh deeply and scrub a hand over my face, ignoring their argument, which seems to be getting thornier by the second. But I can't lie here indifferently for much longer, so I get up and put my hair into a ponytail, pull off Thomas's shirt, and put on my clothes from last night before leaving the room.

As soon as I open the door, I can see Thomas's powerful figure towering over Larry. Both of them turn toward me, lapsing into a deathly silence, which only makes me feel even more awkward. Thomas slowly lets go of Larry's shirt, allowing him to straighten up and run his hands over himself in an attempt to smooth it out.

"Good morning," I murmur, embarrassed. I gesture toward the coffee machine. "If it's not too much trouble, I'll just make a cup, and then I can get out of your hair," I say, sidling past them with my head lowered.

"You can stay as long as you want and do whatever you want," Thomas says in a calm but firm tone that immediately makes me turn to look at him. I see him glare at Larry, who, eyes hidden beneath his tousled curls, bites his tongue.

I gulp and give them a tight smile before continuing to the kitchen counter. I take a pod from the blue tin and insert it into the machine; then I lean on the countertop, tapping my nails against its surface. With my back to the guys, I wait for the smell of coffee to start wafting through the house.

"You took a decaf one," Larry points out. I turn to him, frowning. "The blue tin is for decaf. And the decaf is mine," he clarifies, his voice going a bit shrill.

"Oh, I'm sorry. I had no idea."

A sound from the machine tells me that it's ready. I quickly grab the cup and offer it to him. "Coffee?" I curve my lips up into a smile, hoping to soften him up a bit.

Thomas stands next to Larry, watching this scene unfold. Clearly aware of the severe look Thomas is giving him, Larry shakes his head resignedly. "No, it's fine. You drink that one. But bear it in mind for next time."

I nod, and with the cup of coffee still steaming in my hands, I watch as he puts on his jacket with an embittered air before grabbing a few comics off the table and leaving. As soon as the door closes behind him, I turn around and put the cup back on the counter, rubbing my forehead with a sigh. I don't like people disliking me. And I really don't like causing trouble for people.

Thomas puts his hands on my hips, turning me to face him, and then bends down until he can look me in the eye. "He's not mad at you. He just doesn't like change."

Despite knowing that it's surely unconvincing, I still manage a weak smile. "Yeah, good, I get it. Either way, I'm going to look for a new place to stay. Maybe a room in a house or anything really that has four walls and doesn't require me to rob a bank."

He lets out a chuckle.

"But first I have to go home and change."

"You sure you wanna do that?"

"My work uniform is there, as are the rest of my things."

"Do you want to go right now?"

"My mother will be at the office until six; I want to take advantage of her absence to grab the necessities."

Thomas picks up my gym bag and slings it over his shoulder. "I've got practice in two hours. I'll take you."

I smile tenderly at him, pleased that he wants to spend more time with me, and accept his offer. We leave the apartment and stop at the elevator. I'd like to take his hand, but despite the night we just spent together and the care he's shown me, I'm still afraid of overreaching. So I stop myself.

When the doors open, a group of boys emerges, and it's only when Thomas and I step in that I notice Logan leaning against the wall. His hand is pressed to his ribs; his face is pale and covered in bruises...so many that it hurts just looking at him. My breath catches.

My God.

His lower lip is split, his right cheekbone is swollen, and his eye on that side is half shut with a shiner so puffy the pale blue of his iris is barely visible. My stomach tightens until it feels like I can't even swallow. I am overwhelmed by guilt—I can't help but think that none of this would have happened if I'd just left that room sooner last night.

Logan lifts his head with difficulty, as though even this small movement causes him incredible pain. In the briefest moment when our eyes meet, I see an expression on his face that I never would have expected. He seems almost pleasantly surprised. He even smiles slightly at me, but seeing Thomas next to me, his face becomes grave again.

Thomas firmly entwines his fingers with mine and pulls me behind him, almost like he means to shield me with his body. "Get the fuck out of here," he says to Logan in the kind of voice that would make anyone shiver.

Logan doesn't need to be told twice. Wearing a grimace of pain that intensifies with every step he takes, he walks past us. He casts a furtive glance over his shoulder at me just before the doors close. After planting myself beside Thomas, I stare at him for a long moment, certain he can feel my eyes on him. But he ignores me, choosing instead to glare at the reinforced steel doors of the elevator.

"Thomas…"

He cuts me off, gritting his teeth. "Don't start." He doesn't even bother to look at me. He presses the button for the ground floor, and down we go. I move in front of him, forcing him to look at me.

"He looks bad, Thomas…really bad," I insist. "Tell me the truth: Where did you go last night? Did you go find him?" Only now, with his jaw clenched tight, does he finally lower his eyes to me and give me his full attention. But seeing the ferocity of his gaze, I almost wish he didn't. He neither confirms nor denies anything but instead just stares at me, leaving me to draw my own conclusions.

The elevator makes a sound indicating we've just passed another floor, and I feel the panic rising inside me. "Do you realize he could press charges?" I whisper, not even knowing why, since we're alone in here.

He lifts one side of his mouth mockingly as he crosses his arms over his chest. "I hope he does. I'm dying to make him taste his own blood again."

"You cannot be serious."

He gazes at me with the look of a man who has zero scruples. It always freaks me out to be reminded that Thomas isn't only the guy who takes me ice skating in the middle of the night just to see me smile, but he's also *this*. Impetuous, ruthless, remorseless. Completely out of control.

"Listen to me…" I take his face in my hands, standing up on my tiptoes to do it. "I understand that you are still furious about what happened; I am too. But you should not underestimate the seriousness of this situation. His father is a judge. You could get in trouble. Serious trouble. Maybe if I talked to him, I could keep him from—"

"You're not talking to him," he orders, looming over me, his voice harsh. "If he wants to press charges, let him, but I bet my ass he won't dare, so stop worrying about it." The elevator doors open on the ground floor. "Seems to me, you've got more important things to worry about anyway." He takes my hands from his face, skewering me with a look that brooks no argument. Then he walks out of the elevator, unconcerned about whether I follow him.

He heads for the dorm's exit, and before he can go through it without me, I run out of the elevator to him. "Thomas, wait," I say, grabbing his arm and turning him in my direction. "I'm sorry, okay? I'm scared because I don't want anything to happen to you. I don't want anything to happen to anyone because of me ever again. But I especially don't want to argue with you, not today, not after everything that happened last night. I couldn't stand it." He just stares down at me reproachfully. "Please," I murmur, my voice cracking.

It is then that he sighs, relaxing his shoulders. "I don't want to argue with you either." His features soften almost imperceptibly. "C'mon, I'll take you home."

Neither of us says much during the car ride. I try to keep my mind busy, pushing aside any thoughts about my mother or about Logan's condition, but it's fruitless. I start gnawing my thumbnail, feeling my anxiety increase with every mile, each one of them bringing me closer to my house. Or rather, my mother's house.

Pulling into the driveway, which is still wet from last night's storm, I stare out the window at the porch, where I sat hours ago. It's the same porch where I spent whole summers sunbathing, reading, or just tending to the peonies. Thomas turns off the engine and rests his hand on my thigh. "Still sure?"

I continue looking at the house, worrying at my lip. I have to do this. I straighten my shoulders as if to give myself courage, and I swallow hard. I unbuckle my seat belt and get out of the car without answering his question.

Inside the house, silence reigns. We both leave our bags on the floor, and I put my keys in the bowl on the entryway cabinet. Together, we walk through the kitchen on our way upstairs, but I stop and turn toward Thomas. "Are you hungry? You have practice in less than two hours, and you shouldn't go on an empty stomach."

"I've got these." He shows me the pack of cigarettes he always has on him. "All I need."

"And a real booster for your lungs," I answer sarcastically, pushing him into the dining area. He grins at me while he sits on a stool at the kitchen island. I open the fridge and find it well stocked. "Is there anything you want to eat? I don't know, a sandwich? Maybe some eggs? Aren't athletes obsessed with protein?"

"A sandwich will be fine."

My lips curve into a smile as I get busy. I take everything I need out of the fridge before washing my hands and rinsing the tomatoes in cold water. In a frying pan, I toast two thick slices of bread while I cut the bacon into strips. While I wait for everything to cook to perfection, I grab a plate, put it on the table, and start slicing the tomatoes.

"Are you a good cook?" he asks me, intrigued.

"Good enough. When I was a kid, I liked to watch my grandma or my mother in the kitchen whenever I could."

"My mother always liked to cook for the whole family," Thomas tells me, the spontaneity of this disclosure taking me by surprise. "My house always smelled like fresh-baked sweets, especially on Sunday mornings."

I stop to listen to him with interest, delighted that he is confiding something to me of his own free will for once. He stretches his arms out over the marble counter, his eyes fixed on some point in the middle distance. There is such intense nostalgia in his face that it makes my throat feel tight.

"My sister would get excited every time. She'd start jumping on the bed and singing to herself until she woke everyone up." He chuckles softly. "She was an insufferable little snot when she was a kid. She's calmed down a bit over the years."

I fold my arms over my chest and smile sweetly, perfectly able to imagine this scene in my head. I feel like I can even smell the odor of sweet treats spreading throughout the house. I picture his mother at the stove, cheerful and radiant, intent on preparing breakfast for her family while her mischievous children clamor around her, chasing each other and getting into tiffs. I inch closer to him to reduce the distance between us, though I'd like to do so much more. I'd like to kiss him, to sit on his lap, hold him, and listen to him talk for hours and hours. I want to hear as many stories as I can about his life, about his family. Until I understand him completely. But I promised him that we would move on his timeline, and I intend to keep that promise. "That sounds lovely."

The expression on his face turns hard, as though my comment has upset him somehow. He focuses his eyes on me and shakes his head slowly. "Nothing that happened in that house was lovely, actually."

Coldness spreads through my chest, and my words die on my tongue. I stiffen and frown at him, confused. "What do you mean?"

Thomas shrugs and, clearly trying to end the conversation, jerks his chin toward the stove and scolds me: "Careful you don't burn it."

I can tell from the detached sound of his voice that he's put up his usual walls once again. "I'm going out for a smoke," he says, getting up from the stool to leave.

Time's up.

He gave me a little piece of his past, but whatever impulse led him to do it has gone now, and he has withdrawn into himself. I take a deep breath and close my eyes.

That's okay too, I tell myself.

Baby steps.

Five minutes later, he's back. I am relieved to see that some of his tension seems to have been released. I arranged the crisp bacon on the toasted bread along with the tomato slices and some fresh lettuce, trying to assemble everything in the most inviting way. I've cooked for other people over the years, for my father or for Alex when he'd come by, but I'm surprised by how much I like doing it for Thomas. I can feel his gaze on me the whole time, so I raise my face to smile shyly at him. He has a strange way of always managing to make me feel awkward and nervous in his presence. He knows this. He embraces it.

"What is it?" I ask, licking a bit of bacon grease off my fingertip.

He moves closer, positions himself behind me, and, looming over me with his broad frame, he buries his face in the crook of my neck. Right where the skin is still purple, marked by last night's kiss. He rubs his closed lips over it, producing an animal noise of satisfaction. He dips his cold fingers under the hem of my shirt, lifting it slowly to reveal a strip of my torso, which he caresses.

"I could get used to this, you know?"

I swallow as his vetiver smell, mixed with the odor of tobacco, goes straight to my head. "To what?"

"To you cooking for me," he murmurs. "Although, if we're being honest, I'd like it even better if you were wearing just a pair of lacy black panties." I feel his mouth curl into a smirk. "And some high heels in the same color." His hands tighten on my hips, pressing me into his pelvis. I feel a heat blooming in the low part of my abdomen. "Then, I could satisfy your appetite too."

I hold my breath, unmoving. I am silent, unable to formulate anything like a meaningful sentence.

Thomas rests his forehead on my shoulder and starts laughing. It's a deep, mesmerizing sort of laugh. "It takes so little to make you freeze up," he notes, shaking his head. He turns me to face him before lifting my chin and planting a chaste kiss on my lips. Then he snags a piece of toast and sits back down with a smug look on his face, probably well aware of all the silent insults I'm directing his way as I try to regulate my heartbeat and regain some small measure of control over the situation. Damn him.

We sit down to eat and clean our plates. I ask for help washing the dishes and tidying the kitchen; then we go upstairs to my room. After putting some clothes into an old moving box, I move on to selecting today's outfit. I quickly pick out a pair of white jeans and drape them over one shoulder as I continue hunting for a shirt. Thomas is lying on my bed, propped up against the headboard with his ankles crossed in front of him. Bored, he flips through one of my philosophy textbooks on deductive reasoning.

"Do you really study this stuff?"

"Yeah, it's interesting. And in theory, you should be studying it too." I take two sweaters out of the closet and lay them on the foot of the bed; one is gray, the other baby pink.

"'The mental process by which new information is evaluated subject to generally known concepts is called the deductive method.'" He lifts his gaze from the page and, with a snap, closes the book. "What the fuck does that mean?"

I throw a look right back at him. "In other words, deductive reasoning means starting from a general premise and proceeding toward a specific practical conclusion." Thomas looks even more confused, and so I keep talking, hoping to clarify the concept for him. "It means that, for example, if you were about to give me a book and realized you didn't have it with you, you could *deduce* that you had left it at home."

He stares at me perplexed for a few moments. "That's it?"

"Yeah." I smile, amused. "That's it."

He sits up and pulls on the sneakers he'd taken off previously. "This is why I hate philosophy. It makes something complicated out of something extremely simple."

My phone display lights up with a message from Tiffany. She also wants to know what happened last night. I respond quickly, telling her to meet me on campus, and while I'm at it, I ask if she can give me a ride to the Marsy. Then I put the phone away and decide to wear the baby-pink sweater.

"If you don't like philosophy, then why are you taking the course?"

"I started three years late, but I need the elective credits," he answers calmly. "One course is as good as any other for me."

"Wait, you started three years late? Does that mean you're twenty-two?" I ask, disoriented.

Thomas just nods, facing downward as he ties his other shoe and avoids answering the question I've only implied: *Where was he those three years?*

I can tell he doesn't want to talk about it, so I switch topics. "In any case, wouldn't it have been better to get credits with courses that were more up your alley? I saw your drawings; they're beautiful. You could have picked something in the arts. Or focused on sports."

"You know, I could have." He approaches me wearing a crooked smile. When he's just a few inches from my face, he taps me lightly on the nose with his index finger. "But you weren't in any of those courses."

His answer leaves me speechless. What does *that* mean?

Thomas laughs, watching me. I'm sure he can see the gears turning in my head as I try to figure out what he's saying. "We need to go," he says, only a breath away from my mouth. "I have practice in twenty minutes, and your mother will be home soon too. Should I take you to the Marsy?"

I jerk my head no. "To campus. I need to meet up with Tiffany before work."

"Great, I'll be waiting downstairs." He walks out of the room, leaving me standing there in a daze, staring after him.

Oh, no.

Like hell am I going to let him get away like that! This time, I'm going to demand an answer.

I pull on the sweater at light speed, grab my work uniform and my schoolbooks, and throw it all in my bag before chasing after him. The moving box can wait.

"Thomas!" I call out to him, shouting. But as soon as I hit the first step of the staircase, I see him close the front door behind him.

Dammit!

Don't you run away from me!

I take the stairs two at a time. I grab the house keys, lock the door, and run to the car, pinning him with a look that will not permit silence.

"Tell me."

"What?" He chuckles as he turns the key in the ignition and starts the car.

"Don't play dumb." I fasten my seat belt without taking my eyes off of him. "Tell me why you took philosophy."

"I already said."

I blink in disbelief. "You really want me to believe that you enrolled in philosophy…for me?" That's impossible. He didn't even know I existed before that Monday when he sat down next to me and decided to pester me. "Seriously?"

"Maybe," he answers nonchalantly as he puts the car into gear and we head off.

I shake my head and rub my temples. "Now I know you're lying. You didn't even know who I was."

"Ness, we've been going to the same college for over a year now. You were dating the motherfucker who used my sister. Of course I knew who you were."

Sure, he must have seen me in passing occasionally in the hallways, or maybe at one of Travis's practices. But I doubt he ever took much notice of me. "But you…you never thought about me," I point out.

We slow down as we approach a stop sign. He stops and looks seriously at me. "That doesn't mean I didn't know who you were." He accelerates again.

"But then why? Why would you do it?"

"Who knows?" he replies, giving a distracted shrug. "One day I saw you, and you seemed interesting. And I'll admit that I was a little bit tickled by the idea of pissing off your asshole boyfriend."

"A spur-of-the-moment thing. So that's why?" I ask in a faint voice, trying and failing to understand. "To punish Travis?"

His forehead creases as he frowns at me. "What?"

I shrug. "That's what you just said."

"I said that I liked the idea of pissing him off. I didn't say that's why I did it," he answers, annoyed.

"Then why did you do it?" My voice nearly trembles.

Thomas rests an elbow on the rolled-down window and stares out at the road with an uncertain frown on his face.

"Thomas, please tell me."

He sighs, looking sideways at me and, after a few interminable moments, finally decides to speak. "The first time I ever saw you, I was training with the guys off campus. It was a summer afternoon, and I'd just recently moved to Corvallis." He speaks as though he's confessing this to himself more than to me. "You were sitting on this little wall with Travis's sister. You were reading something, probably one of your super boring books. You just sat there with your head bent over the pages and played with a little bit of your hair…" He gives me a sideways glance and lifts one corner of his mouth. "It was shorter than it is now."

I wonder how it is possible that I have no memory of that day.

"You weren't alone on that wall. There were other girls who were there just to give me flirty looks, trying to get my number or just to get laid. But not you. You never even looked at me. You weren't looking at your boyfriend either. You didn't look anywhere except down at that book. You were shut up in your own little world. Then Travis called over to you because he wanted to show you a shot, and you looked up, smiled a little bit, then immediately went back to reading. But in that brief moment, I got a look at your eyes, and they were the same color as the ocean when it's stormy, and I could see all of that, all that storm, inside of you. You looked so melancholy and fascinating, you were just…gorgeous." He shakes his head. "But you were the team captain's girlfriend, and there are strict rules among guys. When he broke them all last summer by messing with my sister, I felt entitled to break some in return." He turns to face me. "That doesn't mean I was using you to punish him. It just means that I liked you and I wanted you. And I would have made you mine no matter what."

I blink once, then twice. Three times. I am incredulous…and moved.

"Are you about to cry?" Thomas pulls a face, trying to deflate the moment. "I shouldn't have said anything. I knew it; you're too emotional. All I told you was that I've always liked you, not that I dream of marrying you and fathering your kids or whatever."

And there it is, landing on my heart like a ton of bricks. God. Will he ever be able to resist undermining the few nice things he allows to sneak out of his mouth? I cross my arms over my chest petulantly and stiffen in my seat, immediately annoyed. I would like to be even more irritated, but that damned butterfly feeling in my belly won't let me.

He's always liked me.

"I understood what you said; there's no need to clarify. And I wasn't crying; I'm just surprised. I mean, I never realized."

"I didn't give you a chance."

We turn into the campus parking lot and stop. I look at him with a frown. "One thing I still don't understand, though: If you decided to take philosophy because you liked me, then why did you act like such an ass that morning? You were arrogant, rude, and generally unbearable. You ruined the whole lesson for me."

"I liked teasing you; you'd snap at every little thing," he answers, smiling slyly as he pulls the keys from the ignition. "And honestly, that condescending, judgmental teacher's-pet attitude of yours was pretty annoying."

"I–I…I'm not judgmental." I start to defend myself, not entirely sure I'm telling the truth.

Thomas refutes my statement with a sidelong glance.

He starts to open the door and get out, but I stop him with a hand on his arm. He can't seriously think he's going to just drop a bomb like that and then act like nothing happened. I look him straight in the eyes. "Is it true?" I bite my lip nervously before continuing. "Have you always liked me?" I murmur, somewhat ashamed to be asking for confirmation.

Thomas leans closer and rubs his nose against mine while I stare bemusedly into his eyes, magnetic but unknowable. With his warm breath tickling my face, I feel like I could get lost in him so easily that it almost scares me. I swallow nervously, and just as I'm about to be the first to look away, he smiles at me. Just before kissing me, he whispers, "Always."

Four

THREE KNOCKS ON THE CAR window make me start.

When I turn, I spot Tiffany, bent at the waist so her breasts are level with us. There's a fixed smile on her face, her red hair hangs forward, and her floral perfume wafts in through the half-open window.

"You two are worse than a roller coaster," she greets us with an exasperated sigh. I can't really blame her; just yesterday I called her in the middle of the night, desperate to know where Thomas was, and today she finds us making out in his car like two hormonal teenagers.

"Buzz off, Collins. I need to talk to her," Tiff says, dismissing Thomas unceremoniously.

I frown and study the small tension lines on his otherwise peaceful face. Tiffany opens the car door and gestures for me to get out, reaching in to grab my arm. Thomas gives a resigned shake of his head before grabbing his gym bag and leaving. As he walks away, he clicks the door lock and sticks a cigarette in his mouth, giving me a sly smile as he does it. My cheeks flame once again.

"What happened? You seem tense," I ask her as soon as we are alone. She is mangling her lip between her teeth. "Well?" I insist, worried for her.

Tiffany grabs my shoulders and, with a laugh that falls somewhere between delighted and hysterical, exclaims, "I'm coming to live with you!"

I stare at her, unmoving, uncomprehending.

"What?"

"Don't make that face. I'm the ideal tenant: I clean, I organize, I contribute to expenses. Besides, your mother adores me. It'll be fantastic, just you wait and see." She nudges me playfully as I continue to stare at her in shock.

"Tiff, what are you talking about? Why would you ever want to come and live with me?"

"Easy. Because my parents have decided to ruin my life."

"Explain more."

She hunches her shoulders, sighing. "Every day my father has been harping on me about how, from now on, it's my job to continue the family business with him. So much so that this morning he told me I had to go with him on a business trip next weekend."

"What? He can't just do that; he knows you have different plans for your future!"

She gives an anxious nod. "Yeah, but apparently that's not a good enough reason for my dad. With Travis out of the picture, he thinks his only daughter needs a better education, so the business empire doesn't collapse as soon as he dies. I told him that I have no intention of ever working for the company, but he started giving me this whole speech about the importance of family, responsibilities, duty, and blah, blah, blah. 'You're the last remaining Baker,' he told me. 'Having this last name is an honor.'" she grumbles, imitating her father's voice. "Do you know what it really means? This is it for me. No more going out, no more parties, no more fun. No more anything. Just studying and work. Working at a job I didn't choose and don't want!" she bursts out. Some passing boys give us a startled look, and I smile politely in return.

Wrapping an arm around her shoulders, I guide her to a bench near the entrance. "Okay, now let's just take a deep breath and try to calm down," I tell her as we sit.

"How am I supposed to calm down?" she demands, growing agitated again. "My God, I'm a criminology major; I don't want to spend the rest of my life at a desk signing contracts!"

I lean in and give her a big hug, trying to offer her some comfort, because I know that's what she needs right now—to feel that she is not alone and out of options the way I am. "If there was anything I could do to help you, I would," I tell her, petting her hair. "But the truth is...I don't have a house for you to stay in."

Tiffany pulls away abruptly and looks me in the eyes. "What are you talking about?"

I suck in a deep breath, trying to find the right words to explain what happened. Finally, after a long pause, I feel ready to talk. "It doesn't seem real to me either, but last night, after I got off the phone with you, my mother and I got into a fight."

"Well, that's nothing new."

"True, but it was different this time. I spat a lot of nasty stuff at her. I accused her of being the reason nothing ever works out in our lives. I said she was an awful wife, an awful mother, and...the next thing I knew, I was alone on the porch without a home anymore."

Tiff's mouth drops open in disbelief. "There's no way..."

I nod silently, pulling the sleeves of my sweater down over my hands.

"How did it get to that point? I mean, what were you two talking about?"

"Thomas," I admit after a brief moment of hesitation. Her eyes nearly bug out of her head. "But it wasn't just him," I hasten to add. "Victor's moving in with us, and she didn't even bother to give me a heads-up. She already made the decision and just expects me to accept it without even thinking about how I might feel having another man who isn't my dad moving into the house."

"Oh my God...I can't believe I dumped my stupid drama on you while you're going through all of this." She places a gentle, comforting hand on my shoulder. "Where did you stay last night? Why didn't you call and tell me?"

"I was in shock; I didn't know what to do. Then Thomas showed up in front of my house, and when he found out what happened, he took me back to his dorm. The thing is, I can't stay there. His roommate wouldn't allow it, and I can't afford student housing."

"I'm so sorry," she whispers, hugging me. "The atmosphere at my place isn't great, it's true, but you know that we'd be happy to host you."

"Thanks, Tiff," I say, full of affection for her. "But I'm not sure that's such a good idea. Between Travis enlisting and the pressure your father is putting on you, I think my presence might be a bit too much."

"Never think that." She steps back to look me seriously in the eye. "You are always welcome, you know that." And even though I hate to do it, I find myself giving her proposal some serious thought. I let out a long breath, and exhausted by the events of the past twenty-four hours, I agree.

"Everything will work out, you'll see," she reassures me, rubbing my shoulders. "Have you gotten your books and clothes from your house yet?"

"I started filling a box, but I didn't have time to finish," I answer.

"I'll go with you to get your essentials tomorrow before class, after your mother goes in to work, okay? In the meantime, you can borrow my clothes. It'll give you an excuse to finally update that granny wardrobe of yours. Thomas will thank me, I'll bet." Then she jolts, as though she's just remembered something important. "Wait, what does Thomas have to do with all of this?"

I look reluctantly at her, worrying my fingernail; my palms are sweating. "My mother won't accept that he is a part of my life, and I can't accept her continued attempts to control me. I told her that straight up, so she gave me a choice. And I chose him."

Tiff's shocked face speaks for itself. "Does he know?"

I shake my head vehemently. "I told him about the issue with Victor, but he doesn't know that I was really kicked out of the house over him. And he's not going to find out."

"You can't keep a thing like that hidden. If he finds out—"

"He won't."

Tiffany levels an unconvinced stare at me. "Honey—"

I cut her off, feeling a lump forming in my throat. "No, Tiff, I'm serious. If I told him, he would just blame himself and end up pushing me away, because he'd think that would solve the problem. And that's not what I want, not now that I feel like I'm closer to him than I've ever been."

I can feel the weight of Tiffany's scrutinizing gaze. Then she rubs both hands over her face, sighing deeply. "Fine, I'll keep my mouth shut. You'll be safe at my place for now."

"It'll just be temporary, I promise. I'm going to try to get a meeting with the financial aid office."

"For what?"

"I'm thinking of applying for student loans."

"Student loans?" she echoes, disgruntled.

I nod. "My scholarship only covers about half the tuition and fees. With a loan, I could pay for the rest and get a spot in the dorms. With my wages from the Marsy, I should be able to pay it off in a couple of years and make ends meet in the meantime. I've been thinking about it for a while; it should work."

"Wow..." Tiff rubs her temples before shaking her head. "You'll work for who knows how many years to pay back a loan. Have you thought about that?"

I shrug and lower my gaze, trying to ignore the weight I feel in my stomach. "I have to focus on the present; there's nothing else I can do. And, right now, a loan seems like the only possible alternative."

After these words, we both fall into a thick silence, more telling than any verbal reply.

"Hey, here's what we'll do," she says sweetly, after a few seconds. "I'll take you to the Marsy right now, and when your shift is over, I'll pick you up, and we'll have a nice pizza and movie night, the kind you like. We can invite Alex too."

I smile gratefully at her. She smiles back and adds: "I promise you that we will find a solution."

I nod, though I am not at all convinced.

Five

THE MORE TIME PASSES, THE more I lose hope. Finding a place to live in this city seems to have become an impossible task. Four days have passed. Four days of exhausting research, and still I find myself staying at the Baker royal palace—a less than ideal situation. Tiffany was right; her father is loading her up with all the pressure that, up until a few weeks ago, was on Travis's shoulders. And just as I feared, it doesn't feel like her parents are thrilled about my presence at this particular moment.

Alex offered to let me stay with him as soon as I told him about the situation. It's not that the idea of moving in with him doesn't appeal to me, but I'm determined to figure out something by myself. I can't continue to be a burden on my friends. And I refuse to step foot back in Thomas's dorm. As lovely as it was spending the night with him, I have no desire to relive that awkward wake-up courtesy of Larry.

I struggle to put aside my familial and rental problems to concentrate on my reading group's discussion, just like I do every other Saturday morning. The novel we've chosen for this month is *The Scarlet Letter*. A junior named Kate is reading a crucial passage: "'No man, for any considerable period, can wear one face to himself and another to the multitude, without finally getting bewildered as to which may be the true.'"

The phone in my pocket vibrates, alerting me to a new text.
Where are you?

I grin; it's from Thomas, or, as I've dubbed him, the Grinch. I was going to save his number in my contacts under his actual name, but then I thought better of it. I needed something different, something that represented him completely. Something like *Miscreant* or *Arrogant Broodster*. Then I had an epiphany: the Grinch! Surly and bad-tempered to anyone who tries to get close—the perfect nickname for Thomas.

At reading group, I answer.

Do you have much longer?

I look at the clock, which reads 11:37. Twenty minutes, tops.

Can you leave early? Like, say...now?

I shift in my seat, curious. What's wrong, Collins? You missing me?

Come to the fifth-floor staff bathroom. I'll meet you there.

I smother a smile. Students aren't allowed in that bathroom.

Right you are. I can almost see the cheeky smile spreading across his face, delighted with his own response.

So why do you want me to come there?

I want to show you something.

Something?

I waited with bated breath until his answer comes a minute later: The sink.

Huh?

I want to show you how good you'd look bent over it... he adds.

A powerful blush spreads across my face, and I almost drop my phone. I clear my throat, looking around to make sure no one noticed my intense reaction.

I stare, wide-eyed, as the three little dots disappear and reappear on the screen before a new message comes in: ...and make you feel just how much I've missed having you underneath me, being inside you...

I know I've turned entirely red. My hands are tingling, and my heart is pounding. Is he serious? Am I? Do I really want to ditch reading group for a quickie with Thomas in the staff bathroom? Jesus, the burst of arousal that moves through forces me to clench my thighs together as I try to get just a tiny bit of relief from the intense need that his proposition has kindled in me. Well, my body's answer is a loud and clear YES. And it's insane because the Vanessa of a few months ago would never have put a boy ahead of her studies or allowed him to distract her from her precious books.

I take a few deep, calming breaths before replying. I'll let you in on a secret: I've always been fascinated by bathroom fixtures.

It's marked as read immediately, and he responds within seconds with Good girl. I bite my lip, lock the screen, and stick the phone back in my pocket. Then I stand up, feeling my knees tremble as I do.

"Sorry, Kate," I break in, interrupting her reading (which I long ago stopped paying attention to). "I'm not feeling so good; I think my blood pressure is low. I'm just going to go get some air."

I can feel each of the book club members looking attentively at me.

"No problem, Vanessa, go ahead. We'll update you later on the group."

I nod, and as a trickle of sweat makes its way down the side of my face, I hastily gather my things. In seconds, I'm out of the classroom and headed for the staircase that will take me to the fifth floor, and still I can't entirely believe that I'm really doing this. But then, as I turn the corner and prepare to climb the first step, I run into Alex.

"Hey, don't you have reading group?" he says, grabbing my arm to keep me from stumbling.

"Y-yeah," I stammer, caught red-handed. "I'm just…not feeling well today."

"You're sick?" He immediately puts the back of his hand against my forehead to check my temperature. After apparently establishing that it's within the norm, he takes my books out of my arms, freeing me from that small burden.

"Don't worry, I'm okay. I just needed some air," I babble hastily, hoping to sound at least a little credible. Lying to a group of fellow students is one thing; lying to my best friend is different. He knows me so well that it would take him about three seconds to figure out I'm not telling the truth. Fortunately for me, he doesn't seem interested in analyzing my facial expressions or doubting what I'm telling him.

"You're better now?" he asks me. As I nod, I feel my phone vibrate in my bag. I start and then dig the phone out, unlocking the screen to see a new message from Thomas: On my second cigarette now; don't make me light a third. What happened to you, stranger?

My lower stomach tenses as I quickly tap out a reply assuring him that I'm on my way.

"Well, if you're not doing anything else, let me take you to lunch," Alex puts his arm around my shoulders and starts guiding me toward the canteen. "I'm awfully hungry, and I want to ask you for a favor."

I hesitate, then eke out a small: "Right now?"

He cocks his head, confused, and looks at me. "Do you have another commitment?"

Well, sort of... Can the promise of getting bent over the sink in the staff bathroom be termed *a commitment*?

I rub my eyebrow with my thumb and say, "No, I suppose not."

Resigned, I text Thomas and let him know that I've encountered an unexpected situation. Then, with a tense smile, I force myself to follow Alex.

The scent of boiled cauliflower and floor cleaner in the cafeteria makes my nose wrinkle in disgust. Why can't they ever make an edible meal instead of this vomit-inducing swill? On the plus side, the cafeteria is half empty, so we don't have to wait in line.

"So what's this favor?" I ask.

"In a little over a month, it'll be Christmas and Stella's birthday," Alex explains after we load our trays with macaroni and cheese and sit down at one of the tables near the windows overlooking the lawn. "I want to surprise her."

"I love surprises! What kind?" I inquire.

"I haven't decided, which is why I need your help. I want something unforgettable."

"Alex." I look tenderly at him, moved by his sweetness. "I'm more than happy to help you, but I'm sure that, whatever you do, she'll be happy."

"I hope so," he answers, emptying a can of Coke into his glass and letting it foam. "Either way, I was thinking about a trip."

I look at him, wondering why he needs my advice. "That's a great idea; I wish someone would surprise me like that."

"Do you think it's too much? After all, we've only really known each other for a few months."

I hurriedly shake my head. "Not at all. In fact, I think it's a great way for you two to get to know each other better. Do you have a destination in mind?"

"No, that's where you come in. My first thought was Paris, but then I thought maybe that's too much of a cliché, so then I considered Aspen or New York."

"First of all, Paris is never a cliché, but flying to Europe would be a lot," I tell him, digging my fork into the macaroni. "Aspen has its own special charm, with all those wood chalets and everything. I gotta say, though, that the Christmas tree lighting at Rockefeller Center has always seemed like a really magical experience to me. I've always wanted to go skating on that giant ice rink, framed by all those enchanting lights," I continue dreamily.

We finish lunch, evaluating the different potential destinations, and in the end, Alex takes my advice and decides that New York is the place for them. When the cafeteria starts to get crowded, a few of his friends from his photography class invite him to sit with them. He turns to me as though he's going to ask my permission. Since I don't require a babysitter, I smile at him and shoo him away with a friendly shove. I follow him with my eyes until, through the cafeteria window, I spot Thomas outside on the lawn. He's leaning against the trunk of a tree, one knee propped up, concentrating on smoking a cigarette with a copper-haired girl.

I feel a small trembling in my chest. That's not his sister. It's not even Shana. So who is she?

The girl hands him a flyer, smiling and resting her hand on his arm longer than necessary as she tells him something. I stiffen immediately as a burst of jealousy spikes in my chest.

A sick thought bubbles up in my mind: *Is this someone he replaced me with when I stood him up in the staff bathroom?*

Thomas drops his gaze to her hand. He looks almost annoyed but does absolutely nothing to distance himself from her.

God, I'm such an idiot. Did I really sacrifice my reading group time just so I could be present for...*this*?

Dammit, Thomas.

Fed up, I look away from the scene in front of me. Just because Thomas looked after me in my time of need for one night doesn't mean things have changed between us. We aren't together. Thomas is not my boyfriend. And he's not going to be. We are both free to do what we want, aren't we? I have no right to throw a fit if I see him with someone else.

Theoretically.

In practice, I can feel my blood boiling in my veins, and I hate myself for giving him this power, for letting him make me feel so vulnerable. But I push aside these intrusive thoughts and instead take my laptop out of my bag. Time to consult the various rental sites, flagging the listings most likely to be in my price range.

Several minutes pass like this, until I spot movement to my right. Thomas takes a seat next to me, setting his lunch tray on the table.

"Am I understanding this correctly? Did you ditch me to hang out with your little friend?" he snaps, not bothering to hide the irritation in his voice.

"Pardon me?" I answer vaguely.

"He's your 'unexpected situation,' I suppose?" he notes and, from the corner of my eye, I can see him glaring at Alex's table.

"We ran into each other in the hallway; he needed advice, and I didn't want to leave him alone," I inform him, not taking my eyes away from the screen and continuing to scroll slowly.

"So you left me alone."

When I finally choose to look up, the blazing intensity in his eyes gives me a start.

"Looks like you consoled yourself pretty quickly," I reply after a moment of hesitation, flashing him my very fakest smile.

Thomas gives me a puzzled look. "What are you talking about?"

A wave of shame washes over me. I am aware that I might be making a big deal out of nothing here. After all, the girl only handed him a flyer; they probably didn't even know each other. *Dammit*.

I shake my head. "It's nothing."

"You sure? Because I'm getting a pissed-off vibe from you, and I have no idea why you'd be pissed off. If anything, I should be the angry one."

"I'm not pissed off; I'm just..." I pause, chewing on the inside of my cheek. I groan in frustration as I run a hand through my hair. "I'm anxious about the situation with my mother and how I haven't found a solution to the housing problem yet, that's all. And the mood at Tiffany's house is tense, and it's making me uncomfortable."

To be fair, all of this is true. To be completely accurate, though, I'm not brave enough to tell him about the jealousy that is eating me up. Thomas's expression changes, softens, and I feel even more guilty.

"So who was that girl?" I ask abruptly and regret it immediately.

"Which one?" he replies, calmly sipping his Sprite.

"The one you were talking to outside, under the tree," I hiss, resuming my search on the laptop in an attempt to hide how bothered I am.

"Oh, she has a class with my sister, I think. They're handing out flyers around campus."

"Seemed like she really enjoyed talking to you." I force a smile as I turn to face him.

Thomas just stares at me without speaking before a sly grin creeps over his face. "You jealous?"

I snort loudly. "Oh, please. No."

He exhales a guttural sound, much like a laugh, and nods. "Oh yeah. I believe you," he mocks. I give him a murderous glare and think about how much I'd like to strangle him. Fortunately for him, he decides to stop teasing me and changes the subject.

"Find anything new?" he asks, pointing at my laptop.

"All the scams you could want, as usual, and a few affordable listings. Literally just a few" I sigh, demoralized. I close my laptop irritably and stick it back in my bag. "On the other hand, I do have appointments in an hour to see two other rooms on Roosevelt Drive and a studio apartment in one of the university buildings on Walnut Boulevard."

"Do you have a ride yet?"

"I can walk; it's not far."

"I'll go with you."

"Thomas, no. Seriously, there's no need. I don't want you to feel like you have to drive me all over. Also, I like walking, you know? It calms the nerves. You should give it a try sometime," I tell him, smiling.

He gives a snort of amusement before taking a bite of his cheeseburger. "It's cute when you interpret my statements as questions."

I should have given up before I started—nothing I say is ever going to make him change his mind. "Do what you want, but know that you don't have to—"

I don't even have time to finish my sentence before we are joined by two boys. They are both tall and sturdily built, with that innate self-assurance that athletes always seem to have. One of them—the blond—is wearing a hockey jersey and carrying a helmet. The other, with brown hair and no helmet in sight, toys with an extinguished cigarette. They greet Thomas with slaps on the shoulder, and he responds in kind.

"What's up, man?" the brown-haired one asks before they both take seats around the table.

"Aren't you gonna introduce us to this new little gem?" the blond adds. And when he smiles at me, there's a spark of familiarity. I've seen that smile somewhere before.

Thomas lets them hang for a little bit but finally introduces me with his jaw tight, as though he hates doing it. "Ness, this is Blake and Vince. Guys, this is Vanessa."

"'This new little gem'?" I turn my gaze on Vince. He nods, smiling a mischievous smile that highlights the light sprinkling of freckles on his nose. I can't tell if he's making fun of me or trying to be my friend.

"Since when do you screw freshmen?" Blake blurts out with a "couldn't care less" smirk.

I almost choke on my own saliva. "Excuse me?"

Thomas glares at him, his fingers clenched around his can of Sprite. "Don't be an asshole," he warns.

"Pardon him, Little Gem. What you have to understand is, our Blake here has a lot of rough edges. He's more of a proto-man, a sort of missing link, like the kind you'd find being exhibited in a zoo." Vince gives Blake a mock reproving look. "How many times do I have to tell you, that is not how we address young ladies." He pats the top of Blake's head and looks at me as if to say, *There, I've put him in his place.*

Blake himself doesn't even try to apologize. He shoves Vince away with his shoulder and gives me a look of arrogance and superiority. What is his problem? Thomas puts a reassuring hand on my knee and rubs it.

"I'm not a freshman," I say shortly. "I'm in my sophomore year." There is a part of me, the remnants of my pride, that would like to tell them that Thomas doesn't "screw" me at all, but that would be an enormous lie.

"I've never seen you around before," Blake says, observing me without interest.

And thank God for that.

"I tend to keep to myself," I grit out, looking down at my open notebook before closing it and putting it away.

"I, on the other hand, have seen you lots. You were with Baker, right?" Vince breaks in, taking his hockey helmet off his arm and setting it on the table. He crosses his arms over it, waiting for my response.

I take a long look at him, and finally, I realize where I've seen him before. He's the guy who gave Thomas the keys to ice rink on Monday night so that I could skate! Do I thank him? Maybe some other time. Instead, I tuck my hair behind my ears and nod. It's strange to realize that people at this school really only remember me because of my relationship with Travis.

He sticks his hand out. "Nice to meet you. I'm Vince." Hesitantly, I take his hand and shake it in return. I thought we already introduced ourselves. When I try to pull my hand back, he holds on and squeezes it more than necessary. "You're cute," he says, winking at me. As he does it, I can feel my face getting hot. Just as I'm about to look away in embarrassment, a crushed empty pop can hits Vince's shoulder.

"Keep your hands off her," Thomas threatens, his stare brutal. Then he puts his hand on my thigh, curling his fingers around the underside. With a jerk, he pulls me closer to him.

Vince seems amused by this reaction. He cocks his head and quirks a corner of his mouth. "Message received."

"Listen, is everything confirmed for tonight? You're still in, right?" Blake asks, getting out of his chair. Vince does the same.

"Yeah, all confirmed," Thomas answers evenly, licking a smear of ketchup from his thumb and index finger.

Just these three words are enough to make a strange melancholy settle over me, as I silently realize that Thomas and I won't be together this evening. The idea makes me a little sad. A lot sad. Between my classes, his practices, and my move to Tiffany's, we haven't been able to spend much time together. I was really hoping we'd get Saturday night together at least...

"I'm gonna go shoot hoops; wanna join?" Vince offers, pulling me from my thoughts.

"Pass for now. I'm busy," Thomas answers, giving me a brief glance.

Blake scrutinizes me with an irritated sneer on his face before shaking his head. I get the feeling that he doesn't at all approve of my presence in Thomas's life. But if he thinks I'm the Yoko Ono of this situation, he is hugely mistaken.

"Remember, we've gotta take care of that thing for Martinez..." Blake says, preparing to leave. "*Now*."

I look back and forth between them with a frown on my face. But they're ignoring me. Thomas looks up at Blake, and they exchange a long look which both of them seem to understand perfectly.

"Right," Thomas says, massaging his forehead. Then, he turns to me. "Wait for me here? I just need to take care of something, and I'll be right back; it won't be long."

Ever since everything happened with Logan, Thomas has been more evasive than usual. I get the feeling he's hiding something from me, and I'm not sure I want to know what it is. All I know is that there's no point in pushing with interrogations and demands; Thomas won't talk about it.

"I'll wait," I confirm, smiling faintly because what else can I really do? He gives my thigh another squeeze and then walks away with his friends. Blake doesn't even bother saying goodbye. Dick.

In contrast, Vince gives me his second wink of the day and snickers at the look of annoyance on Thomas face. I think I understand his game now: He's not actually hitting on me; he just likes winding Thomas up.

"Hey, who were those guys?" Alex asks me, returning to the table with an empty tray.

"Thomas's friends," I answer, walking with him to return our lunch trays. A few feet ahead, we spot Tiffany, focused on loading her own tray with chicken and a salad, so we beeline for her.

"Have you had lunch already?" she asks, selecting a bottle of water.

Alex and I both nod. Then I check the time on my phone and see that it's half past one. "I'm waiting for Thomas to come back so I can go check out some apartments," I say.

"Really?" says Alex. "I'd like to come along, if that's not a problem. As your friend, I have a moral obligation to make sure that you at least choose a safe place to live."

"Don't you have more classes today?" I ask.

"I've got a global warming seminar at five, but I'm free until then."

"That's perfect, then."

"I would come too, but I have film club after lunch. Today we're watching a new true-crime documentary, and I can't miss it. But keep me updated. Send pics, okay?" Tiffany adds as we walk her to a free table to keep her company. "By the way, were you able to talk to the financial aid office about a loan?"

I nod. "I had a meeting with them this morning. It looks like a loan is my only solution right now."

"Welcome to America, ladies and gentlemen, where money buys every privilege, but if you're poor, you're screwed." Tiffany exclaims angrily to Alex's nodding agreement. I'd like to point out that both of them are far closer to the first category than to the second, but we are interrupted by the sudden appearance of Leila.

"Hey, folks! Do you like snakes?" is what she opens with, sitting down next to us. "There's an exhibition at the Corvallis Museum next Monday, and they have a discount for OSU students," she explains, handing each of us a flyer.

"Blech, no, God forbid," Tiffany says with a repulsed grimace on her face. "All those scales, the forked tongues, and the way they slither all over everything..." She shudders and squeezes her eyes shut. "God, it's disgusting. It's like I can feel them on me!"

Alex and I, however, politely thank Leila for the flyers. This would be a good opportunity to better introduce her to my two best friends. The first—and last—time they met, we were surrounded by the chaos of the basketball game.

"Hey, Leila, do you remember my friends?" I ask her. "Alex and Tiffany?"

"Yeah, of course. You're the photographer guy, right?" she asks, pointing at Alex. "You took a ton of pictures at the last game."

"Yep, that's me," Alex says, shaking her hand with that easy way he has of making people feel comfortable.

He and Leila continue to chat about photography, also drawing Tiffany into the conversation, until Thomas appears in the cafeteria door. With an unlit cigarette waiting between his lips, he props the door open with one foot. He acknowledges his sister from across the room and invites me outside with a jerk of his head.

"He's here. I'll let you know how the appointments go. Later!" I tell Leila and Tiffany, before heading off with Alex in tow. When Thomas notices his presence, his jaw immediately clenches, and he crosses his arms over his chest. I'm willing to bet that the next words out of his mouth will be something like, *He's not getting in my car.* So I pick up my pace to get to the exit before Alex. I launch myself at Thomas and manage to silence him by throwing my arms around his neck and covering his mouth with a kiss that clearly takes him by surprise.

"Please be nice to him?" I murmur.

Thomas jerks his head in annoyance but still doesn't take his lips off of mine. He pushes my mouth open with his tongue, kissing me deeper. He runs a hand over my butt before squeezing it hard, causing an explosion in my body. Under my clothes, every inch of my skin is burning.

Behind us, Alex clears his throat, and I instantly come back to earth. Embarrassed, I detach Thomas's hand. "We're not alone," I say into his mouth. I lower myself back onto my heels and press my hands to his chest to put him at a safe distance.

He looks from Alex to me; then he wraps a possessive arm around me and pulls me back to him, as though trying to establish the boundaries of his territory. "If I want to touch you, I'll touch you," he tells me, soft but firm. "And if your little friend doesn't like it, he can leave. This is the second time today he's cockblocked me when all I want is to be alone with you."

"Uh…how about I wait in the parking lot for you two?" Alex breaks in, clearly uncomfortable.

"Stop calling him my little friend; it's demeaning," I murmur, disheartened, as I watch Alex walk away to leave us alone. "He's my friend, my best friend. We're a package deal. So I would really like you to make an effort to get along with him or least to accept our bond." I plead with my eyes, and Thomas gives me an indulgent look. I smile gratefully at him, and the three of us walk to the car and leave.

I didn't have any great hopes for the apartments I was seeing, but reality somehow undershot my expectations. The visits were all complete disasters.

The first place was a good price, but it was a house share with bunch of musicians—punk musicians—who may or may not have been high on something, considering that in the twenty minutes we spent with them, none of them was able to put together a single meaningful sentence. The second place was also shared, with a guy, a detail which had not been specified in the ad.

Thomas's answer, before I even had time to formulate one of my own, was unequivocal: "Not a chance." He grabbed my wrist and dragged me out to a soundtrack of Alex's soft laughter.

The studio near campus, on the other hand, was really nice. The common areas were well cared for, the internal walls were red brick, and the layout was sensible. But it was too expensive.

So here we are, back on campus again, dropping off Alex for his last class of the day. I'm dying to take a shower before work, and Thomas offered to let me use his bathroom at the frat house. He didn't have to ask me twice. I like occupying his space even when he's not in it. It gives me a feeling of familiarity.

We park in the space reserved for students and climb out of the car. Thomas locks the doors and then hands me his room key. "Please actually lock the door this time," he teases.

I take the key and roll my eyes. "That was just an oversight, sweetie," I say, dragging a smile out of him. Though, honestly, I almost die of shame every time I think about how Finn saw me half naked in Matt's room.

With one sudden movement, Thomas sweeps me up off the ground and sets me on the hood of his car. He positions himself between my legs and rests his palms on either side of my hips, on the still-warm chassis.

"An oversight we don't wanna make again," he says, rubbing his nose against mine. I can feel his warm breath against my lips as I wrap my arms around his middle.

"Worried someone else might see me in my underwear?" I tease in a whisper, letting my gaze fall first to his Adam's apple, covered in ink, and then to the breadth of his shoulders in his black sweatshirt.

"If that were to happen..." he warns, bringing his mouth to my neck, just below my ear. He kisses me softly there, teasing the sensitive skin. I shiver and press my eyes closed, savoring the jolt of electricity that courses through my body. "I couldn't be held accountable for my actions," he continues, his voice raspy, his hands sliding around to the back of my pants. He squeezes my butt and pulls me harder against his hips, all while continuing to lay a trail of kisses along my jawline.

"You're too jealous," I answer, burying my fingers in the fabric of his sweatshirt. He shakes his head slowly, but a small half smile gives him away.

"I just protect what's mine." He takes my bottom lip between his teeth and softly bites it. His deep-green eyes stare into me. "And you are mine."

I'm his?

Maybe.

But not in the way I'd like.

Somehow, without realizing it, I've gotten myself entangled with him, and it suddenly feels so natural and right for me to be here, in his arms, that I stop thinking entirely. I squeeze his hips with my knees as we kiss, our tongues seeking each other out and intertwining. My heart feels like it's doing backflips. I'm getting short of air, but I don't want to pull away from him, not even to breathe. It's been too long since we've been together, and my body reminds me of that fact every time he gets close to me.

Maybe his does too, because Thomas grabs my legs impulsively and wraps them around his waist. I let him do it, feeling almost drunk on him, on his greedy kisses and his incandescent touches, which burn my skin even through my clothes. He slips a hand along the side of my face and into my hair while I clasp my fingers around the back of his neck and pull him closer to me. I can feel the hardness beneath his jeans, pressing between my thighs.

A wave of devastating desire crashes down on me, but I force myself to put on the brakes. "Thomas..." It comes out as a soft laugh. I can taste the mint gum he's been chewing all afternoon. "We're out in the open. People get arrested for this kind of thing, you know?" I lay my hands on his chest, forcing him to regain a modicum of self-control as well.

He detaches himself from my lips with considerable reluctance and his heavily lidded eyes stay locked on my mouth, devouring me with his gaze. "You're a big problem, Ness," he whispers, his breathing heavy and his mouth red from kissing. "A huge problem."

Then, he helps me down from the car and walks me to the frat house. Standing on the front porch, I am suddenly overwhelmed with sadness at the thought of saying goodbye to him.

What a nitwit.

If I told him anything I was feeling, he would call me a whiny little baby. "Well, see you around..." I shift from one foot to the other, nervously playing with the door key and keeping my eyes down so he can't see what's going on inside my head. Thomas, however, gently tilts my face up.

"If you don't feel like staying with your friend tonight, you can come back here. I won't be here, but the boys aren't planning any parties, so you'll be able to rest." He smiles, and I swear I would smile right back at him, were it not for that phrase *"I won't be here,"* which is playing on an infinite loop in my head.

Is he going to be out all night? I try to chase away all the negative thoughts, though I feel the urge to pepper him with questions and advice. I want to tell him to be a good boy, to not get drunk and wind up between someone else's legs. To neither touch nor be touched. I'd also like to ask where he'll spend the night and with whom, but all of those are girlfriend questions, and damn it, I am not his girlfriend. He is free to go where he wants when he wants and be with whoever he wants, and he doesn't need to tell me anything.

My God, this is already driving me crazy.

"Don't worry," I tell him, trying to appear unruffled. "Alex offered to let me stay with him, at least until I find another solution." Something in Thomas changes radically with my words. His eyes grow dark under his furrowed eyebrows.

"Alex?"

I nod. "I told him how things aren't that great at Tiffany's house and that I'm planning to find a place on my own but, in the meantime, I need somewhere stable to crash."

"You had a stable place to crash," he says, his voice suddenly hard. "My dorm. But you said no."

"And you know why. I have no idea how long it'll take me to find a place; it could be weeks, and Larry can barely stand my presence. Plus, he's right when he says that I'm a squatter. I can't risk getting expelled, and I won't make you risk it either."

Thomas doesn't answer. He just stares at me, grinding his teeth before taking a deep breath and closing his eyes. The phone in his pocket rings, distracting him from who knows what grim thoughts. He doesn't take the call, but the air between us has grown heavy. I'd like to kiss him one more time before we go our separate ways, but now he feels too far away.

"Whatever you want," he says flatly. And then he leaves and I'm alone, trying to deal with the strange heaviness in my gut. I watch as he walks down the steps, lighting a cigarette and turning down the path that will take him off campus, his phone pressed against his ear.

Six

"AND SO I SAYS TO him, 'Look, handsome, it's fifty for the full service.' Then he takes out fifty bucks and drops his underwear."

"I don't believe it!"

"And he just stands there, staring at me, waiting for me to get to work. You should have seen his face when I told him I was in the prostate massage business." The two middle-aged ladies burst out laughing over their dry martinis as they exchange anecdotes. When they see me passing by, one of them summons me with a snap of her fingers, demanding another round of drinks without even looking me in the face. I sigh because by now I've grown used to rude customers, and I've learned to put on a pleasant face to keep them from stiffing me on the tip.

It's nearly eight o'clock on another Saturday night, happy hour is over, and the real chaos is about to begin. The tables are filling up, and I find myself running between them like a ping-pong ball flung from side to side.

Sitting at the counter, right under the big LED screen, is James, a regular whose habits and preferences I've come to know well. He's been waiting for his dinner for more than a half hour, yet he hasn't made a single complaint. He just sits there, typing rapidly on his laptop as he calmly sips his beer and munches on an endless supply of pistachios. If all my customers were that patient, this would be a much better place to work.

"Your chicken wings are going to be a while tonight. Sorry, we had a problem in the kitchen," I tell him, giving the bar a quick wipe. Truthfully, there's no problem in the kitchen, except that the cook doesn't care about anything ever since he caught his wife in bed with his best friend.

"Don't worry about me; the pregame always saps my appetite a bit. I'm sure the wings'll arrive by the time the Ducks pull ahead."

I find myself smiling my first real smile since I left Thomas at campus and started my shift. I see my coworker Cassie walk by, and then, as if remembering something, she doubles back and stops right in front of me. She jabs her order pad at me and says, "Before you got here, Maggie told me to tell you that a woman came by asking for you at lunchtime, said she wanted you to get in touch with her. Maggie said she seemed a little off and was kinda aggravating. Very tall, blond, and her eyes were—"

"Blue." We finish her sentence together. Cassie gives me a surprised look. "Yes! How'd you know?"

"She was my mother."

"Your mother? Couldn't she just call you?" Cassie asks, like it's the most normal thing in the world.

"Apparently not." I look sideways at James, embarrassed to have him involuntarily participating in this conversation. But I am relieved to see that he has gone back to his computer and is typing again.

I thank Cassie for the heads-up and continue working, finally able to deliver those chicken wings to James. I wonder why my mother bothered to show up at my job after almost a week, when she knew full well I wouldn't be here. Why didn't she just call me? What does she want? If she's trying to signal to me that I should reach out to her first, she's going to be very disappointed.

Half an hour before the end of my shift, I am surprised to see Tiffany and Leila walk in the door, busily chatting with one another. I arrange the last of the chairs on top of a table and head over to the bar, where I find them waiting for me with twin dazzling smiles.

"Hey, what are you two doing here?" I greet them, giving them both a bit of a shifty look.

"I'm looking for reasons not to go home, and Leila is…" Tiffany looks at her thoughtfully. "Actually, I don't know what her deal is, but we wound up here purely by chance."

"Do you want something to eat? The kitchen's closed, but I could probably get you a sandwich or some pretzels real quick."

"Actually, I'd rather have some of that liquor you keep back there," Tiff answers in mock desperation before sitting down on a stool and resting her forehead on the bar.

"In that case, make it two," Leila adds, sitting down next to Tiffany.

"Something wrong?" I ask her, drying the glasses that have just come out of the dishwasher.

"I'm going home in two days."

"And you're not happy about it?" Tiffany says, lifting her head up off the bar.

Leila lets out a sarcastic laugh. "Any daughter should be happy to go home for a visit, right?"

Not any daughter, believe me…

"Actually, I haven't seen or heard from my parents in a long time," she continues, scratching the rough surface of the bar with her fingernail. "And there are about a million valid reasons to keep on avoiding them, but now that he's on his deathbed, my father apparently wants to atone for all his sins," she finishes softly, staring into the middle distance.

Her words snap me to attention, struck by a sudden feeling of distress. I can feel Tiffany's gaze on me, almost like she wants to ask me if I know anything about this. Truthfully, this is a part of Thomas's life that is completely opaque to me. What sins is Leila talking about? Is this why Thomas has been so hard to pin down recently? And what does Thomas think about all of this?

Every time we even get close to the topic of his family, he shies away and becomes even more indecipherable than usual. If I am an open book, then Thomas is an inaccessible tome hidden deep in the forbidden section of the library.

"Not all parents are good parents," I tell Leila, hoping to

comfort her. "But he's still your father, and I'm really sorry about the whole situation." I try to calibrate my words precisely and put just the right amount of compassion in my voice. If I've learned anything from Thomas, it's that he becomes defensive when he feels like I'm pitying him. I don't want to trigger the same reaction in his sister.

"I can't really be that sorry about it, though," Leila says to my surprise. "On the one hand, I want to be able to go home and forgive him but, on the other hand, I can't help but wonder if it he isn't getting exactly what he deserves."

I'm speechless. Of all the things she might have said, that is one I never imagined I'd hear. But then a half-forgotten memory comes back to me: Leila and Thomas arguing in a campus doorway at the end of September. She was begging him to go home with her, but he refused. He freaked out on her. At the time, I didn't understand—I couldn't understand—but now I am beginning to feel as though I was given a small piece of a much larger puzzle.

"Girls, what is up with all this drama?" Tiffany breaks in, distracting me from my musings. "Have we by any chance wandered into a soap opera? My parents are trying to control my life; you have to go home to your family, but it's the last place you want to be. And that's to say nothing of you." She raises an arm to point at me. "You've been kicked out of your house and forced to go into debt to the federal government so you don't wind up living under a bridge while you finish school," she cries, slapping her hand down on the bar.

We all fall silent. I sigh and slam the glass I was drying down on the bar, making both of them jump. "You know what? My shift ends in fifteen minutes; we should do something."

"Something?" Tiffany echoes.

"Yeah, let's get nuts. We could...I don't know, go to the movies!"

Tiffany raises her eyebrows in confusion. "Is that your idea of a wild Saturday night?"

"Do you have a better suggestion? There's not much to do in this town."

"How about we go dancing?" Leila cuts in, drawing our attention. "I know about this place in downtown Corvallis."

"Now that's a good idea!" Tiffany exclaims, as though she's just been roused from a deep sleep. "I really need to let loose."

I quickly do the math. Between the cost of gas, the door charge at the club, and any drinks, there's no way I'd have enough money to cover it. "Um, I don't know, girls. Now that I'm not living with my mother, I have to save as much as possible."

"Don't worry about it," Tiffany says sweetly. "I've got you. You know it's no problem."

But it *is* a problem for me. It's terribly humiliating for me.

"But if you're not feeling it, that's okay," Leila puts in. "We can go to the movies, go bowling, or take a nice walk by the river."

Tiffany nods along, but James interrupts us to ask for the check before I can answer her. I dash to the cash register to ring him up, and we exchange a few more words about the current score in the game.

"You know, I'm lucky enough to have a job that lets me travel a lot," he tells me, rummaging in his coat pocket. "But I have to tell you that the best chicken wings I've ever had are right here."

I smile at him, pleased that he likes them; then I print the bill and hand it to him. "That'll be fifteen seventy-five."

James takes his wallet out of his pocket, and as he does so, his sleeve rides up, and I can see the tattoo on his wrist, a tiny letter *E*. After giving him his change, I see that he's left a hundred-dollar bill in the tip jar.

"James, wait! You forgot this." I try to hand it to him, sure that it was a mistake, but he won't take the bill.

"That's for you; it's your tip."

I nearly stroke out. "B-but...it's a hundred dollars," I whisper incredulously.

He smiles at me as he adjusts the collar of his elegant knee-length coat and does up the buttons.

"You're a good kid, Vanessa. Keep it. I know you'll make good use of it. See you tomorrow, same time, same place." He gives me a wink and then walks away. I just stand there, open-mouthed with the hundred-dollar bill in my hand, staring at the Marsy's door as it closes behind him.

"Nessy, what happened?" Tiffany asks when I come back over to them.

"A customer just tipped me a hundred dollars," I hiss, still in shock.

"Who?" She turns her head suddenly. "The man who just left?"

I nod, slowly refolding the bill and tucking it into the waistband of my skirt with the rest of my tips.

"And people say servers are underpaid." She smirks. "Now you have no more excuses: We have to celebrate!" She wriggles on her stool, excited.

"Definitely," I tell her with a smile.

"What club were you talking about, Leila?" Tiffany asks her.

"It's called ClubSeven," Leila explains.

"*The* ClubSeven?" Tiff exclaims, her face disapproving.

"What is it?" I ask.

"A nightclub full of maniacs. The people who go there are rotten to the core, and you can't trust any of them. It's not safe to go there alone. Plus you have to be twenty-one to get in, and none of us are."

"You're not wrong about that, but I know the bouncer, so our ages won't be a problem. And we wouldn't be alone," Leila retorts, trying to suppress a grin. "My brother's there."

My breath catches. Thomas is there?

"Oh..." I manage, not sure how I feel about this.

"So...should we go?" Leila asks again.

Tiffany looks my way, letting me decide.

I just shrug, because I don't want to seem like *that girl*. The one who gets all clingy and depressed when she's away from her boyfriend, or stalks him to make sure he isn't doing anything he shouldn't. I can't deny, however, that I do have an intense desire to see Thomas, and knowing that he's out at a nightclub doesn't make me feel very relaxed. And there is definitely a part of me that would like to keep an eye on him...

Okay, so maybe I am *that girl* after all. Damn it.

I sigh, giving in to temptation. "All right, let's go."

Before going to the club, we take a small detour to Leila's dorm on campus, near the Marsy. She offered to lend us some of her clothes, because even if she does know the bouncer, we should still at least *look* twenty-one. Tiffany chooses a ruched blue bodycon dress, which she pairs with heels in the same color. Leila goes for a darker look: a fitted skirt made of burgundy leather and a lacy black crop top under a studded jacket, along with a pair of biker boots.

I want to be daring but not too daring. So I pick a red dress with thin straps and a generous sweetheart neckline. The satin fabric hits me at midthigh and hugs my body perfectly, highlighting the curves of my hips and my round butt. According to Tiffany, the contrast between the dress and my long black hair (which I have decided to wear down) creates a "bombshell effect" that's going to draw everyone's attention. Even though I'm only really interested in catching one person's eye.

When it comes to shoes, though, I remain faithful to my Converse. It's not the best combination, I know, but I like it better this way.

I pay close attention to Leila during the entire hair and makeup operation to see if I can glean any hints about her mood. After what she told us at the bar, I can imagine she's not in a great place right now. But I can see that she is similar to her brother in this: they both tend to appear outwardly impassive and unaffected, while inside of them a war is raging.

Shortly thereafter, we arrive in front of a club illuminated by a large neon palm tree with the words *ClubSeven* flashing intermittently underneath it. We can hear the muffled bass even from outside. I tug the edges of my short jacket tight against my exposed chest and look around at all the people. They linger in small groups, smoking, laughing, and talking. Here and there, kids perch on the hoods of parked cars while an endless line snakes out the front of the club.

None of this seems to be a problem for Leila, who motions for us to follow her and moves to the front of the line, ignoring the shouted insults and protests of the people who have been waiting for who knows how long. When we reach the entrance, we are met by a mountain of a man, his bulging muscles highlighted by his tight black T-shirt. His close-cropped hair gives him a tough look. Tiffany and I exchange a "not bad" eyebrow raise.

"Hey, Marcus," Leila exclaims. "Did my brother get here yet?" she asks, rummaging in her clutch for something.

The bouncer nods. "About an hour ago."

Leila's face lights up in a triumphant smile. "Fantastic!" She leans in close to Marcus's ear and whispers, "Do you think you could let us in?"

The bouncer looks skeptically at Tiffany and me. "You I can," he says to Leila. "You two need to show ID," he orders, pointing a finger at us.

Shit.

"Come on, Marcus. They're my friends. We'll be good," Leila says, giving him a look that would soften a pack of angry hyenas. But he just shakes his head, unmovable.

"You know the rules, JC. You can come in, but they can't, not without ID."

"Who the hell is JC?" Tiff whispers into my ear. I shrug, having no idea.

"Listen, Marcus, she's my brother's girlfriend," Leila adds, pointing at me, and my heart leaps. "And the redhead has a date with Martinez. They're waiting for us, and we're already late."

Hold on a minute... Martinez?

Is this the same Martinez that Thomas and Blake were talking about in the cafeteria?

Marcus frowns, looking surprised. "The guys didn't tell me anything about that."

Leila nods firmly and takes her cell phone out of her clutch. "But it's true, I promise you. So are you going to let us in, or do I have to call them to come get us? You know how Martinez doesn't like to be bothered."

He studies us carefully for a few seconds, cocking an eyebrow, before giving up. He takes our right hands and stamps the backs with the name of the club. Then he unhooks the rope that cordons off the entrance and lets us through. As we pass, Leila gives him a cryptic smile, which he returns.

The thought occurs to me: *Is it possible that those two are...?*

I shake my head. *Don't ask questions, Vanessa. This is a Collins we're talking about; just don't ask questions.*

"Give it to us to straight: You fucking that bouncer?"

My eyes bug out and I whip my head around to give Tiffany an admonishing look.

"No," Leila answers, laughing. "Honestly, after what happened with your brother, I have a hard time trusting men," she finishes in a meek and suddenly insecure tone that causes an uncomfortable silence to descend upon all of us.

Tiffany stops suddenly, looking devastated. "I am so sorry. I didn't mean to be disrespectful. I know it might not mean much to you, but I'm not like him. Well, we are twins, so I am like him in some ways. But you have to believe me when I tell you that I have never been more ashamed than I was when I found out what he did to you." She gives me a sad look. "And what he did to you," she adds. Tiffany takes Leila's hand and smiles at her.

"It doesn't matter; it's over now. And I really like you," Leila tells her, making us all smile.

"Why did the bouncer call you that name?" I ask her as we walk through the long dark tunnel that connects the external and internal entrances.

"JC?"

I nod.

"It stands for 'Junior Collins.' My brother always calls me that, and Marcus overhead it once, and now everybody's calling me that or 'Little Collins.'"

"And who is this Martinez?" Tiffany interjects.

"He's the owner's son. He does some...business out of the club."

The way she says "business" is very suggestive.

"What, is he a drug dealer?" Tiffany asks in surprise. Leila tells her to lower her voice, immediately confirming that Tiffany's suspicion is correct.

But...why is Thomas hanging out with drug dealers?

"And what does that have to do with us?" I ask, although I'm a lot more curious what it has to do with Thomas.

"Oh, nothing. I just had to make up an excuse on the spot to make sure Marcus would let us in."

The hallway forks at the end of the tunnel. Leila guides us to a black door on the left, while I look curiously at the line of mostly boys waiting on the other side. The only thing I can see ahead of them is a red curtain. "Hey, what's on the right?"

Tiffany and Leila both turn to look and the latter replies, "Oh, that's where the strippers perform."

"You mean this is a strip club?" I ask, incredulous.

"Something like that," Leila confirms, chuckling at the shock on my face.

"But there are minors in that line. Is that legal?"

"The word *legal* is open to a lot of interpretation when you have the right connections. Trust me, the less you know about it, the better. Let's go." She takes my hand, and I grab Tiffany's tightly as we walk through the black door.

As soon as we enter the club, we are hit by a wave of heat generated by the huge crowd of people jumping around and going wild to the pounding beat of the dance music. Beams from a strobe light blind me, it stinks of alcohol and smoke, and it's so loud, we're forced to scream to hear one another. Tiffany was right; this place is a jungle.

"Let's go get something to drink!" Leila suggests.

"I'm down!" Tiff answers.

Before I even have time to decline the invitation, I'm being dragged over to the bar. Leila rests her arms on it, summoning the bartender with a wave of her hand and shouting something in his ear. Moments later, three beers slam down in front of us, each with a slice of lime jammed into the neck of the bottle. We toast each other and drink. I feel a rush of adrenaline; the music is roaring so loudly that I can feel the bass vibrating in my chest. I lick beer from my lips and turn to Leila. "Do you come here a lot?"

"No, not that much."

"What about...your brother?" I ask, trying to sound as casual as possible.

"He definitely comes here more than me. There's nothing else like this in Corvallis, so sometimes the guys come here for some entertainment."

Sure, "entertainment"...

I sip my beer and look around, but I suspect it will be impossible to spot Thomas among all these people. I'm just about to let my thoughts completely spiral when Tiffany grabs my hand and drags Leila and me both onto the dance floor.

"We are here to have fun," she shouts at me. "So quit thinking and have some fun!" Tiffany lets loose to the music with moves that make both Leila and me burst out laughing. I envy her vitality, her ability to enjoy herself, to be with other people and just dance without caring about anything else.

Leila joins Tiffany, and I force myself to let go as well. The three of us dance, waving our arms in the air, moving our hips, and laughing like fools. Our thrashing attracts the attention of three boys. Two of them start dancing with Tiff and Leila, and I'm left alone with the third, who puts his arm around me and pulls me closer to him. I instantly tense up. Under the colored lights, I can see his amused grin and his lascivious gaze lingering on my cleavage. On instinct, I pull my jacket tighter around myself and slip from his grasp.

"Gotta go to the bathroom; I'll be right back!" I yell in Tiffany's ear, though it takes two attempts for her to understand me. She offers to go with me, but I tell her there's no need. I make my way through the crowd, dodging a few guys who approach me before I feel someone grab my ass. I spin around quickly, but it's hard to identify a culprit in this crush of people. Yuck.

Suddenly, in the midst of all this confusion, I spot what appears to be a familiar figure in the distance. Squinting my eyes to get a better look, I can see a guy with broad shoulders. His arms, exposed by his black T-shirt, are covered in a series of tattoos. *His* tattoos. My heart is in my throat.

It's him.

Seven

SEATED ON A LEATHER SOFA with one arm thrown over the armrest and his legs slightly spread, Thomas holds a glass of beer. He didn't put any gel in his hair, just the way I like it. When he gets up and raises an arm to greet someone, I see that the dark jeans he's wearing are low-slung enough to reveal the elastic of his boxers. It's a perfect mix of sensuality and audacity—absolutely irresistible. I'm almost angry at the thought that every girl in here gets to admire all this bounty.

Following an uncontrollable instinct, I move toward him. I shouldn't. I should be dancing with my girls and having fun on my own, just like he appears to be doing. But I seem to be drawn to him by some force that is impossible to ignore.

Thomas sets his glass on the table and leans over a boy sitting on the other side of the sofa, pinning the guy down with a knee in his stomach while he punches him in the shoulder. They laugh and clown around cheerfully, and Thomas seems so different from how I'm used to seeing him that it makes me want to hide in a corner and just watch him, enraptured, for the rest of the night. The other boy gets to his feet, and I realize that he's the obnoxious dude I met in the cafeteria today: Blake. Thomas takes his beer from the table and brings it to his mouth.

The closer I get to him, the more I feel a strange sense of anxiety. He's surrounded by at least five other guys, some of them standing, others sitting and drinking or fiddling with something on the table. The psychedelic lights of the club make it tough for me to decipher faces and movements. Except for one, a face I would recognize anywhere.

I feel an electric shock run down my back as a pair of blue eyes intercepts my gaze. They stare at me, alert and confused before a cruel smile spreads across that perfect face. A moment later, Shana reaches out and wraps her arms around Thomas's neck, planting a kiss in the hollow of his throat. My own throat closes as if caught in a vise. I try to swallow and discover that I can't. My beer tumbles from my hand, smashing on the floor, and the urge to run as far away as possible and hide from everything is so strong that I don't even think about it. The last thing I see before I turn and flee is Thomas pulling away from Shana and sitting back on the sofa with the other guys.

I can't believe this.

My heart is thumping wildly in my chest. I speed toward the exit because I have to get some air. I squeeze my eyes shut and shake my head. Why is he here with her? Why didn't he tell me? Why is he letting her touch him? Hug him? *Kiss* him?

After throwing a few elbows here and there, I finally manage to push my way to the exit, but just as I'm about to grab the door handle, Tiffany appears in front of me. "Here, hon!" she says as she hands me one of the two glasses she is holding, filled with some colorful cocktail. "Leila managed to get them from that cute bartender!" She points to a guy behind the bar.

"I–I don't want it. I have to get out of here." I push the glass back into her hands, walking past her to get out the door. Outside on the patio, I breathe in the cold air.

"Hey, what's the matter with you?" Tiff asks worriedly, chasing after me.

"Thomas is here. With her..." I turn to look at Tiffany in shock, my heart beating so hard it actually hurts. "With Shana."

Her eyes widen. "What?!"

I nod, rubbing my forehead. "I saw them together not two minutes ago. As soon as she spotted me, she practically pounced on him.

God…" I shake my head and cover my face with my hands, embittered and disgusted with myself. "I am so stupid."

"Hey!" Tiffany scolds, taking my hands in hers. "You are not stupid at all. Now, you get back in there and have it out with him. And if you can't do it, I will!"

"I can't…" I gasp. "I can't just bust in there like a crazy person and demand an explanation."

"You can, actually. In fact, you have to."

"No, Tiff. He and I are not together. He is not my boyfriend! Thomas can say whatever he wants about how it's just him and me, but do you know what it all really is? Just a bunch of bullshit! In reality, he doesn't feel any obligation toward me, and this is clear proof. And I knew that; I knew it from the beginning!"

"Nessy, don't jump to conclusions…"

"I am not about to pretend that I don't know what just happened in there, and I'm not going to relive what happened with Travis either. If Shana felt free to kiss him, then that's because he lets her do it," I continue, my voice shaking. "I want to go."

"Just listen for a second, okay?" Tiffany sets the cocktails down on a patio table near us and gently grips my shoulders. "You saw exactly what she wanted you to see, because she's a giant bitch. But you can't let one moment ruin your whole evening. The fact that they are here together doesn't mean anything; they have lots of friends in common, and you know it. And if you've decided to head down this path with Thomas, then you have to learn to trust him. I know that after what my brother did to you, it's hard to trust. It would be hard for anyone, but Thomas isn't Travis. He's an asshole for sure, an arrogant one, and he can be a real bastard sometimes, but he isn't Travis. I'm sure he has a good explanation for this."

I give a skeptical snort and cross my arms over my chest—I'm starting to shiver in the cold. "And what explanation would that be? I can't even talk to my platonic best friend, but he can get his neck slobbered on by the girl he was fucking up until a few weeks ago?"

I can see from Tiffany's face that I've made a good point.

"I'm not saying you're wrong, but standing out here brooding isn't going to give you the answers you want. Go in there and deal with the situation. Get pissed if you want. But running away isn't the answer. It never is." She brings her hands back to my shoulders and gives me a firm look. "Don't let Shana get you down. If he's going to have fun without you, then show him you can have fun without him too!"

I convince myself that Tiffany might be right.

We grab our drinks and head back inside the club. I am determined to enjoy every second of this evening to the fullest. To hell with Thomas and to hell with Shana. I down my cocktail in one gulp, rage igniting my chest. The alcohol burns a path down my throat; I close my eyes and let the heat wash over me. I leave my jacket in the coat check and disappear back into the crowd to continue dancing with Tiffany and Leila.

We go completely wild on the dance floor, and after a while, we are joined again by the three guys from before. My friends pick back up with their two from before, while the third gets behind me again. This time, I'm not leaving. I keep moving to the beat, starting to feel a liberating effect from the alcohol coursing through my bloodstream. I slide my hands over my breasts, down my torso, and finally to my hips. I close my eyes, imagining he is here with me and not with her. And then I am picturing her lips on his skin. It hurts.

But I just keep moving, uninhibited. I pull up my hair and let it fall to the side. Two hands rest delicately on my hips. I suck in a breath, deluding myself for a moment that it might be him. But that hope dissolves in a hurry; he doesn't touch me like this. Thomas's touch is devastating, wild, and possessive. When he touches me, he claims every part of me. My back bumps into the stranger's chest as he decides to ramp up our dancing. My backside is rubbing against his pelvis, we begin to move together, and I try to stifle the feeling of revulsion that tells me to get away from him. His lips move closer to my neck, and his hands stray to the exposed skin of my thighs. When I feel his fingers wandering underneath the hem of my dress, I immediately come to my senses.

What am I doing?

I pull myself away from him forcefully and flee. Water. I need water.

I make it to the bar and try to order, but the thumping music and the crowd of people all decidedly taller than me render me invisible to the bartender. After a few failed attempts, I sit on the first open stool I can find and wait for the people to disperse. I can see Tiffany and Leila tearing up the dance floor in the middle of the club; the guys from before appear to have left. I watch as they sway to the rhythm of the music, back to back.

"On the house, babe," a nearby voice says, and a glass full of amber liquid slides down the bar toward me. I take it and look over to find myself faced with a tall broad young man with green eyes. Not green like Thomas's, of course, full of infinite hues and shades; this guy's eyes are just…green.

"Bartenders in places like this never notice people like you," he says.

I frown, a little annoyed. "People like me?"

He gets up from his stool and walks over to me. Placing a hand under my chin, he leans over me with disarming self-confidence, and then, just a couple of inches from my ear, he whispers, "Yeah, people like you. Good girls."

He steps back and brings his glass to his mouth, taking a sip without moving his eyes from mine. He sets the glass back down on the bar and then stares at my legs shamelessly, his mouth hinting at a smile. Uncomfortable, I quickly press my knees together and tug down the hem of my dress but to little avail.

"I'm Jeremy. And you are?" he asks me when he looks back into my eyes again. I don't even have time to tell him to back off before an arm moves between us with such sudden vehemence that it makes us both start.

"She's *spoken for*."

My heart hammers in my chest. Thomas is standing between Jeremy and me with his back to me, and his large masculine hand is gripping the cold steel of the bar so hard that his knuckles are white. I can't see his face right now, but I can see Jeremy's stricken expression, so I can imagine the icy look Thomas is giving him. "And if you don't wanna be hospitalized for a head injury, I'd advise you to get lost."

Jeremy takes a step backward and vanishes into the crowd. But I am far from relieved. How dare he pull this crap after he's the one who came here with Shana and didn't tell me? Infuriated, I hop off the stool and try to leave, but Thomas stops me with a hand on my wrist.

"Where do you think you're going?" he roars.

"Anywhere you're not!" I try to tug my arm out of his grip, but he stops me, pulling me tight against his chest.

"What the fuck are you doing here? You should have told me; if I knew you were here alone, I would have—"

"You would have what? Changed your plans so you could do whatever the hell you want in peace?" I needle.

"What plans are you talking about?"

I cross my arms irritably, glaring at him. "You're here with Shana. I saw you two together."

He stares gravely at me, his face revealing no emotion whatsoever. I don't know whether his unruffled state suggests a clear conscience or otherwise.

"So?"

I raise my eyebrows in astonishment. "And when were you planning to tell me?"

"Tell you what?"

"Oh, for Christ's sake, Thomas! That you're seeing other people, that you're seeing *her*!" I gesticulate wildly, finding myself thankful for the crowd that renders us anonymous.

"I'm not seeing her," he says pointedly through gritted teeth. He's a hairsbreadth away from my face and at the end of his patience. "And if she's hooking up with one of the guys I'm out with and we happen to be in the same group, why is that a problem?"

"It is a problem because a week ago that bitch threw a smoothie on me. It's a problem because every time I run into her, I have to endure her ridiculous attempts at intimidation because she's jealous over you!" I stab a finger into his chest. "It's a problem because, apparently, you can go out on the town with the girl you were fucking up until a few weeks ago and who clearly still has feelings for you, and you can let her touch you and kiss you, but I can't talk to Logan or Jeremy or any other breathing male in my vicinity!" I am yelling now, truly getting out of control.

Faced with his angry eyes, I completely lose my temper. He is the last person in the world who is allowed to be mad right now.

"Yeah, that's right, because you are clearly incapable of recognizing danger when it's right in front of you," he replies with his most punchable face. "Why the fuck did you hide this smoothie thing from me?!"

I stare at him, offended. "I can't recognize danger?" I demand, focusing on the only part of his speech that really seems important to me. "You think I don't know what that guy was after? I would have gotten him to piss off easily if you hadn't barged in. You treat me like I'm this little baby incapable of living in the world, but I don't need to be protected from everything. Just now, I danced with a guy, and hey, would you look at that? I'm still alive."

Thomas takes a deep breath, and a terrible expression comes over his face. "What did you do?"

"Don't give me that look. If Shana is allowed to take liberties with you, then I can too. After all, isn't that how these open relationships work?"

His jaw tenses as he scrubs a hand over his face. His rapid breathing shows no sign of calming down. "She was one who jumped me, and if you had been there, you would have seen that I didn't return the favor. I backed off! And what do you do? Grind your ass on the first dick you can find?" His words hit me like a punch to the chest, leaving me speechless. I'm starting to feel a painful guilty sensation, but why? I'm not the one who screwed up.

"You know what, Thomas? Enough. I...I gave it a try, okay? I tried to make this thing between you and me feel good, but I can't. It doesn't. This isn't for me."

Thomas stiffens, giving me a severe look. "What the hell are you talking about?"

I don't know. I don't know what I'm saying. Or what I'm doing. But I'm like a runaway train—unstoppable.

"You know exactly what I mean," I tell him stubbornly.

For a long time, he just stares at me with no reaction. Then, without another word, he grabs my wrist and drags me away from the chaos that surrounds us.

"What are you doing? Let me go!" I try to resist, digging my heels into the floor, but he just tightens his grip on my wrist.

"Come with me, now," he orders, pulling me into the men's bathroom. He looks around for a free stall, and a moment later, I find myself imprisoned in a tiny metal cubicle with profane scribbles all over the wall. My back is against the door, Thomas's body pressed against me with his forearms on either side of my head.

"You want to end things with me just because you saw Shana sitting with me? I don't give a shit about her."

It's enough to make me laugh. "I can't end anything with you, because technically, we aren't even together, Thomas. I'm just telling you I can't do it anymore."

"You felt otherwise up until this afternoon. What happened to make you suddenly change your mind?"

"Nothing happened. I just realized that this is not for me. So no more messy scenes from now on. No more doubts. No more anything; it's over," I answer, unable to admit that I'm simply jealous. That I've fallen in love.

Thomas's face grows hard as he becomes increasingly enraged. "Bullshit," he says.

"It's over," I say again, almost challenging him.

But he just shakes his head, slowly and more seriously than ever, looming over me again. His mouth is a mere inch from mine. My heartbeat suddenly becomes faster, stronger until it's deafening me. He takes my face in his hands and stares into my eyes. "It's not over until I say it's over," he growls, a breath away from my lips and staring like he wants to devour them. "And I say it's not over. You want me. And I want you. *Just* you." His grip on my face intensifies, and I can feel my skin heating. "Right now, you're out of control and crazy jealous. But so am I. You think it didn't piss me off, seeing that guy drooling over your tits and legs? Or that I'm not dying to find that asshole you danced with and smash his face in?"

His scent, wafting up from his T-shirt, surrounds me. Surprised and maybe even satisfied by his words, I lift my eyes to meet his.

"Fuck, do I want to do that," he continues. "But do you know what else I want to do, Ness?" He spins me around in one sudden movement, and now my chest is pressed to the door, my palms flat against it. My breaths are short and rapid, and his body is crushed against me.

"Thomas..." I start to say, planning to calm him down, but the gentle whisper I'd intended takes on more of a moaning quality.

The rumble of male voices coming in and out of the bathroom instantly triggers a fear that we'll be overheard. But for some reason, that risk only makes everything that's happening more exciting and even seems to amplify the sensations roiling inside me. Thomas brushes his lips over the sensitive skin of my neck, and a shiver runs down my spine. He slips his hands under my dress and crawls his fingers along the flesh of my inner thighs, slowly moving up and up until he meets the damp fabric of my panties.

The panting for breath and burning skin are clear signs of my growing arousal, and they coax a satisfied groan from the back of his throat. "I want to rip this dress off and fuck you until you forget about the existence of other men." He presses me into his pelvis hard, making me feel his erection. An untamable fire ignites within me, and I tremble all over when he starts to slowly move his fingers between my panty-covered lips. The way he sucks and gnaws on my earlobe is almost violent. "Until you understand that the only cock you're allowed to rub yourself on is mine."

I hold my breath. I dig my nails into the door so hard, I nearly scratch the paint. Not giving me time to react, speak, or even think, Thomas takes my chin with his other hand and turns my head for an angry kiss. I moan into his mouth. It's intense, this kiss of his; there's agitation in it as well as presumption but also desire. Yearning. When he pulls away from me, I feel dizzy and hot. He turns me around completely so we can face one another and then continues.

"Fuck it, if they want to look at you, then let them look. But I'm the only one who gets to touch you." He grabs my ass with both hands, lifting me up, and I instinctively wrap my legs around his waist. My back hits the door. My dress rides up to expose my thighs, and I gasp as he rubs his groin against my panties. Incapable of pushing him away, I let him do what he wants. What we both want.

Thomas seizes my mouth, greedily taking it for his own. I get lost in the heat of him and the faint taste of beer as he slides his tongue inside, intertwining it with mine. His breathing is more of a growl as he fondles and squeezes my breast, covering it with his palm. He pulls down the straps of my dress and bends his head to devour my bared breasts. I squeeze my eyes shut and dig my fingers into his hair.

His hands are everywhere until they slip securely underneath my dress. He pushes my panties to the side and begins touching me even more eagerly.

"Don't say it again." He takes my bottom lip between his teeth and bites down, hard. "Never again." He slips one finger inside me, and I contract against it. The rush of pleasure and adrenaline makes me jump.

"What?" I gasp, clinging to his shoulders while he moves me rapidly against him with one hand firm on my ass. "That it's over?"

I provoke him again just to see him tremble with anger just a little bit more. Because I love the way his body reacts. I love the way his pupils dilate and burn with passion. I can't stop looking at him, and he is so goddamned irresistible no matter what the circumstances. Whether he's turned on or pissed off—or, even better, both—he wreaks havoc on every part of me.

"Shut up," he scolds me, panting as he pulls his hands out from between my thighs. And just when I think he's about to fix my dress and put me back on the ground, he takes things to the next level. He unzips his jeans and pulls them down just far enough to release his erection. The air is driven from my lungs. I should tell him to stop. Remind him that someone could hear us at any moment and also that I am not at all the type of girl who gets railed in a sleazy nightclub bathroom. Yeah, I should tell him all of that...but the truth is that the idea of doing that with him right here, right now arouses me beyond belief.

When he lifts me up again, I can feel my heart beating in my throat. He pulls my panties aside once more and rubs himself against me, making me somehow even wetter and greedier. Oh God, I need air.

"I don't have a condom; please tell me you're on the pill," he gasps, pressing his forehead to mine. "I've never gone without one before; I'm clean." Delighted by this confession, I nod. It's both an answer to his question and an offering of consent for what we're about to do. I trust him. And I want him inside me. I want to feel him skin-to-skin, the way no one else ever has.

His eyes are eager, brimming with desire. Without ever taking his gaze from mine, he enters me in one powerful, decisive thrust. I let out a loud sob of pleasure, overwhelmed by my feelings for him. Thomas allows his head to fall into the crook of my neck while he squeezes my ass with both hands, pushing me against him. "Fuck!"

Doing this without a condom is a completely different experience. It's more beautiful, more intense. It creates a physical and mental connection that goes beyond simple carnal pleasure. It's just *more*.

"Have you done it like this before?" he asks, speaking against my neck in a soft voice.

"Never."

My answer apparently pleases him, because he grins. He takes my mouth again and starts pounding into me, wild and possessive, stealing my breath with each thrust. "You're mine, Ness," he says roughly, groaning into my ear. "Every part of you is mine." He kisses my neck, my shoulder, my breasts where they are spilling out of my dress. He bites and then kisses them again. He speeds up his thrusting until he's got me out of my mind. I close my eyes as he slams my back against the cubicle door with each powerful drive into me. It is the most primal sex I've ever had. I cling to him tightly because I need to touch him, to kiss him and to feel what's *mine*.

I'm so aroused that my climax comes almost immediately; just a few more thrusts, and I start to shake. I knit my fingers behind his neck, pressing my cheek against his; with his fingers digging into the flesh of my ass, I explode into uncountable pieces. Thomas keeps fucking me through my orgasm. Then, with one hand, he pulls my dress up, baring me to the waist. He slams into me one last time before pulling out again with a bestial roar. Maybe it's crazy, but a part of me was hoping that he would go all the way and let himself come inside me.

Thomas holds himself and slides a hand up and down his length a few times until he shoots copiously on my belly. His shoulders tremble slightly; he clenches his jaw and tilts his head back. His eyes, half closed and clouded with pleasure, make him more seductive than ever. I watch the hot flow of his spend as it slides down my skin, over my lower abdomen and groin, ending up between my thighs.

Oh God…it's filthy and thrilling at the same time.

He's holding me up with just one arm, still clasping me against him. We stare into one another's eyes, not saying anything, while we both try to even out our breathing. We're sweaty and dazed, covered in hickeys and love bites. Slowly, I loosen my grip around his waist, and when he lets me slide off of him, I can feel my knees shaking like they're made of Jell-O.

Thomas grabs some toilet paper, cleaning me up and wiping his own hand before tossing everything in the toilet. He does up his jeans and observes me. Indecipherable as always, he looks like he's musing on some complicated idea. "It's not over," he states finally, definitively. I look steadily at him for a long moment, but I don't reply. Because it is painfully obvious that nothing is finished between the two of us. My silence only confirms it.

I force myself not to fall into those green eyes as I fix my panties and dress. When I look up at him again, he is still staring at me. I bite the inside of my cheek and ask in a whisper, "What is it?"

He advances on me, forehead wrinkling in a serious expression. "You just got fucked in a nightclub bathroom."

"And *you* just fucked me in a nightclub bathroom," I point out, hoping to get a laugh. But it doesn't work.

"And that's...okay with you?" He seems confused and a little embarrassed. I cup his face in my hands and kiss him.

"It's okay with me because I did it with you. Also, if I remember correctly, I owed you a rendezvous in the staff bathroom. I'd say you've thoroughly collected that rain check."

Thomas presses his forehead to mine and kisses me. Not a fiery kiss like before but slow, just his lips against mine in a tender caress. "If you think I've collected even part of it, then you don't know me at all."

"In that case, I look forward to working off my debt." I grin, finally getting a laugh out of him.

"If you want to get out of here, just let me know," he says encouragingly, brushing my cheek.

"I want to stay. And you're here with your friends; I don't want to spoil your evening."

"By the way, there's something I wanted to talk to you about." He steps back from me and feels around in the pocket of his jeans, eventually pulling out his pack of cigarettes. He gives me a quick look, asking for permission. I agree because, even though we are in a tiny enclosed bathroom, I imagine he needs it.

"This afternoon when I left the frat house, I talked to Matt," he tells me, leaning back against the wall. He lights up a cigarette and releases the first plume of smoke into the air. "He gave me the go-ahead."

I frown, confused. "The go-ahead for what?"

"For you to move into my room at the frat house until you find someplace else."

My eyes widen. "What?"

"It's the best solution right now."

"To come live with you? No way," I say loudly, trying to disguise my shock with a nervous laugh.

Is he nuts?

He gives me an amused snort and takes another drag. "I stay in the dorms during the week; you'd be alone at the frat house. You wouldn't have to worry about a deposit, and no one would take advantage of you. And you wouldn't have to keep crashing with your friends. Think about it; it's not a bad idea."

"But it's a men's fraternity. And the parties they throw aren't really suitable for people who are...me," I point out.

Thomas just shrugs. "The guys are fine. Between class and practice, most of them are out all day anyway. Leila lived there for a while with no problems, remember? Besides, they know you're with me, so they wouldn't even dare to look at you."

The breath catches in my throat. I blink incredulously, positive that I've misunderstood him somehow. It takes me a few moments to recover the power of speech.

"I'm with you?" My voice shakes; my heart is bursting.

He watches the smoke disperse in front of him but doesn't answer me. He just lifts up one corner of his mouth slightly.

Then I push myself forward until I reach him. I lean against him, sliding a thigh between his legs and flattening my hands on his chest. Thomas strokes my backside automatically. "Am I with you, Thomas?" I ask again.

He stares into my eyes in a way that makes me tremble, but I don't look away. I maintain my gaze because I want to hear him say it. He has to say it... But when I realize that he isn't going to, I lower my eyes, feeling a bitter sense of disillusionment.

Stupid... I don't know what I expected. I shake my head and pull away, deciding it's time to get out of here.

"Ness," I hear him say behind me. When I turn, he grabs my hips and pulls me into him. He rubs my lip with his thumb, and staring steadily into my eyes, he says: "You and I, we are together."

Eight

I CAN'T BELIEVE HE ACTUALLY just said it. I bite my lip, incapable of replying.

"W-we're together? Like, together-together?" I look at him, uncertain but full of hope. He just keeps staring at me through the cloud of smoke rising from his lit cigarette. After another very long moment, he nods.

"And you're not just saying that because I yelled in your face that I wanted to end things, are you?" I murmur, staring down at his shirt, almost afraid of seeing the bitter truth on his face.

Thomas tosses the cigarette into the toilet bowl, takes my chin in his hand, and tilts it up. "I told you that I don't do relationships. That I don't know *how* to do them. That they only make trouble. And that's all true." He pauses and moves his thumb delicately over my bottom lip, tracing its contours. "I could tell you that I want you in my life because I desperately need you, but that wouldn't be the truth. I learned the hard way never to need anyone. I want you with me because you, more than anyone else, actually make me believe that all this shit is worth living through."

Even though I find it hard to believe I could mean so much to him, his words make my heart skip a beat. "So now we are…a couple?" I ask again, still astonished.

Thomas lets out one of his usual derisive snorts and nods. I bite my lip again, trying to hold back my expression of joy mixed with satisfaction. I stretch up to give him a kiss, which he responds to by rubbing my bare thighs.

"Do you know what this means?"

"What?" he asks, arching a skeptical eyebrow.

"From now on, you're gonna have to do so many nice things for me. Take me to the movies, go out to dinner with me, buy me flowers, and, most importantly, you will cuddle with me while we watch TV like a good boyfriend." I lay it all out with wild enthusiasm, just to tease him.

"I don't cuddle, Ness," he chides me.

I give him an exaggerated pout. "Well, in that case, you will have to compensate me for the lack of cuddles with lots and lots of gifts. Just so you know, peonies are my favorite flower, I don't like dark chocolate, and if you're ever undecided about what to get for me, a book will always be a safe bet. Well, except for those Russian bricks; I really can't handle those." I keep teasing him, twining my arms around his neck and trying to keep from exploding with laughter. The expression of pure dismay on his face is too hilarious.

"I'm not doing any of that, and you know it. Now, let's get out of here; the stale air is starting to get to you." I imagine he wants to look serious, but his eyes betray him with an amused twinkle.

When I turn to open the door, Thomas grabs the bottom of my dress and tries to pull it further down my thighs with little success. "Did you really have to come here dressed like that?"

I turn and raise my eyebrow at him. "And how else was I supposed to come to a dance club? In overalls?" says I, the girl who once attended a full day of classes on campus wearing her pajama shirt.

He grimaces. "At least that way no one would look at you. Not how they're looking at you with this dress on at least."

I give a resigned shrug and push the door open. On my way out, I meet the eyes of two boys standing at the sinks. They look at me, perplexed. But as soon as they see Thomas emerge from behind me, their expressions change. Their lips twist into sly smiles, and they give him knowing looks. My cheeks burn, and I look down at the floor, pulling some hair over my face to cover my blush. We wash our hands and leave in a hurry.

Once outside, Thomas puts a palm on my back and brings his mouth close to my ear. A little bit of his hair, soft and nice smelling, falls over his forehead and tickles my cheekbone. "Are you sure you want to stay?"

I nod.

"Okay, you want something to drink?"

"No thanks. I don't want to push my limit."

"Come on then, let me introduce you to the guys." He slides his hand over my butt, almost as if to hide it from the depraved eyes all around us. He guides me toward his table, but I stop him just before we get there.

"Wait, I have to find Tiffany and Leila first. I came here with them, and then I disappeared for a long time; they'll be worried."

"My sister's here?" he asks, troubled. "And neither of you felt the need to tell me?"

"I guess not," I reply, shrugging.

He gives me a look that is both irritated and resigned. He's about to say something else, but behind him, I spot a boy waving his arms to attract our attention. In the glare of the strobe lights, I almost recognize him. But yes, of course…it's Vince. And it seems that he's just noticed me as well, because he gives me a sly smile and greets me with a mouthed "Hello, Little Gem." I ignore him, rolling my eyes. Next to him, another boy sips a cocktail. I notice Shana is perched on his lap, but she doesn't do anything except glance in our direction.

Thomas waves Vince away and turns back to me. "Okay, go find the girls, and then come back here," he orders. "I don't feel comfortable knowing you're alone in this place."

He's about to leave, but as soon as I see Shana's triumphant look, I instinctively grab his arm and pull him back to me. He looks surprised. "What's up?"

I stare at him. I look at Shana then back at him. "Don't go over there without me. Let's look for the girls together."

Realizing that I'm jealous, Thomas barely restrains a laugh, which I manage to silence with a menacing glare. Not giving him a chance to reply, I drag him along after me by the hand. We move through the crowd, scrutinizing the faces around us.

Thomas walks right behind me with his hands firm on my hips and his groin pressed against my ass. Every time his hands tighten, he pushes me harder against his body, and I'm overwhelmed by a series of electric bursts concentrated between my thighs. He's doing it on purpose, I know, and so I smile when I feel a slight protrusion rubbing against my ass. Then he bends down to give the hollow of my throat a kiss so languorous that I cannot help the moan that slips from my mouth.

"Just so you know, that first one was just a taste. Tonight, I plan to fuck you so hard that the walls shake," he whispers into my ear. The feeling in my stomach is less butterflies and more like...elephants. Doing somersaults. I lay my hand over his and intertwine our fingers, but I don't have time to answer him, because Thomas is intercepted by Blake. Shockingly, he's rude, giving me only a condescending look and a barely perceptible nod in greeting. God, he really is unpleasant.

As he leans close to Thomas's ear, I move aside and let the two of them talk. The club music drowns out their voices and I can't understand a thing they're saying. They both seem very serious; Thomas even looks worried. They continue to have an animated discussion as Blake is joined by an attractive blond holding two beers. She stands there stock-still, just like me, waiting for them to finish talking.

But this conversation doesn't seem to be coming to an end, and it's starting to bug me. I untangle my hand from Thomas's and mouth to him that I'm going to look for the girls. He looks a little irritated, but he nods and continues talking to Blake. What can they possibly have to say to each other that is so important it can't wait until another time?

I head for the corner of the bar where I think I've spotted Tiffany, when suddenly the girl herself appears in front of me, as though she fell out of the sky.

"Where the hell were you?"

I jolt. Clearly that wasn't her sitting at the bar.

"Uh…" Images of Thomas and me in the bathroom stall, him with his hands all over me flash through my mind. But I try to keep a straight face. "I was with Thomas… We made up," I add vaguely. "We're together now. He even suggested that I move into his room at the frat house," I finish, giving her a toothy grin.

She looks dumbfounded. "It's great that your insane relationship is back to normal and that you've even upped the ante just to make sure you didn't miss anything, but we have a real problem here," she exclaims, her eyes so wide she looks like a bush baby.

"What?" I ask, alarmed.

"Junior Collins is out."

My forehead wrinkles as I look around, as though I'm going to find her here in the midst of all this chaos. "She's gone? But we drove here with her?"

"No, I mean *out*-out." She points at a sofa behind me with a worried look. I turn and spot her. Oh no. Leila is sprawled on the cushions, her head slumped back. She must have drunk herself into a stupor.

Elbowing through the crowd, we quickly make our way to her sofa, where I shake her slightly, trying to wake her up. I give her cheek a gentle slap, but she doesn't react at all. We call her name over and over to no avail, so we try to prop her up to standing. She clearly doesn't agree with this decision, however, because she emits a whining moan and tries to push us away. Perfect; at least we finally got a reaction.

I turn to Tiffany with a dirty look. "Why'd you let her get like this?"

"Hey, this had nothing to do with me. When I saw she was starting to get wobbly, I told her to stop. I even took the drink out of her hand, but the girl is stubborn. She wouldn't listen, and she just kept telling me that she could hold her liquor." Tiffany defends herself with a shrug.

"And you believed her? Come on, Tiff, she's tiny! A glass of wine would have been enough to have her seeing pink elephants."

She runs her hands through her hair and sighs. "Okay, I screwed up. But there's no use crying over spilled booze, right? What do we do about it now?"

"Go to the bar, and get as much water as you can; then go get Thomas. He should be over by the other sofa." I sit down with Leila, brushing aside some of the sweaty strands of hair that have escaped from her French braid and are plastered to her forehead. I gently shake her again, trying to get her to wake up.

Tiffany returns with a large bottle of water and Thomas, who strides past her furiously. "What happened?"

I stand up immediately. "She's drunk; we can't get her to wake up."

He kneels down in front of her and grabs her by the shoulders, giving her a shake. "JC? Open your eyes."

Leila shakes her head and tries to get away from him with a pretty well-placed kick to the knee for a girl who's dead drunk. Tiffany and I trade bewildered looks.

"We should get her home; she needs to sleep it off," I yell, but I'm not sure Thomas is listening. He just keeps calling Leila's name to no response.

"JC, open your eyes, or I swear I'll open them for you," he snarls. Leila remains motionless. Until suddenly, without a moment's hesitation, Thomas turns and grabs the water bottle out of Tiffany's hands and splashes it all over his sister.

"Thomas!" I shout, rushing to the defense of Leila, who, meanwhile, has leapt to her feet at lightning speed. She wobbles for a second, clearly still out of it.

"What the hell? Are you out of your mind? You soaked my entire bag!" she sputters, punching his shoulder.

Thomas doesn't bat an eyelid. He jabs a finger at her and, with the most uncompromising look I've ever seen on his face, says, "I'm taking you home now."

Leila doesn't respond, but neither does she seem at all intimidated by her brother. Without even looking at him, she takes her sodden bag and shoves it into his chest. "You better hope to God that my phone still works!" Then she stumbles past him. The rest of us retrieve our coats and follow her out of the club.

Ten minutes later, and we're still sitting in our parked car in the ClubSeven lot because apparently Thomas can't multitask. He can either yell at his sister or he can drive. And he's chosen the former.

"Shut up, you're gonna give me a headache," Leila snaps, exasperated, in the back seat behind her brother.

"You're so wasted, your brain wouldn't even recognize a headache," he finishes angrily, glaring out the window.

"Come on, leave her be; can't you see she's sick?" I say, coming to Leila's defense. I reach across the seat and give her leg a gentle rub, trying to comfort her a bit.

"She's not sick; she's drunk," Thomas points out, drumming his fingers on the steering wheel.

I give him the side-eye. "It's nothing you haven't experienced before, though, is it? I'm betting you got your first hangover when you were still taking your whiskey in a baby bottle," I say, and I can hear Tiffany laughing behind me.

"This isn't about what I do."

Oh, of course it isn't.

"Hey, people…" Tiffany murmurs.

"Think about it this way," I begin. "If the bouncer hadn't let her into the club, none of this would have happened. And apparently we only got in thanks to you and that… What's his name? Oh yeah, Martinez… So maybe instead you should tell us why your names carry so much weight around here? What are you, some kind of mob boss?"

Thomas dodges my question and glares at his sister in the rearview mirror. "Did you drop his name to get in?"

"I had to…" Leila's voice trails off.

"Either way, this doesn't seem like the time to start lecturing her." I take Leila's side, hoping that Thomas will leave her alone. "She could have been on her way home by now, Thomas. In fact, we all could have been." I snort impatiently, looking at my phone screen, where the clock reads 1:20 in the morning.

"Oh, but now seems like the perfect time to me," he replies.

"Look, you're blowing this out of proportion," I say. "She tied one on... She'll sleep it off by tomorrow. She's eighteen years old, not a child. I'm not saying it's a good thing, and I understand that you're worried about her, but yelling won't make the situation any better."

"Hey, I've gotta..." Leila continues from the back seat, interrupted by Tiffany's voice.

I can't hear what either of them are saying because Thomas admonishes me so harshly that it makes gasp: "Don't stick your nose into things you know nothing about, Ness."

Stung by his reproachful tone, I look down at my interlaced fingers and start worrying at them. "Sorry," I mumble awkwardly. "I didn't mean to—"

"No! Don't even think about doing it in here, not on me!" Tiffany squeals. Throwing open the car door, she jumps out and drags Leila with her. Thomas and I whip around to see what is happening. The two girls move a few feet away from the car before stopping. Leila bends over, her hands pressed to her stomach before...vomiting.

Thomas heaves an exhausted sigh, letting his head fall back against the car seat.

Fifteen minutes later, and we haven't moved. Thomas gave Leila his jacket to protect her from the cold and tried to help her, but she shoved him away rudely. So then I gave it a shot, only to discover that seeing her puke makes my stomach queasy as well. I held out for as long as I could, but eventually I was forced to ask Tiffany to swap with me.

Now Tiffany is holding back her hair and supporting her shoulders, while Thomas and I lean against the car and supply Tiffany with clean tissues and water for Leila.

"You cold?" Thomas asks me, frowning at me slightly. I'm shaking. The cool damp of the night has gotten into my bones.

I nod. "A little..."

He pops the trunk and gets out one of his usual thick dark sweatshirts and gives it to me, helping me pull it on. I'm swimming in it, but it's so warm and cozy, and even smells like him, and I think that I could happily use it as a blanket and sleep under it for the rest of my life.

"Sorry about before," I say again. "I wasn't trying to butt in; I just wanted…"

"To stand up for her," he finishes for me, a hint of gratitude in his voice.

"She came to see me at the Marsy tonight," I say, watching Leila. "She was trying to hide it, but I could tell that something was wrong. I just didn't think the situation would get this out of hand." I look sadly back at him. "I know about your father, about him being sick. I'm so sorry," I murmur, wrapping his sweatshirt more tightly around myself.

"Don't be sorry. That man doesn't deserve anyone's sympathy," Thomas answers harshly. "My sister isn't like me, though. She's sensitive, emotional…a good person." He turns and watches me for a few seconds before continuing. "They begged her to come back home, and even though that's the last thing in the world she wants to do, she can't tell them no. And this"—he gestures toward Leila, who is still being held up by Tiffany—"is just the fallout."

"Sensitivity is the good person's curse," I murmur.

"And indifference is the clever person's armor," he adds, surprising me. He sticks his hands in the pockets of his jeans, pulling out a pack of cigarettes and lighting one.

Yeah, I'd say that's your philosophy exactly, Thomas…

"Are you really going to let her go alone?" I ask, trying to sound as neutral as possible.

He breathes out a cloud of smoke and nods in a melancholy sort of way. "I don't care about that part of my life anymore, you know that."

"But don't you think that she might need you? For better or worse, you're still family," I say encouragingly.

"I lost my family a long time ago," he answers coldly, refusing to look at me.

I don't reply. I'd like to say lots of things and to ask him even more, but I know that this is neither the time nor the place. So I just interlace my fingers with his, lean my head against his shoulder, and whisper,

"The most important part of your family is right here." I look to Leila. "And she will never leave you."

At first when he looks at me, I'm afraid I've said the wrong thing, but then Thomas just rests his head against mine and rubs the back of my hand with his thumb. The little movements echo, I imagine, the twisted spiral of his thoughts.

The silence is broken by shouting from somewhere behind us. We turn around to see Thomas's friends; apparently they are all drunk. They slur indistinctly and stagger around shouting. They're yelling like they're still in the club with deafening music drowning out their voices. Unfortunately, they are actually in a deserted parking lot. There doesn't seem to be a designated driver, and they seem too drunk to summon a rideshare.

"Shouldn't we call them an Uber? They can hardly stand up," I point out to Thomas, worried.

"Dumbasses," he mutters, pulling his phone out of his pocket.

As he begins ordering an Uber, Tiffany advances on us. "I'm afraid we're going to be here for a while, so I'm going to take advantage of this moment of calm to get Leila into the bathroom, get her away from all these prying eyes, okay?"

Thomas agrees with a short nod. "Have Marcus get you the key to the private bathroom," is all he adds.

I help Tiffany lift Leila up, and we escort her to the back entrance of the club.

When I return to the parking lot, I discover that Shana is now here.

She walks unsteadily, using the wall of the club to support her. Eventually a guy, presumably much more sober than she is, puts her over his shoulder, happily clowning around with her. He squeezes her thighs together as Shana licks the side of his neck, giggling. It wouldn't bother me at all, seeing her this way, if it weren't for the fact that, as soon as she notices Thomas's presence, her gaze locks on him and stays there. He's ignoring her, still trying to order a ride, but Shana is undaunted. If looks could talk, hers would be screaming, *Pay attention to me, damn it! Here I am!*

When she notices the vicious look I'm giving her in return, it doesn't bother her one little bit. She just lifts one corner of her mouth in a smug smirk, as if to say she's not afraid of me. Our stares only grow sharper and more tense. At this point, we are basically attempting to destroy one another with the power of our minds. Thomas finally finishes up on his phone and says something to me, but I'm not listening to him. When he turns to face me, probably waiting for an answer, he sees that Shana and I are exchanging nasty looks, downright filthy even.

"Ignore her," he orders.

I don't listen to him. Instead, I cross my arms over my chest and continue to face her with the same menacing vibe she's directing at me. I am certainly not going to be the first to look away.

"Can you believe it? She isn't even trying to pretend she's not obsessed with you. She's just eyefucking you right here in front of me. That poor guy carrying her doesn't even realize she couldn't care less about him." I say the words to Thomas, but I'm staring at Shana the whole time.

He laughs. Perhaps he finds my jealousy entertaining. Too bad I'm not enjoying it at all. Then Thomas rubs my cheekbone with his thumb before sliding a hand down to my hip and turning me until I'm facing him.

"Don't let her get to you, okay? Instead, why don't you tell me what went down between you two?"

I sigh and rub my forehead. I don't want to play the part of the damsel in distress who whines to her boyfriend just because she was bullied by his crazy, jealous ex. But I can tell by the way he is looking at me that he's not going to stop pushing until I tell him what he wants to know.

I hide my hands in the pouch of his sweatshirt and blurt it all out. "Last Monday we had a little run-in in the bathroom at school. And she made a point of telling me that it's only a matter of time before you come back to her. Because that's what you always do." Out of pride, I do my best to sound indifferent. I don't want him to know how much the possibility of that actually happening haunts me.

"Did she really say that to you?" he asks, troubled.

"Yeah. Well, not before tossing a whole coconut smoothie on me in front of the entire cafeteria, but yes." If I think too hard about it, I feel the uncontrollable urge to rush over to her right now and rip every damn strand of red hair right out of her head.

"What the fuck? Why didn't you tell me then?" he bursts out after an incredulous moment.

"Because it didn't concern you," I answer quickly, but I regret my knee-jerk response. I can see from the stricken look he gives me that I've hurt him. I hang my head, feeling guilty.

He rests one hand on my waist and tilts my chin up with the other. "It does concern me. Everything that happens to you concerns me."

I shrug, as if it was no big thing. "There's nothing you could have done about it anyway. She hates me because she wants you, and that's not going to change."

Thomas pauses, seemingly to think about this. Then, in a reassuring voice, he says, "That stuff she told you is bullshit. Total bullshit. I wasn't with her because I had some romantic interest in her. I was with her because she was around whenever I wanted and because she was cool with what we were doing. But she always knew that it was just sex."

I get what he's trying to tell me. They were both using each other, but apparently one of them was lying about it, and it's not hard to guess who. I let out a heavy sigh and shake my head. "Can we not talk about this anymore?"

Thomas hesitates, seemingly about to say something in reply, but instead goes along with my request. I check the time again to see how long it's been since Tiffany and Leila went to the bathroom, and I see that more than ten minutes have passed. Even Thomas seems worried, darting quick looks between the back of the club and the small rowdy group of his friends.

"Hey," he says then, in a softer voice. He pushes a strand of hair behind my ear and stands in front of me. "I didn't tell you that stuff to hurt you; I told you because I want to be honest with you. No secrets between us. You're my girlfriend now, right?" He gives me a crooked smile, fully aware of the effect those words have on me. Like an idiot, I find myself grinning back at him, biting my lip, trying to hide it. "I don't want her bullshit getting inside your head," he finishes, lightly touching my face.

I look up and smile at him. "It's okay; I get it."

"You sure?"

I nod. I want to trust in what he's saying; I want to trust him. "But just so you know, she's still staring at you."

He doesn't even turn around to check and see if it's true, just gives a sly grin and slots his mouth over mine before pulling back to look into my eyes.

"So let's give her something to look at," he suggests, his voice rough. I give him a questioning look, but I don't even have time to answer before his hands are on my hips. He pushes me up against the car door and presses his body to mine. He captures my lips with a passionate, hungry kiss. He slips his tongue into my mouth as he drags his fingers through my hair. My mouth chases Thomas's, my tongue rubbing gently against the piercing in his.

We kiss for what feels like an endless amount of time, one of his hands resting firmly on the back of my neck and the other kneading my ass. The moment I pull away, I can feel the total lack of air in my lungs. I stare up at him, thoroughly bewitched. Absolutely lost. His face is cocked to one side, his half-closed eyes watching me with such intensity that it makes the butterflies burst forth in my stomach again. I touch his stubbly cheek with my fingertips, the rest of my hand almost entirely swallowed by the sleeve of his sweatshirt, and I curl up against him, tucking my head underneath his chin.

Thomas wraps his arms around me before checking over his shoulder. "She's not looking anymore," he tells me. "In fact, she's not even here."

I smile because I realize that I don't even care anymore. I close my eyes and breathe in his scent, welcoming it, getting drunk on it. He's warm like a toasty bed at the end of a long day, and he smells like the grass after it rains. He smells like home. "I don't know if I've ever told you this, but this is absolutely my favorite place in the whole world."

I feel his chest jerk with a flimsy laugh. "What, in my arms?" he asks sweetly.

I nod silently, nuzzling myself further into his body. "You make me feel safe, Thomas. You make me feel at home." A strange sort of warmth fills my chest. Thomas doesn't answer, but I don't need him to. It's enough for me to feel his arms tighten around me as he holds me even closer, for him to press a delicate kiss to the top of my hair.

Nine

"YOU TWO FINISHED?" VINCE'S VOICE interrupts us. "Because we're all pretty hungry, in case you were wondering."

Thomas and I break away from one another and turn to look at him. Vince slaps Thomas on the shoulder. "Man, I gotta get something to eat; I might pass out."

I take note of the slow, careful way he pronounces every word: he may not be quite as obliterated as the others, but he's pretty close. Thomas grits his teeth and answers him in an irritated voice: "I'm not taking you anywhere, Vince. I called a ride for you ten minutes ago; he'll take you back to campus as soon as he gets here."

Vince gives a wobbly head shake. "Are you nuts? How am I gonna pay for a ride? Sexual favors? Nah. Plus I need to digest some food as soon as possible; otherwise I'm gonna collapse."

"Then go eat," Thomas retorts, inviting him to leave with a wave of his hand.

"To tell the truth, I'm a little hungry as well," I interject with a shrug.

Vince turns to Thomas with his hands on his hips, triumphant. "Yes, see! Are you going to tell her no too?"

Thomas ignores him and just looks at me, cocking an eyebrow. "Didn't you have dinner?"

I shake my head. "We came straight here after I got off work."

He scratches his forehead with his index finger before sighing resignedly. "Fine. What do you want to eat?"

"A big plate of empanadas, extra beef, extra spice!" Vince answers excitedly on my behalf.

"I didn't ask you," Thomas hisses through gritted teeth, never taking his eyes off me. I try to stifle a laugh because their bickering has taken on a real Shrek and Donkey vibe. If I shared this thought, Thomas would probably ghost me on the spot.

"Anything's good," I say simply. "Although, I don't think there are a lot of options at this time of night."

"What a coincidence!" Vince says, clapping his hands together. "I just happen to know of a little place near here that is part of a chain of Mexican restaurants and is open twenty-four hours a day, seven days a week!" he continues, drawing Thomas's ire.

With a smile and a shrug, I decide to back Vince up. "Sounds good to me."

Thomas frowns at me. "You sure? We can look for something else. We don't have to just go where he wants," he says, shooting Vince a dirty look.

I'm about to tell him that Vince's suggestion seems like a good one, but we are interrupted by the girls coming back toward us. Tiffany—who is also looking disheveled and exhausted—is holding Leila up with an arm around her waist.

"Hey, how are you feeling? A little better at least?" I ask Leila, going to meet them.

"It's a shit show," she says, barely managing to keep her eyes open. Her brow is heavily furrowed, and her voice is shockingly low and shaky.

Vince follows the girls with his eyes, bewildered. "Dude, what the hell's up with your sister?"

Thomas just sighs and shakes his head, refusing to discuss the topic. "Come on, JC. Get in my car so I can drive you home, and we'll come back for yours tomorrow," he says, pulling the car keys out of his jeans pocket.

Then he gets into the driver's seat, puts the key in the ignition, and starts the SUV. The girls take seats in the back, and I move around to the passenger side. Out of the corner of my eye, I can see Vince following me, but the moment he puts his hand on a door handle, Thomas leaps out of the car. He leans his forearms on the roof and says: "And what do you think you're doing, Vince?"

Vince looks over the roof of the car at him and replies as though it's the most obvious thing in the world: "Getting in."

"To my car?"

"I can't drive in this condition; you have a moral obligation to take me with you."

"Nope."

"You will, though."

"I called you a ride."

"And, as you can see, it's not here."

"So I'll call you another one."

"Or you could stop being a dick."

My eyes dart back and forth avidly between the two of them. I am thoroughly enjoying this dialectical ping-pong between alpha males.

Finally, Thomas gives in, bowing his head. When he looks up, he points a finger at him. "If you mess up my car, you're dead," he threatens.

Vince laughs, but when he notices the seriousness of Thomas's face, his smile disappears.

I hop in as well, my head still fuzzy from everything that went down tonight. We leave ClubSeven behind us, along with the bass vibrations that dissipate into the night and shouts of young people in the parking lot.

Both of the girls want to go home instead of hitting the Mexican place—they just want to curl up under the covers. We make a pit stop on campus to take Leila to her room before heading to Tiffany's house.

"Thanks for taking care of Leila tonight," I say when we drop Tiffany off. I squeeze her tightly, and she hugs me back.

"It was the least I could do; I still feel bad about letting her get like that," she answers mournfully as we pull away from one another.

"Eh, it wasn't your fault. In fact, I'm the one who's sorry for putting that on you. Leila's having a rough time right now, and she probably would have gotten drunk regardless," I say, rubbing her shoulders in what I hope is a comforting way.

"And thanks for letting me stay at your place. I don't know what I would have done without you," I add, glancing up at the sprawling palace behind her, which stands out starkly against the rest of the neighborhood even with the lights off.

"Anything for you," she answers. "Have fun with that grouchy boyfriend of yours. And if you ever need an escape, you know you can always come back here." She gives me a weary but sincere smile. I watch as she disappears into the large front garden, and only when the solid wooden front door closes behind her do I join Thomas and Vince back in the car.

We walk into the restaurant at two in the morning. Surprisingly, it's full of people. It's so hot inside that I immediately take off Thomas's sweatshirt. From here we can see there's a free table at the back of the room, so we head for it. As we step forward, I can feel the eyes of some of the men in the room gravitate to my legs, making me uncomfortable. It's terrible to realize that a girl really can't wear a short dress without having to deal with slimy looks from men. Adult men, in fact, who look old enough to be my father.

Behind me, Thomas and Vince are muttering something in each other's ears, and as if reading my mind, they move to create a kind of human shield around me, trying to hide as much of me as possible with their bodies. I speed up my walk, and though I can't know for sure, I can feel the dirty looks Thomas is giving to the lookie-loos.

When we get to the table, I hang my purse and the sweatshirt over the back of my chair. Thomas moves to sit next to me, but Vince beats him to it with a feline pounce.

"Move, Vince," Thomas demands, looming over his friend.

Vince tilts his head upward innocently and answers, "Why? There's an empty seat right there in front of us." He's really trying to hide it, but the grin pulling up the corners of his mouth just gets more and more obvious.

Thomas puts one palm flat on the table and the other on the back of the chair currently occupied by Vince; then he lowers himself down until the two of them are eye to eye. "Move," he orders.

The blond boy sighs, rolling his eyes. "See how aggressive he is? What do you see in him?" he asks, turning to me. Nevertheless, he gets up and takes the seat across from us. "It's all the tattoos, isn't it? I know that's it. You know, if I wasn't terrified of needles, I'd be covered in them too, and then there'd be no hope for all of you," he says, pointing a finger at Thomas in an intimidating fashion.

I try to stifle it but I can't help but laugh. "Well, you know, all these muscles don't exactly hurt either," I tell him, rubbing Thomas's left bicep mock-worshipfully. Thomas just shakes his head in resignation.

"Hey, Little Gem, I've got those too. Take a look at this." He shrugs off his jacket and lifts his shirt up to show off his rock-hard abs, even slapping them with his hand a few times to illustrate. He gives us mocking smile, absurdly pleased with himself.

I pretend to gasp in surprise, pressing a hand to my chest.

"Truly admirable, Vince, I am deeply impressed. Seriously, you're looking pretty good. Actually, you know what? This combination you've got going on, with the angelic face, big baby blues, and the breathtaking physique you've been hiding under your baggy T-shirts? It's really putting you over the top."

His eyes gleam. "Over the top, you say?"

I nod. "For sure! I mean, yeah, he's got all these tattoos and that bad-boy vibe that turns a lady's head, but I'll let you in on a little something." I lean toward him as though I'm about to impart state secrets. "Despite what you may think, every woman is secretly attracted to the nice guy." I sit back, composed, a smile on my lips.

"Are you kidding me? So how the fuck do you all end up in the arms of these ungrateful oafs?" He points at Thomas, who, exhausted by this conversation, just shakes his head.

"Because these oafs know what they're doing, loser," Thomas interjects.

Vince snorts and lifts his eyebrows. "Oh, you know what you're doing? How so?"

"You really wanna know?" Thomas answers.

They stare at each other for a fraction of a second, almost as though they are communicating telepathically, and then Vince mimes a retch. "Ah, Christ's sake, no!" he answers, disgusted.

Thomas and Vince get up and stride to the counter to place our food and drink orders—three waters—before coming back to sit down. Vince orders the extra-hot beef empanadas. Thomas chooses enfrijoladas, which, if I understand the menu correctly, are folded tortillas covered in black bean sauce, cheese, and salsa. I would be trapped in my usual indecision if Thomas didn't just go ahead and order for me: the chicken fajitas, an order of empanadas, and the nachos.

Thomas rubs a thumb along his forehead and wrinkles up his nose. "I ordered you a lot of stuff, Ness. I wonder if you can eat all that."

"I'm hungry," I answer decisively.

"Little Gem, they serve generous portions here," Vince agrees, also sounding skeptical.

I look away from him and back at Thomas. "I'm hungry, though."

After a moment of silence—during which they exchange another doubtful look—they shrug.

Another patron strolls by from across the room, apparently on his way back from the restroom, and gives me a smile that would be polite, except for the few seconds his eyes linger on the neckline of my dress. I clear my throat uncomfortably while staring at the menu. As soon as I finish, though, I'm startled by a glacial voice, full of disdain.

"Are you fucking kidding me right now?"

I grab Thomas's thigh underneath the table out of instinct and squeeze it tightly, willing him to not make a scene.

The guy turns in Thomas's direction, confused. "I beg your pardon?"

Thomas looks at him with blazing eyes. "Oh, you'd better beg, because if I catch you looking at my girl's tits one more time, I'll make sure that the next thing you see is the lid of your fucking coffin."

A vast disheartening silence settles over all of us. I put my face in my hands, while Vince presses his fist into his mouth to keep from bursting out into laughter. *There's nothing funny about this*, I want to snap at him.

"I–I wasn't...I wasn't looking..." the guy stammers, trying to defend himself, embarrassment written all over his face. Thomas doesn't let him finish, though, but instead abruptly points across the room.

"Go back to your seat; you're done here," he orders him angrily.

The guy doesn't need to be told twice—he vanishes immediately. Thomas must be able to feel my indignant look on the side of his face because he turns his irritable gaze on me. "That guy couldn't take his eyes off you."

"It didn't seem that way to me. But you do realize that you can't threaten to murder anyone who looks at me, right?"

"I feel like we've already addressed this topic," he declares arrogantly, lightly brushing his jeans as if clearing away invisible crumbs.

"Thomas, I'm not joking."

"Neither am I," he fires back insolently. "Let me try to understand you here; what were you expecting me to do? Just ignore the fact that he was undressing you with his eyes right in front of me? Am I supposed to pat him on the back and buy him a beer? Or maybe I'm supposed to slip him your number and invite him to shoot his shot? Maybe if he plays his cards right, he can see the rest of you tonight too?"

I stiffen, eyes wide with hurt. I must have misheard him. I must have *seriously* misheard him. I harden my gaze and channel all my fury into my voice. "What did you just say to me?"

"Woah, woah... Okay, folks...I know we're all a little amped up tonight, but let's try to keep calm. Let's all just take a deep breath, have a nice drink of water, and pull ourselves together here." Vince's eyes move from me to Thomas as he nudges our respective water glasses toward us. "Let's try not to end tonight in a fight, thanks."

"Apologize to me right now."

"*Me* apologize?" Thomas exclaims, grimacing as he turns to face me.

I nod emphatically.

He breaks eye contact and gives Vince a derisive look, shaking his head at me.

"Do you even realize what you just implied about me? Do you think I'm slutty?" I ask through gritted teeth.

But the only thing that comes out of Thomas's face is an arrogant snort.

"Bro, I am begging you, for the love of God, just tell her you're sorry so we can get past this," Vince pleads, exhausted.

But Thomas ignores us both, playing with one of the thick steel rings on his thumb. And that's the last straw for me.

"Thomas, if you don't apologize to me, I swear I'm leaving." And this time, I am completely serious. I don't care if his arrogant pride prevents him from taking anything back, humbling himself, or apologizing. Nor do I care that his lack of impulse control means he often says things he doesn't really mean. I'm not going to sit here and pretend he didn't just insult me.

Thomas's back straightens at my threat to walk out of the restaurant. "You're not going anywhere," he snaps. "And if you want to avoid this kind of scene in the future, here's some advice: the next time you leave the house"—he scans my body—"get dressed first."

I stare at him, blanching, while Vince closes his eyes and gently *thunks* the table with his forehead.

"I am dressed," I reply icily, giving him the dirtiest of looks. "And that was a real asshole thing to say. So you're hypocritical as well as sexist! The fact that I'm wearing a short dress doesn't give anyone the right to leer at me like a creep. And it doesn't give you"—I stab a finger at him furiously—"the right to make me feel like I've done something wrong and brought this on myself. Move; I'm getting out of here."

Thomas chews on his lower lip, scrubbing his face with his hand before exclaiming, "Come the fuck on! I know it's not your fault, and

I know it's not the dress. Obviously, it's not. I'm just pissed because that guy wouldn't take his eyes off you. I wasn't trying to offend you or be disrespectful."

I stare back at him, my eyes narrowed to slits. "That's it? That's your apology?" I demand with a disdainful air.

"Bro," Vince says, laughing across the table, "you must have a real primo dick, because you sure are terrible at this."

My eyes nearly bug out of my sockets, while my cheeks redden. Thomas drinks his glass of water in one gulp, leaving a single mouthful, which he splashes at Vince. "Knock it off. I'm not good at this sort of thing," he says defensively before turning back to look at me. "I am sorry, truly. I didn't mean what I said, about you...about the dress..."

I look at him for a long time. His eyes are full of what appears to be sincere regret. I heave a long sigh and point at him. "Fine, you get a pass this time, but you have got to stop reacting like that."

I'm half-expecting him to come back with one of his typical quips, all *I do what I want, blah, blah, blah*, but instead he just gives me a look halfway between a smile and a grimace, and nods. Then, to completely dissipate the tension, our number is called, and Vince goes to the counter and comes back with our meals, steaming hot and looking delicious. I immediately realize that Vince was telling the truth: These portions are generous. But the boys are extremely incorrect if they think that I won't be able to put away every last bit of this bounty.

"Mmm, that smell..." I close my eyes and inhale, ecstatic.

We devour our dinner while chatting in an atmosphere that is, finally, relaxed. Vince does get a little hot under the collar when he tells Thomas about some disagreement between the football guys and the soccer guys, the latter of whom are about to "catch an ass whupping" as he says, if they don't chill out. He asks me what I think, but I'm honestly too busy savoring my empanadas to pay attention. I spout something vague in support of him and keep eating.

After Thomas clears his plate in record time, he declares himself full. Spreading his legs slightly, he rests one hand on his abdomen, while the other lies along the back of my chair. As he talks to Vince, he twirls strands of my hair around his fingers. It's something he does often, and I get the feeling that it relaxes him. And every time he does it, I melt.

Every now and then he turns to watch me eat and smiles. It's embarrassing, being watched as I fall on my food like a hungry lioness on a gazelle, but he seems to find it entertaining. Maybe even cute, judging by the look he gives me.

Despite the guys' lack of faith in me, I manage to finish everything on my plate, even if it does feel like I'm literally going to burst. By the time the bill comes, it's a struggle to even stand up. Thomas, who never misses an opportunity to laugh at me, cracks up over the mournful faces I make while complaining about having eaten too much. We fight over the bill a little, but in the end, he prevails and gets dinner for us all.

After leaving, we take Vince back to his dorm on campus, and then, after a short walk through the rows of now bare trees, we arrive at the frat house. The place that will be my home for the next few months.

Ten

"I'M SO TIRED, THOMAS. I don't think I can do it."

"Don't be dramatic. You've done it a million times."

"It's different this time. It feels like they're never-ending," I whine.

"There aren't that many."

I stare at the tall staircase before us and then slide my gaze over to Thomas. "I can't."

He snorts. "Next time I take you out to eat, you're getting a salad," he teases. I don't have time to answer before he lifts me up with disarming ease, one arm under my knees and the other behind my back.

I wrap my arms around his neck, and as we walk up the stairs, old memories start to flicker through my mind. Memories of the night it all started, when, seeing me shaken and wounded after the breakup with Travis, Thomas invited me to a party at this very frat house. I was looking for a distraction, some way to numb the pain, turn off my brain, and forget. But it was more than that. There was always an awareness there, some part of me that wanted, more than anything else, to be with Thomas. It was only with him that my heart seemed to start beating again, the pain went away, and I was finally able to feel good.

Eventually, I'd gotten so drunk that I couldn't stay on my feet, and it was Thomas who put an end to the ridiculous show I was putting on. He took me in his arms and carried me up to his room. And against all the odds, I never wanted to leave again.

"Why are you laughing?" he asks me, bewildered.

I rest my head on his chest, snuggling in.

"Memories," I whisper gently.

When we reach his door, Thomas puts me down and reminds me that I still have the keys to his room.

"Right." I didn't give them back to him after stopping by this afternoon for a shower.

Once inside, my gaze is drawn to the poorly made bed. I try to ignore the shiver that runs down my spine when I think back on the two of us between those sheets… Everything was so different just two months ago.

I find myself looking at the room through new eyes, in a way I'd never imagined I would. It's no longer just Thomas's room, but mine now as well… I let my gaze wander over the empty sofa, the desk to my left scattered haphazardly with books and sketch pad, across the black walls that surround us. God, those walls are tragic. It's going to take some getting used to.

"I must admit, I'm always surprised by how neat you are. Not a thing out of place," I note, chuckling as I step into the middle of the room.

"What were you expecting?" Thomas grins, shutting the door behind him.

"Oh, I don't know…" I turn around, my wrists crossed behind my back. "Bottles of booze, thongs hidden here and there, bong residue on the floor…" I joke.

"Nah, I'm the quiet type. A real homebody," he says mockingly.

"Yes, of course. The shy, reserved sort, that's you." I give him a suggestive look before turning my eyes back to the bed. This time, however, the shivers down my spine are cold ones as I dwell on just how many girls took a turn in there.

"I'm going to need new sheets," I inform him, pointing at the mattress.

Thomas frowns so hard his eyebrows almost meet over his nose. "Those are clean; I changed them today. What's the problem?"

"You can't seriously believe I'm going to sleep on the same sheets that have played host to every female creature in the county?"

Thomas cocks his head at me with a sly smile. "You've done it once already, and it didn't seem to bother you then."

I give his shoulder a playful slap. "Well, that's because I was drunk, and I had other stuff on my mind. I'm clearheaded right now, and you can bet your fine behind that I'm not getting into that bed knowing what you did there with me and God knows how many others."

Thomas takes off his shoes, and with his typical cocky self-assurance, he also whips off his shirt. My lips fall open when I see his sculpted chest. Suddenly my throat feels very dry and very, very hot.

His face, Vanessa, look at his face!

I shake myself, meeting his eyes again, and see him snickering at me. Caught red-handed.

"None of the women I brought here ever used my bed, didn't even sleep with me," he admits, and I can't help laughing.

"Uh, I'm pretty sure that's not the case. You said so yourself, remember? That this room is your personal harem?"

"And it was, but we just used the sofa. Once the festivities were over, they would leave, or I would leave if they ended up falling asleep here."

I immediately turn to the scene of the crime with a disgusted grimace on my face. I look back at him silently for a few seconds, with an expression that screams, *Just how stupid do you think I am?*

"No lie, Ness," he adds, as though reading my mind. "My sister ended up here most of the time, when she didn't want to be alone in the other room. I can assure you, she would have beat my ass if I tried to make her sleep in the same bed where I got it on with the other girls."

The other girls.

You've got to take your medicine, Vanessa: the past is the past, and you can't change it.

"You let me sleep there, though," I point out, moving closer to him.

"For you, I made an exception."

"Why?" I whisper, just a breath away from his lips.

"Because you were the only one I wanted in my bed."

My heart beats wildly in my chest as Thomas wraps his arms around my waist and kisses me.

"Mm-hmm, tell me the truth: You prepare these lines in advance, don't you?"

"Fuck, you got me."

We both laugh, and when we break apart, I take a moment to look more carefully at the room. "To be honest...it feels strange being here with you," I say in a low voice. I glide my fingers along the smooth surface of the desk as I approach the window with slow steps. I fixate on a streetlamp in the distance, dimly illuminating the dark night. "So much has changed since the last time we were here together..."

I trace meandering lines on the wet glass with my index finger. "When I woke up beside you that morning, I swore to myself that I'd never set foot in this room again. And now..." I sigh, thinking back on all the fights with my mother and their disastrous consequences, which have led me here. "I'm going to live here."

I turn to face Thomas. He's leaning against the doorframe, arms crossed. I meet his eyes, and in those emerald depths I see nothing but melancholy and regret. I give him a tight smile, trying to lighten the mood, and sit down on the edge of the bed. "Life's funny sometimes, huh?"

He joins me, sitting down next to me with his elbows on his knees. He stares at the floor, and I get the feeling he'd like to tell me something, but he remains locked in his silence.

I lie back on the mattress. "She came looking for me at the Marsy today," I murmur.

Thomas turns, his brow furrowed. "Your mother?"

I nod silently, staring up at the ceiling.

Thomas falls back as well, sliding his arm under my neck and tugging me closer to him. I nestle into his shoulder. "Did you two talk?"

I throw my leg over his and rest my arm on his chest. I slide the pad of my finger over his pectoral muscles, tracing the contours of his tattoos. "No, she came by when I wasn't there."

He strokes my hair, giving me a sense of peace and tranquility that is beyond value. "Maybe she thought she'd find you there?"

I shake my head. "She knows my shifts. She's playing games with me now, don't you see?"

"Did you trying calling her to find out what she wants?"

I lift my head a bit to get a better look at his face. "No. And I don't intend to, Thomas. She has my number; she could call me at any time, but she doesn't." I let out a nearly inaudible snort and shake my head again. "Believe me, she's not looking for an explanation; she just wants to make things worse. She probably can't figure out why I'm not on my knees at her front door, begging her to let me back in." I let my head fall back and continue to slide my finger along the ouroboros that covers his abdomen, following the circle all the way around. We remain silent for a bit.

"Ness," Thomas says finally, sighing loudly. "I'm the last person who should be giving you this kind of advice, but I think you should talk to her. Whatever happened between you, this is no good for either of you. You should both find a way to put aside your differences and stop this pointless war."

I stop tracing the lines of his tattoos, growing serious. "I'm not going to war with her," I say bitterly. "If anything, she's the one doing that to me. She's unbearable. She's never open to conversation; she just steamrolls people. You saw the way she talked to you when you came to our house. She didn't even know you. Do you think you were the first person she treated that way? No, it's how she is. You can hear it in the way she talks about people; she always has to be a cut above everyone else, looking down on them…"

"You're losing time with her that you can never get back," he interrupts, looking me in the eye. "For what? Some petty disagreement? Is it really worth it?"

"I didn't create this situation, okay? She's the one who cannot accept that she's no longer in control of my life. And am I understanding you correctly? Are you defending her?" I demand, propping myself up on my elbows.

Thomas gets into a sitting position, and I mirror him, never taking my eyes off of him.

"I'm not defending her. I'm trying to keep you from someday regretting the choices you're making right now in the heat of the moment."

I stare at him, increasingly confused, and I wonder if he isn't talking more to himself than to me, if that wasn't exactly what happened to him. After all, we all have our burdens to bear, and Thomas seems to have a lot of weight on his shoulders.

"That won't happen," I assure him. "I've forgiven my mother for lots of things, but she crossed the line this time."

He doesn't answer. Instead, he bows his head and looks at the floor, brooding on unknown dark thoughts.

"What's wrong, Thomas?" I take his face in my hands and force him to look at me. A shadow moves over his features, as if he's being tormented by something. After a few moments of silence, he answers me.

"Have you ever looked into your mother's eyes and seen nothing but contempt for the daughter that you are?"

His question catches me off guard, and I feel a pain lancing through my heart, so intense and unexpected that, for a moment, I struggle to breathe.

"No..." I manage vaguely, my voice barely audible.

"Then believe me, you're lucky."

He pulls my hands from his face and stands up, ready to flee from me and this conversation, but I stop him. I pull him back down, my eyes glistening after what I just heard. "Did that happen to you, Thomas?"

He stares at me, more serious than I've ever seen him before. "A lot worse than that has happened to me."

My mouth drops open, even though my lungs feel empty of air. My heart is pounding relentlessly, and I feel like my palms are starting to sweat.

"What happened to you?"

Thomas stares at me obliquely, letting only his mistrust show in his face. "Nothing you really want to hear about," he argues, looking away.

"No, I want to." I wrap my shaking hands around his arm. "I want to know everything about you."

"Actually, I don't think you do. Because if you knew the whole truth, you'd never look at me the same again. You'd see me for what I am. And what I am, Ness? You wouldn't like it at all."

"That could never happen." I straddle the middle of his body and take his face in my hands again, staring into him. "My eyes will always look at you just this way, do you understand? Always." My voice trembles a little bit, but I continue: "You can talk to me about anything. Confide all your secrets in me, confess all your sins... I will be here, by your side. I promise you, Thomas. I promise you I won't leave."

When he lowers his eyes, he looks so unexpectedly vulnerable that I feel a sudden urge to wrap my arms around him. But I resist that impulse, because I know that kind of gesture in this moment would make him feel pitied.

Thomas sighs, sliding a hand over his face, while I feel an unpleasant anguished sensation growing in my chest. *Talk to me*, I beg him silently. And then, to my enormous surprise, he actually does.

"Remember that night I came to the Marsy drunk?"

I nod, focused on him.

"That wasn't an isolated incident."

"What do you mean?"

He hesitates for just a moment but keeps talking. "I mean, I've been in that situation a lot in the past."

"You're someone who likes to drink, that's obvious."

Thomas shakes his head, running a hand across his forehead. "That's not... It's not just that... It's more complicated than that."

"Complicated?" I frown, trying to follow his train of thought.

He nods, giving me a dark look. "I'm an alcoholic, Ness," he adds quickly, watching my face.

This revelation hits me like a bolt from the blue. *Alcoholic*, I repeat over and over in my mind as I stare at him unblinkingly.

Impossible...

Thomas is not an alcoholic. He likes a few beers every now

and then, true, but he…he's just not an alcoholic, I try to convince myself.

"That can't be…"

Thomas just nods.

"H-how…how did it happen?" is all I can manage.

Thomas shrugs miserably, as if not even he can answer that question. "My sister claims I got my looks from our mother and my alcoholism from our father. A genetic defect," he confesses.

"For as long as I can remember, he's always been drunk. And he was a mean drunk, a real mean drunk. The clearest memories from my childhood are screams, begging, and pleading, and the terror that we felt whenever he'd come home."

My God…

"Your father…he…did he hi…" The words die in my mouth, I can't bring myself to say them. I can't give voice to that monstrous possibility. Thomas nods, understanding without needing me to finish the sentence.

"I was four years old the first time it happened. My mother was in the living room, I remember that she was ironing something while I was on the floor, playing with these toy cars. My father came back late from work that night. He was hungry and he started a fight with my mother because he wasn't happy with the dinner she'd made." His voice is heavy with resentment.

"He started yelling, so my mom made me go sit on the sofa and turned the TV up and she told me not to move from there, not for any reason in the world. The two of them shut themselves in the kitchen to argue, but the door was open a crack. I did everything I could to focus on the cartoon on TV instead of the deafening noise. Pans being thrown around, pounding on the walls, plates shattering, and then my mother's whispered cries… I was too little to understand what was happening and too scared to stay put like I'd been told." He lets out a sigh full of misery and keeps going.

"I remember running to the kitchen door, sticking my head in through the little crack and…I saw it. The worst thing I'd ever seen. My mother was curled up on the ground with blood running down her temple, begging him to stop. She was pregnant with my sister at the time. And the more she screamed, the more he hurt her, until she couldn't catch her breath. Until she passed out.

"My father realized I was there because I started crying. I was fucking terrified. And it was only then that he stopped. Ignoring everything I'd just witnessed, everything he'd just done, he just walked past my mother's body on the floor, threw me aside on his way out of the kitchen, and left the house."

He holds on tight to my thighs as I blink away tears. "My God... all of that...it's awful."

"Over the years, episodes like that started to become almost normal. My father kept my mother at home and didn't let her go out much so no one would get suspicious if they saw her. For me, he'd explain away the bruises, saying that I was a troubled boy and that I was always getting into fights. He didn't touch my sister, probably because if people saw marks all over a little girl, they'd be alarmed. Instead, he got in her head. He'd insult her every time he saw her. If he saw her leaving the house in clothes he considered too short or tight or whatever, he'd say, 'You're growing up to be a whore,' and throw condoms at her. That was how he talked to a ten-year-old girl. Ten fucking years old," he repeats angrily.

Horror and disgust sweep over me, taking my breath away.

"My sister spent years fighting panic attacks and self-loathing. She got so ashamed that she wouldn't even leave the house anymore. She'd just stay locked in her room, while downstairs, our father drank and drank until he exploded, taking it out on Mom and me."

"Did you ever report him?" I murmur brokenly.

Thomas shakes his head.

"My father is a cop, and the county sheriff is his good friend. And obviously the sheriff believed every single lie my asshole father fed him. And if that wasn't enough, my mother was scared of the repercussions a complaint might have had."

"Oh my God. Did she ever consider taking the two of you and just making a run for it?"

"Of course she did. But she knew that he would kill her if she ever tried. She's got a scar on her neck to remind her."

The gravity of these confessions makes me feel lightheaded. But I need to prove to him that I can be strong. "I can't imagine the hell that must have been…"

"The worst kind. That house became a cage with no escape route for my mother and my sister. I, on the other hand, spent as little time there as possible. But all that time out in the world without any sort of guidance, constantly searching for some way to push down all the anger I had inside…I was adrift. By the time I was fourteen, I was on a dark path. Feeling so pissed off all the time made me look for conflict everywhere. I would get into fights just because I wanted to hit someone and get hit. I wanted to suffer and make other people suffer too. It made me feel alive. If people refused to attack me, then I'd start something. And I remember it so clearly; with every punch I threw, it was his face that I pictured hitting, beating until my hands were bloody. It was always my father's face. But it was never enough.

"The torment was eating me up more each day, and I only found one way to soothe it: alcohol and drugs. They gave me the relief I needed. My pain and my rage toward that bastard faded, and the sense of impotence that ran in my veins, constantly reminding me of how useless I was, how I couldn't do anything to change things…it disappeared. Life was still shit, but it hurt less. It was more bearable."

I can sense the shame he feels as he tells me this truth, and my heart aches for him.

"I can't remember a single day in the next four years when I didn't get high or blind drunk. Nothing mattered to me anymore. Not my mother or my father or even Leila. Not even myself. In fact, I'd had it with all of them. I was mad at my mother for giving us such a shitty father and for not being able to get rid of him. I was mad at my sister for continuing to believe that, sooner or later, it was all going to stop, that he was going to repent his ways and get his head on straight. And I was angry at myself because, out of all of us, I was the most like him. So much that it scared me. And then, instead of staying with my mom and protecting her, I did nothing but add to her worries. As if living with my father every day wasn't enough to earn her a break. No...she had to deal with me too. My fuckups, the constant fights that broke out between my father and me. And with every day that passed, each time I'd come home so high I could hardly stand up straight, I would see a little more pain and disappointment fill her eyes. She had tears in her eyes and hatred in her voice, and all she would say to me was, 'You're just like him.' Like *him*, the animal that had ruined her life; ruined all of our lives. And do you know what the worst part was? Deep down, there was a part of me that knew she was right."

I scowl, feeling his pain.

"You haven't heard the worst part yet. Maybe you'll think differently once you do," he says with a bitterness that I've never heard in his voice before. "One night four years ago...everything changed," he continues. "There'd been yet another fight at home that night. I got physical with my father in a way I hadn't before. The neighbors called the police about the screams. My mother had completely given up, Leila was horrified by our bloody, swollen faces.

"So before I did something that I would have regretted probably for the rest of my life, I ran out of the house. I was headed for the only place where I could go to vent the way I wanted." He pauses and I look at him, urging him to continue, grasping his hands tightly.

"I knew this guy who organized underground fights. I was so out of my mind that night that I managed to beat three huge guys in a row. I didn't escape unscathed—I was actually in really bad shape—but I felt euphoric. I was riding high on adrenaline, but the anger was still there too. It never gave me a moment's peace. The only way to truly stifle it was to...."

"Drink," I finish for him, and he nods.

"I chugged whatever shit was being passed around in the back room before I left...then I got on my bike and headed home. It was on my way back...when the accident happened."

I flinch. "The accident where you got the scar on your side?"

He nods. "The road was dark and empty. It had been raining all night, and the asphalt was wet. By the time I saw it coming, it was too late. This truck came out of nowhere, or maybe it was there the whole time, and I was just too drunk to see it. I remember that he was going fast, but I wasn't fucking around either. The truck swerved into my lane just for a split second, and when I tried to dodge him, the wheels went out from under my motorcycle, and I crashed right into the guardrail. It happened in a snap. When I opened my eyes up again, there he was, lying on the road a few feet away from me, dying."

I flinch again. "He?"

"That's what I didn't tell you before: I wasn't alone that night. It wasn't just me on that bike."

A chill runs down my spine. "Who else was there?"

Thomas doesn't answer me. His stare is fixed on our entangled legs. Absent. Gone.

"Thomas." I touch his fingers to his cheek, shaking him. "Tell me: Who was with you?"

It seems like an eternity, the seconds that pass before he gathers the strength to look me in the eye and speak again. But, when he finally does, I'm frozen.

"My brother."

Eleven

I REMAIN MOTIONLESS. PARALYZED. "WHAT...?"

Thomas is breathing deeply. He moves me off his legs, as if to reject any sort of human contact in this moment. As if he cannot stand it.

I sit on the end of the bed staring down at the floor, while around me, it feels like the room is spinning. Thomas stands up and starts pacing, running his hands over his throat and the back of his neck. His breathing becomes increasingly labored. He's moving like an animal in a cage.

He grabs his pack of cigarettes from his pocket and puts one in his mouth, lighting it. Then he goes to the window and opens it, leaning his forearm on the frame above his head and inhaling deeply from the cigarette. "That's the first time I've ever said it out loud," he murmurs a few seconds later, and I jump a little bit at the sound of his voice.

"His name was Nathan..." I can see Thomas's back rising and falling in an irregular rhythm, as though speaking right now is costing him a great deal of effort. "And he was thirteen."

My heart aches for him. He was just a little boy. Another moment flashes into my mind: *"I'm grieving, Ness. And it's my fault."* He was drunk when he told me that just a few weeks ago, and I thought it was the liquor talking. But in reality...

"He...he never should have been with me that night. I knew where I was going and what I was going to do there. I knew it was no place for him, and I knew my mother would slit my throat if she knew I was taking him out in the middle of the night with me when I was in that state. I didn't want him to come, but arguing with him was pointless. When he got an idea into his head, there was no changing his mind, and I was too pissed to even try," he continues in a voice shot through with anguish while clouds of his smoke rise skyward.

"He wanted to come with me because he was afraid that, with the headspace I was in, I was going to get into some kind of shit. And I don't know...I really don't know what was going through my mind when I let him. I just wanted to get out of that goddamn house as fast as I could. So I took him with me, not realizing that neither of us would be coming back that night."

My tears are really flowing now, and this time, I don't try to stop them.

"He died alone, on an empty wet road in the dark, just a few feet away from me. He was screaming my name, begging for me to help him, and I couldn't so much as lift a fucking finger to get to him."

It feels like the world is collapsing in on me. My head spins as blood pounds in my ears. I instinctively press a hand to my chest, feeling the rapid, convulsive beat of my heart.

"Ten days later, I woke up intubated in the hospital," he continues, wrathfully tossing his cigarette out the window. "My sister was sitting next to my bed. The first thing I did was ask for him, but all I had to do was look at her eyes, and I knew everything she couldn't bring herself to say out loud. My brother was gone. They'd already buried him."

Silence falls over the room. He wasn't even able to go to the funeral...

"He was dead," he adds, with a cruelty in his voice aimed squarely at himself, "because of me."

At these words, my head jerks up, anguished. My throat is burning, and my breathing is still erratic. I feel numb, but I can't just let that go unchallenged. I wipe my eyes and go to him, wrapping my arms around him from behind. He tenses up as soon as he feels the contact, and I take a step back. "Don't say that, Thomas," I murmur brokenly.

He gives me a sour look over his shoulder. "I took him with me, even though I knew I was putting him in danger. I got drunk and drove the bike," he says, staring straight ahead.

"But it was the truck that forced you off the road," I murmur.

Thomas rests his forearms on the windowsill, and I realize for the first time that it's absolutely pouring outside. "If I'd been sober, my reaction time and my reflexes would have been faster. I might have been able to avoid the whole thing."

"You were on a motorcycle in the dark on a wet road; you would have ended up off the road either way."

I hear him inhale sharply through his nose. The idea of him just a breath away from me and near tears, struggling to bear all his pain and remorse, sends me shattering into a thousand pieces. I hurry to his side and turn him, forcing him to look at me. His eyes are reddened, but his face is dry. My God...I wish there was something I could do, anything. I want to soak up all his pain and free him from this torment because seeing him like this is killing me. I stand up on my tiptoes to take his face in my hands, and I look him straight in the eyes. "Don't blame yourself for your brother's death. You can blame yourself for driving drunk, but not for your brother dying, because that wasn't your fault."

He grabs my wrists roughly and shoves my hands away from his face. "Don't do that," he orders coldly. I'm willing to take the risk of getting all his wrath vented on me if I can prevent him from torturing himself like this.

I square my shoulders and try not to be intimidated by his glacial stare. I grasp his face firmly again and hold him steady, forcing him to keep looking at me. "It wasn't your fault," I say resolutely.

"Stop it."

"It wasn't, Thomas."

"Do you think you're going to make me feel better?" he shouts at me, clenching his hands around my wrists. "Do you know what I see every night just before I fall asleep? It's his eyes, full of fear as he took his last breath!"

My vision blurs again, but I don't want to cry. I don't have the right. All I can think is, *How can anyone survive with a burden like this on their conscience? How much misery can one human being take before they implode?* When his grip on my wrists slackens, I barely notice the slight burning sensation. "You lost your brother; you lost a part of yourself..." A tear runs down my cheek. "But if I've learned anything from being abandoned by my father, it's that the only way to get past pain is to face it." I put my hand over his heart, which is pounding like a drum. *How much suffering do you carry in here, Thomas?* "You have to forgive yourself. You have to find the strength to do it."

He exhales shakily. "What if I don't want to forgive myself?"

"Why wouldn't you?"

He takes my hand away from his chest but still holds it in his own. "Because that's the price a monster like me ought to pay."

Oh, Thomas...

"You are not at all a monster," I reassure him, staring into his eyes. "If you were, I wouldn't be here with you. Your sister wouldn't be with you. If you were a monster, my heart wouldn't want you."

His green eyes, hard and tempestuous, pin me to the spot, but he doesn't say anything. Instead, he sits down on the floor with his back to the wall and his forearms propped up on his knees. I yield to his silence, sitting down next to him, and we stay that way for a long time, saying nothing to one another, lulled by the sound of rain on asphalt outside.

"What if my mother was right? What if I really am like him? My father?" he asks me, suddenly shattering the silence. His face is a mask of disgust.

"You're not," I answer immediately, no hesitation.

"How can you say that? You don't know him."

I turn my gaze on him as he stares skeptically at me from under his eyelashes. "But I know you, and I know that you would never do all the horrible things he did to you."

He releases a pained breath and leans his head back against the wall. "I take after him. At the pool party, when I jumped Travis...there wasn't a single part of me that wanted to stop. Not with Logan either. I never want to stop. I don't know what happens to me in those moments. My brain goes haywire. I can't hear anything; I can't see anything; I can't feel anything. The anger and the bloodlust take over completely; it's out of my control." He scrubs a hand over his face, frustrated, adjusting his forelock. "Jesus, I'm a fucking mess."

My thoughts tangle restlessly. A normal person would probably be running away after a revelation like this. But not me. Despite everything, I can't be afraid of this. So, moved by an instinctive need, I perch on his legs to get a better look at his face. His gaze strays for a moment to my exposed thighs, but I don't care. I lightly touch his eyebrows with my thumbs. Gently, I run my index finger down his straight nose until I reach his stubbled jaw. Even though he's watching me with disarming gravity, I can see his face soften and his breathing slow, as though my touch is giving him the comfort he needs.

"You should get as far away from me as you can, Ness," he whispers in a small voice, twisting a strand of my hair between his fingers while his other hand skims my ribs.

"I won't," I answer in a low voice, continuing to touch his face, so tired and worn by what he has told me. "I'm not afraid of you, and you shouldn't be either. You are not like him. You're not evil. You're just a boy who grew up surrounded by evil. And it marked you. It made you impulsive, aggressive, lost, at times… But there is goodness in you. A kindness that your father never had, and it makes you different from him. I can feel it." I brush my finger across his lips and lock eyes with him.

I can see a veil of uncertainty behind his eyes. "You can be good to me. Caring with your sister, tolerant of your friends." I smile faintly, thinking of all the times Vince taunted him this evening and how Thomas just let him do it. "You're a good person; you just have to realize it." I trace his cupid's bow with my thumb and stare at him, hoping my words convince him. I can tell from his furrowed brow that I haven't had the desired effect. I draw closer, cautiously touching his lips with my own. "Do you hear me?"

He puts both hands on my hips, preparing to push me away. To reject what I'm saying. But he has to, he has to believe me. He has to understand that this is the truth. This and nothing else. I take his face in my hands and press my forehead against his.

"You are a good person, Thomas," I repeat in a delicate voice. Then I give him a slow kiss. "A good person."

"Ness, stop it," he says with an exhausted sigh, his Adam's apple bobbing. But I don't stop. I kiss him again, more insistently this time, forcing him to surrender. His lips open to mine, and his hands tighten on my hips.

"You are a good person," I tell him endlessly against his mouth, kissing him, touching him, holding him tight to me. I wish I could do more. I wish I could make him feel good, free his mind from all the things that torment him, and chase away the demons that haunt him night and day. I want to be his escape from reality.

I know there's only really one thing that can make him feel better now. And so I let it happen. I slide my hands down, rubbing his shoulders, and then the warm skin and tense muscles of his sculpted abdomen as I trace his lips with my tongue.

Thomas bites my lip with a grunt. I can feel his teeth in every part of my body. Our breathing is suddenly labored. The bulge pressing up against my panties gives me a warm sensation that makes my lower abdomen throb.

I run my fingertips along the seam of his jeans, and I hear him suck in a breath when, with unusual boldness, I tug his zipper down. I'm just about to slip my hand into his boxers when he grabs my wrist to stop me.

I open my eyes, confused, and find him staring at me, his eyes half closed and suffering. "You don't have to…"

"I want to…" I murmur shamelessly, watching his mouth. It's red and wet from our kissing. But Thomas shakes his head. He zips himself back up and straightens the hem of my dress, trying to cover me up as best he can.

"If I let you keep going right now, it wouldn't be for you; it would just be for me. And I don't want that."

"But I do," I say. "If that's what you need, to lose yourself in something, then go ahead. But do it with me. Get lost with me."

The furrow on his forehead deepens. Despite the flicker of heat I can see in his eyes, wariness wins out, and he hesitates. I lean in close to his ear until I'm brushing it with my lips, kissing it. "Do you remember what I asked you to do the first night we were together, right here in this very room?" He shakes his head almost imperceptibly, and as I begin to grind against him in slow movements, I feel him start to tremble beneath me. "I asked you to help me forget." My mouth trails down to his neck, pressing one wet kiss after another to it. "And you did. You did it exceptionally well. Now, let me help you forget."

I grab both his hands and place them on my thighs, sliding them up under my short dress until they reach my buttocks. Automatically, his fingers sink into my flesh, and Thomas thrusts his pelvis against mine. I close my eyes, overwhelmed by a flush of pleasure.

"You're not gonna like it this way," he growls, an inch from my ear.

But I do like it this way.

I like it every way, when it's with Thomas.

I smile a little against his ear. "Touch me, Thomas. I want you to touch me the way only you can." I whisper it to him, taking his earlobe into my mouth and sucking it. Thomas stiffens, his grip on my ass tightening, burning me like a brand. I continue to tease him as I move my hands over his groin and rub his erection through his jeans. I pull a half-choked moan from his throat.

"I want you right here. On this floor right now. With the rain in the background and your hands all over me," I confess, inching his zipper all the way down. His eyes, lit up with greed, catch on my hand before slowly coming up to linger on my face.

And that's it.

For him and for me.

Thomas crashes into my mouth and stabs his tongue forcefully inside. There is no delicacy in this kiss. No respect. There is only desire. Hunger. Claiming. The next moment, I find myself prone on the floor, caged by his body. I flex my knees around his hips. I dig my fingers into his hair and kiss him back with the same enthusiasm. He grabs my wrists, clamping them together above my head with one hand while he bites my lip so hard that it makes me moan in pain and pleasure.

He runs his other hand along my stomach until he hits my thighs. I part them, and his fingers move expertly over my panties, lingering on one heated, quivering spot. "Is this how you want me to touch you?" he pants into my mouth.

My body is on fire as I nod. My hips buck, desperate moans issuing from my throat as his thumb puts more pressure on my clit. I struggle to free my wrists from the grip of his hands, but I don't struggle too hard, because feeling immobilized underneath him makes everything more thrilling. He continues to tease me with the palm of his hand. Finally, Thomas pulls aside my panties and unhesitatingly presses a finger inside me.

I can feel my breath catch in my throat from the intensity of the desire that overwhelms me. He withdraws his finger only to push it back in even deeper. I arch my back until my torso is pressing against his bare chest. I squeeze my eyes closed and bite my lip.

"You're so fucking beautiful, Ness," he breathes, giving me an indecipherable look. Then he seizes my mouth. He kisses, bites, devours the flesh on my jawline, dipping down to my covered breasts and then back up to my lips again. All the while, he keeps fucking me with his finger—in and out, in and out. My internal muscles tense and burn with every stroke as an unbearable pleasure grows between my thighs. God, I just want to grab his shoulders, dig my nails into his back, touch him everywhere, but he won't let me.

Before I know it, he stops pleasuring me and withdraws his hands to his jeans, pulling down his boxers just enough to free his erection. He rubs it slowly against my panties as I writhe, desperate for more contact. And since I can't use my hands to bring him closer, I lock my legs more tightly around his middle and pull him against my body. The longing ache between my legs has to be soothed, but Thomas gives me no relief. He tugs my panties aside and draws close to my opening before moving away immediately, only intensifying the unbearable feeling down there. My God, I need more. I want him deeper, inside me, just like in the bathroom at ClubSeven.

As if reading my mind, Thomas releases my wrists and turns me over roughly, grabbing me by the hair. Then he pushes me to my knees on the floor, a position that won't allow for kissing or any other emotional connection. He grabs my panties again, finally tearing them away, and then, without further delay, he sinks into me. My breath catches.

My scream bounces off the walls of his room. His breathing is more like a growl as he pulls out and slams back into me, making me scream again and again. I can't help it—I am no longer in control.

"Good girl, use your voice; let me hear how much you want me."

He moves inside me, back and forth, harder, faster. My body is on fire with arousal. The bursts of pleasure are so intense that my legs nearly give out. He holds my hair in one fist while his other hand runs along my hips, pushing my dress up to my waist. He reaches my covered breasts and eagerly pulls the satin fabric down, nearly tearing it in an attempt to bare me. A moment later, he tears my dress off entirely and tosses it into a corner of the room.

He bends his head to bite my shoulder and lick my neck. Then he wraps an arm around my waist, cupping a breast in one hand and squeezing it. He gives me a strong push, forcing me to arch my back. I can feel his panting on my shoulder blade. He moans—low, raspy, virile. I can feel his boiling flesh melting into mine, inch by inch, and I abandon myself to pleasure.

Thomas slips a hand between my thighs and strokes between my wet folds, teasing my clit. The rhythm of his thrust gets more intense, and—my God—I can feel it everywhere, right down to the pit of my stomach. My thighs tremble, I can feel my skin beading with sweat, and I'm panting. My head spins wildly. I want to kiss him, to feel his warm chest against mine, to fall over the edge with him.

Thomas just keeps thrusting violently into me, until the room fades away around us. There are just our bodies now. I can feel my muscles tense, my chest shaking through a series of spasms, and I hold my breath as I let my orgasm detonate. The intensity of it is so overwhelming that I'm briefly afraid I'm going to collapse on the floor, but Thomas's arm around my waist stops me. He also tightens his grip on my hair and pulls my head up, forcing me to turn my face toward him. He takes my mouth in the same greedy way he's slamming his hips into my ass until with one final short, decisive thrust, he releases me, leaving me to hold myself up on my unstable arms. Then he pulls out, squirting hot liquid on my lower back and ass. As his grip on my hair gradually slackens, he pants so deeply that it gives me chills.

Finished, he rubs the back of my neck, pulling my hair off my back. He gets up to retrieve a hand towel and cleans us both. He tosses it to the floor, turns off the light, and comes back to pick me up, helping me to stand up despite my stiff, trembling knees. I am still being wracked by small tremors; my breathing is labored and fragmented.

When I've gotten to my feet, with my back pressed against his sweaty chest, I can feel his erection prodding my ass. "I want you again," he grunts against my ear. He lifts me up, and I wrap my legs around him, clinging to his body, sore but satisfied. "But this time in my bed."

He lays me down on the bed while he remains standing in front of me.

He fully removes his jeans and boxers, and, with unusual delicacy, parts my legs and stares avidly at the place in between, where I'm still wet with both of our fluids. I bite my lip, fighting the urge to snap them shut out of shame. Only the darkness of the room keeps him from seeing my blush.

Thomas lowers himself on top of me, rubbing my calf and moving up toward my inner thigh, where he begins to alternate gentle kisses with hungry bites. Then he reaches my mound, where he lingers, making me arch into him.

"It wasn't just for you," I find myself whispering, my hands tightly gripping his hair. Even in the darkness of the room, I can see his eyes meet mine. He props himself up on tense biceps and smiles at me almost imperceptibly. Then he begins to slowly nibble along my ribs with his teeth, rising further until he closes his warm lips around the soft flesh of my breast. My stomach tightens, and so do my fists in his hair as I shiver.

"No, it wasn't," he confirms, moving on to my other breast.

"It would have been okay if it had been," I reassure him, stroking up and down his broad back. His boiling chest presses against my breasts, and I'm surrounded by the savage smell of him.

"When I fuck you, I want to be present." He buries his face in my throat and licks it. A thrill of arousal makes me dig my nails into his flesh. Thomas grabs my thigh, drawing it aside and pushing himself in between my legs again. I gasp. I pull his face down against me until our lips met as he begins to move inside, slower and deeper this time. For a split second, I feel the intense need to confess everything to him: how insanely in love I am with him, with this broken and damned boy, with all the parts of himself that he thinks are flawed or beyond redemption. But something holds my tongue.

I'm afraid it's too big a revelation for him right now. Too important and too binding. Instead, I just luxuriate in his kisses, welcome his thrusts, and love him in secret. I draw my free hand along his muscular arm, touching his chiseled chest and narrow hips. With just my fingertips, I brush the long irregular scar on his side before stroking it gently, yearning to just relieve a little bit of his pain. But then I feel him go rigid, as if my touch is costing him some effort.

He stops and looks down at me, troubled. I stop touching him immediately, fearing his response. I can remember the first and last time I tried to touch him there, and he had such a negative reaction that I haven't tried it again. Faced with his penetrating stare, I gulp. I'm about to apologize when I'm interrupted by his voice.

"Don't stop," he mutters, seeming almost surprised at himself. Hesitating slightly, he grabs my hand and places it back on his scar. He kisses me more forcefully, grinding me into the mattress. He holds my ass, filling me with ever more determined thrusts until a powerful electric shock seizes me from head to toe. As I reach my third orgasm of the evening, I plaster myself against him and scream so loudly that I'm almost immediately embarrassed.

After two more powerful strokes, Thomas stops, overcome and spasming. He grabs my hand and intertwines our fingers. He raises our linked hands above my head, and flexing the muscles in his back, he comes deep inside me. I can feel it pulsing inside; my body contracts rapidly. It is the most intimate moment I've ever experienced.

"Fuck, Ness..." he blurts, his movements slowing as the intensity of his orgasm begins to wane. When I open my eyes back up, I can see Thomas's half-closed eyes, his hair soaked, chest sweaty, wracked by labored breaths. He collapses on top of me, burying his face in my neck. He's gasping for breath but still careful not to crush me.

It takes him a few minutes to recover, finally lifting his head to rest it on mine. He stares at me for a few seconds, stroking my hair, pulling damp locks away from my face. "I won't be able to do without it anymore."

"Without what?" I ask, still panting.

"This." He kisses me softly, his lips parted. "You. Us."

My chest tightens until it feels like my heart is going to explode. "You won't have to do without it."

He just keeps staring at me as though he'd like to say something else but can't. In the faint moonlight that lights the room, I spot a hint of worry on his face.

"Is something wrong?"

He shakes his head, rubbing my cheeks with his thumbs. "Just swear to me you won't leave."

There's a dark edge of desperation in his voice that makes my breath catch. I look deeply into his eyes and say, more seriously than ever: "I won't, I promise." I kiss him and he reciprocates more intensely. Then, he stretches out next to me and we roll on to our sides, lying face-to-face. We are both tired and worn out. Seeing my goose bumps, Thomas draws me close to him and covers us both with the sheet.

"You want me to close it?" he asks, jerking his head toward the open window behind me. I shake my head. The sound of the rain and the feeling of the wind moving over my body is blissful. I want to keep enjoying it. Instead, we close our eyes and fall asleep, clasped tight, as the beating of our hearts blend together.

Twelve

WHEN I WAKE UP THE next morning, the weather is gloomy. The gray sky seems to make everything feel a bit melancholy. I'm still wrapped up in Thomas, who sleeps with my head tucked under his chin and his arms wrapped around my back.

He didn't sleep peacefully the night before; dredging up memories must have shaken him. He writhed and held me the whole time, as though he was trying to use my presence to soothe some of his torment. I pull away from him a little and just watch him sleep, gently touching his cheekbone, then his forehead, where a slight expression line forms as soon as my skin touches his. Even when he's unconscious, I get the feeling that he is still in conflict with himself.

A delicious smell emanating from downstairs coaxes me into leaving Thomas's warm and welcoming bed. With great care, I slip out of his hold and walk to the bathroom on my tiptoes. I put a little toothpaste on my finger and quickly brush—or rub—my teeth. First item on the to-do list: bring all my personal stuff over here. I wash my face and put my hair up into an everyday messy bun. Looking in the mirror, I can see some minor dark circles underneath my eyes. Considering the time we finally fell asleep, that's to be expected. What catches my eye instead are the unmistakable marks Thomas has left almost everywhere on my body. Signs of what he did to me last night in the bathroom at the club, on the floor of his room, and then again in his bed. I pass my fingers over each bruise—my breasts, my belly, down to my thighs—and I smile, biting my lip. They don't hurt; in fact, they bring back the memory of what I felt in the moment I received them: happiness.

Back in the room, I stumble upon my ripped panties. I pick them up and examine them with pursed lips, sorry for the ignoble end that Thomas gave them. I toss them into the trash can next to his bed and pick up Leila's dress while I'm at it. Second item on the to-do list: buy Leila a new dress. I hope she won't hate me for returning this one in such a state. Having nothing else to wear, I put on Thomas's shirt and a pair of basketball shorts that I find folded over the back of his desk chair. Perfect, I look like an actual mess.

With a shrug, I exit the room and head downstairs, humming as I go, feeling ready for some refreshments. I'm coming down the last few steps, when suddenly five pairs of eyes snap to me. I freeze immediately, my throat so dry that I can hardly swallow. I clasp my hands protectively over my middle as five frat boys look me up and down, grinning all the while.

Matt stands at the stove, busy scrambling eggs with a dish towel tossed over his shoulder. Two guys with curly blond hair sit at the counter behind him, books open in front of them. Both of them are barefoot and wearing dark track pants with white tank tops. Another boy stands in front of the open fridge with a carton of milk under his arm and an empty glass in his hand. The last one is in the doorway fully dressed, ready to leave.

"Well, well. Good morning, princess. Did you sleep well?" Matt asks me. The other guys chuckle under their breaths.

"Um, yes, I did." I look down, trying to hide my embarrassment.

"Lemme see," adds a familiar voice from the living room. I turn my head and see Vince heading right for me on the staircase. He plants one foot on the first step and leans his elbow on the handrail. He quirks one corner of his mouth and says loudly, "Heard you two set off some fireworks last night." He waggles his eyebrows.

Fireworks?

I remain frozen, unspeaking, digesting his words. Then, as I begin to understand, I can feel my cheeks start burning. Oh, no.

No, no, no, no.

They heard us.

"Just so you know, it's not a problem for us. We're guys; we get it," one of the curly-haired boys at the counter chimes in, lifting a spoonful of Froot Loops to his mouth. My eyes immediately snap to him. "But you should be made aware—just for the future, you know?—that the walls in this house are very, very thin."

Jeez. If, in the past, someone told me that I would one day find myself doing the walk of shame in front of the mocking eyes of five frat-house residents, I never would have believed them.

"Uh...well, I–I..." I stammer like an idiot, having no idea what to say in this situation. *Excuse me? I'm sorry? It won't happen again?* God, how embarrassing.

With a barely audible laugh, Matt jumps in and briefly introduces me to everyone in the room. He explains that there are still a few guys missing, but that, generally, these are the people I'm going to be living with from now on. Then he slides the scrambled eggs onto a plate already loaded with strips of bacon. He puts the pan back on the stove again and melts some butter in it before placing a few slices of egg-soaked bread on top.

I clear my throat awkwardly, and despite the blush burning my face, I cross into the kitchen and make an effort to introduce myself to the boys. They greet me politely before returning to their rooms. Alone with Matt and Vince, I sit down on a stool. Vince sits next to me with a sly look on his face. I glare at him, hoping he'll knock it off.

"I didn't know what you'd want for breakfast, so I just made the first thing I could think of," Matt informs me as he finishes toasting the last slices of bread.

"Thanks so much; this is great," I answer, pleasantly surprised.

"Bro, I suggest you beef up your portions. This girl here is used to ingesting enormous quantities of food..." Vince teases.

Stifling a groan, I tilt my head to the side to look at him. "It's not even ten in the morning; why are you here?"

"Because me and that peacock you've been banging all night go running every Sunday morning," he answers nonchalantly, stealing a slice of my bacon right off my plate. He eats it in one bite and licks his greasy fingertips.

"You're going for a run?" I ask in disbelief. "But it's raining; you're going to catch a cold."

He bursts out into laughter, followed by Matt, who is busy adding more food to my plate. What did I say that was so funny?

"Little Gem, who do you think you're talking to?" Vince loops an arm around my neck and pulls me closer to him. "We're *men*; a little bit of water won't make us sick."

I roll my eyes; what can I say in the face of this gym-bro machismo?

"Okay, then. But I still think it's a bad idea. Especially after last night." I wiggle out of his hold and turn back to my breakfast, which I begin attacking with gusto.

After trading some more small talk with the boys, Matt tells us goodbye, and Vince sends me upstairs to let Thomas know he's here. Back in the room, I close the door behind me. Seeing Thomas still asleep, wrapped up in the sheets, I'm seized by an intense urge to creep into the bed next to him.

I go over to the bed and lie down on it, my back against his chest. He buries his face in my hair and emits a soft noise of appreciation. He loops his arm around my middle and slowly climbs a hand up to my breast, cradling it.

"I like you in my clothes, but I much prefer you out of them," he murmurs, his voice low and guttural. My forehead wrinkles. He's awake? I turn to face him and smile. His first thought upon waking is my naked body? Typical perv.

"Good morning," I whisper, throwing one leg over his. He squeezes it with one hand, and I take a moment just to admire him. His eyes are half closed, his lips are swollen, and his hair is a messy tangle. God, he's beautiful. Even like this, with his face all sleepy and numb, and his wild look.

"You've gotta stop sneaking out of my bed all the time. I don't like falling asleep with you and then waking up to find you gone." He tightens his arms, tugging me even closer and pressing his naked body against mine. "Where were you?"

I grin at this small unexpected confession. "Downstairs. Matt made breakfast." I trace the outline of the tattoo that he has on his bicep, an hourglass wrapped in barbed wire with three tiny butterflies trapped inside. "Vince is here too," I tell him. He nods. I move my hand to his shoulder, continuing to touch him. I can feel some raised scratches under my fingertips. I run my hand over them again before realizing that they're just the marks that I left on him last night. I blush at the thought. I drop my eyes and my hand, overcome by conflicting emotions. Embarrassment, yes, but also satisfaction. I'm not a possessive person, or at least that's what I've always thought. I've never felt the need to mark a guy's body like before, but with Thomas, it's different. Everything is always different with him.

"What's up?" he asks, looking seriously at me.

"You're...covered in scratches," I manage.

"And you're covered in bruises," he answers, unable to hide the hint of guilt in his voice. "Do they hurt?"

I look up at him and give my head a decisive shake. "Do yours hurt?" I ask awkwardly, not meeting his eyes. A low, spontaneous laugh is his only response. Then he slides a hand under the shorts I'm wearing, rubbing my thigh and butt cheek. He grabs me firmly and rolls me on top of him.

"I wish you'd hurt me like that every day," he says slyly, pressing my hips down against his morning wood. When I feel a tremor between my thighs, I gulp.

"Always such a pervert," I tease him, patting his chest.

"You like my perversions, admit it," he murmurs provocatively. His hands remain firmly on my ass while I try to remain unmoved by his touch. I shake my head, only attempting to deny it because I don't want to let him win. But the truth is, his depraved side stirs feelings in me that I didn't even know I had.

"Liar. Did you forget that every time I do this"—he gives my ass an illustrative squeeze—"you get soaking wet?"

"Thomas!"

He laughs at my indignation, and I try to wriggle off of him, pretending to be annoyed. He holds me down, circling my waist in an iron grip. I try to free myself, but instead we find ourselves improvising some sort of weird wrestling match. Eventually, I end up pinned beneath him, my back pressed into the mattress and my forearms held down firmly on either side of my head. Thomas torments me with nips along my throat. I buck my hips in futile protest, and my groin accidentally rubs against his. This brief contact is enough to set us both off.

Thomas gives me an intrigued look, and when he sees that I'm not trying to move away, he stifles a grin and presses down harder onto my body, increasing the pressure on my core. I can feel every nerve ending alive with tension and pleasure as he lifts up my shirt and takes it off. Then he returns to my open thighs. "I bet that if I checked right now," he says, laying soft kisses on my stomach, "I'd find you all ready for me." He lifts his head up to look cheekily at me. And I'd tell him that he's wrong, except for the inconvenient fact that he's goddamned right.

I have a wild longing to feel him inside me, but I have no intention of putting on another show for the denizens of the house, so when Thomas tries to glide his hand downward, I block him. "We can't."

He stares up at me, brow furrowed so hard, his eyebrows are drawn almost together. "We can't?"

I bite my lip and shake my head. "The house is full of guys. And before, when I came down for breakfast, they made it pretty clear that last night…well, we weren't quiet," I tell him.

He shakes his head. "So?"

"Thomas, they *heard* us," I insist.

"Ness." He settles his body weight on his forearms, which are planted on either side of my hips. "You realize you're in a frat house, right? Do you have any idea how much moaning and squawking I've heard through these walls?"

"Is that supposed to make me feel better?"

"No." His lips are back on my belly, and he begins kissing me again, gradually moving lower. "It's supposed to make you realize that no one gives a shit what we do." Before I can answer him, he pulls off my shorts, and I'm left completely nude under his hungry gaze. An appreciative groan comes from deep within his throat. I know I'm blushing again, just like every other time I've found myself underneath him, naked and vulnerable.

"No panties?"

"Well, last night someone thought it would be a good idea to reduce them to shreds."

"That someone had an excellent idea," he answers brazenly.

I can't suppress a gasp when his hot tongue licks along my inner thigh, teasingly close to my most intimate parts. He grasps my exposed breast in one hand and rubs circles around my nipple until it stiffens. I instinctively arch my back and tighten my grip on his hair. The friction of his stubble against my inner thighs makes me shiver.

Without ever removing his gaze from mine, Thomas presses another moist kiss to my mons, glancing over my clit, which is throbbing so hard, it hurts. "Please, don't torture me this way," I pant, unable to stand another moment of this suffering. My body burns as I get wetter and more aroused. I squirm, longing for his tongue, his hands, his entire body.

"I want you to do something for me," he says, in a voice rough with desire. He observes my every reaction as he continues to kiss, bite, and lick me. "Will you?"

I nod. *Anything you want*, I think.

"I want you to touch yourself for me, Ness."

My eyes widen, taken by surprise.

"I want to watch you do it," he adds, sliding his tongue along my sodden folds. My breath catches, and my heart skips a beat.

I don't speak. I don't know what to say. I've never done anything like that before, and he knows it. I told everyone at Carol's party during that stupid game of Truth or Dare. Thomas can sense that I'm getting nervous, so he takes my hand and positions it between my legs. My heart begins to beat more anxiously.

"Relax," he says softly, rising back up to my lips. "There's nothing wrong with it." He kisses me intensely, using his tongue to share my own taste with me. His erection is pressing hard against my belly, and another volley of heat bursts between my legs. Thomas shifts his weight to his right forearm, and he takes his shaft in his other hand, slowly gliding it up and down himself.

When I look up and meet his eyes, I see pure desire along with sweet encouragement. So I take heart; I try to shed the prudishness that has always held sway over me. Although I'm still hesitant, I press my fingers to my slick folds, imagining that he's the one doing it.

"Tell me what you're thinking about," he whispers, staring down at my crotch and watching as I begin to move my hand in sync with his.

I swallow, and with no small amount of effort, I force myself to blurt out the truth: "You. I'm thinking about your hands on me."

Thomas quirks a corner of his mouth and sucks so greedily on my nipple that I moan. I touch myself with more urgency, the need to have him inside me rising. My clit throbs as pleasure spreads throughout my body. His guttural pants against my neck make me shiver. My back arches, pressing my breasts against his chest, which is rising and falling faster and faster.

Immediately, his lips are on mine and my body trembles. Oh God, I'm coming. I can feel the force of my orgasm burning up the back of my thighs, clouding my brain. Thomas masturbates himself faster, which tells me that he's also on the edge. But then, from behind the closed bedroom door, Vince's voice interrupts us.

"Bro, move your ass and get downstairs. We're already late."

I freeze and stare at Thomas, my eyes wide with panic and my body trembling with adrenaline.

"Fuck. I'll be out in a minute; wait downstairs for me!" he growls between gritted teeth, throwing a murderous look at the door before returning his gaze to me. "Don't stop," he whispers into my ear with his deep voice. "Keep touching yourself."

He bites my neck, and still pleasuring himself, he gets on his knees and puts his hand over mine, urging me to move. He pushes two of my fingers between my lower lips, moving them up over my clit and down again.

"Oh God," I moan, tossing my head back against the pillow. I try to withdraw my hand and let him keep going on his own, but he holds it firmly and continues to direct my movements, faster now. I can feel little electrical zaps running down every nerve I have. And then Vince's voice comes crashing down on us again.

"A minute is not long enough for you to finish what you're doing in there, and we all know it," he says. "I've already been here twenty minutes, so either you come out of that room right now, or I'm leaving."

We both stop moving. I feel my orgasm slipping away for a second time.

Thomas, with his jaw hard, mutters a quick "Fucker" and gets out of the bed, leaving me with a profoundly empty feeling. I cover myself with the sheet as he moves toward the door with determined strides and slams it open. Vince is there, leaning against the doorframe, and his face immediately screws up in disgust at the sight of naked Thomas.

"What the…? Dude, cover yourself up for Christ's sake,"

Thomas stabs a finger at him. "You owe me a fuck, you got that?"

"You mean…you and me?" The grimace on his face deepens. "No, I'm good."

"You're an idiot," Thomas answers. "Now I'm going to take a shower. An ice-cold shower."

"If I don't see you downstairs in two minutes, I'm gonna leave—"

Thomas slams the door in his face before Vince can finish and then stalks irritably to the bathroom.

Unsettled and dissatisfied in a way I've never felt before, I watch him vanish. I stare up at the black ceiling while I listen to the sound of running water in the shower, and I blink incredulously at the absurd situation we've found ourselves in. Scratch that—the absurd situation that Vince has put us in. Goddammit.

I snort and flop back on the mattress, and just when I'm about to give up on an orgasm this morning, Thomas reappears in the room. He advances on me, his face tense, and grabs me by the hips. With one single movement, he hoists me up over his shoulder, carrying me upside down. "Thomas! What are you doing!" I squawk in surprise.

"Taking a fucking shower."

Before I can answer, I find myself backed up against the bathroom tiles, my legs wrapped around Thomas's waist, his hands on my ass, and his hard-on pressed against me. Water from the shower streams over us, forcing me to blink repeatedly and maybe gasp a time or two. Thomas stares at me with a longing that makes me tremble. He pushes his hair back with a jerk of his hand, but a strong jet of water sends it falling right back over his forehead. He's somehow sexier than ever. Then, he pounces, kissing me passionately.

"I want you so much," he breathes into my mouth.

"I was under the impression that we didn't have time for this," I gasp, clinging to his shoulders.

He pulls back from my mouth a bit and, with a small smile, moves a sodden bit of hair from my temple to behind my ear. "I can mix business with pleasure." He slides into me with a moan. He braces himself against the tile and begins to move against me. I tighten my legs around him, and our breathing speeds up. And then he kisses me. He kisses me in a way he never has before. It's stronger, needier, deeper. My heart is thundering so hard, I'm afraid he can hear it.

"Thomas, I…" I'm breathing heavily as he thrusts purposefully into me, causing my stomach to tighten like a vise. He bends his head to vigorously suck my breasts.

"I–I…" I want to tell him, I need to tell him how much I love him, but those three words, so small but so powerful, are trapped on the tip of my tongue. I can't do it. It's fear. My own fear. Fear of not having my feelings reciprocated or of watching him slip through my fingers because those feelings are too big and too demanding for someone like him to deal with.

"What's wrong, little one?" he asks in a broken whisper, just an inch from my lips.

I stare into his eyes, my hands linked around his neck. I try to find the courage to just spit the words out, but…

"Nothing…it's just that…I…oh God…" I tilt my hips forward. "I'm…going to…come…" I'm amazed at how quickly I reach orgasm as I dig my fingers into his back and squeeze my thighs tighter around him.

"I know you're coming." His chest is flush against mine, and the glass of the shower is fogging up as he dominates me with the sharp, perfectly placed movements of his hips. "I can tell by the way your eyes get blurry, how your muscles tighten up and your body starts to shake." He seizes my bottom lip between his teeth and tugs it gently. "And, goddammit it, you should see yourself like this. You're so beautiful."

His words are enough to shatter me into thousands of pieces, to make me explode with pleasure. He loses control almost immediately after, and our mouths collide in a searing kiss, swallowing one another's moans. With one final thrust, Thomas squeezes my ass hard and, staring deep into my eyes, comes inside me. I'm breathing heavily, left at the mercy of an orgasm that has untethered me from reality.

He holds me against the wall for a few moments longer, his forehead on mine, his fingers clutching at my ass as the water streams over our bodies. "I did it," he says finally in a scratchy voice.

"Did what?"

"Got you in the shower with me." He smirks, making me laugh. Then he slides out of me, lowering me back to the floor.

"You didn't give me much of a choice," I answer with a grin, feeling my legs start to relax. He grabs his vetiver-scented shower gel and lathers up his hands. Then, he turns me around and begins to wash me, starting from my shoulders and moving down, massaging my entire body with slow, calm movements. It's wonderful to share such an intimate moment with him. Thomas draws circles on my lower stomach with his fingers before moving up to my breasts. He fondles them while his lips brush my neck, and he whispers to me about how he loves my tits. His erection is still pressing against my butt, conjuring all sorts of indecent ideas. Before I can communicate any of them to him, however, Thomas brings me back down to earth.

"We have to get out of here, or I'm going to fuck you again. And then Vince will kill me for real." He laughs, and I suddenly come to my senses. I swallow dazedly with flushed cheeks as I stare at the shower tiles, blinking repeatedly. He slips a hand between my legs and draws his mouth close to my ear. "But when I get back, I fully intend to pick up where we left off." He turns me around again and *boops* my nose.

I nod and give him a woozy smile.

We rinse off and get out of the shower. I wrap a towel around my body, and Thomas does the same. "Are you seriously going for a run in this weather?" I ask him when we get back into the room, my head still buzzing.

He nods, rubbing his hair with a towel. "You can come along too. I wouldn't mind working out with your sweet ass swaying in front of me."

I smile and shake my head over his typical dirty jokes. I sit down at the foot of the bed and watch as he strips off his towel and walks, casually naked, to the dresser. Biting my lip, I watch as he puts on his boxers and a pair of gray sweatpants that hug his thighs and ass in a way that makes me want to jump right back into the shower with him and stay there all day. God, what the hell is wrong with me? I need to chill out. So I take a deep breath and move my gaze anywhere else, to the still-open window, the glass streaked with rain. The bad weather doesn't seem to want to quit, but I don't actually mind. I get up and go to the window, pulling my hair over one shoulder so I can untangle it, and I lose myself in watching the rain as it hits the asphalt.

Thomas approaches me from behind and wraps me a hug, kissing my neck and resting his chin on my shoulder. "You really do like the rain, huh?"

I nod. "I like the smell the wet ground gives off after a rain. It's called petrichor. That's a lovely word, isn't it? And I like the sound of the raindrops on the pavement and the big rolls of thunder that feel like they're shaking everything. It gives me this deep, peaceful feeling..." I pause briefly. Then, moved by the scene before me, I keep going. "It's overwhelming, powerful, wild. The sky looks dark and grim, but you can't help but stand there and watch it, enthralled."

"A yes would have sufficed," he teases me.

I turn away from the window and tilt my face back toward him. I give him a little nudge in his side, and he lets out a weak laugh.

"Do you like it?" I ask, nuzzling into him.

"I prefer to stay in bed under the covers when it rains." He smirks, and I shake my head.

"You're hopeless," I chuckle.

Thomas backs away from me and goes to the closet, where he retrieves another of his black sweatshirts. "There's a game Friday night," he tells me, pulling the sweatshirt on. "You coming?" He continues with forced lightness, as though trying to give the question as little import as possible. Still, I thrill as I realize that he wants me there. It's a happiness that is almost immediately dampened when I realize that unfortunately, I can't come.

"I have work on Friday after class," I tell him regretfully.

"Shit, that's right," he answers.

"But, hey, maybe I can swap shifts," I say, moving toward him.

"Nah, don't worry about it. Don't fuck up your schedule for me; it's just one game, it's not that important."

"Yes, it is," I insist, just a step away from him. I look deep into his eyes. "I promise you that I'll do everything I can to be there."

He shrugs his shoulders indifferently. "If you want, but you don't have to."

It almost makes me smile. I stretch up on tiptoe to take his face in my hands and kiss him. "No, I don't have to, but I want to. I want to be there to cheer for you. For my boyfriend," I tease. He rolls his eyes and lets out a long-suffering sigh. Grinning, I wrap my arms around his neck and kiss him again.

When I finally let him go, Thomas pulls his ubiquitous black bandanna from a drawer and twists it around his wrist. Curious, I ask him, "Is there a reason why you always wear that?"

He seems to go rigid at these words. "It was his," he answers with a grim expression, looking down at it.

For a few moments, it is totally silent in the room. Then, I get it.

His.

His brother's.

Nathan's.

My breath catches. "Oh, I–I didn't...I didn't realize that. I'm sorry."

"Never mind," he says, downplaying it with a suddenly cool and impersonal voice. "I'm going now; see you later."

He goes to the door and leaves, dismissing me with air of detachment. He's sealed up once again in his shell, barricaded behind the walls he builds to keep the world out. And though I've struggled in the past to understand why, everything is much clearer to me now.

Thirteen

WHEN I'M ALONE, I FIND myself struggling to cope with everything that Thomas has told me. Part of me always knew there was a dark broken place inside of him, but I never imagined it went so deep. I would like to think that his having finally found the strength to tell me about it is a first step toward overcoming that pain and feelings of guilt, but after watching him withdraw into himself again, I'm not so sure. After last night, neither of us brought the subject back up, and I don't really feel like pushing it any more.

I get rid of my towel and put Thomas's clothes back on. Then, I text Tiffany to see how she's doing after our rough night. She answers that, apart from a mild headache, she feels fine. I take the opportunity to ask for another favor: Could she do the move for me? Maybe it's a cowardly thing to do but, right now, I'm not ready to go back to that house and risk getting into yet another argument with my mother. Besides, even if I wanted to go out, I don't have anything to wear here. She agrees, so I ask her to fill as many boxes as she can (especially with my books) and bring them over to me.

I psych myself up enough to also call Alex and update him before asking him to give Tiffany a hand. Though skeptical about the new situation between Thomas and me, he doesn't back out and assures me that they'll bring my stuff over as soon as possible.

While I wait for reinforcements, I try to make the room a bit more presentable. I carefully make the bed, collect some of Thomas's clothes scattered here and there before folding them and putting them in the dresser. Finally, I clean up the bathroom as well. When I finish, I feel particularly satisfied as I admire the shiny results.

After a couple of hours alone, I hear a car horn from the frat's front yard. Looking out the window, I can see Tiffany parking her Ford Mustang. Both she and Alex get out of the car, pop the trunk, and start unloading boxes. Tiffany, in a short tight black dress and tall rain boots that make her look effortlessly chic, says something to Alex and gestures nervously while he does his best to cover her with his umbrella as she carries the first box in. I slip on my Converse and go downstairs to lend a hand.

"Wow, did Collins paint his bedroom to match his heart?" Tiffany snarks when she enters the room.

"What were you expecting? Butterflies and unicorns?" Alex grins as he sets a box down on the desk and shakes out his wet hair.

It's a little uncomfortable, hearing her say this. His heart isn't black; it's broken. But between those infinite cracks, there's a light that not everyone gets to see.

"Thomas isn't that bad," I say defensively, trying not to take it personally.

"Of course he isn't. We are talking about the same Thomas Collins who drives you crazy on a daily basis? Right, Ness?" Alex asks, exchanging an amused look with Tiffany as they both take off their muddy shoes.

I drop my box on the floor and stand up, tucking my hair behind my ears as I look my friends in the eyes. "You don't know him. Not like I know him, and well, I am completely aware that he isn't the easiest person in the world, but—"

"Hey, retract your claws, tiger," Alex interrupts, coming over to me. "I didn't realize you were so sensitive about him." He puts an arm around my shoulders, hugging me and kissing my head before ruffling my hair with a jerk of his hand.

"Yes, hun, chill out, we're just joking. Mostly…" Tiffany says with a smile and a wink.

"I'm chill. It's just that…trust me, there's more to it than you know," I argue, shrugging.

To defuse the sudden tension, I change the subject, and we all end up laughing when I tell them about the morning welcome the frat boys gave me. Trying to sound casual as I unpack a few of my beloved books and put them on an empty shelf above the desk, I ask, "So…did you see my mother?"

They both nod, but only Tiffany answers. "Yeah. It was obvious that she wasn't expecting us, and she didn't say a word the whole time."

"Playing the indifference card," Alex agrees.

"Exactly. Before we left, though, she did ask me where you were."

Alarmed, I freeze midair with a book. "And what did you tell her?"

"That you came to stay with me, which is true. I thought it would be better not to update her on subsequent developments."

"You thought right," I answer sadly.

"Are you sure everything is okay?" Alex asks me, thoughtful.

"I'm sure. I'm just tired of her and her childish games," I confess, staring at the shelf, which is now nearly full of books.

"What games are you referring to?"

"Yesterday she came by the Marsy when I wasn't there. Apparently she asked one of my coworkers to have me call her." I shake my head bitterly.

"Your mom is consistent, I'll give her that," Alex says.

I sigh and let the topic drop.

After unpacking everything, we decide to reward ourselves with three delivery pizzas, which we devour sprawled out in bed while watching *Fast and Furious*.

"This is without a doubt the best pizza I've ever eaten in my life!" Tiffany says, chomping into her last slice.

"I don't even know how you can eat that. What kind of psychopath puts cream cheese on a pizza instead of mozzarella?" Alex says indignantly. "If my nonna saw this, she would lose it." As the grandson of an Italian woman, Alex is a bit of purist when it comes to Italian food.

"Before you bad-mouth it, don't you think you should try it?"

Tiffany lifts the slice of pizza closer and closer to Alex's face, before suddenly spreading it around on his mouth, chin, and cheeks. The two of us burst out laughing, while Alex gets his revenge by tackling and tickling us. We wriggle, between laughter and tears, and in all the excitement, my shirt rides up a little over my stomach. Alex takes advantage of the exposed strip of skin to escalate the tickling.

Right at that moment, the bedroom door opens. We freeze. In the doorway, I can see Thomas and Vince. Alex's head immediately swivels toward them.

"Hey!" we all exclaim at the same time, a bit awkwardly.

"Holy shit, people. Is this another one of my recurring sex dreams?" Vince starts.

Thomas doesn't let out so much as a breath. Paradoxically, it is this moment, when he shrouds himself in silence and restricts himself to merely slaying a person with his eyes (which is what he is currently doing to Alex) that all my senses snap to attention. I bound out of bed and go over to him, straightening my T-shirt.

"So, how was your workout?" I smile at him and stand on tiptoe to kiss him, but he doesn't smile back. He remains impassive with his lips pursed, arms motionless, looking sideways at me.

Alex and Tiffany also get out of the bed and pick up the empty pizza boxes before joining us at the door. Tiffany gives me a smacking kiss on the cheek and bumps Thomas with her shoulder. "Collins, a word of advice: repaint these walls. They're disturbing. Much like your face right now," she jokes in an obvious attempt to lighten the mood.

"That's what I like about them," he says, lifting the corner of his mouth, and I can tell that he isn't mad at her. The murderous look he gives to Alex standing beside me similarly leaves no doubt about his feelings there.

"Nessy, we're headed out. Call if you need anything," Alex tells me, trying to mask his unease with a sweet smile that warms my heart.

I nod, giving his arm an affectionate squeeze.

"Hey…man," Alex continues, turning to Thomas. "I hope you haven't gotten the wrong idea here; I assure you that we—"

"We're not friends," Thomas snaps, cutting him off, his voice devoid of any emotion.

"Thomas!" I say, taken aback.

Alex runs a hand through his hair. "That's true, we're not. But I don't want there to be any misunderstandings. I just want to say, Vanessa and I are just friends," he repeats.

"Friends," Thomas repeats mockingly, crossing his arms over his chest. "Were you being friendly when you stuck your tongue down her throat at the pool party?"

This shocks everyone. I can see Tiffany cover her eyes, and Alex blushes.

"Wow, this shit is starting to get interesting," says Vince, who is apparently enjoying the show. Too bad it's time for it to end.

"Thomas, knock it off!" I order him.

"Relax." Alex puts a reassuring hand on my shoulder. "It's fine; I'd better get going anyway."

"Yeah. You'd better," Thomas answers harshly, ignoring my warning. He steps back to clear the hallway, never taking his eyes off Alex.

When Tiffany meets my anxious gaze, she mouths the word *men*. Alex gives me a final nod before disappearing down the stairs with Tiffany. Vince turns to watch her long slender legs go by, and when he snaps out of the trance they've put him in, he runs after her like an excitable little dog to see if she needs a ride home.

Thomas closes the door behind them, and as I stare back at him, I can feel an immense anger rising up inside of me. "What the hell is wrong with you?"

"What's wrong with *me*?" he asks, his eyebrows rising. "I come back here thinking I'm going to find you alone, and instead, I catch you letting that idiot feel you up in my bed. Is this normal behavior for you?" He pulls off his shirt and throws it on the desk, revealing a powerful, virile body soaked in sweat.

I put my hands in my hair and clench my fists. I can't believe he's really going to make a jealous scene about this. "He wasn't feeling me up; we were just messing around!"

Thomas steps toward me, and I can hear the anger in his voice when he says, "And while you were 'just messing around,' did it ever occur to you that you were wearing a fucking T-shirt with nothing underneath?" His dark gaze settles on my breasts.

Frustrated, I let my head fall back and heave a loud sigh. "He has been my best friend since I was six years old, do you get that? I've already told you, he's like my brother!"

"But he's not your brother," he interrupts me sharply.

"Nothing bad happened; you are making a mountain out of a molehill. Also, he's dating someone!"

He laughs, but there's no trace of mirth in it. "His girlfriend will be pleased to find out that, in her absence, the two of you enjoy swapping spit and rolling around in bed together," he taunts me.

"Thomas," I chide him with a hard look.

He gives me an arrogant look up and down and then shakes his head, waving one hand to dismiss me. "Let's just stop this right here. It's always the same story with you anyway; I tell you that I don't trust someone, and you flip out because you see everything through rose-colored glasses."

"No, it's because you see a potential threat whenever someone breathes near me!"

"Yes, and I'm fucking right!" he shouts, punching the desk. Then he turns and heads for the bathroom, so I rush after him.

"Where are you going?"

"To take a shower."

"You're not going anywhere while we're still talking!" I yell at him.

"I don't want to listen to you. So if you wanna talk, talk to yourself. It'll probably be the best conversation of your life." He slams the bathroom door so hard, the frame shakes, and then audibly locks it.

I slap my palms against the wood until I feel them tingle. "Thomas, open this door! You can't just do this!" I keep raining down blows on the door and screaming his name until, finally, I give up. Exhausted and anxious, I pull on a sweater and go downstairs.

Vince is on the couch, still in his running gear, along with some guy I've never seen before. They're playing Xbox on the huge TV.

"Everything all right, Gem?" Vince asks, giving me a brief look.

I nod vaguely, pulling the sweater tighter around me.

"This is Kyle," he informs me, pointing to the boy next to him, who is still too engrossed in the game to take his eyes off the screen. Kyle just nods at me, maneuvering the joystick as if it were a steering wheel.

"Vanessa. Nice to meet you," I say without enthusiasm.

When Vince asks if I want to join the game to "get humiliated by yours truly," I decline with a smile and promise to save the humiliation for another day. I glance around, uncertain what I should do. I could also go out for a walk, but it's still raining outside, and to be honest, I don't really feel like it.

So, with a sigh, I head for the kitchen and look around for something to nibble on. As I do, I take the opportunity to familiarize myself with the new space. I open the pantry and find it stocked with sweets and snacks. Seeing the sacks of sugar and flour, and a bar of chocolate, I decide I could make a cake. I retrieve the butter, milk, and eggs from the fridge, and grab two pears from the fruit basket. I dig out a large mixing bowl and get to work. I break the chocolate bar into small squares and put them in a saucepan to melt over low heat. In the meantime, I peel the pears and cut them into slices. I mix the melted chocolate with the rest of the ingredients until I have a batter. Then I pour the whole thing into a buttered pan and arrange the pear slices on top. But the sound of wood creaking makes me lift my head and look out the kitchen doorway into the living room.

Something vibrates in my stomach when I see Thomas coming down the stairs shirtless, barefoot, wearing just his sweatpants. His hair is messy, and his chest is still wet. His face is a dark cloud. He glances into the living room, where Vince and Kyle are still on the couch. He ignores them and enters the kitchen instead, filling the room with his freshly washed smell. He doesn't say anything, just grabs a can of Coke from the fridge. He pops the tab and brings it to his lips, his gaze fixed on me the entire time. Meanwhile, all of my attention is focused on the movement of his Adam's apple as it rises and falls with each swallow. I grit my teeth and look away. I'm still mad at him, dammit! He can't just freak out and then cut me off like that every time he gets suspicious about something.

I walk past him, pretending not to notice his presence, and slide the pan into the oven. Then I start washing all the dishes I've dirtied. He leans back against the kitchen cabinet next to me, watching my every move.

"I thought you'd left," he says after a while, his expression indecipherable and his voice low.

I frown and raise one eyebrow as I continue washing the bowl. "I was tempted to."

Thomas scrubs a hand over his face in a frustrated fashion. "I would have deserved it."

Well, for once we agree on something.

He gives a yielding sigh and puts his hands on my hips, turning me to face him. My soapy hands are dripping all over the floor, but neither of us can manage to care. "I'm an idiot," he admits.

"Yup, you sure are," I confirm, trying to sound mad, but something in his regretful eyes makes it impossible.

"I shouldn't have reacted like that. I just never know how to handle this...this thing," he says, gesturing between himself and me.

"What thing?" I ask, bewildered.

He looks around, hesitating as if trying to find the right words to express himself. When he looks back at me, he cups my face in his hands and buries his fingers in my hair, pulling me closer to him. "In the past, if someone wanted to take something that belonged to me, I was willing to just give it to them. Because I didn't feel like anything really was mine." I'm about to break in and tell him Alex has no intention of taking what belongs to him, but he doesn't let me. "With you, it's different. Seeing you laugh or joke around or even just talk to someone other than me...it makes me crazy, Ness. And I don't give a shit if it's your best friend, a student in one of your classes, or a customer at the Marsy doing it. It's an impulse that I can't control.

Because you're mine…" He clenches my hair into his fist and presses his forehead against mine, staring into my eyes with a disarming intensity. "You feel like mine."

A shiver runs down my spine.

"You are an idiot, Thomas." I cinch my arms tighter around his waist, barely holding back a smile. The smell of his bodywash tickles my nose. "Alex is one of the people I care about most in the world. But I've never looked at him the way I look at you. I've never looked at anyone the way I look at you," I admit, rubbing his back.

We fall silent for a few seconds as his eyes roam over me. Then he shakes his head. "You just keep sticking with me, despite all the headers I take." He pauses and stares intently at me. "Sometimes I think you're the crazy one."

I lift my eyes to meet his and promptly get lost in that emerald abyss. "Sometimes, I think that too," I admit in a whisper.

Thomas strokes my cheek, and without another word, he kisses me. It's a slow, sweet, hypnotic kiss. Our tongues move languidly against one another, his lips warm and enveloping.

"Promise me you'll be nicer to him from now on," I murmur into his mouth.

Thomas just keeps kissing me, holding me tightly as if he's afraid that, if he doesn't, he'll watch me slip away from him. "I can promise that I'll try," he answers hoarsely, nibbling at my lip. "Can't promise I'll succeed."

It's not exactly the answer I was hoping for, but it still seems like an acceptable compromise. Without any warning, he grabs me by the thighs and lifts me up. I automatically wrap my legs around his waist and my arms around his neck. His lips curl into a small smile as he carries me out of the kitchen and toward the stairs. My eyes fall on the dishes yet to be washed and the oven, which is still on. "Wait, the cake is going to burn!" I point out.

"Vince," Thomas shouts, climbing the staircase. "Check on the cake."

Vince grumbles something that I can't hear but can clearly imagine.

When we get upstairs, Thomas closes the door behind us and sits me down on the desk, before...

"What the fuck...?" he says, looking at the pile of books and DVDs behind me, which I arranged earlier and which now take up most of the shelf.

"Um, yeah, see...I didn't mention it to you, but I had my friends bring some of my stuff over."

Thomas takes a look around, only now appearing to realize that the room has been colonized by books. He looks back at me with a raised eyebrow. "Did you bring your entire library, Ness?"

"No! No, no, of course not. Not my entire library," I answer hastily. "Tiff and Alex were careful only to bring me the essentials."

"The essentials?" he repeats skeptically. "My room has been completely invaded," he says, taking another quick look around. There are books and TV series box sets everywhere, to say nothing of the clothes; we managed to fit as much in the empty drawers as we could, but the rest are still sitting around in boxes on the floor.

"Oh God, did I...did I screw this up? I probably should have asked your permission first. I'm not trying to take over your space; it's just that I needed clothes, and I can't really feel at home without my books..."

Thomas stares at me, dazed, and I am briefly afraid that he's about to kick me out, but then he explodes into laughter, resting his forehead on my shoulder.

"I–I'm sorry. I should have told them just to bring a few changes of clothes and leave the rest."

"Ness," he says, raising his head, but I'm too embarrassed to listen to him.

"Believe me, I did not do this to try to put down roots or something. And I totally understand if this is all too much for you."

He says my name again, but I don't let him get a word in edgewise. "I can get rid of it all, no problem. I can call Tiffany and ask her to take some of the boxes back to her place. In fact, you know what? I'll call her right now." I start to scramble off the desk, but he stops me with his hands on my thighs.

"Ness."

"Yes?"

"I'm fine with this."

I look at him, confused. "You're fine?"

He nods, tucking a strand of hair behind my ear. "When I offered you the room, I figured you would bring stuff. I'm just surprised by how much you managed to get over here. Honestly, I don't mind the idea of having your things around."

"Are you sure?"

He grins. "I'm sure."

"Because if you aren't, I can make it all go away—" I don't finish my sentence because Thomas pulls me into him, stifling all my replies with a kiss that leaves me breathless. I melt into his arms and part my lips. Our tongues move and entwine with passion and sweetness.

"Just out of curiosity…" His voice becomes a rough purr as he lowers his head to lick my neck; I tilt my head back. "Are Momo, Nina, and Sparky around here somewhere?" he asks, letting his hand wander beneath my shirt and setting my skin aflame. I nod and feel his chest rise and fall in gentle laughter. "And that ridiculous mask you wear to sleep?" He returns then to my mouth, licking and nibbling my lower lip.

"Yes…" I gasp, my brain foggy, lost in desire.

"And tell me…" He runs his fingers over my breasts. I suck in a breath when his thumb reaches my nipple and begins rubbing it with slow circular motions. It's a pleasure so intense that it almost hurts. "What about the pink pair of pajamas with the teddy bears on it? The ones I had so much fun taking off you when I made you come in my mouth that first time?"

"T-that's here too."

He abandons my breasts, grabbing my ass and pulling me to him with a jerk. I feel an immediate rush of heat wash over my body.

"Do you remember what I told you before I left?"

I nod breathlessly. Of course I remember it. It's only all I've been thinking about.

"I'm a man of my word," he murmurs, kneeling down with a

ravenous gleam in his eyes. He lifts up my legs and puts them over his shoulders. He runs his hands up my thighs until he finds the waistband of my pants, and pulls them down so slowly that it might drive me insane. When he realizes that I haven't put on any underwear yet, he grins at me.

Eyes glued to me, he kisses my thigh in a slow, sensual form of torture. My inner muscles clench, and I let out a groan. His tongue keeps going until it reaches the apex of my thighs. When the cold metal ball of his tongue piercing teases my clit, I begin to shiver. When his tongue ventures inside me, I writhe against him. I fist his hair in my hands, pulling hard as a jolt of electricity shudders through my entire body.

Groaning, I toss my head back and squeeze my eyes shut.

"I want you to look at me," he demands the moment my eyelids close. "The whole time." His hands press firmly into my ass. Stunned, I straighten my head and do what he wants: I look at him. The green of his eyes darkens as he goes back to pleasuring me with his tongue, each movement more intense. Without breaking eye contact, he continues to tease and lick me, unlocking wild arousal within me. I can feel my heart racing; it's throbbing in my ears when, with one firm stroke, he reaches the place that sets me alight.

Thomas smiles with satisfaction and keeps at it like he's just found the key to paradise. My arousal is at its peak when I tighten my hair in his fingers, urging him on. He reacts by sucking my clit into his mouth again before teasing it with repeated gentle strokes of his tongue, which make me explode into his mouth in a series of spasms.

I need to scream, but I suppress the urge by biting my lip. The orgasm completely overtakes me, and neither of us look away from each other for the whole duration. It feels like I've been trapped, like we're chained to each other. It's an inexplicable sensation, what I feel when his mouth moves against me, and I can see in his hungry eyes all the pleasure he's feeling as he makes me come.

I'm trembling from head to toe, but I know that I won't reach the highest peak of pleasure until he owns me completely. That's why I indulge in the wet kiss that Thomas leaves on my mouth. I let him pull off my shirt, pick me up, and lay me down on the bed, waiting for his next move. Standing in front of me with a grin lifting the corner of his mouth and his head slightly tilted, he examines my entire body. Resting one knee on the bed, he grabs his erection and moves his hand slowly up and down it, all the while continuing to stare at me. I lose myself as well, examining his naked body, and I thrill when, in a gruff voice, he orders, "Turn around."

My heart feels like a restless animal, pacing inside my chest as I do what he says.

"Get on all fours, and brace yourself against the headboard," he continues in a low voice. I can feel the mattress bowing when he comes up and bends over me, pressing his naked body against mine and kissing my shoulder blade. He sucks on my earlobe until my back arches. He slides down my body, running his tongue along my spine, kissing the curve of my ass, saying finally, "I want to take you back here."

I gasp, feeling my ability to think clearly faltering. "Okay…"

He wraps an arm around my waist and pulls me tight against him. "I mean, back…back…"

What?

I stare at the wall in front of me for a few seconds before I realize what he's talking about. Then my eyes go wide, and I whirl around, sitting up. "No! I have no intention of crossing that line!"

He laughs like he was anticipating my reaction. "Do you trust me?"

"Yes, but—"

Thomas stops me, taking my face in his hands and running his thumb over my lower lip in a gentle caress. "I would never do anything that would hurt you. Only pleasure, Ness, pure pleasure."

I look at him, overwhelmed by a thousand conflicting emotions. Embarrassment. Hesitation. Fear. Excitement. Curiosity. But above all else, a sense of belonging. It feels like there's a part of me that would be willing to do anything with him, experience everything, push every limit, and lose myself with him in every possible way. But I can't deny that I'm also afraid.

I nervously chew my lips as he lays me gently down on the mattress.

I can feel his erection touching my sex. That small contact halts my breath and reignites the flame inside me that was briefly dampened.

"Relax. We don't have to do that right now. When you're ready, you'll tell me. So…" He smiles, lowering himself down to my breast to nibble my nipple before sucking it so hard I gasp. "Until then, I'll just enjoy taking you from behind the old-fashioned way." With one movement, he flips me over onto my stomach and lifts up my hips. I shift my weight onto my knees and let out a small cry mixed with a laugh when he bites my ass cheek and slaps it.

"You have the sexiest ass I've ever seen; you can hardly blame me for dreaming of making it completely mine every time I see you like this in front of me." He leans over me, caressing the cleft of my butt. I shiver, trembling. With one hand, he pulls my hair away from my back and grasps it in his fist. He pulls me back, forcing me to tilt my head, unconcerned with being too rough. With his other hand, he strokes my belly, reaching down to my clit and beginning to stimulate it. He slides one finger into me, and I grip it tightly. He pulls it out and then penetrates me again, deeper this time. Every time he repeats this movement, my body is more and more inflamed. I move my hips eagerly against him, pulling a low, guttural groan from him. "I'm gonna fuck you so hard, Ness."

He bows over me, licking my neck, grabbing my hip with one hand. I love Thomas's voice when he's deep in his arousal. It's enough to make my legs spread automatically. I clench the sheets in my fists, and then, with a short thrust that leaves me breathless, Thomas is inside me.

Fourteen

IT'S BEEN FOUR DAYS SINCE I moved into the frat house, and things with Thomas seem to be going weirdly well. We're both busy at school with classes and practice, but we manage to make time for each other. When I'm working, he comes to the Marsy with his friends and waits for my shift to end, and then we go back to the frat, where we spend every night together. It's like neither of us can do without the other anymore, and that sense of belonging to one another only gets stronger each day.

I'm so happy, it feels like I'm walking on air, even now when I'm climbing the last of the steps leading to the dean's office. That is, until the thought of what I'm about to face brings me back to earth.

I lift my skirt up a bit, so I won't step on the hem with my Converse. In my other hand, I hold a paper cup full of steaming coffee. Arriving in front of a closed door, I take a seat on one of the empty chairs in the hallway, waiting. I cross my legs and check the time on my wristwatch: 9:45 on a Thursday morning. My appointment is at 9:50.

I take a deep breath and sip my coffee. I tap my feet nervously. I take another sip, set the cup down on the chair next to mine, and gather my hair up into a messy bun. Then I think about it for a minute and realize that I can't show up in front of the dean looking like this. I undo the bun, detangling my hair with my fingers and tucking it behind my ears, trying to play it cool. I drain the last bit of my coffee and toss the cup into the trash can on my left. Damn, I'm nervous. I have no idea why the dean has requested to see me, and the urgent way he summoned me only makes me more anxious. I check the time again: 9:48. I stand up and start pacing.

I'm guessing it has something to do with the student loan I inquired about. Maybe he wants to tell me that, unless the rest of my tuition for next semester is paid, I won't be able to attend classes. That would be terrible. What am I talking about? That would be a *nightmare*.

I don't have time to formulate any other thoughts, because then the office door opens. I turn and am faced with the secretary, who invites me in with a wave of her hand. "Miss Clark, please come in; make yourself comfortable."

Dean Campbell is on the phone, leaning back in his black leather chair and staring up at the ceiling. With a grave expression, he gestures for me to sit down. The secretary goes over to a pitcher of water on a table in the back of the room and fills two glasses. Then she returns, placing them on the desk in front of us before leaving us in total silence. I sit down hesitantly in the chair in front of the dean, separated only by an expensive-looking desk with paperwork scattered all over it.

After a few minutes, during which he continues to talk to the person on the phone about a potential reorganization of campus security, the dean gives me an apologetic look and a "be patient" nod. I look around, tapping my fingers on my legs and turning my attention to the framed pictures hanging on the wall: degrees, various certificates, different portraits, and some family photos. Including one of his two daughters in formal wear, immortalized on prom night, and another of him looking happy and carefree with a woman who must be his wife.

"Miss Clark." The dean's sharp voice makes me jump. I sit up straight and give him all the attention I can muster. "I apologize for the wait, but today seems to be a day full of inconveniences that I have to prioritize." He straightens the knot of his tie and puts both hands on the desk. "So how are you doing?"

"Good, I think, thank you." I give him a very tense smile. I'd like to dispense with all these pleasantries and get right into it. The dean runs a hand through his gray hair before deciding to get to the point. "It's been more than a week since we talked about the difficulty you've been having in paying your tuition." He gathers up some loose papers from the desk and puts them in a folder. "If I remember correctly, I advised you to apply for a student loan. Is that right?" Oh my God, I knew this was going to be bad news. I can't believe it; I'm about to be kicked out.

I nod to him, trying not to show the anguish coursing through my body. But it doesn't work, because when I finally speak, my voice is clearly shaking. "Yes. I've been researching, and I have an appointment with the financial aid office next Monday."

"So you haven't started the process yet?"

"No, but I will do it as soon as possible." I wring my hands as panic overwhelms me more and more.

The dean throws his hands up triumphantly. "That's great news, Miss Clark!"

"Excuse me, h-how?"

He picks up his glass of water and takes a small drink. "Yesterday afternoon, something rather unusual happened. The university received a check from an anonymous benefactor. As requested in the accompanying letter, we've used this check to pay the entire remaining balance of your tuition as well as your room and board."

My jaw practically hits the floor.

"What?" I hiss, in a state of shock.

Dean Campbell nods and hands me a packet of papers. "Here, this is your transaction receipt and invoice. The fee has been paid in full, which means that from this moment on, you are free to use all the related services on campus. No worry about grades either, although even if there were, it wouldn't be an issue. I know for a fact that you are an excellent student." He says it so proudly that it sounds like he's talking about one of his daughters.

I leaf through the documents, my mouth still open in shock, as I try to listen to what the dean is saying while also focusing on the words on the pages. I shake my head. "I–I…don't understand. My scholarship doesn't cover room and board. Besides, I don't know anyone who has enough money to pay the entire balance..." I lift my head. "This is definitely some kind of mistake."

"Are you Miss Vanessa Clark?"

I nod, bewildered.

"Then I can confirm it is no mistake."

"But....can I at least know the name of this benefactor?"

"Along with the check, we received a formal request to remain anonymous. We are required to protect the donor's privacy, or we would be in serious trouble."

"I still don't understand; this feels absurd..."

"There's nothing to understand. Someone must be very passionate about your academic training. Leave this office and celebrate; today is a good day for you, Miss Clark."

I find myself outside the office door, my eyes still glued to the documents. My brain is short-circuiting, unable to form a single meaningful thought. What the heck just happened in there? An anonymous benefactor has paid a huge sum to ensure that I'll be able to continue my studies. I can't figure out who the hell it could be. Only three people—my mother not included—even know about the situation.

I quickly pull my phone out of my bag and text Thomas, Alex, and Tiffany the same message: My full tuition and housing has been paid by an anonymous source. Do you know anything about this?

It isn't long before I receive their respective responses.

Tiffany: WHAT?!

Alex: An anonymous benefactor? How is that possible?! That's what I'd like to know.

Thomas (after a few minutes): I don't know what you're talking about.

I reply to everyone: I just left the dean's office. I have a receipt in my hands right now.

Tiffany: Maybe your mother?

Me: Can't be. She doesn't even have half the amount. And after our recent history, she'd never do it.

Tiffany: Right, that is weird. But hey, why does it matter who actually paid? The important thing was that it got paid! This is fantastic news. Now, if you'll excuse me, I have to find a fingerprint on a fake disemboweled corpse. I'll text you after class, love you!

A notification sound alerts me to a new text from Thomas: I was just coming to meet you when your idiot friend intercepted me. No point in telling him to fuck off, so now we're in front of the auditorium. Hurry up before I kill him.

Me: I'm coming. Be nice to him…please.

I toss the papers and my phone into my bag, and quickly head for the elevators. I take the corner too fast, though, because I collide with a navy-blue sweater-clad chest. When I come out of my daze, I look up to find two blue eyes staring at me in shock. Logan. Great, this day is full of surprises.

Recently, Logan has started to orbit around me again, in class, in the library, during lunch periods. Thomas's presence must have kept him from actually approaching, and that's probably for the best. I can't deny that I'm still ashamed about everything that happened to him because of me. His bruises are healed now, and fortunately he didn't press charges against Thomas like I was afraid he would. But I can't forget the things he said about Thomas and the way he tried to keep me from leaving his room that night.

"Sorry, I didn't mean to slam into you," he apologizes, as shaken as I am.

"Don't worry, it's my fault. I was in a hurry, and I wasn't paying attention."

I look everywhere but at his eyes, and for a moment, neither of us dares to speak. Then Logan tucks his hands into his pockets and breaks the silence. "So how have you been? We haven't had a chance to talk since that night…" He rocks on his heels, visibly uncomfortable.

"Oh, I'm fine, thanks. And you?" I manage, shifting my weight back and forth from one leg to the other.

"I've got no complaints. The life of the average American college student isn't that bad." He chuckles.

I huff through my nose. "Yeah, tell that to anyone who developed stress acne when they couldn't keep up with the coursework."

He gives me a big grin. "They're probably taking the wrong courses, don't you think?"

I smile back at him, more relaxed. Part of me appreciates that he can still talk to me like this, like nothing happened after so much did indeed happen. On the other hand, I'm astonished. My boyfriend beat the crap out of him, and I never spoke to him again, not even to apologize. He probably should feel some resentment toward me; it would be justified.

I shrug. "I don't know; every course is the right course for me." I put my bag back on my shoulder, and nudged by curiosity, I add: "What brings you here?"

"Meeting with the school counselor." He points at the door next to the dean's office.

"Is everything okay?"

He puffs out his cheeks and blows out a heavy sigh. "I need to rework my class schedule," he answers shortly. With some uncertainty, he turns to the coffee machine a few paces away from us. "Can...can I get you a coffee?"

"Actually, people are already waiting for me..." I say, a little awkwardly.

"Maybe some other time?" he asks hopefully.

"Oh, okay, I....honestly, I don't think that would be a good idea..." I don't want to be rude, but I don't want him to get the wrong idea again. And I really don't want to mess up my relationship with Thomas over a stupid coffee. So I give him a smile and go to leave, but he gently grabs my arm.

"Vanessa, wait, please... I'm just asking for one meetup. Just one, in broad daylight, wherever you want... I just want to tell you how sorry I am for coming between you and Thomas the other night."

"Don't worry about that; there's no need. I know you're sorry, and so am I." I pull my arm back. "Let's just forget all about it."

"The truth is, I can't. I can't forget..." I hear him whisper, his head bowed. Does he mean he can't forget the events of that night or that he can't forget...*me*?

Something tells me that's exactly what this is about, and I force myself to obliterate any hopes he might have. "Logan, I know I handled our situation poorly, and I disrespected you by hanging out with Thomas while you and I were seeing each other. But...I'm with him now. I'm in love with him, and that's not going to change. So if there's even a small chance that you still have any interest in me, then I think the best thing for you to do is to stay away from me."

"I don't want to stay away from you; I just want—" he starts to say, sounding dejected.

"No," I interrupt him abruptly. Maybe I seem rude, but he has to understand the situation. "I'm sorry about everything, truly. You're a good guy, and I am sure that you are going to find the right person for you very soon. But that person isn't me." I don't give him time to answer, though I can see the disappointment in his face. Instead, I head for the elevators so I can go find Alex and Thomas.

Thomas and I sit in his tree house, our legs swinging in the air, two cans of Coke and some fries between us as we watch the starry sky above. We came here after class, and now I'm enjoying the light breeze that caresses my face, tousling my hair a bit. To protect myself from the cold, I'm wearing one of Thomas's heavy sweatshirts, which falls below my butt. Lately, I've been finding myself stealing them more and more often.

I'm telling him about my latest adventures at the Marsy when his phone rings. He answers it with his usual surly voice. "Hey...yeah, everything's fine, you? Don't worry about it; I'll make sure nobody touches anything." He smiles and then turns to look at me. "She's fine too. I'll give you to her; she's right here."

I frown and ask him who it is in a low voice. He mouths "Leila" before handing me the phone, adding: "She wants to make sure I'm behaving myself." He shakes his head in resignation as I grin.

Thomas has been agitated since Monday, when his sister went back to Portland, and he's been in touch with her constantly these days to make sure that being with their parents isn't upsetting her too much. Although he doesn't show it, I can tell that he's tormented by the idea of her being alone there with them.

"Hey!" I exclaim, putting the phone to my ear.

"Did my brother tell the truth? Is he behaving?"

"He's doing his best." I chuckle, glancing at Thomas, who glowers in return.

"Maybe I should leave more often, then," Leila answers with humor.

"But how are you doing? Are you keeping up with your classes? Do you need me to get some notes from your classmates?"

"Right now, I can follow along online without a problem. But I do have a favor to ask you."

"I'm all ears."

"You remember that I'm on the editorial staff of the university newspaper, right?"

"Of course. I read your article about accidents caused by cell phones. You did a great job. I saw that it was republished in the *Corvallis Gazette-Times* and the *Albany Democrat-Herald*. What an achievement!" I glance at Thomas, excited about his sister's success.

"Oh, thanks so much," she answers shyly. "But I do have a small problem. I'm supposed to deliver an article next week about the police's abuse of power in this country. But being here in Portland is slowing me down a lot; I can't focus the way I need to. And I was wondering if you could...well, if you could help me?"

I feel my heart start pounding at the prospect, and in a rush of enthusiasm, I answer her before really thinking. "That would be an honor!"

"Oh my God, you'll really do it?" she exclaims, relieved.

I nod, as though she can see me, while I keep Thomas's curiosity at bay with a wave of my hand.

"Of course! I've never done it before, but I've always wanted to. Do you already have some material I could work with?"

"Yeah, I've collected several sources and put together some notes. A lot of notes. I'll email you everything tonight. Thanks, thanks, thanks!"

"Don't thank me," I answer, grinning. "Instead, tell me, do you think they'll let me join the staff to work on this article, even if I'm not regularly a part of the paper?"

"I'll let them know, don't worry. I'll tell them you're taking my place until I return."

"Great!" I rub a hand on my pants, brushing off some grains of salt with my fingers. Hoping I don't sound too intrusive, I ask, "So… how are thing going at home?" Next to me, Thomas stiffens almost imperceptibly.

Leila sighs. "That's another reason I called… The hospital admitted our father this morning after a respiratory crisis."

I feel a cold chill but, after what I've found out, I can't say I'm actually sorry for the man.

"I've put off telling Thomas for a while but, I think it's time."

"I get that. I'll pass you back to him, then?"

"If you don't mind, I'd like to talk to you about something first. Can you move away from him?"

Thomas and I are currently stuck in a house on top of a tree, suspended twenty feet in the air. "Uh…not really," I answer, trying to sound casual so I don't arouse his suspicion.

"I'm making this hard for you, aren't I? Sorry, that wasn't what I wanted. I just feel like I need to talk to someone about it. Someone who won't freak out the way my brother probably will."

I'm starting to get nervous, imagining the worst. "I'm listening; talk to me," I encourage her, pressing the phone more tightly against my ear.

"Our mother wants to see him. She wants to see Thomas, now that our father isn't at home anymore."

Oh, that's all? My shoulders immediately relax. "That sounds like a good thing to me."

"Not for Thomas, as you know. I would really appreciate it if you could convince him to accept her invitation." Leila knows that her brother told me everything about their childhood. But she probably doesn't realize that, after that night, we never broached the subject again. I don't want to make him feel harassed, but I also know that he and his mother haven't been in touch for a long time. He told me that the first time he took me to this tree house.

"I don't think…"

"Thomas listens to what you say, much more than you think. It feels like, after so long, I might finally have my mother and brother under the same roof again. I don't want to watch this opportunity slip away just because he's a hothead."

My heart is aching. I can only imagine how much suffering Thomas's obstinate refusal to come home is causing her. I bite my lip. "Okay, okay, I'll do it. Or at least, I'll give it a try."

I can hear her sigh deeply. "Thank you so much. You are the best, I swear, the best! I won't ask him right now so I don't dump too much on him, but I will soon. Now you can hand me back to my idiot brother. I've already taken up too much of your time."

Gathering my courage, I hand him the phone and wait for the truth to hit him, prepared to soften the blow as best I can.

"Hey, is everything okay?" I ask in a whisper as soon as Thomas hangs up. He brings a cigarette to his mouth and takes a long, deep drag, the center of his forehead wrinkling slightly. Then he stubs the cigarette out in a small ashtray, starting at some point in the middle distance. I know his mind is wandering off somewhere else, far away from me, but I want him here. Right here with me.

I put a hand on his shoulder and rub it. "Thomas…"

He turns with a start, making me jump as well.

"Are you okay?" I ask again.

He nods. "I'm fine. You wanna go home?"

"No, I like this place. It relaxes me." I shrug, breathing in the cool evening air of the woods. I crouch down next to him and wrap my arms around his neck.

"They admitted him to the hospital this morning..."

"Yes, Leila told me. Do you want to talk about it?"

He shakes his head. "Did she say anything else? She seemed a little weird on the phone."

"Um, not really. She just asked me to fill in for her at the school newspaper while she's away," I answer vaguely. He gives me an uncertain look. I don't know if he senses that I'm hiding something from him, but for whatever reason, he decides to drop the subject.

We stay cuddled there in silence for a little while. Until, trying not to appear too nosy, I decide to take a chance. "Thomas, I know we haven't talked about it since the other night but...would you like to tell me what happened after the accident?"

He doesn't release his hold on me, but I can feel his body stiffen.

I rub his back gently. "You don't have to tell me if you don't want to. But if you feel the urge to talk...well, just know that I'm here." I press a soft kiss to his jaw.

He reciprocates with his lips against my hair. "No secrets, right?"

It's the promise we made each other two nights ago when, lying together under the covers, I opened up to him and told him all about my father: the pain his abandonment caused me and the sense of helplessness I felt when I watched my parents gird their loins and go to battle with each other.

"No secrets," I repeat, grateful that he seems ready to take the same step forward.

Thomas runs a hand through his hair, takes a sip of his Coke, and begins: "After I woke up from the coma, I stayed in the hospital for a little over a month. My mother never once came to visit me."

His confession makes me shudder, and I wonder how that could be possible. She had lost a son, true, and she must have been in excruciating pain, but there was still another son who needed her. That son was alive; he survived and was lying in a hospital bed. He didn't deserve to be there alone.

"The only good thing about that time was that my body was forced to go through a kind of detox," he continues, pulling me back from my sad thoughts. "By the time I was discharged, I was clean. I made myself a promise when I left that hospital. I was going to take the second chance I'd been given, and I'd go straight. I had to do it, not just for myself but for my brother, who was gone. But more than anything else, I felt like I owed it to my mother. It was the least I could do after what she went through. After what she'd lost. But when I got home, the situation was even worse than I expected.

"Leila said something to me, but it wasn't until I got back that I realized my mother had fallen into an intense depression. She spent days in my brother's room. Lying on his bed with his clothes in her hands, just staring at the wall. She refused to eat or speak. She didn't even go to parent meetings at Leila's school. All she did was sleep, doped up on psych meds. I could see this woman who looked just like my mother, but there was no real trace of her left. There was just emptiness in her eyes." He hesitates a moment before starting to talk again as I feel a stab of pain in my gut.

"I tried everything I could to get close to her, because I needed it. I needed her desperately. But the harder I tried, the more I saw nothing but an accusation in her face. She never said it, but it was as clear as day when she looked at me. The only thing she saw was the boy who had taken her son's life. The better son, who deserved to live much more than I did."

"Thomas...I–I don't think she..." My voice is shaking so hard that I can't finish the sentence.

"That's how it was. Believe me. She couldn't stand to see me in that house anymore...or maybe she did want me around but couldn't find the strength to forgive me. That was when I realized that I had to back off. I wanted to leave, but I couldn't. I couldn't go anywhere for two years because of my sentence, so—"

"Wait, what? Your sentence?" I interrupt to ask, my head snapping up in surprise.

He nods. "I was charged with manslaughter."

My eyes widen as I sit up straight. "But it was the driver of the truck who ran you off the road!" I insist, my voice anguished.

He sighs, running a hand over his face, and looks at me. "I was driving the bike while intoxicated, and the accident resulted in the death of a person. The driver of the truck didn't stop, so…" He leaves the sentence hanging there, trusting that I'd be able to intuit how it ends. I rub my forehead, my heart thumping.

"My God! So you've…have you been to prison?" I shudder just thinking about it.

He gives a weak shake of his head, and I let out my held breath. "That would have been the right sentence, but no. During the trial, my lawyer made a big deal about how young I was, telling the jury that I was definitely a troubled boy but not irredeemable. He argued that there was no need to send me to prison, because my prison would be the burden of living the rest of my life without my brother, drowning in grief and guilt. I guess that made them feel some kind of pity for me, because they lowered the charge to involuntary manslaughter. I got two years of community service and probation for driving under the influence, plus some of the fights I'd gotten into in the past. Then I had to make up the year of high school that I'd missed because I had to prove I was a 'good citizen,' or they'd have sent me to jail. I went straight until my sentence was over."

I stare at him in shock. "And then what happened?" I ask, guessing from the dark tone of his voice and the tense expression on his face, that the story didn't end there.

"What happened was that, despite all my efforts to keep my nose clean, the situation escalated again. Things at home were out of control. My father always blamed me for my brother's death. For how my mother was, for the failure of our whole family. After the accident, he actually started drinking more, if that was even possible. He still hit my mother; the only difference was that now she didn't react. She was basically catatonic at that point.

"In the end, it was just like it always was: that bastard and me coming to blows. After a few months, I'd completely fallen back into my old habits. That house...that life...it had become this vicious circle that was impossible to escape. Leila found herself forced to take care of all of us. She tried to fill my mother's shoes...but she was still just a teenager. The life she was living wasn't right for her. She should have been going out with friends, pining for some douchebag who broke her heart...certainly not looking after a couple of alcoholics and a severely depressed woman."

"And you'd started drinking heavily again?" I guess.

"I'd also started using hard drugs again." A glacial silence settles over us; then he rubs his hand along my thigh and says, "Listen, what I just told you...I'm not saying this to justify what I did. But when you live a certain kind of life and you hang out with a certain kind of people in an unhealthy situation like mine, it becomes really difficult to resist temptation. Especially if you don't want to resist temptation. My brother was dead; my sister was miserable; my mother...she... I had lost her for good. And it was all my fault. Getting high was the only way I could just not think about it all for a while."

"And you haven't heard from your mother since you left?" I ask, testing the waters.

He nods.

"Did you ever try calling her?"

"And tell her what? Her silence since I left speaks loud enough. She has no interest in knowing where I am or what I'm doing or how I'm doing. I probably did her a favor when I walked out. Apparently things are better at home now, which just proves that my leaving freed her from another burden that was weighing her down for too long."

"He hasn't hit her since you left?"

Thomas shakes his head no.

"How do you know that?" I ask.

"My sister kept in contact with Mom, and she reassured Leila about it."

So this is why Thomas refuses to show hide nor hair at home... he's afraid that going back would light the fuse, and everything would explode again.

"Do you know what I think? I think that, despite everything, she still loves you with her whole heart. A terrible thing happened to all of you, but I bet that she's been thinking about you all this time," I say, drawing on the information that Leila entrusted to me.

He answers with a derisive snort, staring down at the bandanna on his wrist. Still, despite all the resentment he clearly feels, I can detect a little bit of agony in him as well.

"What made you decide to start over?" I asked, trying to step back a bit.

"This one night…" He stops. "One night, I almost OD'd." He turns to look at me with shame in his eyes. "Leila found me passed out in my room. When I woke up in the hospital, she was there and she was terrified. She was crying, and she begged me to stop because she couldn't stand the thought of losing another brother. Three days later, I decided to check myself into a facility."

It takes me a second to digest this information. "You went to rehab?"

He nods. "I was there for six months. It was hard, but I wouldn't have done it otherwise. As soon as I got clean, I left Portland. But the temptation is always there. I still drink—I just can't help it—and I smoke lots and lots of cigarettes. They help curb the impulse to get high. A cigarette for every bump of coke I'd like to do."

I stay silent and motionless as I stare at him. And then a memory pops into my head: *"Nicotine keeps a lot of my impulses at bay. Things I wouldn't be able to control otherwise."* He told me that the first night we talked outside the gym on campus. At the time, I didn't know what he was talking about. I couldn't have imagined.

"But the night you came to the Marsy, you were drunk on Jack Daniels…and you spent the next morning drinking and smoking pot…"

Thomas lets out a sigh. "That was the anniversary of my brother's death. That night I…I wasn't thinking straight. I'd brought you here in the afternoon, away from everyone and everything, because I wanted you to be with me. To be just *for* me. And I don't even know how you did it, but you somehow managed to ease some of that sadness that was fucking with my head. You were good for me, Ness. So good that I didn't want to be without you. You turned out to be the perfect antidote to all the poisons my body craved. But then I went to the Marsy and saw you with Logan, and I don't know what happened. I wanted you to be with me, and you were with him instead. I was feeling so many different things, this frustration mixed with anger, and all I wanted to do was drown myself in alcohol and loneliness. The next day, I saw you slipping through my fingers with so much disappointment in your eyes, and I realized that I was fucking everything up again."

I'm overwhelmed by these revelations, by a power over him that I never knew I had.

"I...I didn't want to make you feel bad..." I say regretfully. If only I'd known that night...

"You weren't the problem. I was angry at myself. For everything I'd done and what I was continuing to do. You showed up at my dorm that morning, and damn it if you weren't the last person who should have been there. Because I knew that I was going to say or do something to hurt you. But despite all that, you were also the only person I actually wanted to see."

I stare into his eyes, and all my stupid drama with my mother seems so trifling. I feel like an idiot for complaining to him about it. I lower my head, but he puts a finger under my chin and lifts it up. "I was right, wasn't I?" he asks, with a hint of sadness in his voice.

I blink confusedly. "About what?"

"About how you'd never look at me the same again. I don't blame you if all you see now is a guy who doesn't deserve your respect. I know I don't deserve it, I know I'm a bad person, but..."

"You have my respect, Thomas. Because, despite all the ugliness that surrounded you, you found the strength to pull yourself out of it." I take his face in my hands and bring my lips to his. I brush them with my own, close my eyes, and kiss him. When our mouths pull apart, I rest my forehead against his. "The first time we talked, that night outside the rec center, I told you something. I said you're human and humans all make mistakes. What matters is that you find the strength to overcome them. And that's what you're doing. You should be proud of yourself."

I kiss him again, harder this time, and I feel a tear run down my face, which he quickly wipes away. Now that I know about everything he went through, everything that happened to him and how much it cost him, I'm amazed he found the strength to tell me about it. And I know that, despite everything, my heart belongs to him, and I will do everything in my power to help him find the peace he deserves.

Fifteen

"'I OFFER MYSELF TO YOU again with a heart even more your own than when you almost broke it, eight years and a half ago. Dare not say that man forgets sooner than woman, that his love has an earlier death. I have loved none but you. Unjust I may have been, weak and resentful I have been, but never inconstant. You alone have brought me to Bath. For you alone, I think and plan...'"

Leaving the bad memories behind us, Thomas and I are watching the starry sky, taking advantage of the new moon to look for constellations. I know this wasn't a casual suggestion on his part. A few nights ago, when I told him about my father and how much he'd hurt me when he left, I'd also told him about how much I'd loved sky-watching with my dad when I was a child.

Now, I lie on top of Thomas, my legs stretched out between his and *Persuasion* resting on my belly. He has one hand tucked under his head, and he rubs the back of my neck with the other, while I use my phone's flashlight to read aloud all about Anne and Frederick's heart-wrenching love. One he immediately makes fun of, naturally.

"Is this your idea of a romantic love story, Ness?" he teases.

I pull my eyes from the page and back to him. "Jane Austen does much more than just tell a banal romantic love story. She delves deeply into the psyche of the characters, exposes all their hypocrisies, and describes how love can triumph over resentment."

"I still think these books do you more harm than good," he needles me.

I roll my eyes, surrendering myself to the idea that I will clearly never be able to make him care about books. I close the book and set it aside, changing the subject to tomorrow's basketball game. "Have you ever thought about having a plan B, other than basketball? I mean, you say you don't like studying, but you're not doing badly at all."

"Nah, why should I? I'm a basketball star," he answers, cocky as ever, making me laugh and shake my head at the same time.

"So that's your secret dream? To be a basketball star?"

"I don't have any secret dreams. I've never had any, didn't have the chance to cultivate them. College was never in my plans. For a while, I thought about working for my uncle in his tattoo shop, but then life took me in a different direction."

I raise myself up slightly to look at him, intrigued. "But you came to Corvallis with a basketball scholarship, so you must have had something in mind?"

He rolls his eyes but tolerates my third degree. "Not really. I've always been good at basketball. Even in high school with all the bullshit, I managed to perform pretty well. I quit the team after the accident, and I only started playing again in my last year of community service because my coach encouraged me. For some reason, he'd decided to take me under his wing. During that time, a talent scout noticed me, and my name started to get around. But obviously I fucked that all up with my second relapse. Coach knew I wanted to get away from Portland, so when I finally got clean, he put in a good word for me with the athletics department at OSU. He had some old friends there, and they brought me here. Basketball was my one-way ticket out of Portland," he concludes.

I figure I've done enough investigation for today, so I turn off my phone flashlight and rest my head on Thomas's arm. Together, we rest and watch the sky, side by side. Suddenly, I point to a cluster of brilliant stars and exclaim with childlike excitement, "Look, Thomas! It's Cassiopeia!"

"Mmm, I don't think so," he says doubtfully.

"No, it is. Here, look closer." I point my index finger in the direction of my gaze. "Do you see those two small pyramids next to each other? They form a letter *W*?"

Thomas squints, concentrating on those luminous dots light-years away from us and nods slowly.

I draw my index finger downward, as though I'm tracing the constellation on a piece of paper. "A little bit down here is Andromeda, Cassiopeia's daughter, and there to the right is Perseus." I sigh, still gazing up. "You know, according to the Greek myth, Perseus saved Andromeda from Cetus, the sea monster," I say in a passionate whisper.

"Okay, nerd, I guess you found it," Thomas admits, smiling. Then he adds, "Let me guess: Those up there are Ursa Major and Ursa Minor, right?" I scan for the two constellations, fascinated by the spectacle of the night.

"You're right, that's them. The star at the end of Ursa Minor is the North Star, which is visible all year round," I whisper dreamily.

When I turn around, Thomas is watching me. And the way he's looking at me makes me tremble. Like I'm the best thing in his life. Like he's found his place in my eyes. His place to retreat to when he's in need of shelter. His place where he can feel free to be what he wants, what he is, with no masks and no defenses.

I smile again and wonder if it will always be this way. If my heart will always thump in my chest with the force of a hurricane every time he's near me. If my cheeks will flush red every time he gives me one of his smiles. If my hands will always tremble from the feelings he stirs in me. I hope so. I hope I get to feel this way for the rest of my life, because I can't remember ever being happier than I am right now.

I feel the wind suddenly pick up, and before I know it, the sky is clouding over. Strands of my hair start to fly around. Thomas tucks one carefully behind my ear, and just as I see him part his lips to tell me something, a drop of water lands on my cheek, and I blink rapidly. We both raise our eyes to the sky, surprised. Another drop. And then another. Within a few moments, we are getting drenched by a downpour.

How the hell is this possible?

"Shit," Thomas says, standing up on the platform. "Rain wasn't in the forecast." He moves the soaked hair that falls across his forehead with a jerk of his head and holds his hand out to me. "Come on, let's go home." The rain is falling copiously on us now. I stand up as well. I pull my sweatshirt sleeves down to completely cover my hands and then rub them against my face, trying to dry off as much of the water as possible. But then I burst out laughing.

Thomas looks at me with a priceless expression on his face. Somewhere between astonishment and amusement. "Are you going crazy?"

I stare up at the sky and close my eyes, letting the rain fall on my face. I remember when I was a little girl and I would always beg my father to let me play in the rain. My mother never did, but he would indulge me. I would jump and run around with my arms spread out wide, like an airplane in flight. I could splash through puddles for hours on end. I feel now just like I did back then, like a happy little girl. "Don't take me home; let's stay here," I say, talking loudly over the sound of the rain.

He raises an eyebrow at me. "We're surrounded by trees, Ness. Are you trying to get toasted by a lightning bolt?"

I shake my head no, fully enjoying this moment. "I just want to feel free."

Thomas just shakes his head and smiles at me, amused. With my own smile on my lips, I lean into him and kiss him. He runs a hand through the sodden hair at the back of my neck, kissing me back with the same passion. Our lips fuse together, tongues entwined. We devour one another.

I stand up on my tiptoes and wrap my hands around his damp face while our hearts beat in time to the rain. My God...if I had the power to stop time, this is without a shadow of a doubt the moment I would choose: me, Thomas, and the rain.

It's 11:45 on Friday morning. Since I have class in the afternoon, I've managed to convince Maggie to swap this shift with me so I can be at Thomas's game tonight. The place is nearly empty. What few customers are here work on finishing their breakfasts, mostly tuna sandwiches and scrambled eggs. And I dust the bottles of alcohol on the shelves behind the bar with a smile on my face, thinking back on the magic of last night under the downpour.

"Vanessa Emily Clark." The voice behind me is followed by the thump of a purse hitting the counter, making me start. I turn around quickly. Before me, I see my mother, dressed to the nines as always. Long wavy light hair falls to her slim shoulders. Her face is perfectly made up, her lean and willowy body clad in a suit with a gray knee-length skirt and a white blouse underneath the jacket.

"M-Mom, what...what are you doing here?" My voice comes out so low that it's barely audible. I'm holding a bottle in one hand and a cloth in the other as I stare at her, blinking repeatedly. It takes a few seconds before my brain starts working again.

"The question isn't what I'm doing here; it's what are you trying to prove?" Her high-pitched voice draws the attention of some customers.

"What?"

"I came here last Saturday. I'm guessing they told you," she answers shortly.

"Of course they told me," I say, still not understanding the reason for her visit.

"So why haven't I heard from you?"

After a brief moment of confusion, the light dawns. I press my palms to the counter and stare her down. "How did you know I'd be covering this shift today?" I ask her suspiciously.

She shrugs one shoulder nonchalantly. "I've been following you."

"What?" I ask, shocked.

"I've been doing it for a few days. Does that surprise you? It shouldn't. You disappeared, Vanessa. What did you expect me to do? Sit quietly in the corner while my daughter was most likely blowing up her future hanging out in a shady frat house with bad company?"

I cannot believe this. This is why she's here now? She just wants to give me one of her lectures? I look around irritably and mutter, "Do you realize how insane it is to hear you talk about blowing up my future when that's exactly what *you* did?"

Her eyes narrow, and she sets her lips in a hard line.

I know her well enough to know that right now she's trying her hardest not to lose control. She tucks a lock of hair behind her ear and stares steadily at me. Chin high. Shoulders straight. She parts her lips and takes a deep breath. "I didn't come here to fight."

No, of course not.

"Then what do you want?" I put my hands on my hips.

"I want to talk to you. I haven't heard from you in almost two weeks!"

I grimace. "That's not my fault!"

"Listen, the situation got out of hand that night for the both of us. I never wanted to strike you or to kick you out, but I was hurt by what you said, and I acted on impulse. However, as you are too stubborn to understand that my warnings and rules are for your own good, it's clear to me that it's time for us to make up."

I stare at her, amazed. "Now you want to make up? After you put me out on the street? If you really cared about me, you would have done something before I was forced to find a solution myself!" I argue, pressing a hand to my chest.

"You never gave me the chance! You did everything you could to keep from being found. You even sent your friends to get your things so you wouldn't have to see me!" Her face reddens with anger, and her icy blue eyes pierce me with a stern look.

"Oh, I'm so sorry if I was a little bit hurt and upset after my mother kicked me out of my house!" I hiss. Some of the customers are starting to give us concerned looks. My God, how embarrassing. I'm airing all my personal and family problems here at work.

Just when I think this situation couldn't get any more humiliating, I hear the heavy tread of footsteps on the stairs. Derek, my boss, walks into the room and gives the customers a fixed smile. A smile that clearly says, *Please excuse the scene my waitress is subjecting you to. My soon-to-be-fired waitress.*

He joins me behind the bar, and I am too ashamed to even look him in the face. I'm sure he's about to read me the riot act, but he surprises me by placing his hand somewhat hesitantly on my shoulder and turning to face my mother.

"Mrs. Clark, pleased to meet you," he says, holding out his hand.

"White. I'm Ms. White," she insists, returning the handshake haughtily.

"Oh, yes, of course. Pardon me, Ms. White," he corrects himself politely.

I just stare at the bar, willing myself to sink into the floor.

"Unfortunately, I'm going to have to ask you to discuss your personal matters outside. Vanessa, you can take your break if necessary; I can take care of things here."

I don't dare look up at him. I know my cheeks are burning. I have never been more mortified in my life. A mother-daughter fight in my workplace... God, not even in the worst soap operas. My mother snatches her purse and steps back.

"That's not necessary," she says. "I'll talk to my daughter when her shift is over."

She's not planning on staying here until then, is she? I don't want her hanging around.

"My shift finishes at two p.m. I still have two hours left," I answer as calmly as I can, even as inside I'm melting down.

"Perfect. In that case, I would like a martini while I wait." She grins. She sits down on a stool and taps her light-pink-polished nail on the wood.

I look at her, narrowing my eyes, before giving up. It's no use. She's not going anywhere. Derek tightens his grip on my shoulder, almost as if to give me courage. "I have some work to do upstairs; are we good here?" he asks me.

I nod. "Yes, definitely. I'm so sorry; it won't happen again."

"Great." He releases his grip on my shoulder and steps back. "Ms.

White, although I would have liked to meet you under better circumstances, it was still a pleasure." He excuses himself politely and goes back to his office.

I glare at my mother, who doesn't bat an eye, before turning around and grabbing a cocktail glass. I make her a martini. To top it off, I toss in a green olive. My feeling of humiliation is once again giving way to a mounting anger even more explosive than before.

"Are you really sure you want to wait here until the end of my shift? Because if you do, you'll be forced to see Thomas when he comes to get me." I grin wickedly, her cocktail in my hand.

"Oh, really? I should have known they'd let anyone into this bar," she says calmly.

I stifle a groan of frustration as I slam her glass down on the bar, causing some of the liquid to slop over the edge. "Your martini, Ms. White. You're welcome." I hand her a napkin with just as much bad grace.

"I see you still need some practice. How do you get tips when you're so clumsy?" she retorts, scowling at me.

I resist the urge to sigh and ignore her instead. It's going to be a very, very long afternoon.

I spend the remaining two hours of my shift running up and down the bar, serving all the customers in my section. My mother remains seated at the counter, making occasional demands, while I just keep mulling over a thought that recently leapt out at me: *Was she the one who paid my school tuition?* Her sudden visit has me suspicious.

When I change after my shift, clock out, and leave, she's already waiting outside for me. Right there in front of her car, purse clutched tightly under her arm. I walk toward her, glancing around the Marsy's parking lot. Thomas isn't here yet. When I reach her, I cross my arms over my chest and face her. "It was you, wasn't it? Did you pay my tuition when you found out I was moving into the frat house? How'd you do it, huh? Did you mortgage the house? Get a loan from the bank?

Take a handout from Victor? Anything to keep me away from him, right?" I can feel the outrage rising inside me.

"What in the world are you talking about?" she asks me, frowning. She seems sincerely confused.

"I'm talking about the tuition that magically got paid, giving me access to all the university's services, including housing."

She stiffens and seems even more surprised. "Someone paid your tuition? I don't know anything about that."

Her harsh mask is collapsing, but I can't trust her, not anymore. I snort loudly, not even looking her in the eye. "Yeah, sure. It happens yesterday, and then today you show up at the bar; am I supposed to believe that's a coincidence?"

"I couldn't have paid that amount even if I wanted to. You know that." She pauses and thinks for a few seconds, and then, it's as if a light bulb has suddenly flickered on. "Unless..."

"Unless what?"

Her eyes are fixed on the asphalt, and what she is thinking seems to disturb her more with every passing second. She looks up at me, and I see a strange emotion flicker in her eyes. Offense? Resentment? Whatever it is, it's definitely not good.

"Who did you tell?"

I knit my eyebrows. "I'm sorry, what?"

"You must have told someone; a thing like that doesn't just fall out of the sky!"

She's getting way too agitated. I decide to tell her the truth, to try to reassure her. "Only Thomas, Alex, and Tiffany know. And none of them would do something like that without my knowledge."

"They must have told someone else!"

"No, Mom, they didn't. But why are you so worked up about it?"

"My daughter's tuition gets paid by God knows who, and that shouldn't bother me?"

"It bothers me too, if you want the truth, but whoever did it requested to remain anonymous."

"That's even more ridiculous. I swear, I am going to find out who it is," she continues, completely out of control.

I sigh and bite down on my lip in an attempt to calm myself as I rub my throbbing temples. With a much less aggressive tone, I ask her, "Why are you here anyway?"

My mother looks me in the eye and lowers her defenses as well. "To apologize to you and try to make up for it, if you'll give me the chance. My door is always open for you, no matter who you decide to hang out with. I'm sorry I made you doubt that. But I want you to come home, Vanessa."

I was expecting almost anything other than hearing her say those words. It does make me sad to see her like this, but I can't help but feel a bit like a puppet dancing on her strings. And for once, I almost wish my pride would win out. But then I think back to these last few days with Thomas and everything he told me about his past. I know that there are much more serious reasons for a mother and daughter to stop speaking to one another. I hate to admit it, but I think he's right. It's not worth keeping up this estrangement over an argument that got out of hand.

"Well, I'm glad to hear you say that. I think I owe you an apology too. I know I hurt you, and I shouldn't have. But I'm not coming home," I tell her. "And before you say it, Thomas has nothing to do with it. I plan to move out of the frat house now that I can stay on campus. I think I need to finally get a place of my own where I can concentrate on my studies."

"I think that's a good decision. But I would still like to spend time with you, if you agree."

I shrug uncertainly. "I honestly don't know, Mom. Nothing's changed since last time. I'm still with Thomas, and you still hate him. And I have no intention of getting into a situation where I spend time with my mother just to listen to her spout more nastiness about my boyfriend. Thomas doesn't deserve that."

She rolls her eyes but then composes herself. She studies me carefully, as if considering how to propose something to me. I give her a questioning look, until she finally says, "What about dinner?"

I cock an eyebrow because I can feel there's more to this.

"Dinner with the both of you," she adds.

My eyes bug out. "W-what?"

She looks away for a second, staring at some vague point behind my shoulder; then she looks back at me. "You and I are very different in some ways but very much alike in others. You've fallen in love with that boy, and you're not going to let anything or anyone interfere. Where he goes, you go. I understand that. But you're my daughter, and I'm not willing to jeopardize our relationship again. So I'm giving you the chance to prove me wrong about him."

I study her with a certain mistrust. "What is this? Some sort of weird reverse psychology technique? Are you pretending to host a family dinner, when the only real purpose will be to analyze his every move and wait for him to screw up so you can show me how unsuitable he is?"

"No reverse psychology. Just a mother trying to get to know her daughter's boyfriend a bit better."

"After the last time you met, when you had zero qualms about calling him a potential serial killer, I don't know if he wants to see you at all, let alone have dinner with you."

She clicks her tongue against the roof of her mouth, rolling her eyes again. "Oh, come on, let's not make a big deal out of that. I'm sure that boy's heard much worse things said about him."

And precisely as she says these words, I hear a motorcycle pull into the parking lot, about twenty feet away from us. I turn and watch Thomas put both feet on the ground. Leaving the engine running, he pulls up his visor to look in our direction. I nod at him, and he nods back.

"I'll think about it," I say, turning my attention back to my mother.

She notices him. They don't acknowledge each other. But the judgmental expression on her face as she stares at his motorcycle is telling. After what feels like an interminable moment, she turns back to me without letting any emotion show on her face. "Okay, you think about it and talk to him about it. When you've made a decision, let me know," she tells me with a sad smile.

"Okay, I will," I answer, returning her smile a bit uncertainly and tucking my hair behind my ears, discombobulated by this conversation.

We say our goodbyes a little awkwardly; then I walk toward Thomas, who doesn't take his eyes off me. Behind me, I hear the sound of my mother's car door closing and the screech of tires on pavement. When I reach him, Thomas takes off his helmet, puts an arm around my waist, and kisses me. "What'd she want?" he asks, glancing over my shoulder.

"To talk," I answer with a heavy sigh. "I think she's trying to reestablish contact with me, in her way." Admitting it out loud makes it even more ridiculous. "And apparently...she's been following me these last few days."

Thomas's eyes go wide.

"Yup. She really has." I shake my head in resignation. "And to top it all off, she suggested we have dinner."

Thomas scrutinizes me carefully. "That's a good thing, though, isn't it?"

"Yeah, maybe... I don't know," I say, shrugging my shoulders uncertainly. "She wants you to come too."

His head snaps back in surprise. "Me?"

"You don't have to come. I didn't confirm anything yet; I just told her I'd think about it. But I think that's plenty for today, I still have two classes and basketball game to cheer during," I finish with a much more serene vibe, which earns me a smile from him. I put on the helmet he hands me, climb onto the seat, and we head for campus. Me to my philosophy class, Thomas to an extra pregame training that gets him out of the day's classes.

"In previous classes, we've talked about Nietzsche, examining the cardinal points of his philosophical works. Today, we will do a final overview before the upcoming exam. Ready to get started?" Professor Scott asks as he paces the room, tapping his pen against his chin. "So we have established that Nietzsche's philosophy can be grouped into three eras. Can any of you tell me what those are?"

I raise my hand.

"Miss Clark, go ahead."

"The first is the Schopenhauerian period, which is when Nietzsche wrote *The Birth of Tragedy*. In that text, he argues that art and chaos are opposing forces each required for fullness of being. It builds on a Greek theory whereby man is divided into two parts: Apollo, who represents rationality, clarity, order, and harmony, and Dionysus, who embodies irrationality, disorder, a lack of moral limitations, and ecstasy."

"Good." He smiles at me. "Anyone else? Yes, down in front."

While Philip answers by delving into the Enlightenment phase, I am distracted by a familiar voice behind me. I don't need to turn around to know that it's Logan. He usually avoids talking to me during Professor Scott's class, because Thomas is always sitting next to me. But not today.

"Hey, you're really into Nietzsche, huh?" he whispers to me.

"He definitely knew what he was talking about," I murmur, turning my head away slightly.

"Really?"

"Absolutely. Haven't you read any of his work?"

"I think I should probably start; Professor Scott will probably kick my ass if I don't," he answers with a laugh.

"Oh, he definitely will. He's a hard-ass," I joke, trying and failing to hide my discomfort. I don't understand how he can talk to me so easily after yesterday, when I basically shot him down again for a second time. He's willing to take his lumps, I have to give him credit there. And he must have a heart of gold; it's not every person who can keep their wounded pride in check like that. Before he can say anything else, however, I raise my hand to answer a question about the doctrine of eternal return, thereby ending my conversation with Logan.

At the end of class, when the room is nearly empty and I'm gathering the last of my books into my bag, Professor Scott waves to get my attention. "Miss Clark, can I have a few minutes of your time?"

"Of course." I put my bag over my shoulder and join him at his desk. "What's up?"

He puts some files in his briefcase, closes it, and looks up at me. "I just wanted to tell you that I'm very pleased with your academic performance. Perhaps you already know this but, I wanted to tell you anyway: You are the best student in this course. One of the brightest at this school, apparently."

"Oh, thank you." I tuck my hair behind my ears and try to tamp down the blush that is surely already coloring my cheeks.

"But as you know, not all students have such high-level abilities. There are those who need some extra help. So I wanted to propose something to you: Would you be willing to make yourself available for some tutoring sessions? You're an attentive and patient girl, and it's clear that you love philosophy. Obviously, this type of extracurricular activity is great for your CV, which never hurts if you are, for example, aiming for graduate school scholarships."

Okay, I'm convinced.

"How many sessions would it involve? My current classes keep me pretty busy, plus I work in the evenings six days a week. Having it on my résumé would be nice, but I'm not sure I'll be able to find the time to dedicate myself to tutoring the way I'd like."

"The number of lessons will mainly depend on how quickly the student is able to pick up the basic concepts."

"Sure, of course. Well…" I take a deep breath, putting on a smile. "I'd be happy to help someone out."

"Excellent choice. I'm sure you won't let me down. I'll notify the designated student today." He smiles back at me, and we walk out of the classroom together.

Sixteen

BEFORE HEADING TO THE ARENA, I stop by the frat house to take a quick shower. I put on a pair of black leggings, my Converse, and Thomas's black sweatshirt with *Go Beavers* on it. I could have worn my own, but stealing his sweatshirts has become a habit now, and I refuse to stop. Besides, he likes it. I scrape my hair into a high pony and head out.

"I'm sorry, what do you mean you aren't coming to the game?" I chat on the phone with Alex as I walk down the path that leads to campus. As I do, I rummage through my bag, searching for some snacks to munch on, but apparently I haven't stocked up lately.

"Well, my parents are going out to dinner tonight, and Stella's going to be FaceTiming me soon. So I expect to be busy for a while."

Oh, hold on a minute—is he saying what I think he's saying? "Are you telling me you're leaving me alone in that insane crowd to have FaceTime sex?"

"Well, when you put it like that..."

"God, Alex, this is high treason, you know that, right?"

Once I get inside the student union, I bask in the warmth of the common area. It's November now, and the temperature change from outside to inside is marked.

"Hey, I know I'm bucking our tradition, but I promise to make it up to you with the best pistachio ice cream you've ever had," he says, and I picture him giving me an angelic smile.

When I reach the first floor of the student union, I immediately head for the vending machines. I greet a passing girl from my English lit class with a smile. "It's okay, don't worry about it. In fact, tell her hi from me. Wait. I mean...not while...oh, you know what I mean!" I can hear Alex laughing on the other end.

A beep tells me that a message from Tiffany has come in. I pull the phone away from ear for a moment and read the notification: Where are you? The game is about to start! Oh, no!

"Listen, Alex, I gotta let you go. I begged Tiffany to come with me to the game, and she's waiting for me," I tell him hastily.

"Cool. Keep me updated on the outcome. Actually, only do that if we win."

"Will do. Have fun, you crazy kids..." I say suggestively.

"Count on it," he answers mischievously before hanging up. I put my coins into the machine, punch in the code, and naturally the money-gobbler leaves me high and dry. I pound the glass again and again.

"Admit it, you hate me! Just give me my Reese's, damn it!" Impatient, I give the machine a hateful glare before running to the cafeteria. I grab a bottle of water, a bag of pretzels, and a bag of chips from near the register. I pay, throw everything in my bag, and run like the wind down the long walkways, slaloming off other students on their way to the coliseum when...

"Vanessa!"

I cannot believe it. Again. I'm really making a habit of running into him like this.

"Logan..." I manage, turning to look behind me.

"Are you okay? You look like you just saw a ghost," he says, adjusting a tuft of his gelled hair as he approaches me.

"No. I mean, yes. I'm fine. I just wasn't expecting to see you there. And I'm in a bit of a rush." I clutch my bag against my side.

"Are you going to the game?" he asks, looking at the building behind me.

I nod. "Yeah, it's starting in a minute."

"Oh, I won't take up too much of your time, then. Really, I just wanted to say thank you."

"What for?" I ask, wrinkling my forehead.

He gives me a gobsmacked look, like he expected me to already know. "For agreeing to tutor me."

I stare at him wordlessly as I feel a wave of panic wash over me. "What?"

"Do you remember when we ran into each other yesterday in front of the dean's office?"

I nod.

"I was actually there to talk about my grades. Philosophy was tanking my GPA, but they gave me the option of having remedial lessons with a tutor. I couldn't help but think of you."

I just keep staring wide-eyed at him, unable to say a word. The person I'm tutoring is Logan? That can't be right. "B-but…why…why did you bring up my name?" is all I ask him.

He gives a casual shrug, hands tucked into the pockets of his jeans. "Well, because you're the best in the class. I would have been stupid not to pick you."

"If I knew you were the person who was behind it, I wouldn't have agreed to do it," I confess brusquely. I feel as though I've been ambushed here.

He gives me a strange look. "Wait, are you mad? What's wrong, Vanessa? Why are you reacting like this?"

"Do you even have to ask?" I take a step back, annoyed.

"Is it because of what happened between Thomas and me?" he guesses, his mouth twisting as he lowers his voice. "I've already told you that I'm sorry about that, okay? I never wanted the situation to degenerate that way. I'll apologize to him too if necessary. But we're not just talking about you and me here. We're talking about my education. This is exclusively about studying, nothing more. He'll understand."

I laugh nervously and shake my head. "No, he won't. And you

know what? I don't even want to put him in a position where he needs to understand."

Logan crosses his arms over his chest and lifts his chin in irritation. "So this is how it works between the two of you? He has final say over what you can and cannot do with your life? Wow, that doesn't sound like a toxic relationship at all," he taunts me, getting angry. Then he hangs his head and presses two fingers to the center of his forehead, blowing out a puff of air. "I don't get you." He looks me in the eye, as serious as I've ever seen him. "You said yes. That means it was a good opportunity for you. You'll get an extracurricular for your résumé, which you presumably need. And I need to get my average up. Giving up something that you need and even want to do just because your boyfriend is too jealous to let you do it is stupid. Thomas should not be an impediment to your plans."

The only impediment here is Logan, who is well and truly the problem right now. Any other guy would have been fine. Sure, I would have had to deal with Thomas's jealousy, but in the end, I could have talked him into accepting it. But he won't with Logan. He won't even try.

I run my hands through my hair. I close my eyes and try to calm myself with a deep breath. When I open them again, Logan is looking at me with an irritated frown on his face.

"It's not about him," I say. "My choices aren't dependent upon Thomas; it's just that—"

"You know what, Vanessa?" he interrupts me bitterly. "I can find another tutor and still catch up. The only one losing something here is you." Before he leaves, he gives me a long glare, full of resentment. And when I find myself alone, staring at a potted succulent on a windowsill a few feet away, I feel almost guilty for the way I treated him. I attacked him unfairly, and though I hate to admit it, Logan isn't completely wrong. I would be the one losing out. This is the last year I am free to figure out what I want to do with my future, which path to take. Padding my résumé for potential grad schools is an attractive idea. Why must my life be this constant struggle between right and wrong?

The roar is deafening as I walk into the arena. The entire crowd is in a frenzy. Immediately, I spot Vince clowning around in the front row with a couple of freshmen and that obnoxious Blake. I try to find Tiffany but am forced to throw in the towel. I text her instead: If you're in the gym, send up a smoke signal. I can't find you.

Her answer comes a few seconds later: Third row, center. I head for the third row, scanning the various faces until I catch a glimpse of a girl with copper hair waving in my direction. I grin at her.

"Hey, I'm here!" I plop down next to her and kiss her powder-scented cheek.

"Where were you?" she asks, pushing some of her locks off her face.

"I was hungry, so I stopped at the café in the student union to refuel." I pull the chips out of my bag and hand them to her. I'd also like to tell her about Logan, maybe ask her for advice, but I don't think now is the right time. I just want to enjoy the game and not think about it all for a little while at least.

"Where's Alex?" Tiff asks, pulling me from my thoughts.

"Forget about him; he's not joining us today. He's busy with Stella," I answer, putting my bag between my feet.

The arena's loudspeakers announce the guys' entrance to the court, accompanied by the wild cheers of the audience. Players from both teams, the Beavers and the Stanford Cardinals, stand at opposite ends of the court. Their coaches follow them, ready for the traditional pep talk. My eyes immediately find Thomas. Because how could I do anything else? He stands out among the rest. The well-defined muscles, the body covered in tattoos, the tousled hair that falls over his forehead, and the confidence that shows in his every movement. He's wearing his black-and-orange uniform with his number (12) and his last name printed on it as he turns his attention to the coach, who is talking animatedly to the team.

Thinking back on the last time I was in this arena, a shiver moves down my spine. If, just two months ago, someone told me that I would be here today not to watch Travis play but to watch Thomas, I certainly wouldn't have believed them. Yet I couldn't ask for anything more.

When the coach walks away, Matt whispers something to Thomas, clapping him on the shoulder. He laughs and nods before rubbing his forehead with his wrist, the one wrapped in his brother's bandanna. He takes a glance around the audience around him. When he spots me, he gives me a wink, quirking the corner of his mouth. I respond with a radiant smile and a pounding heart.

"Come on, Thomas!" A cry of encouragement comes from one of the front rows. I frown and lean forward to see who it is. Tiffany does the same. It's Shana. Obviously. She's flanked by the spineless friends who follow her everywhere like dogs on leashes.

She turns toward me, as if she'd felt my riled-up look. She narrows her eyes and stares at me with barely concealed contempt, giggling wickedly. "The view is so much better from down here," she informs me in a loud voice.

I stifle a sigh of frustration and force myself to ignore her. I am not going to fall into her trap. But Tiffany must feel differently, because she shocks me by grabbing a handful of chips from the bag and throwing them at Shana's hair.

Shana's head snaps around, her mouth and eyes all wide open as she tries to tidy herself up with no small amount of effort. Her friends can barely restrain their laughter. "What is your problem, you ugly bitch?" she shrieks. Tiffany points a finger right at her.

"Next time you try to low-key flirt with my best friend's boyfriend, I won't throw just chips at you. You know, the aim is so much better from up here," Tiff warns her.

Shana gives us a hateful sneer and raises her middle finger before turning her back on us. Tiff and I exchange looks, our mouths quivering. And in the end, we give in. We burst out laughing unrestrainedly.

"You don't need to defend me, you know," I point out as soon as we compose ourselves.

"I definitely needed to." She rubs my arm, smiling tenderly at me. "Do you think I don't know how that bitch is always messing with you? You shouldn't let her. Actually, do you know what you should do? Teach her a lesson. You can't keep being treated this way."

I'd like to tell her that fighting isn't really my style, but the game is about to actually start. The guys move into their positions. The referee positions himself into center court with the ball in his hand. A moment later, he tosses it into the air, opening the first quarter.

Twenty minutes later, our team is leading by twenty-three points. Tiffany takes advantage of the break to go to the bathroom. I, however, pass Shana on my way down the stands toward my boyfriend, who is chatting with Matt and Finn while wiping sweat from his forehead with the hem of his T-shirt.

"Hey, champions, you're doing great," I say as I stop at the bottom of the stairs behind the sidelines. Thomas comes toward me, leaving his friends behind. He sees the Beavers sweatshirt I'm wearing—his—and smiles smugly. He grabs my chin and kisses me like the two of us are the only people in the gym.

"You haven't seen anything yet," he answers when we break apart. He wraps his arms around my hips, and I lock my wrists around his neck. I look up at the scoreboard behind him.

"At this rate, you'll have this one in the bag," I exclaim gleefully.

"Don't be fooled, the other team is smart. They're saving their energy to kick our ass later."

"Oh." I fall silent, hunching my shoulders. "You think they'll come back in the second half?"

"They'll try. But all this time, we've had them thinking this is our A-game. They're gonna be pretty surprised to find out we can play even better." He smirks.

I give him a look of exaggerated admiration. "This is the exact kind of cunning I could use when playing *Battleship* with Alex. Nice move, my friend."

"Friend? Is that what we're back to after all this bullshit?" he answers, amused.

I snort, patting him on the chest. "As if you were ever my friend."

"That's because I never intended to be," he says, a grin on his lips and, before he can plant another kiss on my mouth, Matt joins us and laughs as he rests an elbow on Thomas's shoulder.

"Folks, I don't want to break the spell here, but we do have a game to win," he says, dragging Thomas away by the arm.

They return to the court, Thomas walking backward and looking me up and down with such intensity that I feel naked. Then, he mouths a rather dirty observation about my legs wrapped in my tight leggings and what he plans to do with them after the game. I smile and bite my lip, knowing that my cheeks are burning.

There are seven minutes left in the game, and we're sitting at fifty-seven to sixty-two, in the Stanford Cardinals' favor.

"I can't believe we're getting beaten like this," I tell Tiffany, down in the dumps. "Thomas did tell me that the other team was smart." But just as I'm about to surrender to despair, something in the game mechanics turns back on itself. Our boys manage to put up one basket after another until, in a very short span of time, they've tied up the game.

We only need one more point. Just one more and the game is ours. The players' faces are pouring sweat while the scoreboard counts down from sixty seconds. A new kid, Travis's replacement, throws the ball to Thomas, who catches it halfway down the court.

Fifty seconds.

Thomas moves like lightning, passing his opponents until he gets close enough to the hoop and prepares to shoot it. Two Stanford boys block the shot. One recovers the ball and runs for the opposite hoop.

Forty seconds.

Thomas is right on top of the guy, and when he tries to pass the ball to his teammate, Thomas takes it back.

Thirty seconds.

Thomas runs for the basket again. The squeak of his sneakers rubbing against the floor and the almost tinny sound of the ball bouncing are the only noises I can hear. Thomas gets close to the hoop but, once again, he is shut down.

Twenty seconds.

"Collins, pass to Tucker! Pass to Tucker!" their coach shouts, seeing that he's in trouble. Jason Tucker holds up his hands, ready to catch the ball and score, but Thomas doesn't listen, continuing to guard the ball while his opponent hovers closely behind him. Thomas dribbles, looking for an opening.

Ten seconds.

"Collins! To Tucker!" the coach shouts again, waving his arms now as the veins in his neck throb and his face reddens.

In the space of a second, Thomas bounces the ball to his right then to his left, confusing the boy behind him. He passes it under his legs, spins around and, with a leap, tosses it toward the basket. His opponent jumps along with him and grazes the ball with his fingertips; it hits the backboard but doesn't immediately go through the hoop.

Five seconds.

The ball spins on the rim. We all watch with bated breath.

Three. Two. One…

"And the Beavers pull off a nail-biting victory!" the commentator bellows as we all leap to our feet in celebration. Matt hits his knees and shouts with happiness. The guys pile on Thomas; Finn grabs his face with both hands and presses his forehead against Thomas's, screaming like a lunatic.

The opposing team disappears quietly while we all take to the court to celebrate. As soon as he spots me running for him, Thomas moves toward me and smiles in that way that makes my stomach coil up. He hugs me tightly, and I throw my arms around him as he twirls me. And then we kiss, surrounded by the rapturous crowd.

"Chug! Chug! Chug! Chug!" shouts a group of drunk guys on the lawn, urging Finn and Vince to guzzle as much beer as possible from the kegs they are currently attached to. Through the open kitchen window, I see that Finn appears to be getting himself upright. I worry that Vince is going to collapse on the wet grass at any moment if someone doesn't wave the white flag soon.

After the game was over, we all went to the frat house to celebrate the team's win. The house is now packed with athletes and students from every department. Tiffany decided to get in on the bacchanal and is now playing beer pong. Her parents are out of town for the weekend, so she can finally breathe a little easier.

I, on the other hand, am sitting on Thomas's lap on a stool in the kitchen, eating a slice of leftover pizza from one of the half-empty boxes scattered around the table. Thomas refused to participate in any sort of drinking game, which made me proud of him. Now he's got his arms wrapped around my waist as he talks to Matt.

"I gotta admit, that was a great plan, dude," Matt says, hopping up on the kitchen island to sit.

"What plan?" I interject, eyebrows raised.

"To make those Stanford assholes think they were winning," Thomas explains, taking out his pack of cigarettes and pulling one out. He gestures for me to get off his lap with a light pat on my thigh because he knows that the smoke bothers me. So I take a seat on the stool opposite him. He lights his cigarette and takes the first drag, tilting his head to the side.

"Are you telling me that everything you did out there...it was just a strategy?"

He nods, pulling my stool closer to his so he can steal a bite of the pizza slice I'm holding.

"You took a big risk."

Our conversation is interrupted when Matt sees a drunk couple intent on tearing each other's clothes off in a hidden corner between the pantry and fridge. With a grossed-out look on his face, he jumps off the counter and bullies them out of the kitchen. "What the fuck?

This is a house, not a brothel!" he complains, grabbing a new can of soda from the fridge.

"It's not? Since when?" Thomas taunts him sardonically.

"Since I said so," Matt answers. But all his credibility vanishes the moment two girls from the theater department appear in front of him and, without too much coaxing, lure him out to dance.

"Like I said," Thomas tells him with grin, watching Matt disappear into the living room.

I turn to look at him. "You don't have to stay in here. If you want to go and have fun with the others, you can."

Thomas laughs and shakes his head. "I could, but I'd much rather be doing"—he drags his lips across my throat, leaving a hot trail of kisses that makes me quiver—"this."

He turns his gaze to the window, where Vince has flopped on the ground and is making a disastrous attempt to get back on his feet. We both burst out laughing at the pitiful scene. Then, Thomas pulls me back onto his lap, until I'm sitting astride him. He presses his forehead to mine and touches my cheek with his thumb. He captures my lip between his teeth and nibbles on it until my mouth opens, allowing our tongues to touch.

"And what if I had a better alternative to offer you?" I murmur, my lips moving against his. He responds by tightening his hold on my hip and pressing me down onto his pelvis. I can't hold back my moan.

"Better than having you here on my lap, feeling your pussy purr on my cock?"

As he says it, a heated burst of desire blooms between my thighs. Increasingly filthy thoughts creep into my head.

"You led your team to victory today. You deserve to be rewarded."

"And how do you intend to do that?"

"Take me upstairs and find out." I lick my lower lip and then bite it, watching Thomas's pupils dilate as his Adam's apple bobs up and down. He grabs my hand and, in just a few seconds, drags me upstairs into our room and locks the door behind us. He flattens me against the door, grabbing the back of my neck. He presses his tongue into my mouth and kisses me with everything he has, setting me aflame. I love the way he does this, so strong and decisive. The way he touches me, how he infuses just the right amount of possession into every movement.

"So..." he says against my lips. "What sort of reward are we talking about here?"

"Whatever you want." I press my body against his, feeling my nipples aching for more intense contact with him.

"Be careful what you offer me, stranger. You know very well that I might want a lot more from you than you're really willing to give." He grins as he continues devouring my mouth. He slides a hand underneath my sweatshirt, grasping my breast. He squeezes it hard and presses down on the hot and swollen nipple. Wild moans escape my mouth as I realize I want it. No matter what, no matter where, I just want it.

"Why are you still wearing pants?" I rasp. I'm giving him a green light, but Thomas stops. Breathing heavily, he looks down at the fly of his jeans, and when he looks back up at me, a strange gleam lights up his face.

"If you want it, then come and get it."

I blink at him for a few seconds, feeling a wave of awkwardness come over me. He wants me to be in control.

"H-how am I supposed to do that?" Stunned, I ask him the dumbest, most idiotic question possible.

"Well, I do have a weakness for strippers..." A lustful smirk curves his lips as he takes a step back. "Also, sexy waitresses with amazing legs, long black hair, and angel faces."

I cock an eyebrow and stifle a laugh. "Do you seriously expect me to do a striptease?"

He's messing with me; he knows how awkward I am. And he's clearly having a lot of fun. But I can mess with him too, if I want.

So I decide to demonstrate.

I put my hands against his chest and push him down on the foot of the bed, making him fall into the mattress. He sits and spreads his legs, leaving me room to stand between them. As if compelled by some mysterious force, Thomas grabs my ass. I lean over him, and a few inches above his mouth, I whisper, "I'm not going to strip, Thomas. But if you want it..." I put my hand over his and slide it up my thigh until it meets the fabric of my leggings. "Then come and get it."

I straighten up, pulling his hand away from my crotch just as he was starting to apply pressure. He squeezes his eyes shut, barely suppressing a groan of frustration as I smile mischievously at him. *Shoot and score.*

"Otherwise, I'll have to take care of myself." I step back, shrugging one shoulder casually. "You've taught me pretty well," I add, bolder than ever before.

His gaze devours me. Thomas gets up slowly and advances on me, like a tiger would its prey. A tremor shakes my body. He grabs me by the waist and, with a sudden movement, turns me around. His erection is pressing against my ass. His fingers are sinking into my skin. My stomach is in knots. With one hand, he brushes my hair aside, his lips grazing my neck.

"I am dying to watch you *take care of yourself* right in front of me," he murmurs. "But first, you're gonna need to be fucked enough times that I won't have to take you again." He licks the crook of my neck and kisses it, making me shiver. "Again..." He bites me. "And again..." He slides a hand to my belly, slowly slipping it beneath my leggings and under the elastic of my panties. He cups a possessive hand over my mound and presses on my clit so hard that I can't get any air into my lungs. I know that he could make me come at any moment now, just with these small touches. I arch my back against his chest and rub against his jeans. Feeling his excitement makes me burst with a desire to have him inside me...in a different way.

I turn around, my brain hazy with lust, and I kiss him until I'm breathless. "I want to taste you, Thomas," I breathe, my heart pounding like a drum at the thought of it. "Really taste you."

I fumble with his belt and pull down his zipper. He gives me a confused look through his eyelashes. Then, he understands my intentions and his mouth is all over me. He kisses me, holds me, consumes me, pressing me into his hips. Then, I pull back and begin taking his clothes off impatiently, as if I were unwrapping a long-awaited gift.

He does the same for me, leaving me completely naked under his burning gaze.

I grab his already-open jeans and pull them down to his ankles. I run my hands along his muscular, tattooed thighs. I can see him throbbing in his boxers, and I smile in satisfaction. I take them off, freeing his erection. A searing heat radiates from between my legs. Compelled by an irrepressible need to touch him, I wrap my hand around his erection and begin to massage it slowly, up and down. The movement makes his abs tense and his mouth fall open. Thomas squeezes my butt cheek hard, a rough move that forces me up on my tiptoes. Our groins collide. Our noses brush. My heart hammers uncontrollably in my chest.

He grabs his erection, covering my hand, and starts rubbing it against my wet slit. He bumps my clit with the tip, sending me into ecstasy. "Where do you want it?" he asks. I bite my lip again, staring down at the cock moving between my thighs before I look back up at him.

"In my mouth," I whisper, my lips touching his, completely shameless.

Thomas smiles. He covers my cheek with his hand, rubbing my lips with his thumb. He observes them, enraptured.

"Get on your knees," he orders. I swallow loudly and moisten my lips. I pull my hair out of its elastic, because I know how much he likes it down, and I lower myself to the floor. I try to beat back some of the nervousness that pervades my body now that I'm about to do something I've never done before. I know I'm probably going to look inexperienced or maybe even clumsy in Thomas's eyes, but I don't care. I want to make him feel good. I want to give him the most pleasure I possibly can and to give myself completely to him.

I look up at him through my eyelashes, and he looks back at me in such a savage way that it's like he's got the most sensual creature he's ever seen right here in front of him. "I've wanted to feel those lips on my cock since the first time I saw you." He threads his fingers through my hair. "Take me in your mouth and give me the best postgame reward I've ever gotten."

Bolstered by his encouragement, I put my hand on his thigh for support. I open my mouth and run my tongue over his tip. Thomas grips my hair in his fist and chases my movements with his hips. His hoarse breathing echoes around the room as, with each thrust, I take more and more of him. "Holy shit, Ness, it's…" I hear him groan as I lick him unceasingly, not even needing his hands to guide me now.

"It's what?" I whisper, running my mouth along his entire length. A tortured sound issues from his throat.

"It's fantastic." With every movement of my tongue, Thomas's legs tremble. "I want to feel you all way down," he growls through gritted teeth. A hot burst of desire rushes through me from head to toe. Though I'm hindered a little by his size, I try to do as he asks. I lock my eyes on his as I relax the muscles of my throat, giving him the chance to do whatever he wants with me. He smiles sweetly at me, and then, with his hand gripping my hair tightly, he begins to fuck my mouth with vigor.

Moans of pleasure reverberate in his throat. I love having this kind of effect on him. I love feeling him lose control. I love watching him at the peak of pleasure with his head tossed back, eyes closed, and his mouth slightly open. But above all else, I love *him*. Captivated by all these feelings, I accept every one of his thrusts, and a hot gush soaks my inner thighs. The urge to touch myself, to soothe the heat that burns between my legs is becoming more intense, more desperate. I bring my fingers to my clit and start moving them in small circles. Thomas gropes my breast, pinching my nipple hard between his thumb and forefinger. He does it a second time and a third. Every nerve ending explodes as an ecstatic orgasm overwhelms me, shattering me. I squint my eyes, and for a moment, my knees turn watery. He holds my hair in an iron grip, urging me to keep going.

"I'm gonna come…" he gasps breathlessly. "If you don't want to…" he mutters, his brow furrowed in an almost pained expression. I won't take my mouth off him. I want to feel him burst inside me. I want to taste it. I shake my head, keeping my eyes on his because I want to watch him come apart and relish every part of him.

I continue sucking, never slowing until the hot, thick proof of his orgasm pours right down my throat. "Fuck…" A sound of pure satisfaction comes out of his mouth, and a dizzying heat spreads through my body. I swallow every last drop while his fist in my hair continues to move as his orgasm winds down.

Still kneeling on the floor, I wipe the corner of my mouth and stare up at him, waiting for him to catch his breath. I'm suddenly nervous. Did he think it was good? I have no yardstick with which to measure, while he, on the other hand, has way too many.

Thomas lowers himself down to me. He's panting. He's all sweaty, disheveled hair and crimson cheekbones. He's simply magnificent. He moves some damp strands of hair off my forehead and kisses me deeply, moaning into me, "Your mouth is gonna be the death of me." That gets me up on my feet. He takes me in his arms and kisses me again, chasing away all of my insecurities. When he pulls back, however, I watch his expression turn serious and frowning.

"How many times have you done that?" He looks at me, waiting for an answer, while I think I might actually die of shame.

Why is he asking me this? Maybe I was wrong. Maybe he didn't actually like it.

"Just once…with you." My voice comes out trembly and unsure. All my boldness is gone.

He raises a skeptical eyebrow. "Bullshit."

"No, it's the truth," I answer, embarrassed, wringing my hands and hoping to move quickly past this topic.

"How is that possible?" he demands.

I shrug, not sure what to say. "I've never felt the urge to do it with anyone before you."

"Are you telling me that I was your first blowjob?" he says loudly, with all his innate refinement and a smug grin flitting around his mouth.

"That makes you feel pretty pleased with yourself, doesn't it?" I move closer, wrapping my arms around his neck.

He smiles, absolutely full of himself. "So pleased."

After we got ourselves back together, we left the room and headed downstairs with the full intention of having fun. Instead, we wound up sneaking away again to a different corner of the house, teasing and provoking each other like a couple of hormonal kids. I think I've developed a sort of "Thomas addiction." The more I'm with him, the more I seem to need him. And when he's not around, it feels like I'm going through withdrawal.

When our ardor seems to have finally cooled a bit, he gives me a pat on the butt, and we go back to the kitchen to get some more of that leftover pizza, which no one else has touched since we left. He sits me on the kitchen counter and positions himself between my legs.

"Have you decided anything about that dinner with your mother?" he asks me suddenly.

"No, not yet. Basically, there's a part of me that wants to go. But I know her too well; she's definitely going to end up saying or doing something that will make me feel bad. It's always been like that between us. One step forward, ten steps back. Only, this time, I don't think I have the strength to make it through another battle."

"That doesn't mean it has to happen that way. Maybe this time is the right time," he suggests. It always surprises me to hear him trying to negotiate for a reconciliation between my mother and me. And it makes my heart ache a little bit too. He, more than anyone else, knows how painful a parent's absence can be.

"If you want, I can be there," he adds in the face of my silence, playing with the ends of my hair.

I give him a confused look. "You mean at the dinner?"

He nods confidently.

I raise my eyebrows in surprise. "You'd really come to my house to have dinner with my mother?"

He looks unhesitatingly into my eyes. "Do you want me to be there?"

I don't even need a half second to think about it. Of course I want him there. Having him there would mean the world to me.

"Yes. Your presence would make me feel better."

"Then I'll be there," he answers, and my heart threatens to burst from my chest.

He has no idea how much this gesture means to me. I smile at him and hug him tightly. I want to say something more than just thank you, but suddenly, all I seem to feel is terrible guilt. I remember my conversation with Logan, our encounter yesterday, and the fact that Thomas knows nothing about all of it. I've kept it from him, and although I had a good reason, I know that I can't make a relationship work with lies of omission. He's trying really hard to open up to me. To let me feel a part of him, of his world. It's not fair; he needs to know about Logan, and he needs to know now.

I pull back just far enough to lock eyes with him and clear my throat. "Thomas, listen, I have something to tell you—"

His phone vibrates in his pocket. I can't believe it. Excellent timing, as usual. He takes it out, checks the name on the display, and answers it. "Hey. What? No, wait, it's too loud here; I can't hear you."

He puts the phone against his chest and brings his mouth close to my ear. "It's my sister; I'm stepping out for a minute. Don't disappear, okay?"

I nod, just a little apprehensively.

The moment Thomas walks out the door, I see Tiffany collapse on the sofa in the living room. Her cheeks are slightly red, her hair is sweat soaked, and her mascara is smudged. I head over and sit down next to her. "Hey, are you okay?" I try to hold back a laugh as I take in her not exactly pristine condition.

"Hell yeah, I am. I won four games! Then my head started spinning, and I realized it was time to throw in the towel. I'm thirsty. Thirsty for water, lots of water. Would you go get some water for me?" She straightens up a bit and tries to wipe the smeared makeup off with her fingers.

"Sure, I'll be right back." I pat her knee and go to the kitchen for a nice glass of cold water. When I get back, she drains it in one gulp. She's tipsy, and it shows, but I'm relieved to see she's not completely wasted.

"Who chose this terrible music?"

I cock an eyebrow as I hand her a tissue to dab herself dry. "You don't like Hendrix?"

"Too noisy for my current condition," she whines, squinting.

I laugh out loud, but in truth, I can't shake off this creeping feeling of distress. I stay silent for a moment before deciding to speak. "Hey, Tiff? Do you think you have a little bit of sobriety left to dedicate to your best friend?"

My request seems to goad her a little, as she suddenly sits up straight. "Of course. Shoot!"

I sigh deeply, putting the tissues back on the coffee table in front of us, and sink back against the couch cushions, watching all the drunk people around us.

"On my way to the arena, I ran into Logan," I confess. At the mere mention of his name, Tiffany screws up her mouth and rolls her eyes. She never liked him.

"What did he want?"

"To tell me some good news," I say, devoid of enthusiasm.

"Which was…?"

"Long story short, I'm supposed to be his philosophy tutor."

Tiffany puts her hand over her mouth in disbelief and utters a tiny whispered "No…"

"Yeah…" I answer apathetically.

"Does Thomas know?"

"No, not yet. Honestly, I'm not sure what I'm going to do…"

"Give up the tutoring," she says immediately.

I give her a disconsolate look. "But do I want to give up the boost to my résumé, which might just get me through this semester without going completely insane?" I don't think I've ever felt more helpless in my life. Whichever choice I make, I end up losing something.

"Then do it," Tiffany says with the exact same conviction she just used a minute ago to suggest that I back out.

I shake my head. "Thomas will be furious."

"Oh, sweetheart, of course he will. But it's not like you can help it," she says, giving me a sympathetic look. "Remember, you're doing it for yourself, and if he really cares about you, he shouldn't be able to do anything but support you."

As hard as it is to believe all of that, I hope with all my heart that she's right.

I scrub my hands over my face and start thinking of the hundred thousand ways I could tell Thomas that I'm going to have to start taking time away from him and dedicating it to Logan, when Tiffany alerts me.

"Uh-oh, trouble incoming."

I take my hands away from my face and look at her uncomprehendingly.

Her eyes are fixed to the front door. "Sir Tedious himself has entered the room and is headed right for us." I turn around quickly and see Logan advancing on us with long decisive strides.

My ears are ringing; all the voices around me seem muffled. All I can really hear is the sound of my own breathing as it gets heavier and heavier.

Seventeen

WHEN LOGAN GETS TO ME, I jump up like the cushion underneath my butt just caught fire. I move my alarmed gaze from him to the front door, where I am expecting Thomas to appear at any moment.

"Logan, what are you doing here?"

He runs a hand through his hair, his eyes wandering around the chaotic room. It feels like he's looking for someone. "I...wanted to talk to you, actually."

"I thought we already did that," I answer with a trembling voice. From the corner of my eye, I can see Tiffany getting up off the sofa. She puts a hand on my shoulder and squeezes it as if to give me courage before walking past the both of us and vanishing out onto the lawn. Knowing my friend, she probably went to find Thomas and keep him out of the house for as long as possible. At least, I'm really hoping that's what she's doing.

"Yes, true," Logan continues. "But I didn't like the way we left things. I realized I was pretty rude to you." He sits down on the sofa, and I turn to look at him.

Logan rests his elbows on his knees, rubbing his forehead with a clenched fist as if pausing to reflect on something troubling. Then, his blue eyes turn attentively to me. "I don't like this situation that has been created between the two of us. We don't speak, we avoid each other like the plague. And any time we do get near each other for some reason, like this morning in class, you are clearly uncomfortable."

I shut my eyes and sigh. "Logan, we already talked about this—"

"Let me finish," he interrupts me, irritated.

I fold my arms over my chest and nod for him to go ahead.

"I like you, okay? It would be pointless to deny it. But, believe it or not, I've made my peace with that. And when I told you before that this would just be about studying, I was being sincere. I want you to be my tutor, Vanessa. I want you because you're good. The best, actually, and you know it. But I also realize that I've put you in a difficult position, and that's why I'm here. I want to clear the air with Thomas once and for all."

He seriously came here to talk to Thomas? Not a chance. At least, not before I do.

"I want to reassure him that I'm not going to use this as an excuse to try to get with you. And I also want to apologize for goading him that night at the Marsy and for not waking you up when you fell asleep." He pronounces the last part with a certain embarrassment, slumping his shoulders as if just saying it out loud has made him feel about as big as an ant.

"I know it's an awful excuse, but I was so excited to be with you that night. Instead, I was confronted with a painful truth that got my head all turned around. But I want you both to know that I'm ashamed of what I did," he finishes in a gloomy tone, hanging his head like a beaten dog.

His low, suffering look conveys all of his misery to me. There's a small part of me that doesn't want to blame him at all. It's clear that he was hurt, and everyone does things they regret when they're being driven by anger and pain.

"Okay, I agree. I'll be your tutor," I say, overcome by guilt.

He lifts his eyebrows, just as surprised as I am to hear me say those words. "You'll really do it?" he asks, almost incredulous.

I nod. After all, it's really just a matter of giving him a little help with homework, right? But I do want to make one thing clear. "I will help you, Logan. But if you do or say anything that makes me regret this decision, our sessions will end immediately."

"I won't do anything like that, I promise," he says fervently.

"And the meetings will be held exclusively on campus in a study hall," I add. I chew on the inside of my cheek and suck in a deep breath, terrified that I've just made the wrong call. But then I try to convince myself that I'm just blowing the whole thing out of proportion. No, Thomas certainly won't be jumping for joy when he hears about this, but he'll understand. He'll have to understand.

"Of course."

"Okay. Then, I think we should meet on Monday before class to see where you are and draw up a plan of attack. We should also schedule the meetings, and you'll have to—"

"What meetings are you talking about?"

I jump when I hear his voice from behind me.

Logan leaps to his feet, eyes widening. I turn slowly toward the towering figure behind me, who is currently staring me down with fire in his eyes and his jaw clenched painfully tight. The familiar sadness in my chest mixes uneasily with my growing anxiety as I try to think of a way to explain everything to Thomas as quickly as possible while making sure he doesn't misunderstand anything.

"Hey! Uh...that was quick. How's Leila? I hope everything's okay?" I give him an extremely tight smile; even my knees are quivering. You could cut the tension with a knife.

"I asked you a question," Thomas insists rudely, arms crossed over his chest. The imitation smile vanishes from my face. I tuck my hair behind my ears and swallow hard, preparing myself for the worst.

"Look, I can explain everything, but you have to promise me that you won't get mad when—"

"Don't blame her; it's my fault," Logan interjects from behind us.

Thomas's menacing glare snaps to him. He pushes past me and stands in front of Logan, looming over him completely. I suck in a sharp breath, and I can feel my hands shaking with fear as Thomas grabs Logan by the collar of his coffee-colored polo. The tips of their noses are nearly touching.

"You're stalking her. You stick to her like a fucking tick. Tell me, are you stupid or just suicidal?"

Logan automatically raises his hands in surrender. "I didn't come here to fight. I came here to apologize to you."

"I wouldn't wipe my ass with your apologies," Thomas growls frostily. Then, before anyone can stop him, Thomas punches him right in the cheekbone. Logan tumbles onto the sofa. The people around us, who were drinking and dancing, now turn to stare at us.

I jolt, clapping my hand over my mouth. Thomas starts to lunge for him again, but I grab his arm and pull him back. "Are you insane?"

"Tell me why he's here, at my frat, with you!"

I want to answer him, to explain the situation, but the words lodge in my throat. Before I can push myself through it, Logan answers for me.

"I'm here because I didn't want Vanessa to agree to tutor me before I'd clarified the situation with both of you," he mumbles miserably, touching his injured cheek with his hand.

"What the fuck are you talking about?" Thomas snarls through gritted teeth.

For a moment, I am perfectly still, as if time has stopped. Then I grab the bottom of my sweatshirt, which covers me to midthigh, and start twisting it anxiously. "Listen, I–I...I was just about to tell you in the kitchen, right before your phone rang, remember?"

"You were going to tell me what?"

Logan moves closer and gives me a surprised look. "Wait, he didn't know yet? I thought you'd already told him."

If the icy stare I level at Logan could talk, it would be saying, *Shut your fucking trap!*

The hurt that I see in Thomas's eyes is killing me.

"I'm sorry," Logan murmurs again. "I never intended to make a mess like this. I came here to fix things, but instead I've only made them worse." He gives me a heartbroken look and shakes his head. He pushes past Thomas and starts to leave but halts halfway. "One last thing, then I'll stop bothering you." He approaches me, feeling for something in the back pocket of his jeans. He takes out a small floral-patterned notebook. My class notebook!

"It slipped out of your bag when we met up yesterday. I wasn't able to return it to you because you'd already left. I apologize again for all of this." His eyes flick back to Thomas, who is still glaring at him. Then he walks away, leaving me speechless with my hands still outstretched, holding the notebook.

Thomas gives me a look filled with resentment. I don't even have time to say anything before he turns his back on me and heads for the door.

"Thomas! Stop, please!" I beg, running after him. He ignores me and continues walking away with determined strides, pushing aside anyone who blocks his path. I knew this was how it was going to go!

Before he gets out the door, I try to grab his arm, but he jerks away from me. I can't figure out whether he's running after Logan or away from me. But all my questions are answered when he gets out on to the lawn, and I hear him shout: "FALLON!"

Thomas reaches out and grabs Logan by the back of his shirt. He shoves him up against a tree to the right, pressing a forearm into his neck. I stop just a step away from them, frozen with fear. "Whatever you're planning, I swear to God I will make you regret it."

"I–I'm not planning anything. I–I don't know what you're talking about," Logan tries to say, his hands pushing against Thomas's wrist in a futile attempt to free himself.

"Thomas, enough, please, just leave him alone." I shove my way between the two of them and try to separate them, but Thomas won't let me.

"You know. You know exactly what I'm talking about," he insists, sneering in such a malevolent way that it makes my skin crawl. Then Thomas steps back and, never taking his eyes off of Logan, allows him to go with a promise contained in his menacing stare: *You are a dead man.*

Logan staggers away from us. His breathing is shallow, and he's stifling a cough as he rubs his neck with one hand. His face is purple, twisted with fear. I stare helplessly at him, completely desolate.

Once we're alone, Thomas rests his hand on the trunk but otherwise remains still. He doesn't speak and neither do I. I watch his chest rhythmically rising and falling as I wring my hands and chew on my bottom lip. Finally, I get up the courage to speak. "You shouldn't have done that. He only came here to apologize..." I point out, aware of the risk I'm running. But there is no way I'm going to just excuse his violence.

Thomas takes a cigarette out of his pack, lights it, and inhales greedily. "You're right," he says. "I should have done much worse."

Without another word, he starts off for a low wall, far from the chaos that surrounds us. I follow him unthinkingly. He sits down, breathing in cigarette smoke and flicking the ash between his feet. "I only asked you for one thing. Just one. To stay away from him." He looks up at me. "How is that so difficult for you?" His voice is thick with anger.

I take a cautious step closer to him. "I did stay away from him. And you know that. But this morning, when I was offered a tutoring position, I didn't know that he was the student. If I knew—"

"What would you have done?" he interrupts me brusquely. "Would you have said no?"

"Of course I would have!"

"Then do it now." He shrugs irritably. "Say no."

I give him a bewildered look. Is he seriously asking me to give up an academic project just because he can't control his jealousy? That's wrong! Inevitably, that conversation I had with Logan before the game pops into my head. Is what he suggested about us true? Does Thomas really get the final say in all my decisions? And am I going to let him? I don't want it to be that way between us. He has no right to make choices about my life; I'm his girlfriend, not his property.

"I need the extracurricular," I answer decisively, crossing my arms over my chest and not even trying to hide my irritation.

"Get it some other way," he orders with the determination of someone who is not willing to hear any objections.

My eyebrows arch in amazement. "And how exactly shall I do that? Overload myself with more activities? What about my job, Thomas? Did you perhaps forget about that? I don't have the time! Tutoring is the best alternative right now."

"Okay, then change students!" he exclaims, throwing his arms out wide in frustration.

"I can't! Professor Scott assigned Logan to me because he trusts me, and I gave him my word that I'd work with him. How is it going to look if I back out now? What am I supposed to tell him? *Hello, Professor. You know what? I've changed my mind about your offer; I can't do it anymore because my boyfriend disapproves?*" I burst out. But my reaction only fires him up further.

He leaps off the wall in one movement, using his height to loom over me. His jaw is tight. His brow is furrowed. For the first time, I'm almost afraid of him, but I stand firm. "After everything that went down, are you really still trying to convince me that he's okay?"

I neither confirm nor deny this.

Faced with my silence, Thomas just snorts and stares mercilessly at me. "Christ, I can't believe this." He shakes his head, eyes lowered. "I am trying every way I can think of to keep my cool around you. But you're making it so fucking hard for me!" he shouts, punching the wall next to us. I gasp, staring horrified at his damaged hand, the knuckles skinned. He's completely out of control. I feel exhausted and empty. Drained of all energy. But also disappointed. And angry; Thomas isn't making the slightest effort to put himself in my shoes. He's being selfish and he has no faith in me or my judgment.

"What am I supposed to do? Huh? Do I have to give up this assignment because you don't like Logan?"

"Fuck off, Ness! It's not like you're giving up the presidency; you're taking a pass on a fucking tutoring gig!"

"But at the moment, that's how I need to play the game!" I make an agitated gesture.

The veins in his neck are getting larger as Thomas sinks his teeth into his lower lip and exhales through his nose. "You know what? If you want to do, then do it," he pronounces, an inch away from my face. "But just know that you're being a hypocrite. You threw a fit when you found Shana and me in the same club, but now I'm supposed to be cool with this?"

My eyes open wide. "Are you seriously equating Shana with Logan? I only went out with him a few times, and we never even went further than a dumb kiss. You and Shana were fucking up until the other day!" I shout.

"Yeah, and maybe I should go back to doing that. At least when I was fucking her, things were easy!"

I stagger back, as though I've just been pierced through the heart by a bullet. I stare at him, frozen in the face of such cruelty. He's impassive. He tosses his cigarette to the ground and grinds it out with the toe of his shoe. He gives me the kind of contemptuous look he usually reserves for those who dare to challenge him. And I feel a profound emptiness in my stomach. In my heart. I feel so cold and so far away from my Thomas. It hurts so bad, it feels like dying.

My vision blurs as I watch him turn his back on me and walk away. I'm too stunned to do anything. My heart urges me to run after him, to cling to him with all my might and beg him to stay. But my head won't let me. My head is loudly telling me not to follow him because I don't deserve this spiteful treatment.

My throat tightens into a knot when I hear the wheels of his motorcycle on the asphalt. Probably because, right up until that moment, a small part of me was hoping he wouldn't get on it. Hoped he would stop right before and come back to me. I sink down to the earth, destroyed, and lean back against the wall where, until recently, Thomas was. The smell of him still lingers: vetiver, trees, soap. Mixed, inevitably, with the scent of tobacco.

I cradle my face in my hands as hot tears roll down my cheeks. Right now, I want nothing more than to rewind time and go back to when we were sitting in the kitchen, laughing and playing, so close to one another.

"Holy cow, you pissed him off good this time."

The slurred commentary makes me leap to my feet. I glance around, hastily wiping away my tears, but I can't see anyone.

"Back here, Little Gem."

I frown. There's only one person who insists on calling me that. I lean over the stone wall. Lying there on the ground, weakly curled up into a ball, is Vince.

"What the hell are you doing down there, Vince?" I ask, my voice cracking as I sniffle.

"I was looking for a place where I could fall apart in peace. The problem arose when I could no longer get up under my own power. So I stayed here. It's not so bad… There's the stars…the leaves on the trees, dancing like feathers in the wind…the autumnal breeze shriveling my balls. And then everything started spinning, and it felt like I was on one of those rides for kids. You know the ones, with the little horses that look at you with crazy eyes?"

"Tell me, on a scale from zero to alcoholic coma, how much did you drink?"

"Less than you might imagine."

"You wouldn't know it from looking at you."

"That's because I can't hold my liquor."

"It does seem that way," I answer. "Wait for me, I'm coming over."

"Where are you expecting me to go?" I hear him grumble as I hop over the wall to meet him.

I kneel down at his side and examine him. "If you know you can't handle alcohol, why did let yourself get like this?"

"Do you know the Brooks twins?" he begins in a thick voice, his eyes slowly opening and closing.

I nod. Who doesn't know them? With their olive complexions, green eyes, and long wavy black hair, they're probably the most sought-after girls at Oregon State.

"Well, they promised to spend an entire weekend with whoever could do a keg stand for the longest."

I raise my eyebrows. "That's it?"

He frowns and looks at me like I'm an alien. "I'm sorry, did you not understand what I said? An entire weekend. With them. With the Brooks twins."

I shake my head in resignation. "You're an idiot. You all are, in fact. You let yourselves get duped."

"What are you talking about...?"

"None of you were ever going to spend the weekend with them," I say simply, pulling some of the dried leaves out of his hair.

"But, they said...they..."

"Mm-hmm" I nod, humoring him. "They always say. And then you, you knuckle-dragging troglodytes with sawdust for brains, you always fall for it."

"Ah, I'm still too drunk to keep up with you, Little Gem, but I think you're right. They made fools of us." He chuckles, rubbing his face.

We stay silent for a while, sinking into the quiet that surrounds us. Beyond the wall, the sounds of the party are far away. All we can hear is the wind in the trees and the faint sound of blink-182's "First Date" coming from the frat house. The damp night air forces me to roll the sleeves of Thomas's sweatshirt down until they drape over my fingers. I wrap myself in the soft, heavy fabric. Then, my thoughts turn right back to Thomas and that hateful burning feeling starts up in my eyes again. I'd like to leave because the urge to cry is getting overwhelming, but I don't feel good about leaving Vince alone, especially under these circumstances.

He taps me on the arm with his index finger, and when I turn to look at him, his eyes are still half closed. "You wanna talk about it? I'm drunk but I'm still a really good listener."

I'm so worn out that it takes me a few seconds to even understand what he's talking about. "There's not much to say."

"I know that lunkheaded clown too well to give much weight to the things he says when he's angry."

I shrug, letting out a shaky sigh. "I'm trying not to, but it's too hard sometimes."

"Did you argue about a guy? That Logan dude?"

I pull my knees up to my chest, resting my chin on top of them. "You know him?"

He nods sleepily. "More or less."

"You might not know, but the two of us dated for a little while. And Thomas never liked him," I explain as I twist some blades of grass between my fingers. "When I broke things off with Logan, he tried to change my mind. It's kind of a complicated story, honestly, and I feel confused every time I think about it. In the end, Thomas and Logan got in a physical fight. Actually, that happens just about every time they get within a few feet of each other."

"Little Gem, far be it from me to stick my nose into things that are none of my business, but I think you should listen to Thomas."

I look at him and scowl. "I should let Thomas's jealousy interfere with my academic career? That's not how a relationship is supposed to work."

"True enough. But that Logan guy has weird vibes. Feels like he's hiding something, something big. I wouldn't want my girlfriend to hang out with someone like that either."

"'Someone like that'? There's nothing wrong with Logan, I can assure you," I say defensively, wiping my dirty fingers on the fabric of my leggings.

"Oh, come on, haven't you noticed how he's always by himself and doesn't talk to anyone? Nobody knows anything about him. And he's not on social media at all; doesn't that strike you as suspicious?"

"Not having socials doesn't make a person weird, Vince," I say in an irritated mutter.

"But not having friends does," he insists.

"He's just an introvert. So am I. Since when did being a private sort of person become a crime? And he does have interpersonal relationships. He and I dated for a while, for example. And I know for a fact that he does have friends," I add, thinking back on the roommate he plays *Call of Duty* with and the guy he went to pick up when his car broke down.

"Hey, I wasn't trying to upset you. Just keep your head on a swivel, okay? Thomas is an asshole, but he's not actually stupid. If he wants you to stay away from Logan, he probably has his reasons," he answers, yawning with a relaxed air.

"His 'reasons' don't hold up. He's just jealous, and that's okay; I understand that. I mean, I would be too. But..."

"Jealousy is one thing; concern is another."

"What are you trying to say?"

"Just what I said. And maybe what I shouldn't have said. Shit, I'm too drunk for this conversation."

"Do you know something that I don't?" I press him. But he doesn't answer me. "Vince, spill!"

"No, nothing, just...trust him. He knows what he's doing."

"Do you mean Thomas? Is he doing something behind my back? Vince, if there's something I don't know, I demand you tell me!"

"Stop trying to weasel information out of the drunk guy. You... you just be careful, okay?" he slurs as he rolls onto his side and curls into a fetal position.

"Be careful of what? Of Logan?" I'm getting increasingly nervous as I get no response from him. "Vince! What are you trying to tell me? Is Logan 'homicidal maniac' bad or 'shoplifts candy' bad? Because there's a pretty big difference between those two things."

No answer again. I give him a vehement shake but to no avail. Apparently, he's passed out. I am left with my mouth hanging open, speechless, heart thumping, and, frankly, slightly nauseous.

What the hell does all of this mean?

Eighteen

ONCE I REALIZE THAT VINCE is beyond my help, I am forced to call for backup. Matt puts him over his shoulder and takes him back inside while I go to find Tiffany. I tell her all about the predictable disaster that ensued between Thomas, Logan, and me, and only after saying goodbye to her do I finally go back upstairs.

Shut up within these four ink-colored walls, I do nothing but ruminate about Vince's insinuations. And though I was distressed at the beginning, after thinking through everything and reviewing all of Logan's behavior toward me, I decide that it was all just based on stupid prejudices. Caught in my spiraling thoughts, I realize only now that it's three in the morning. I've heard nothing from Thomas. Sitting up in bed, I start chewing my fingernails as I stare at the clock radio on the bedside table.

What if something's happened to him?

He wasn't thinking clearly when he got on his bike; he was blinded by anger. What if…? I don't even want to think about it. Panic is just about to seize my brain when suddenly the bedroom door opens, and Thomas appears before me.

I leap to my feet. His forehead is beaded with sweat, and I can tell his heart is racing. "Where have you been?" I shout.

"Shh! Are you nuts? You'll wake up the whole house."

He closes the door behind him and leans back against it. He bows his head, narrows his eyes, and frowns. I can't tell if he's irritated or in pain. I do see that he can barely stand, and he's got an unlit cigarette pressed between his lips.

I examine him carefully from head to toe. I fold my arms and ask, "Have you been drinking?"

He massages his temples and answers me with a nod. He rests his head back against the door and looks at me through his eyelashes, chin high. "Am I grounded?" he taunts.

"You shouldn't have done that," I say simply through gritted teeth. I swallow the lump of bitterness in my throat and try to keep a lid on the anger that threatens to explode out of me.

"I'll bear that in mind for next time." He gives me a wink as he fumbles in his jeans for his lighter. He eventually finds it and lights the cigarette with a sneering, extremely punchable look on his face. And I can feel my palms tingling from nerves. I take a deep breath, trying to calm myself down.

"Where have you been?" I repeat more steadily.

He takes a drag from his cigarette and replies with a vague hand gesture. "Here and there."

I raise my eyebrows. "Did you drive like this?"

He sighs, emitting a barely audible growl. "Knock it off. It's late. My head's killing me, and the last thing I need is to be asked a bunch of fucking questions. I'd like a little quiet." He bends over to take off his shoes, tripping over his own feet.

So we have an argument, he vents all his anger at me in the worst possible way, then he goes and gets drunk. He stays out all night and now he'd "like a little quiet"? Like hell!

"And I would like an answer."

"Fuck, I can't stand you when you're pushy like this. I was at ClubSeven, and no, I didn't drive. Happy now?"

My heart stops momentarily. He left me here alone so he could go get drunk and cut loose at the same club where I just found him with Shana. And even though I make an enormous effort not to let my imagination run away with me, I just can't do it. I swallow thickly as

I feel the familiar burning sensation in my eyes. I bite my lip to try to stop my trembling.

Don't cry, Vanessa. Don't you cry.

He gives me a long impassive look, saying nothing, just smoking. In fact, I can't even really say for sure that he's actually looking at me. He looks so...hazy.

"Was she there too?" I ask, regretting it even as it comes out of my mouth.

Thomas licks his lower lip with the tip of his tongue and then bites it. He appears to be thinking hard. "I'm fucking angry, and I've had a few too many. But I didn't forget that I'm with you."

I feel every joint in my body relax at once.

"Can we talk?" I whisper, approaching him slowly.

Thomas lets his arms fall loose to his sides. "For what purpose? You're still gonna do what you want to do, right? You always do. All the time, you wanna know where I am, what I'm doing, and who I'm doing it with. But when it comes right down to it, I never get to know what you're doing."

I grimace. "You always know what I'm doing!"

"Bullshit. I know what you're doing when you're with me, but when you're not, I don't know anything. At the club, you made up your mind about Shana and me after watching us for, what? Five seconds? And then, without even giving me the chance to explain, you drew your own conclusions and decided that grinding on the first person who came along was the right thing to do. You invite your little partner in crime over here, conveniently forget to tell me, and then when I get home, I catch him in bed with you. And now I find out you've been seeing Logan and you're hiding the fact that you're going to tutor him." He stubs out his cigarette in the ashtray, takes off his sweatshirt (which reeks of alcohol and sweat), and tosses it onto the desk. "I don't know shit about what you do, much less why you do it. What I do know is that if I did even one of those things, you would have pointed your little finger at me and called me a heartless bastard."

He goes over to the bed, and for a moment, I think he's decided to put an end to this conversation by going to sleep. Instead, he grabs a pillow and heads back toward the door. I am even more agitated. "Where are you going?"

"Downstairs."

Is he joking?

"What? I don't want you to go downstairs, Thomas." I reach for him, grabbing his arm. "I'm sorry about everything. About the misunderstanding with Alex and about dancing with that guy the other night. It was a stupid, childish thing to do. I know, I get that. But I'm sorry. And I'm extremely sorry about this whole thing with Logan too. I swear, I was going to tell you, but…"

"You were going to tell me? When were you going to tell me?"

"In the kitchen, right before your phone rang…I was just about to tell you!"

Thomas gives a sarcastic snort. "You were only going to tell me because you had no other options. You expect transparency, sincerity, and honesty from me, but where is any of that from you, huh?"

I stare fearfully at him, profoundly shocked by the truth of what he is saying. I've been so angry at him all night. And now, I'm just angry at myself. I'm just so stupid. A stupid, pathetic screwup who probably deserves to spend the night alone feeling sorry for herself. Because the truth is, I always end up making the wrong call. And it's for that reason that, when he walks out the door, I let him.

Fresh off a night of bitterly weeping, I thrash restlessly in the bedclothes. My phone has been ringing nonstop for I don't know how long. But this time, instead of stretching my arm out to the bedside table and rejecting the call, I grab the phone irritably. An unknown number flashes on the display.

"What?" I answer in an unsteady voice, sitting up on the edge of the bed.

"Hey, finally! It's about time," an irritated and not-at-all-familiar voice exclaims. "You're Clark the sophomore, right?"

"Um...yeah, that's me. Who am I speaking with?"

"I'm Athena. I've been instructed to give you the keys to your new residence. And considering that this is also my Saturday and I don't have time to waste, the sooner we can get together, the sooner I can get out of your hair. Tell me where you are so I can meet you."

I press my hand to my forehead, staring bewildered out the window, absolutely stunned. *Keys? Residence? What is she talking about?*

"W-what?"

"Tell me where you are so I can meet you there. I'm not going to say it again; I don't have all day. It'll be a short meeting, trust me. Just long enough to sign some paperwork, get you the keys, and show you your new apartment."

I get up and start pacing the room. Of course, I'm so dumb—my new residence! Only now do I remember the conversation I had with the dean and the rental contract he gave me.

"Right now I'm at a fraternity house, but—"

"Woah, woah, woah. I'm not setting foot in that den of brain-dead drunks."

"I can come to you; that's no problem. I have a session with my book club on campus at eleven. I apologize for the inconvenience; I didn't know we were supposed to meet up today. If I had, I would have been more prepared," I explain.

"Yeah, well, I wasn't notified until the last minute either," she says, still slightly annoyed. "Either way, I'll be waiting for you in front of Howell Hall in half an hour. Is that enough time for you?"

"Wait, I'm living in Howell?" I burst out in amazement. It's undoubtedly the best residence hall on campus, completely made up of full apartment-style suites instead of just shared rooms. It's owned by a university benefactor, who rents the apartments to the university community by application only.

"Daddy made your dreams come true, eh?"

"Ah, no. I don't actually have a—"

"Sure, fine, whatever," she interrupts. "I'll be waiting for you there in twenty minutes."

"Wasn't it half—"

Too late. She hung up.

Still in a daze, I put my hair up into a bun, go to the bathroom, and, after brushing my teeth, hop in the shower. I put on a pair of high-waisted dark jeans and a turquoise cashmere sweater. I head downstairs, hoping that Thomas will be more willing to talk this morning after sleeping on it. I don't want to leave the house before I clear the air with him.

When I get down to the kitchen, I find a full plate of breakfast on the stove with a Post-it note next to it, which reads, *Hands off this plate. It's for our girl,* and is signed, *Matt.* I grin because his little everyday thoughtfulness warms my heart. Next to the plate, I find a thermos full of steaming coffee. I cup my hands around it and stick my nose into the top, breathing in the aroma.

I move into the living room, noting the disgraceful condition of the house. It's 9:25, and obviously everyone else is still asleep. Some of them are on the floor. Some, like Vince, are on the sofas, where he's lying like a corpse with one limp arm dangling down. Someone's even passed out on the beer-pong table outside on the lawn. God...what a disaster. The guys are going to have a lot of cleaning to do when they finally wake up.

With a pang of hurt, though, I realize that someone is missing... I don't see Thomas anywhere. Did he leave already? Without saying anything to me? No, he wouldn't have done that. *Yes, he would, you moron. Of course he would have done that*, the little voice inside my head responds.

I squat down in front of the couch where Vince is sprawled out and give his shoulder a firm shake. "Vince, wake up!"

"Mhghfg..." He mutters something incomprehensible before rolling over, still in the arms of the alcoholic version of Morpheus.

"Vince, open your eyes. I need to know where Thomas is."

"I dunno. Now let me sleep, I'm begging you..."

"Are you sure? Is it possible that you heard him leave, or maybe he told you where he was going...?"

"Ah..." Vince swears, rubbing his eyes with his thumb and

forefinger. "You're a menace, Little Gem. I have an all-time hangover, and here you are tormenting me first thing in the morning with this shit. I don't know where he is. If he's not here, he probably went out."

I check my cell phone, hoping to find at least one text to explain his absence, but there's nothing. Vince gives me a pitying look. "Do you want my advice? Let him cool down for a little while. As soon as he calms down, everything will be fine. You'll see."

If he was intending to reassure me, he hasn't remotely succeeded. In fact, the only thing his words have done is reawaken the anger that I pushed aside.

"Let me see if I have this right," I snap. "I'm supposed to just wait until he calms down? I already spent a terrible night worrying about him, waiting for him to come back to me while he was out having fun! It doesn't work that way!" I yell, not caring if I wake the others.

I stride away from Vince with determined steps, blood pounding in my temples as I head for the door.

"Where are you going now?" he asks wearily, still lying on the sofa with his head bent to keep looking at me.

"I'm moving out!" I leave the house, slamming the door behind me.

I walk down the path toward Howell Hall, flanked by red maples and aspens. Anger has my whole body trembling. The cold wind makes a mess of my hairstyle, strands sticking to the corner of my mouth.

About five minutes later, I heard Vince's still-sleepy voice from behind me. "Hey, hey, slow down, come on!"

"What do you want?" It's more of an accusation than a question, and I continue to walk briskly, arms folded tight.

He pulls alongside me, keeping pace. "I've got nothing to do, so I thought I'd keep you company."

I give him a sideways look. He's wearing the same clothes as yesterday, now much dirtier and more malodorous. His hair is disheveled and wild, his blue eyes still swollen and red from lack of sleep.

"I don't need company. Just go back to the house and sleep. Or bathe. Whatever you think is more important."

"Are you insinuating that I stink?" He lifts his right arm and brings his nose close to his armpit. "Shit. Yeah, I stink," he confirms, his face twisting into a grimace of disgust. But then he gives a shrug, as though it doesn't really bother him all that much. "So where are we going?"

"*I'm* going to Howell," I grump through gritted teeth.

"You're moving in there?"

I nod, staring straight ahead.

"Dope. That dorm is full of next-level pussy. I have a feeling I'll be visiting you frequently, Little Gem." He rubs his hands together gleefully.

I don't even bother answering; I'm in no mood to indulge his idiocy.

When we arrive in front of the building, a girl is waiting for us, tapping her foot with a listless air. She has a cup of coffee in one hand, some papers clenched under her arm, and a set of keys dangling from the fingers of her free hand.

"Hey!" I move toward her with a smile, trying to show her nothing but serenity. "Are you Athena?"

"Cute…" Vince whispers in my ear, earning himself an elbow to the ribs.

"In the flesh," says the girl with electric blue eyes in front of me as she brushes her honey-colored bangs away from her face.

"I'm Vanessa; it's so nice to meet you."

"Little Gem, you drag me out of bed, I sacrifice my morning for you, and you don't even bother to introduce me?" Vince interrupts, pushing aside my hand and inserting his own to shake with Athena.

"I'm Vince; it's a pleasure." A sideways smile forms on his face, creating a dimple in his right cheek. Athena scrutinizes him without interest and frowns, not remotely impressed by his attempt at flirting. She pulls her hand out of his grasp. But Vince doesn't seem demoralized by her rejection. On the contrary, it seems to wind him up even further. So much so that he gives her a cheeky smile, and the moment she turns to lead us away, he follows close behind her.

"Cute and tough. I think I've just fallen in love," he whispers to me again, his eyes locked on our guide's backside, for which he receives another elbow in his side.

"Ow! Thomas is a bad influence on you; violence is your first instinct now!" He rubs his side with a grimace while I feel a pang in my heart at the mere mention of Thomas's name. Vince seems to understand this, because he puts an arm around my shoulders as if to console me.

"So the building has four floors," Athena breaks in as she moves toward the elevators and presses the call button. "The apartments are occupied only by second-year or international students, no freshmen."

The elevator doors open, and the three of us walk in. Vince just stares at Athena, but she pointedly ignores him. She pushes the second-floor button, takes a sip of her coffee, and continues talking. "You can use the laundry for free, but you need to buy all your own laundry supplies. Newspapers are left outside the door every morning, and your mail will be delivered to you at Arnold Service Center." She doesn't stop talking until we get to the second floor. She's the first out, leading the way to apartment F22.

She puts the key into the lock and lets us into what will be, from now on, my new residence. "And here we are; welcome to your little home." She smiles at me without the slightest bit of enthusiasm. I wonder how many times she's had to repeat this same spiel.

I pause to look around at the dove-gray walls that surround me, the slightly worn flowered sofa, the wooden table with a bowl of fruit already in the center, and I feel an immediate sense of ease.

"As you can see, the living room is pretty small but welcoming. The bathroom is in the back," she informs me, pointing to a door. "Bedroom is that way." She gestures at another door to my right. "And here we have the kitchenette, small but practical."

"Damn..." I whisper, turning around slowly. My eyes land on a television affixed to the wall. "Does that work?" I point to it a little hesitantly, remembering the one in the freshman dorm that was completely useless.

"Of course it works. Now, if you don't mind, can I get you to sign these forms?" She hands me the stack of papers she'd been holding under her arm. "The first one is registering you for a mailbox; the second is confirming you got the keys. The RAs are two other girls and me; you can get our numbers down in the secretary's office or from this instruction packet. If you need anything, just call, we'll be happy to help you."

The way she says it, I find it hard to believe that she would be "happy" to do anything. I nod and grab the pen she hands me. I put the papers down on the table and begin to quietly read through them before signing.

A few minutes pass before, suddenly, I hear Athena's wearied voice snap, "You know there's other stuff to look at, right?"

I turn quickly to see her and Vince facing each other.

"You're cute," Vince answers, winking at her with that cheeky grin that he refuses to put away. His arms are crossed over his chest, and he has the confident air of someone who likes what he sees and isn't afraid to show it.

"Yes, I'm aware," she answers, raising her chin. She's just as confident as he is, if not more so. "But that doesn't give you the right to keep your slimy creeper eyes glued to my ass."

"I wasn't..." he babbles, caught off guard.

"Ah-ah," she admonishes him, pointing her index finger at his face. "Don't try to deny it; I know it's true."

"Well, in my defense, that ass really was made to be stared at," Vince says with a cocky grin.

"Vince!" I leap up, red-faced, while Athena irritably gathers up the papers from the table and shoulder-checks him out of her way. Before she walks out the door, she stops and pulls a flyer from the pocket of her white skinny jeans. She hands it to me without much conviction. "There's a party tonight on the top floor. Nothing big, pretty quiet in fact. You're invited, if you want to come."

"Oh, thank you for that, but I have to work tonight. I don't think—"

I don't have time to finish my sentence before Vince snatches the flyer from my hand and answers for me. "We'll be there."

Both Athena and I glare at him.

"You don't even live in this building," she says.

"And how do you know that?"

"I've never seen you here."

"You're seeing me here right now."

Athena raises her hands in surrender, shaking her head and sighing. "Do what you want; I don't care. Have a great day." Her gaze drifts over Vince's body and she adds, "And for God's sake, take a shower. You smell like a distillery."

When we're alone, I slap his shoulder with the back of my hand. "Wanna tell me what's going on in your head?"

"Right this minute? Are you sure you want to know?" He gives me an exaggeratedly innocent grin.

"You're a pig!" I exclaim, trying to hold back laughter.

"Oh, but look at that; is that a smile I see on your little mouth?" He pinches my cheek gently with his thumb and forefinger.

I try not to smile to avoid giving him the satisfaction, but in the end, I break.

"Well, Little Gem, it's time for me to pack it in," he says, glancing around. "This isn't so bad. Compared to my place, you're living in a palace," he jokes, moving to leave. But before he can turn the door handle, I stop him.

"I'm sorry, where do you think you're going?"

"To sort myself out; I've got to get rid of this hangover," he answers casually, stretching his arms behind his back.

I shake my head no at him. "You insisted on coming here with me, you embarrassed me in front of that girl, and you accepted an invitation to a party on my behalf without my consent. You're nuts if you think I'm going to let you off the hook that easily," I say, looking down at my wristwatch.

He crosses his arms over his chest, frowning. "What do you have in mind?"

"I'm expecting you back here at twelve o'clock sharp," I answer.

After meeting with my reading group, I put Vince to work for an hour, forcing him to help me move. It leaves a bitter taste in my mouth, because I really wanted to settle into my new apartment with Thomas. But apparently, I don't always get the things I want.

When we finish, I thank Vince for his help by offering to buy him lunch and then set him free. I take another shower before deciding to go down to the newspaper's office. I spend a few hours wading through news articles and opinion pieces about the police's abuse of power, occasionally pausing to peek at my phone. I pretend I'm checking the time but, actually, I'm hoping to see a text from Thomas. A vain hope.

At the stroke of six, I transfer all the material I've found onto a USB stick and leave the editorial office for the Marsy, where I begin my shift. Sometimes, I'm afraid that I'm going to end up losing my mind between all these commitments, but I have to admit that I like always having something to do. It keeps me busy and my mind occupied. And right now, I need that to avoid thinking about *him*.

Nineteen

"FOUR ORDERS OF SPICY CHICKEN wings for table eleven, plus two pitchers of light beer," I tell Maggie quickly as she passes me on her way to the bar. It's James's usual order, but it's not for him; this Saturday, for the first time since I've started working here, he hasn't shown up at the bar.

I seat a family with kids at the last open table. I set the table, hand them their menus, and take their drink orders.

"Ugh, I don't know about you, but I hate 'em," Cassie exclaims, irritated. She leans back against the bar and looks out at our customers.

"Who do you hate?" I ask curiously when I get to the taps.

"Them," she says, gesturing with her head at the family I've just seated. "How much do you wanna bet that, in another five minutes, those brats'll be running around all over the place screaming like maniacs?"

I shake my head. "They're just kids, Cassie. Give them some paper and crayons, and it'll be like they aren't even there," I reassure her. From the look she shoots me, I don't think she's persuaded. I hand her some blank sheets of paper and a cup full of markers, and urge her to bring them over. She rolls her eyes but humors me.

When she returns, she fills two glasses of Sprite and asks me in her usual strident voice, "Hey, what happened to your boyfriend?" She looks up, scanning the room. "It feels kinda wrong, you know, not seeing him here," she finishes in a vaguely sly tone of voice that I don't appreciate at all.

I repress a grunt of frustration. I don't have anything against Cassie, but she takes a little too much interest in Thomas's personal life. She's always asking me about him, how he's doing, what he's doing. And then there were the many times I've caught her undressing him with her eyes, probably when she thought I wasn't watching. And of course, there's the fact that I don't actually have the faintest idea where he is today.

"He's busy," I say simply, not looking at her as I put the mugs of beer on a tray and take them over to table eleven, where I find Matt, Finn, and Vince, along with some other kids from school. I set the glasses down on the table and notice that Vince is waving the flyer that Athena gave me this morning in Matt's face.

"Howell Hall, tonight, half past ten, are you in?" I hear him demand.

"Howell?" Matt echoes, confused. "Why would anyone from there invite you? Those people are snobs; if you don't belong to their little clique, you're out. Fuck them," he says, before taking a pull from his mug and wiping the corners of his mouth.

"No one invited him, actually. He invited himself," I say, inserting myself into the conversation. Matt gives me a questioning look, so I clarify: "This morning, I went to get the keys to my new suite in Howell. Vince demanded to come with me and got obsessed with the girl who was showing us around. Which is why he's now acting like a stalker."

"Hey! I'm not a stalker. There was a definite vibe between us."

I almost laugh right in his face. "A 'vibe'? She gave you the brush-off from start to finish. And how can you blame her? This morning you were looking like a college-edition Frank Gallagher."

Everyone at the table bursts into laughter while Vince affectionately whacks me on the belly with the flyer.

"I assure you the vibes were there, and you would have seen them too if you weren't so bummed out today. I'll prove it to you tonight," he grins, a devilish glint in his eye.

I shake my head and leave them to their conversation while I go over to an elderly couple's table to collect their empty plates. When I put them back behind the bar, the front door jingles, and my heart momentarily skips a beat. Because yes, I am furious with Thomas, but even just seeing him would put my mind at ease. Instead, what I see when I lift my head just makes me even more anxious.

Logan.

He's the last person I want to see right now. I take a deep breath as I watch him take a seat on the stool right in front of me.

"Hi," I greet him tonelessly, rinsing a glass under a jet of warm water. "Can I get you anything?"

"Yes, a tonic water, thanks." His head is bowed and his shoulders hunched. He looks like a kicked puppy when, actually, he should be angry at me and at Thomas for the beating he received. But he doesn't seem to be the slightest bit resentful. And, seeing him like this, I'm starting to feel that annoying sense of guilt growing inside me again. How cruel would it be to stay mad at him after the way he was treated?

"Sure, I'll get it right away." I pour a glass for him, and he immediately lifts it to his mouth. I move over to the cash register, where I print out a customer's bill. But then our eyes meet for a split second, and I look away like a coward.

"You're mad at me, aren't you?" he says softly, drumming his fingers on the wooden surface of the bar.

"No, of course not," I answer hesitantly.

"You are. And you have every reason to be. It was stupid of me to rush in and run my mouth like that without making sure you'd told him first."

"Look, what's done is done. Let's not dwell on it, okay?"

"No, it's not okay. I know I made a scene. If you've decided to back out and don't want to tutor me anymore, I understand. I don't want my presence to screw up your life, Vanessa. I've been thinking about it all day, and I realized that you were right. I shouldn't have asked you to do it. Thomas is apparently convinced that I have bad intentions, and I don't think he'll ever believe otherwise. I don't know what I was thinking..." He gets up from the stool, leaves a few bills for me on the counter, and turns to go, looking defeated.

I glance at him out of the corner of my eye as I wipe down the bar, but I can't remain impassive in the face of his unhappiness. "Logan," I call out to him before he can leave the room.

He turns around with his hands tucked into his pockets.

"I haven't changed my mind, okay? I said I would help, and I'm going to. I just...I don't want to talk about it anymore, okay?"

He nods submissively. "Okay. You're always so good. I don't deserve it."

"Do you know what you really didn't deserve? That," I say, pointing at the bruise on his cheek. "I'm sorry. And I'm sorry that it always seems to end that way between the two of you."

He rubs his cheek, inclining his face slightly. "Ah, it's nothing. Don't worry about it." Before he leaves, he smiles at me, and I do my best to smile back, but all I can manage is a grimace that only vaguely resembles a smile.

Once my shift is over, Vince drags me to the party at my dorm. He's been following me around all day, and I don't get why. I tried to convince him to go without me, but he wouldn't listen to any of my objections. "I'm not going to let you hole up in your room all night being depressed," is what he said.

To be clear, that was not my intention. I would have merely curled up in my bed and surrendered to the darkness and silence of my lonely room on what would have been my first official night in my new apartment...by myself. Without him. For the second night in a row. And yes, at that point I would have almost certainly burst into tears. Okay, I admit it, I would have been depressed.

"So you made it. I'd almost counted you out," Athena says when she sees me emerge from a long dorm hallway crowded with students.

"Work kept me later than expected, but yeah, I decided to take the plunge." I smile at her a bit awkwardly, toying with my hair. I'm not quite sure how to act with her. If it were Tiffany in front of me, I'd give her a hug, but Athena seems a bit aloof to me, and I don't have the guts to give it a try.

"Yeah, and I see you brought your friend too." She turns her attention to Vince, who is gorging himself at the snack table.

"Yeah, sorry… I couldn't talk him out of it."

"Don't worry about it; I don't know why I thought you could. At least he had the decency to get cleaned up this time," she points out, chuckling. "In terms of the party, as you can see, everyone's spread out a bit in the various rooms." She gestures at the open doors on either side of the hallway, a different genre of music coming from each one. "In G13 they're playing some poppy stuff; wanna come by and cut loose a bit?" she suggests.

"Um…I don't think I really have the energy to jump around to 'There's Nothing Holdin' Me Back.' I think I'd rather get something to eat."

Vince interjects himself into the conversation, wrapping an arm around Athena's shoulders. "Good evening, Athena. While my friend here may be tired, I have all the energy you need."

She wriggles free. "No, thanks. See you around, Clark."

I nod and smile gratefully at her. I give Vince a pleading look, silently begging him to behave like a civilized human being. Or at least like a properly domesticated animal. Athena heads for G13 with Vincent hot on her heels. I may have been imagining it, but I could have sworn I saw the littlest smug smile on her face when Vince put his arm around her.

After an hour of uncomfortably rejecting numerous pitches and invitations, I swallow the last sip of orange soda from my plastic cup and decide that the time has finally come to leave this party. I'm not in the right mood for this at all. Everyone around me is having fun in one way or another, while here I am just sitting in this uncomfortable chair, repeatedly checking my phone in the hopes of getting a call from him. I feel a bit pathetic, but damn it, it's 11:45! Is it possible that it just hasn't occurred to him to reach out?

Annoyed, I search for Vince to tell him that I'm going to leave. I find him in a room where R&B music is playing. To my great surprise, I see that he's dancing with Athena. I just shake my head, amused. Maybe he was right about the vibe after all.

I leave him to enjoy the rest of his evening, and I head for the elevators with my stomach in knots. Once I get back to my room, I slump down on the floor. It's as though the whole day's worth of feelings is finally free to explode. I hate myself for this. I hate having no control over my emotions. Never being able to stop myself. I take a deep breath, sniffle a little, and try to calm myself down.

I toe off my shoes and put the bag with my work uniform in it on the sofa. I undo my hair and lie down on the bed. It smells new. I stare up at the dark ceiling, not even bothering to take off the clothes I've been wearing since this morning. Noises from the street and the other apartments filter in, despite the windows all being closed. I can hear the roar of motorcycles racing down the pavement and the honking of cars. From the next room, I can hear some girl yelling at her boyfriend. Apparently he spent the whole night messing around with his friends instead of being with her. I check my phone for the thousandth time since this morning. Still nothing. I feel like I've traveled back in time to when I was still with Travis.

I sigh and rub my face. *Enough! This is ridiculous!* I refused to call him at first out of pride, but the worry is eating me up inside. I'm just about to dial his number when someone knocks on my door, startling me. My fingers freeze and I frown. Is it Vince?

Hesitantly, I open the door, but the person I find in front of me is not who I expected. Thomas looms in the door, wearing his leather jacket and leaning against the frame. He has that rebellious tuft of hair, which always insists on falling over his forehead, his cheeks are a little bit red, and his weary green eyes are fixed on mine. Even all messy like this, he is breathtakingly beautiful, and I hate him all the more for it. There's a wave of warmth washing over my body, and I can't understand what is going on in my brain right now. Emotions chase one another with such violence that it leaves me stunned. Relief. Anger.

Joy. Disbelief. When I recover from the initial shock, however, it's clear that anger has prevailed.

I snort contemptuously before I speak to him. "Look what the cat dragged in. But you've come to the wrong place; I don't want you here. Go back to your room." I start to slam the door in his face, but he blocks it with his hand.

"Ness."

God, I don't think I'll ever get over the effect his voice has on me, all warm when he says my name. But no, this time I have to stand strong. I won't let it enchant me.

"What the hell do you want?" I say fiercely, crossing my arms.

"We need to talk," he begins with a serious look on his face. His voice is low; he sounds anguished.

"Oh, sure. Now that you've decided it's time to talk, you assume I'll automatically agree?"

"I didn't feel like talking to anyone," he answers miserably. My eyes go wide. I am about to completely lose my temper.

"I am not *anyone*, Thomas! I'm your girlfriend, in case you forgot."

"I know."

"No, it doesn't seem to me that you do know. You spent the night out drinking while I cried over you. You've ignored me all day, and now you show up here hoping for what? My forgiveness? Maybe my understanding?" I shake my head fervently. "Well, you're not going to get it."

"Listen to me…"

"No, you listen to me!" I am a raging river, unstoppable. It's as though all of today's accumulated rage has finally found an outlet instead of just eating away at my insides. "I made a mistake, okay? Probably more than one. But you have also made a lot of mistakes with me. Yet, despite all your temper tantrums, despite the nasty things you say to me or the unflattering comparisons you make, I have never shut you out. Not like you, pushing me away yet again. You…you just pull back into yourself, Thomas. You shut out everything around you. And I'm tired of being pushed away. I am your girlfriend, and I want to be yours all the way. Otherwise, this is all just a huge waste of our time."

He stares at me, motionless. His jaw is clenched. His eyes are blazing. Then, without asking my permission, he walks past me into the suite, planting himself in the middle of the room. I glare at him, but I don't fight him, because if we are going to have an argument, I'd rather do it inside the apartment than in the dormitory hallway.

"You know I'm not good at this stuff; you've always known that. I don't know how to make a relationship work...not the kind of connection that you want to have with me. I don't know how to do it. I break things; I don't build them. You knew who I was from the beginning, Ness; you knew...and you still said yes."

I frown, clucking my tongue indignantly against the roof of my mouth. "So because I said yes, you think it's okay to be an asshole like this?"

"No! But how do you not understand that I'm trying here?" He puts his fingers to his temples, frustrated. "I'm trying as best I can, but sometimes it feels fucking impossible, and I just screw up one thing after another. Today, I needed to be alone. I had to get my thoughts in order, away from everything and everyone. Do you think I like the way I reacted? That I feel proud of the things I said? The person that I am?"

"I don't know," I answer, arms still crossed over my chest and refusing to look him in the eye.

"You don't know?" He seems shocked, maybe even wounded.

"No, Thomas, I don't know. Whenever I start to think I understand something about you and we're making some progress, you turn it around on me, and everything goes upside down."

He sighs, wiping a hand over his face. He turns his back to me and puts his palms down on the table in the living room. "I wish I was different than I am. You don't know how much I wish that, Ness. You don't know how exhausting it is to live with myself every day of my life. It's a constant battle, and I always lose in the end."

The suffering that I can hear in his voice renders me mute. And I wish I had the strength to stay angry so I wouldn't be moved by his words. But I don't. I hurt for him. For how he feels, *what* he feels. For the part of him that wants to be different but never can manage it. Now that I know what he's going through, I can't ignore it. I walk over and put my hand on his shoulder. "I'm sorry you are feeling this way, but I really would have preferred that you talked to me about it. Instead, you just cut me out. It can't work like that," I explain to him, calmer now.

"I lost control but not for the reason you think," he admits, turning to face me. "Not entirely, at least."

"Why, then?" Thomas doesn't answer, so I find myself forced to push him. "Tell me. Why did you do it?"

After what feels like an eternity, he lets out a trembling breath. "Yesterday, before Logan showed up, I talked to my sister."

I frown, alarmed. "Did something happen? Is your father...?"

"He's still alive," he answers, taking another breath. His Adam's apple moves laboriously as he swallows. "My mother wants to see me." He sits down in the chair, staring into space. His chest moves up and down in irregular jerks. "I'm going home tomorrow."

I stare at him, paralyzed for a few seconds. "You said yes..." I say incredulously.

"Yeah, but I regretted it immediately," he answers, putting his face in his hands.

I kneel in front of him and gingerly uncover his face. "I think you were right, though. This is a big step forward, Thomas."

"Actually, it's bullshit. I was jacked up from winning the game, you and I were in a good place, and it didn't seem like such a horrible idea at the time. Only once I'd hung up and my head cleared a little did I realize that I'd just made the biggest mistake of my life. I came over to talk to you about it..." He lowers his eyes, rubbing the back of his neck. "And then what happened, happened."

"If your instinct was to say yes, maybe that means part of you is ready to..." The more I talk, the harder he shakes his head.

"I can't go back there, Ness. To that house. With my mother, my sister. Confronting all those memories. The memory of my brother..."

My stomach clenches so hard it almost takes my breath away. In the face of all this pain, none of my anger seems to matter. I take his face in my hands and force him to look me in the eyes. "Yes, you can, Thomas."

He shakes his head again. "You don't get it… That place hurt me."

"That place is your home. It was your father who hurt you, and he isn't there now."

Thomas stares at me for a long moment without speaking. He searches my face before putting his hand over mine and squeezing it. "I know you have a million good reasons to be pissed at me. I hurt you, I know I did, and I won't try to justify my behavior. You may not believe me after what I said last night, but I need you more than you could possibly imagine, Ness."

I can feel my heart pounding in my chest. Even though he put me through hell today with his absence, he's being sincere right now. I can see it in his eyes. I let out a breath I didn't even realize I was holding. "You drive me crazy, Thomas. You don't even know how much. I disagree with at least three-quarters of the things you say and do. And you should know that I am still very angry with you. You're going to have to find some way to actually make it up to me this time because, yes, you hurt me. Deeply. But I think I've hurt you too, many times since we've known each other. I wasn't intending to, but I don't consider myself an innocent in this…" I am about to tell him that, despite all our screwups, I am here for him, with him, and that I will be for as long as he wants, but I don't have time, because he interrupts me.

"Come with me."

I stare at him in astonishment for a few seconds, just blinking. "What?"

"Come with me," he repeats in a serious voice. Is he actually asking me to go with him to his parents' house?

"Thomas…you haven't seen your mother for a long time; don't you think it would be better for everyone if you two had some time to yourselves?" I offer in a soft voice.

"I need you by my side."

I can't stop staring at him in shock. He wants me there with him. He wants my support, my presence. It's a huge step that I wasn't expecting from Thomas, especially now that I know what it means for him to set foot in that place again after all this time. I can't tell him no. I don't want to.

"Okay, I'll come with you."

"DO YOU REALIZE THAT OUR country has the highest incarceration rate in the world?" I start off indignantly as Thomas concentrates on driving toward Portland. "And that's to say nothing of the incidents of police brutality! There are millions of cases of physical and psychological violence, corruption, and abuse of power committed against American citizens, especially in communities of color. It's infuriating! How is it possible that we are in the twenty-first century, and we still can't stop this national shame?" Before vehemently shutting my laptop, I make sure to save the file with all my documentation for the article I'm working on. I've decided to take it with me so as not to waste precious time, and I can have Leila take a look at it when we get there.

I put the laptop back in my bag along with a packet of documents I've gathered. I take my water bottle out of the BMW's cup holder and sip from it while I watch Thomas from the corner of my eye. He's nervous. I can see it in the way he drums his fingers on the steering wheel, in his skittish look, and in the way he keeps fiddling with his tongue piercing almost compulsively. Plus, I know he didn't get a wink of sleep last night.

Last night, after I told him that I would go with him, he held me tightly in his arms, trying to convey with his body everything he couldn't express in words. And I did the same. I held on tight to his powerful shoulders, running my fingers through his hair and along the back of his neck with soft touches. We stayed like that for a while until I asked him to stay and sleep over in my new apartment. We spent the night together. Admittedly, there was a small part of me that didn't want to do that, because, after our argument, I would have liked to have demonstrated a little more backbone. But that would have been completely pointless. In the moment, neither of us was capable of living up to some moral principle. All we knew was an irrepressible need to feel one another, to touch one another, and to belong to one another. Because that's how the two of us find peace: being together. And together, we also find the strength to face anything.

We've been driving for about forty minutes, and I've been trying to make conversation the whole time, but all I've gotten from him are lazy grunts.

"You hungry?" he asks impassively, his eyes fixed on the road and his right hand on the steering wheel. "There's a truck stop a few miles ahead."

We left the house without breakfast this morning. Thomas didn't feel up to it; he was already very anxious, and I skipped my usual bowl of cereal in solidarity. But now I'm so hungry that I could plow through the snack sections of every convenience store in the state of Oregon.

"I am, a little bit."

"Just a little, eh?" He takes his eyes off the road for a few seconds to look at me. "So that wasn't your stomach that's been growling ever since we left…?" He laughs softly, one corner of his mouth tilting up slightly. I rub his shoulder and find myself laughing along with him, charmed by his smile.

We pull into the truck stop, park, and get out of the car. Thomas takes a few bills out of the pocket of his black jeans and puts them in my hand. "Here, get what you want; I'm gonna take a piss."

I roll my eyes in exasperation. "*To pee*, Thomas. People say, *I'm going to pee*, or better yet, *I'm going to the bathroom*. Also, I have a job, I think I can pay for my breakfast." I hand the money back to him and head for the doors with a triumphant grin. "Do you want anything?" I ask him before going inside.

He doesn't reply as he tucks the money back into his pocket. "Nah," he says finally, "I'm good. A cigarette will be enough for me right now."

I cock an eyebrow. "You sure?"

"Yeah, go on. I'll meet you in there." He urges me on with a wave of his hand.

When I get inside, I head straight for their small café area. When the waitress takes my order, I get an English muffin and a coffee. I sip it while watching a music video on the TV mounted on the far wall. The moment I bite into my English muffin, my phone goes off.

"Vanessa, this is your mother." Her strident voice makes my ears ring.

"Yes, I know; you're in my contacts. What's up?" I answer, wedging the phone between my shoulder and my ear as I swallow my bite.

"I haven't heard back from you about my dinner invitation."

"It's only been two days, Mom. And I've been really busy." It's partially true. And partially not. In actuality, I just haven't made a decision yet.

"Of course, I understand that. But I would hope that amongst the thousands of commitments that populate your days, you could find a small opening for your mother, maybe? It would mean so much to me, Vanessa."

I can't help but give a snort inside my head because I can see the game she's playing. The same one as always: trying to make me feel sorry for her and then playing on my guilty feelings because she knows it will always work on me. "Okay, Mom. I accept your invitation. Or rather, we accept. Thomas will come too, as you suggested, but I can't tell you when. Right now, I'm struggling to catch my breath between work and school commitments. But I promise you that I will do my best to make time." I take a drink of my coffee and immediately wipe my mouth with a napkin.

"Okay, I'll be waiting for you call, then. In any case, I was thinking of making a reservation at Maple Garden. Does Thomas eat meat?" she asks with a breeziness that feels so out of place for her, especially when she's talking about the boy she kicked me out over. But I choose to ignore this. I suppose this is her way of apologizing and trying to make a new start.

"I thought we were going to eat at home? But either way, he doesn't have any food restrictions; anything will be fine."

"Eating at home was the plan, but then Victor and I thought it might have felt too formal."

So Victor will be there too...fantastic.

There's a moment of silence, and then she adds: "Tell me, how are you doing? Is school going well?"

"It's challenging, like always," I answer vaguely, dusting muffin residue from my shirt.

"Well, you know, hard work always wins in the end." It's a mantra of hers that I know by heart.

"Yeah, I hope that's true. At least then this will all have been worth it." I glance quickly at my wristwatch and decide it's time for me to go. We exchange a few more pleasantries before saying goodbye. I finish my breakfast, put a tip on the table, and go to the register, but when it's my turn to pay and I'm just about to reach for my wallet, Thomas materializes at my side. He asks the cashier for a pack of Marlboro Reds and, without giving me a chance to do anything, also pays for my breakfast. The checkout guy gives him the receipt, and he crumples it in his fist before slipping it into his pocket with a sly little grin. I glare at him, but he ignores me, deliberately.

As we head for the exit, he drapes an arm around my shoulders and kisses my left temple. "You always complain that I'm not gentlemanly. But when I do some gentlemanly stuff, you still complain. You women are all the same, never happy."

"I hate those kinds of generalizations; don't compare me to other women. Also, sorry, but as far I know, you don't work. How do you pay for all this?" I gesture to his car before getting into it. "The bike, the car... How do you always have cash on hand?" I fasten my seat belt and stare at him, waiting for a response.

"I run a human trafficking ring," Thomas nonchalantly turns the key in the ignition and starts the car.

"Ha-ha," I reply, not amused at all.

"I've had the bike for a while," he answers with a more serious expression. "It got pretty beaten up in the accident, so before I left the city, I had my friend's dad fix it up. He has a garage. As for the rest of it, my grandparents left a small trust fund for Leila and me that I was able to access when I turned twenty-one. Since I already had the basketball scholarship, the first thing I did was buy this car. But it spends more time with my sister than with me."

"Why did you decide to fix the motorcycle instead of getting a new one?"

"Because the last memory I have of my brother was on that bike."

I feel a pang in my heart that I try to ignore. "Were you ever afraid to drive it again? After the accident?"

Thomas shakes his head, staring out the windshield with his left elbow resting on the glass of the rolled-down window. "It's an outlet that I need. I like pushing limits. I like taking risks. And I like to cheat death. Even basketball doesn't give me the spike of adrenaline that I get when I take the bike out at top speed."

"You like cheating death even after what happened?" I murmur, gulping.

"Especially after what happened," he answers gravely, and I can tell from his suddenly darkening look that it's time to close this topic.

We spend the rest of the trip in silence: him lost in his own thoughts, me working on my article but always with one eye on him, trying to spot some microscopic change in his face. After another hour of driving north, we finally get to Portland. The atmosphere hovering around us isn't what I would have chosen, but getting to delve into what was, until recently, his world, his nuances and habits, makes my heart swell. And that's why, when he suggests we take a tour of the city, I enthusiastically agree. Even though I realize what is behind his proposal: fear of setting foot back in what was once his home.

We cross the red bridge over the Willamette River and pass by the downtown buildings that gleam in the midday sun. We park and walk away from the city center, along small streets covered in dry leaves that crunch under our feet. Eventually, we find ourselves in front of his old high school. Thomas tells me about all the trouble he made and the teachers he got into scrapes with. Then we come to a large open lot that local kids used as a meeting place. They came every weekend to work on their bikes, fixing them up and improvising small neighborhood races.

From there, Thomas takes me to an empty and neglected basketball court with cracks all over the asphalt and a rusty hoop without a net. There's a miraculously still-inflated ball abandoned under a cement bench. Thomas grabs it and starts dribbling with his right hand.

"Me and some of the guys used to spend whole afternoons here." He tosses the ball at the hoop, sinking it on the first attempt with impressive ease. The ball returns to him in two bounces. "He always came along...my brother..."

Another dribble.

Another basket.

"He'd sit right there." He points to the bench in front of us. "And he'd cheer for me." His voice breaks a little bit, as though he can see the boy sitting there now. His eyes grow moist. "He believed in me," he continues. "He was probably the only person who did. The only person who was truly convinced that there was a future in this thing that came so easily to me. He was so sure that, sooner or later, someone was going to notice my potential, and then I'd be rich and famous, and he'd spend the rest of his life in the lap of luxury thanks to me and my success. In the end, he was partly right. Someone did notice me. But I have yet to become rich and famous." A bitter shadow of a smile curls his lips while he struggles to tear his gaze away from that bench.

"He said that?" I ask, taking his hand and entwining our fingers before resting my head against his chest. Thomas nods. "It's not a bad plan. He clearly knew his stuff," I answer tenderly.

He cocks his head to the side and observes me for a long moment. I'm forced to tilt my face up to look him in the eyes.

"What's wrong?"

"Nothing. Just he...he would have liked you. A lot. The whole book thing and the good manners..." He tucks a strand of hair behind my ear before sliding his fingers down my neck. "He would have been so into you. He used to scold me every time he heard me swear. Not to mention all the incredibly boring books he was always trying to convince me to read."

I swallow thickly as I feel my heart fluttering and my eyes stinging. Thomas cups my cheeks with his big hands and gently rubs my cheekbones with his thumbs, wiping away the tears I didn't realize I'd shed. "Don't cry, Ness."

I shake my head. "I–I'm not crying," I lie, sniffling. "It's…it's just that…I'm so full of sadness for you, for everything you've had to go through. For what you lost, the suffering you've been forced to endure every single day of your life. I wish so much that it wasn't like this for you. You don't know what I would give to ease your heart and offer you some peace or relief. You have no idea what I would give, Thomas, to let you experience happiness—real happiness. I want that more than anything in the world."

He looks at me, his eyes now cloudy with coldness. "I don't want you to feel that way. I've learned to live with it. I had to."

I take his hands in mine and give them a tight squeeze. "Sure, but what did it cost you?"

He doesn't answer because we both know what the answer is. It cost him everything. His innocence. His humanity. His childhood. Everything has been infected with feelings of guilt and sorrow that will never go away. Never. Because pain changes you forever.

We are both silent for a few moments, then Thomas steps back, frowning. He kicks the ball with a dull thud, brushes past me, and says, "I'm hungry; let's get out of here."

I just stand there, dazed and staring into space. Only now do I realize that I've unwittingly upset him again. I just can't bring myself to accept there's a part of Thomas that will always be broken. Doomed. That his unhappiness was twisted by his father's monstrous nature, and that, now, he will be forced to spend the rest of his life haunted by his regrets.

We walk silently, turning onto a narrow street that heads slightly uphill. Thomas's phone rings several times, but he keeps rejecting the calls. He walks beside me with a determined stride and lowered eyes, though he still holds my hand.

"Where are we going?"

"To eat."

I take a quick glance down at my outfit, hoping I don't look too sloppy with my turtleneck sweater, black skinny jeans, and the ever-present white Converse on my feet.

"Oh. I thought that Leila and your mother were waiting to have lunch with us."

"Change of plans."

My eyes widen. "In the sense that you don't want to go there anymore?"

"In the sense that I don't want to go there right now."

"Shouldn't you at least give them a heads-up?" I ask in a soft voice.

He turns irritably to me. "I already did."

I don't insist; I don't want to push him. I just follow him and pray that his bad mood can be assuaged by a hot meal.

We arrive in front of a pub famous, apparently, for its gigantic sandwiches. I stop to check the day's menu, written on a blackboard at the entrance.

"I recommend the roast chicken one. Joseph's food is unsurpassed," Thomas informs me.

"Okay then, I'll go for the roast chicken sandwich."

As we enter, we are greeted by the smell of ancient wood. The carpet under our feet is patterned in red and green geometrical shapes. The walls are claret colored, and the furnishings are vaguely Irish in style. The room is packed; waiters rush from one side of the place to the other, each holding more plates than seems humanly possible. Maybe I should consider getting some private lessons from them? We look for a free table and, spotting one, sit down.

Thomas seems at ease here, which reassures me. But we don't even have time to open the menus before a loud sound explodes through the room, making us both whirl around.

"Well, I'll be damned!" A plump woman in her fifties with her graying hair pulled into a bun comes toward us, both her mouth and eyes wide open. She's wearing a black uniform, complete with a sauce- and oil-stained white apron over it. As soon as she reaches us, she attacks Thomas, wrapping him in a bone-crushing hug as she ruffles his hair. Strangely, he lets her do it.

"Big fella, this is a surprise!"

"Hey, Miranda," he says, fixing his hair a little bit awkwardly. This is a completely new sight for me.

I put the menu down, lean my elbows on the table, and enjoy the scene before me. I give Thomas a mischievous grin, which he responds to immediately with a look that says, *Not a single word.*

"I'm just passing through. I didn't know you were working here," he continues, turning to Miranda.

"Is that your polite way of telling me to get out of your hair?" she whispers teasingly, putting one hand on her hip and using the other to pat Thomas's shoulder.

"No, of course not. It's just that the last time we saw each other, you were a cocktail waitress at Star's Motel; what happened in the meantime?"

"Ah, the usual stuff, son. Gerald had a little problem with the tax man and, less than a week later, we found ourselves out on our asses. That sweetheart Nolan put in a good word for me with Joseph, so now I'm here. Fortunately, Gerald got hired on as a garbage collector. Not so bad, eh?" She grins ironically, and then, when she turns in my direction, she gives a little gasp. "And who might this lovely lady be?"

"Vanessa. It's nice to meet you." I smile at her, holding out my hand.

"A beautiful name for a beautiful girl." She winks at me. "So tell me, are you two here…together?" she asks slyly, nudging Thomas's shoulder.

I give him an uncertain look, waiting for him to say something but ready, in my heart, to be disappointed. To my enormous relief, that doesn't happen. With his eyes on mine and his hand stroking his stubbly chin, Thomas nods decisively.

"You don't say..." Miranda exclaims, incredulous. "I take it you finally got your head on straight." Then, she turns to me. "Do you know, I've known this boy since he was six years old? I watched him grow up alongside my son, the two of them getting into all sorts of things together." She takes Thomas's cheek between her thumb and forefinger, pinching it as though he were still a little kid. "That reminds me, does Ryan know you're here?"

He shakes his head, folds his arms over his chest, and slides down in his chair a bit, spreading his legs slightly. "Not unless my big-mouth sister told him."

"Come by and see him if you can. I'm sure he'll be happy to see you again. He won't say it, but he misses you. We can all see it" she admits with an air of melancholy and a concerned look on her face.

"I will." He smiles gratefully at her, covering her hand on his shoulder with his own.

"You heard about your old man, didn't you?" Miranda finally asks him.

Thomas stiffens, and his jaw tightens. He nods, with a darkened downward gaze.

She sighs, tightening her grip on his shoulder. "I'm glad to see you here. Finally back home, with your people... The neighborhood wasn't the same without you, big fella. You never should have left."

"It was necessary," he hisses through clenched teeth. He's doing everything he can not to be rude right now, and it's clear he's only putting forth this effort for her. He respects her. He doesn't want to risk hurting her feelings. I wonder if Miranda knows all the horrible things Thomas's father did.

"I understand, son, I understand. Just, this time, please do one thing: Come say goodbye before you leave. Don't just disappear into thin air."

He promises her that he will. Then we order our lunches and eat them in near silence.

After we finish eating, we take a walk around the neighborhood. Thomas is continuing to stall. Not that I blame him; I myself am starting to feel a lump in my throat at the idea that, sooner or later, we are going to walk into the house he ran away from and never looked back.

After wandering around aimlessly for a while, we sit down on a low wall near a fountain shaped like a sailboat. We linger there, resting in the quiet and staring into space. Thomas, with a blank look on his face, starts smoking a cigarette. The wind begins to pick up as the sun sets, coloring the river in the distance with shades of red. It's now five in the afternoon.

I decide to speak. "Thomas…"

"Not yet," he cuts in, already knowing where I'm going with this.

"It's starting to get late. If not now, then when?" I try to say it gently.

"When I feel like it."

"What's holding you back? What are you afraid will happen there?" I caress his cheek tenderly, trying to conceal my own anguish. "I'm here for you, so talk to me."

He scrutinizes me carefully, his features tense. Almost like he's annoyed by my care for him.

"I'm not afraid of anything." He moves my hand away from his face and hops down from the wall. He stands in front of me and, grabbing my hips, helps me down. "I just don't feel like going over there, that's all. Not yet," he stresses, adamant.

I give up with a sigh, tucking my hair behind my ears even as the wind tosses it into my face. "All right. But on the off chance that you don't feel like going at all anymore, I really think you should at least tell—"

He presses his index finger to my chapped lips, silencing me.

"I will go to the house, okay? I promise that I will. But I need more time. I need it, Ness." He pauses for a moment, and his expression grows even more melancholy. Then he rubs a hand over his face, as if to chase the bad thoughts away. "I haven't seen her in over a year. But for me, it feels like just yesterday. It feels like it was yesterday when her eyes were begging me to just disappear for good. This place is bringing it all back to me. All the things I tried so hard to forget. Do you want to know what I'm really afraid of? Myself. Because ever since we left Corvallis, I've had an insane urge to crawl into a bottle and just destroy everything. And the more time passes, the closer I get to that moment, the stronger that urge gets. But I don't want...I don't want to fuck it all up. I don't want to give in to this impulse that is eating me alive. And that's why I'm telling you that I need more time."

His confession catches me off guard, leaving me speechless for a moment.

"I'm s-sorry, I...I'm sorry you're feeling like that, I know this isn't easy for you. None of what you're experiencing is easy. So if you need more time, I get that." I twine my fingers with his and raise myself up on my tiptoes to plant a kiss on his lips. "Take all the time you want. We can stay here, or if you'd like, we can walk or just drive around... What I'm saying is that I'm with you. Completely at your disposal."

He presses his forehead to mine, wrapping an arm around my waist. "Completely at my disposal, eh? I'll have to keep that in mind..." He lifts the corner of his mouth. It's the suggestion of a smile, but it doesn't reach his eyes. "Before I go, there is someone I'd like to see."

"Who?"

"Ryan, Miranda's son," he explains as we start walking again.

"Miranda said you guys grew up together; is that true?" I ask.

He nods. "His uncles were our neighbors. For a while, Miranda, Gerald, and Ryan lived with them. When I was a kid and my father would come home drunk, I'd go out and sit on the porch steps to avoid listening to the screaming. I'd always see him there on the other side of the fence, determined to play with this deflated ball. I didn't realize it then, but we were both looking for a quiet place. Me, to get away from my father, him from his huge messed-up family. The first time we ever spoke to each other, I was watching him try to play with that ball for the hundredth time, and I decided to throw mine to him. We started passing it back and forth, and ten minutes later, we were friends. From that moment on, we were inseparable."

"Then what happened?"

"What happened was that I left."

"And you haven't heard from him since?"

He shakes his head. "No, I left without even saying goodbye. Chickenshit move, I know, but it was for the best. Or at least it was best for me. I never really tried to put myself in his shoes. I was sure he'd understand. He knew about everything that I was going through, because he was having a hard time too. And he knew that I'd been toying with the idea of leaving for a while, but the way I just left him behind along with everything else..." He glances around. "Well, I'm not proud of it."

"I'm sure he'll be happy to see you."

"Sure, probably. But that won't stop him from giving me a good belt in the face for disappearing on him like that. Of course, then he'd offer me some ice for the bruise and a beer," he says, looking amused.

"Should we call in reinforcements?" I answer in mock worry.

"Nah, he's a gentle giant, incapable of holding a grudge. Just like me, right?" he teases with a sideways glance at me.

We walk a couple more miles before stopping in front of a closed tattoo parlor. Thomas puts his face close to the window, and using his hands to shield his eyes, he peers inside.

"It's Sunday; they're closed. We can try again tomorrow."

But it's like talking to a brick wall. Thomas starts knocking on the glass, and I roll my eyes, shaking my head. Does he ever listen to anyone in his life?

"See? I told you, it's closed," I say again, folding my arms over my chest and shivering a little bit from the cold.

He shakes his head, unconvinced. "I know him; he's definitely in there sleeping."

I raise my eyebrows and get closer to the door as well. "Sleeping? At work?"

He nods. "This is my uncle's shop. I told you about it, remember?" He looks at me, and I confirm with a nod. "He hired Ryan on to work for him a few months before I left, and I remember that he'd always rather nap in the stockroom than go home." He knocks again.

"He doesn't like his house?" I ask innocently, peering inside.

"His 'house' was a filthy room in the disgusting motel where his mom worked."

That stops me in my tracks. The motel he mentioned to Miranda earlier? The one where they had "a little problem with the tax man"? "Whoa, what a situation..." I mutter with a grimace.

"You have no idea." Thomas is now banging his fist continuously against the window. Then, a tall muscular figure with electric green hair shaved into a mohawk appears. He's got tattoos all over, even on his face, and when he moves to open the door, I instinctively step back, alarmed.

"Don't you know how to read a fucking sign? We're closed..." he shouts, slamming the door open with a bang, but the rest of his sentence dies on his lips when he realizes who is standing in front of him. His eyes widen and he shakes his head in shock. "Holy shit..."

Thomas and Ryan just stare at each other, neither saying a word. Thomas rubs a hand over his chin and looks him up and down. "Huh. I thought it'd be worse. You still dress like a drug trafficker, and I remember the hair being longer, but on the other hand, I see that you've still got all your teeth. So that's something," he teases.

"You ugly son of a bitch! You roll back into town after more than a year, and you can't even give me a fucking warning?" For a second, I'm afraid that a fist is actually about to hit my boyfriend's beautiful face, but then Ryan's chiseled features soften, giving way to a warm smile. He gives Thomas a big hug, patting his back.

"You know I love a surprise," Thomas answers, returning the clasp. I observe this moment from a few steps away, as though I am watching it on TV. I notice how alike they look: the same height, strong physiques, their tattoos like a second skin, and both of them exude a dark allure that can inspire awe at first glance. But unlike Thomas, who only wears a couple of thick-banded rings and his brother's bandanna on his wrist, Ryan has thick chains around his neck and matching metal bracelets.

"What happened to you, man? We thought you'd gone missing!"

"Yeah, I wish," Thomas answers, making him laugh. Ryan shifts his gaze to me, not bothering to hide his surprise. When Thomas realizes that I'm getting embarrassed, he comes to my aid and takes my hand, as if to reassure me.

Ryan looks at our interlaced fingers, stares at his friend, and says, "Oh shit. Please say you didn't come all this way to tell me you're gonna be a dad?"

Thomas and I both start, our eyes bugging out. "What? No!" we answer in unison as Thomas abruptly drops my hand.

"Don't you think I've got enough bullshit in my life?" He claps Ryan on the shoulder and brushes by him, going into the tattoo parlor.

Twenty-One

"SORRY FOR SHOOTING MY MOUTH off just now, but I don't put anything past him."

You don't put anything past him, including knocking a girl up? Reassuring.

"No problem, don't worry about it." I should stop staring at him, it's really not polite, but all those tattoos are mesmerizing. "That tiger looks great; does it have some meaning?" I ask, unable to keep my curiosity at bay. I point to the left side of his head where the drawing starts, ending around the back of his neck.

"Of course. Every tattoo has a meaning. In the Chinese zodiac, the tiger embodies strength, power, and passion," he explains as we pass a spotless counter with some sketchbooks, a laptop, and some binders on it.

"And why did you choose to put it there?" I glance around in search of Thomas, who appears to have vanished only to emerge from a storage room holding three cans of Sprite.

"It was the only open space left," Ryan laughs, gesturing for me to sit on one of the couches in the middle of the room.

Thomas pops the three cans, hands one to me, and then starts chatting with Ryan as if their period of separation never happened. They reminisce about the old days together; then Ryan tells us about how he's putting some money aside because he'd like to open his own tattoo studio in California. He acknowledges the opportunity that Thomas's uncle gave him but believes that the time has come to spread his wings and fly.

As I drink my Sprite and listen to them talk, I notice how Ryan avoids asking about the real reason Thomas and I are here in town. I'm sure he knows about Thomas's father and his situation, and he probably doesn't want to prod the wound. After a while, I decide to leave them to their conversation and wander around the shop, examining every detail, from the adjustable bed covered with a disposable sheet of paper to the stainless-steel tray set up next to it with a tattoo gun and a few packages of needles. I linger over the art on the walls. The more I look at them, the more familiar they seem. Only after a few moments do I understand why... Lotus flowers, a dragon shaped into an ouroboros, an hourglass wrapped in barbed wire...they're the same designs that Thomas has tattooed on himself. These are his drawings. I smile to myself at the idea of his uncle putting them on display for the public. He has every reason to be proud.

I move at a snail's pace, bewitched by the art surrounding me, until I find myself staring at a small display case full of piercing hardware of all varieties, small colorful gems, and leather bracelets. My eyes land on the lightest one: strips of leather twisted around silver threads to form an elegant, delicate braid with a clear stone in the center.

"See something you like, Ness?" My boyfriend's lips brush my cheek and make me shiver as he grabs my hips.

"More than one thing. In addition to this bracelet, I couldn't help but admire all the designs." I cast a glance around at the walls. "They're your work, right?"

He studies them with a look that's difficult to decipher, a mixture of discomfort and nostalgia. Then he nods.

"They're beautiful, Thomas." I put a hand on his chest as I turn toward him.

"They're just drawings."

"But they're your drawings."

He rolls his eyes, kisses my forehead, and tells me we can go.

"Don't disappear again, you hear?" Ryan says to Thomas as we tell him goodbye before leaving the shop. "And give me a call if he isn't treating you right," he advises me in a good-natured sort of way as he shakes my hand. I smile, assuring him that I will.

As soon as the door closes behind us, Thomas realizes that he's forgotten his cigarettes inside. So, while he goes back for them, I wait outside for him. As I let my eyes wander, I realize there's a man nearby, fifties, with a goatee and a put-together vibe. He's leaning against a car door on the other side of the street with his arms and ankles crossed, and he's looking in my direction. Even though it's dark, he's wearing sunglasses, so I'm not sure if he's looking at me, but he makes me uncomfortable either way.

I hug myself and glance around. It's almost half past six, and there's not much traffic on the road around here. The stranger gives me a weak smile and waves a hand at me. Yeah, he's looking right at me. I watch as he crosses the street toward me. Suddenly, a whole range of shiver-inducing scenarios start playing out in my head. I step back until I reach the tattoo parlor's door, running into Thomas's chest as he emerges.

"Hey, Ness, what's wrong? You're pale." He takes my face in his hands, examining me carefully.

"I–I don't know. There's this man who—" I try to explain, but I'm interrupted by the man's voice.

"It's my fault. I must have spooked her; I didn't mean to."

When Thomas raises his head, his face changes radically, turning hard. He lets out an exasperated sigh, and I hear him swear under his breath. "The fuck is this? A reunion?"

"What?" I murmur, unsettled and confused.

"It's great to see you again too."

I turn slowly to face the person who, up until just a few seconds ago, I thought was a creeper. He puts his glasses on the top of his head and keeps talking. "Your sister told me you'd be here today, but I wouldn't have bet a single dollar on you coming back. I'm impressed." The man shifts his gaze to me and smiles. "My apologies, I didn't mean to frighten you. I'm Robert, this troublemaker's uncle. But you can just call me Rob. You're Vanessa, right? My niece told me a lot about you."

Oh. His uncle. This is Thomas's uncle. The owner of the shop I was attempting to take refuge in. I give him an embarrassed smile.

"Yes, I'm Vanessa."

Rob steps forward and shakes my hand with a smile. I shake in return, and I have to admit that I'm starting to feel a bit overwhelmed. In the space of just a few hours, I've already met three different people who each, in one way or another, represent an important part of Thomas's life.

With both of his hands clasped around mine, he looks me in the eye and says seriously, "Thank you for all you've done."

"What...what did I do?"

"I know perfectly well that if my nephew is here today, you are the person that I have to thank."

"Can we cut the shit?" Thomas breaks in, giving him a sharp look. He pulls a cigarette from the pack and brings it to his mouth, frowning. "What are you doing here?"

They stare at each other a long moment. Then, Robert raises both hands. "Came to see my nephew, didn't I? I knew you'd come find Ryan. You look good," he notes, patting him on the shoulder.

Thomas snorts. "If you say so..." he mutters, cigarette clenched between his teeth.

"Were you headed somewhere? Can I get you a drink? There's a bar around the corner," his uncle suggests.

"No, we're busy," Thomas says shortly, and I give him a glare. But his uncle seems used to his disposition and doesn't appear to pay it any mind. In fact, he seems to have expected it. I'd always imagined, from the few stories that Thomas told me, that his uncle was something like a mentor to him. Yet, Thomas seems irritated by his presence now. Though, not to the point of just walking away and leaving him here as he would have under different circumstances.

"Thank you, maybe some other time," I answer politely.

He smiles at me, nodding, and then shifts his gaze to Thomas. "So...have you already been by to see your mother?"

Thomas shakes his head, looking at an undefined point to his right while exhaling cigarette smoke.

"Are you going to go?" his uncle asks him with a grave look.

"That's what I'm here for, right?" my boyfriend mutters, putting out his cigarette under his heel.

Not feeling the need to say anything else, his uncle approaches him and pats him on the shoulder again. "Everything will be fine, don't worry."

"Yeah, all great," he answers angrily, grabbing my hand. "Come on, let's go."

Robert steps back to let us pass, but just after we say goodbye and leave him behind, he calls us back. "Thomas, wait!"

We turn around.

"Don't you want to know which hospital he's in?"

I feel Thomas's hand squeezing mine, hard enough to make me squirm a little. When he notices that, he drops my hand immediately. He moves slowly toward his uncle, seeing red. "Are you joking?"

"Thomas...with the state he's in, there's a good chance he's never leaving that hospital."

"And you know how much I fucking care!" he rants.

Some passersby on the sidewalks turn to look at us. Robert squeezes his arm tightly, as if to communicate to him that he's trying to tell Thomas something particularly important and he needs to listen. "Has it ever occurred to you that it could be good for you? Not for him—screw that bastard—but for yourself? To free yourself from the weight of all that—"

"How dare you come here and say that to me," he interrupts, jabbing a finger at him. "That weight you're talking about isn't going to go away if I have a heart-to-heart with that son of a bitch. Save the feel-good speeches for my sister, not me!"

For a moment, we all just stare at each other in silence.

Robert shakes his head, and I spot a glimmer of regret in his eyes. "Do you think this is easy for me? Do you think that, after what I found out, I don't want to—"

"And what did you find out?" Thomas lets out a derisive laugh, cracking the knuckles on one hand. "You think you know everything, but you don't. Do you seriously think alcohol was his only problem? That it was just the drinking? And the accident was the trigger? No, but that's what she wanted to you to believe. Because she was terrified of what he would do to her if people knew the truth. But deep down, you always knew that something was wrong, didn't you? All those questions you'd ask JC and me when we were kids, all the extra attention you gave us...I didn't understand it until later. But like the coward you are, instead of taking action and doing something about it, you just put your blinders on instead. I get it, making enemies of the cops in this country is scary. But she was your sister, your blood. You should have done more."

Robert takes a step back, as if Thomas's words have physically struck him. I watch them eye each other, not knowing what to do. Thomas looks for all appearances like he's about one step away from attacking his uncle. Robert, on the other hand, is looking at Thomas with a pity in his eyes that makes me shudder. And I...I'm deeply troubled. Was it really like Thomas said? Was his uncle aware of everything that Thomas's mother was going through and just chose not to do anything to end that horror? Goddamn, she's his *sister*.

Thomas grabs me firmly by the wrist and pulls me away. This time, he doesn't pay any attention when Robert once again begs him to stop.

"Did your uncle really know what he was doing to her?" I ask when we get back to the car, wringing my hands.

"He suspected," Thomas answers a few moments later. "He tried to get information out of us when we were together. Especially from me because I spent so much time with him in the studio. But when everything got worse after the accident, Mom convinced him that it was all because of grief, and that alcohol was the only problem. She left everything else out. I think he accepted that version because it was easier to believe that the police officer who was married to his sister became an alcoholic after losing his son, rather than admitting he'd always been one. And if that wasn't enough, my uncle was involved in some shady business at the time that gave him the money he needed to keep the tattoo parlor going. My father knew all about it. And if my uncle had tried to do something, he would have thrown my uncle in jail in a second, taken away everything he'd built, everything he'd sacrificed for all his life, and left his family destitute."

"I...I don't know what to say..."

"There's not much too say. This shit is my life, Ness. Now you get why I wanted to keep you out of it." The way he says it and the silence we immediately sink into after chill my blood.

We continue our drive, not speaking. Road signs tell me we're heading for the southeast area of the city. We pass through a dimly lit tunnel. When we exit, we take a sharp right, and after a few miles, Thomas parks the car in front of a run-down duplex. The grass in the front yard is overgrown; the fence is rusty. Siding is falling off the facade.

He turns off the engine and just sits there, his hands clenched on the steering wheel as he scrutinizes the two-story house in front of him where, through the curtains, the light gleams.

Discomfort tightening my throat, I unbuckle my seat belt and grab my bag out of the back seat. I open the door and put one foot down on the asphalt, but when I realize that Thomas hasn't moved an inch, I get back into the car.

"Hey, are we...are we not going in?"

He takes a deep breath and shakes his head feebly. "I don't know if I can do it." The despair in his voice makes me shiver.

"Thomas..." I murmur, with all the softness I would use to address a frightened child. I put my hand on his leather-clad shoulder. "Listen, I know that today has been harder than expected. And if the pressure is too much, we can get out of here at any time. Even now," I reassure him. "However, we have come all this way... You're just a few steps away from seeing her again after all this time. Give yourself a chance. You're not alone. You have Leila and me with you."

Even though he continues to frown at the house, my words seem to have given him enough strength to take that first step. We get out of the car and walk over to the fence, which creaks when we open it. The sky above us is black; the air is getting colder and colder, typical of an autumn night. We cross the small yard, and when we reach the door, Thomas stands motionless with his hands in his pockets, just staring at it. From inside, we can hear the muffled sound of a TV. He's still frozen. I give him all the time he needs; I don't want to make him feel that he's being forced in any way to do something he isn't completely ready to do.

"This place isn't so bad, you know?" I say, glancing around and trying to ease the tension. "Though I don't have a lot to compare it to because I've never set foot outside of Corvallis. Except for the time I flew to Washington with Alex and his mom. Though in that case, we spent most of the time in the hotel with the babysitter. I mean, of course we went out some of the time, and it was a lot of fun when we did." I stop talking when I run out of breath and clasp my hands behind my back.

He frowns at me. My blathering must have irritated him even more. *Congratulations, Vanessa, you're so great at lifting people's spirits.* Thomas backs away onto the porch, and I follow him. He brings a cigarette to his mouth, shields it from the wind, and lights it. Then he leans his elbows on the wooden porch railing and blows out a mouthful of smoke. I watch him survey the surrounding area, lingering on a small neglected storage shed at one end of the yard.

"This place sucks," is all he says before taking another long drag from his cigarette. I don't answer him. We stay like this until he finishes his cigarette and tosses the butt over the railing, all in complete silence. Then, he looks at me, taking my chin between his thumb and forefinger and rubbing it delicately. He rests his forehead against mine and traces my jawline with his fingers. "I got you something."

I start. "For me? What? When?" I murmur in surprise, our lips brushing against each other.

He quirks a corner of his mouth in a smug, if weary, grin. From his jacket pocket, he produces a leather bracelet. The bracelet that I saw at his uncle's shop. He got it for me. I stare at him in disbelief, moved. He takes my arm, pulls up the sleeve of my jacket, and ties it around my wrist.

"Don't think I don't know how much it cost you to be here with me. You had to change your shifts at work and push back all your other commitments. And after what I said to you at the party, you didn't have to. You could have told me no. It would have been more convenient for you. At least you could have spared yourself that awkward scene just now." He takes a deep breath. "I don't know how this evening is gonna go, Ness. Honestly…I really don't know. But I do know that I haven't really shown you how much your being here today means to me. You are the only thing that feels right in a sea of wrong, and if something—anything—happens to make you question that, just think back on this moment. Think about this bracelet, which is just my way of saying thank you. Thank you for staying with me, despite everything." Not giving me a chance to answer, he puts his soft, warm lips over mine. He twines his hands through my hair with a sweet calm that dissolves all the accumulated tension of the day. And then, with a trembling exhalation, he breaks the kiss, moving a few inches away. I feel the ground falling away under my feet.

"Now we can go in," he says, touching my cheek.

Leila opens the door for us. "Oh my God, thank you; you came. I was afraid you weren't going to show up again." Her incredulous big green eyes flash at me. She grabs me by the shoulders and pulls me to her, giving me a tight hug. "Come in, come in, it's freezing out there."

Thomas crosses the threshold with a certain apprehension, and his gaze starts darting around like a caged puppy. His chest rises and falls in an agitated fashion. He seems lost, and his shoulders are tense. I'm sure he's currently fighting the urge to flee.

The moment the door closes behind us, he entwines his hand with mine and holds it in a firm grip. Needy. I look up at him, surprised by this all-too-spontaneous gesture. If I know anything about Thomas, it's that when he has difficult feelings, he retreats into himself. But now, instead, everything about him is telling me just one thing: *I need you.*

I reinforce my own grip and wrap my other hand around his forearm to reassure him. To make sure he knows that I am here. That he's not alone. And that he can do this.

"How was the trip?" Leila asks, gesturing for us to follow her into the living room. Unlike Thomas, she seems extremely calm, as if this was just a normal family dinner. Thomas gives an absent-minded nod, busy examining every corner of the house with a scrupulous eye.

"It was smooth sailing," I break in. "Sorry for running late. We took a mini tour of the city, and Thomas was nice enough to take me to lunch at—"

"Joseph's," she finishes, interrupting me with a smile.

"Yeah, how did you know?" I ask her, smiling back.

"He loves that place; we used to go there all the time." She gives her brother a warm look, which he does not reciprocate. An awkward silence descends upon us, and I rush to break it, telling Leila that I brought all the material for the article so I can get her feedback on it.

"Are you by yourself?" Thomas's rough, hoarse voice seems to burst into the room.

Leila shakes her head. "Mom's upstairs changing. She's changed five times since she heard you were coming. She couldn't relax; you should have seen her..." She shakes her head, and the corners of her mouth tilt up in a tender expression. "She also made stew, your favorite." She gives his shoulder an affectionate shove, in an attempt to thaw a little bit of the frost that her brother has brought in with him. But he remains unmoved.

"It's not my favorite," he answers, giving her a dirty look.

"Oh, please, who are you trying to kid? You always asked for it when we were growing up. For your birthday, for Thanksgiving, for Christmas! Don't tell me you don't remember!"

"Do you wanna know what I remember? The plates going flying if that fucking stew wasn't seasoned just right. Look at that wall, Ness." He points to a yellowish wall behind Leila's back with an obvious crack in it. "There's still a mark."

"Thomas..." his sister murmurs, ashamed, her hands on either side of her head.

"Thomas what?" he demands with a raised eyebrow. "How can you stand there laughing and joking like nothing ever happened? What is wrong with you people? This was a bad idea; I shouldn't have come here." He lets go of my hand and moves for the front door, opening it and barreling out.

"Thomas, please." Leila grabs his arm. He lets her. He just halts in the doorway. I watch him from the background. "I know you have a lot of ugly memories in this house; I was there for them. But I am begging you not to leave. Mom has been waiting all day to see you. She started cooking that damn stew at seven this morning. Seven o'clock, Thomas. She was so sure you would be here for lunch. She packed it up and put it aside for you, and she wouldn't even let me have a bite of it. I'm begging you, please don't do this to her. Don't do it to me."

Thomas shifts his gaze to me, and we stare at one another for a good long moment. I silently plead with him to listen to his sister, but it's all for naught. He's determined to leave. "Ness, let's go home," he orders shortly.

Dejected, I release the breath I was holding and comply with his wish without arguing. Just like I promised. "If that's what you want," I murmur in a small voice, walking over to him.

"Don't look at me like that," Thomas says, softening toward his sister, who is now staring at him with glittering eyes and her arms crossed tight over her chest. He moves to her, taking her face in his hands and tilting it up. "I wanted to try. I promise you, JC, I had the best of intentions. But being here...I can't breathe."

Leila takes a deep breath and brushes a tear off her cheek. With the slightest movement of her head, she nods.

Thomas kisses her forehead, whispering, "I'm sorry. Call me when you get back to Corvallis."

He takes my hand and starts to pull me out of the house, but a weak voice calls his name from behind us, stopping him in his tracks.

Twenty-Two

NO ONE MOVES. THOMAS IS holding his breath. After a moment, I very slowly turn to see a slender and incredibly beautiful figure. His mother. Her eyes are the same bright green as her children's. Brown bangs cut across her forehead while the rest of her hair falls straight down her back like a waterfall of dark silk. Her skin is snowy white but marked by time and suffering. Like the scar at the base of her neck, which is only partially covered by her white shirt and slim pearl necklace.

Thomas's mother is paused halfway down the stairs. With one hand, she holds the rail while the other is pressed against her chest. "You came…" she whispers, observing him with shining eyes. She descends the steps slowly and, in a tragic tone, murmurs, "But you're already leaving…"

Thomas turns and holds her gaze. He doesn't say anything; his hands are in his pockets, his lips are compressed into a hard line, and his eyes are full of warring emotions. "It's better this way."

"Please don't go," she begs, drawing a little bit closer to him. "I can't stand to see you leave again."

"Wasn't so difficult to watch me leave last time." The moment he says it, I can see on his face that he regrets it, but he tries not to let that show.

His mother hangs her head, overwhelmed, her eyes cloudy with tears.

"I was sick, so sick. I didn't know what I was saying or doing. It wasn't easy to crawl out of that black hole...but I did it, and I never stopped thinking of you two." With a marked hesitation, she grasps Thomas's arms, as if to make sure he's really there in front of her and isn't just a figment of her imagination. Discomfort is clear in Thomas's eyes, but he doesn't fight her. I'm willing to bet he needs this physical contact too.

"There wasn't a single day, not one...when I didn't pray to God and ask him to take care of you while you were away." I see her chin trembling and tears appear in the corners of her eyes. Thomas looks down at her warily. I wish so, so much that he could find the strength to push past his pain and let himself forgive.

"We've managed on our own," he says, his voice overflowing with years of accumulated suffering.

"I never had any doubt that you would. Your sister has always been safer with you than anywhere else." She swallows hard. "But I am your mother, and what happened to us...it was horrific for everyone. There isn't a day when I don't think about him. Or a day when I don't miss him. But I should never have let my pain make you feel unwanted. You were not unwanted. I made a mistake, a grievous mistake, letting you go. All I ask is that you let me find a way to make up for it, to make up for all the lost time... That's all I ask."

Thomas's truculent glare softens almost imperceptibly as he takes a deep breath. My shoulders relax as well, certain that the tension in the air is about to melt away. After a long moment of silence in which Thomas simply observes his mother, he nods. His mother's eyes light up with joy and deep feeling. She takes his hand and strokes it with trembling fingers.

Then, turning in my direction, she exclaims, "Oh, how impolite..." She wipes tears from the corners of her eyes with her fingertips, trying to compose herself. "You'll have to excuse me... I haven't even introduced myself. I'm Lauren Collins, and I'm so happy you're here as well," she says, holding out a hand to me.

"I'm Vanessa. It's a pleasure to meet you, Mrs. Collins," I answer, shaking her hand.

"Please, call me Lauren." Our handshake quickly turns into an affectionate hug that makes me feel welcome. I hear her faintly murmur the words *thank you* a few inches from my ear. I smile at her and tell her that she has nothing to thank me for.

We move to the kitchen, where Lauren goes to the stove to heat up the stew. While Leila takes a bottle of water out of the fridge, Thomas and I sit in silence. The atmosphere is still pretty tense. Leila pours four glasses of water and hands them out to us. Their mother stirs the stew some more before turning in our direction, her back against the kitchen counter.

"You know, Mom," Leila says brightly, clearing her throat and looping her arm through her mother's. "Vanessa is the girl I was telling you about…Thomas's girlfriend," she explains, giving us a sly look with smirk on her face. Lauren watches us tenderly but, seeing my blushing cheeks and her son's tight face, she decides not to push.

"JC, why can't you shut your mouth?" Thomas scolds her with a surly look on his face. Then he takes the pack of cigarettes out of his jacket, ready to stick one between his lips, but his mother gives him a look that must have dissuaded him because he sighs—almost grunts, really—and frustratedly stuffs them back into his pocket.

"Well, it's hardly a secret," Leila says nonchalantly, sipping her water.

"What? Your inability to mind your own business?"

She sticks her tongue out at him while their mother gives them both a soft look. As if she missed this everyday normal interaction more than anything in the world.

When Lauren tells us that the stew will be ready soon, Leila and I start setting the dark wood table in the dining room. Every now and then, I peer out of the corner of my eye into the kitchen. Thomas is still sitting there, on the stool with elbows propped up on the kitchen island. He's shaking his foot with an anxious look on his face as he continues to glance around the room. His mother is with him, and she's talking to him, but I'm too far away to hear what they're saying. Thomas nods a couple of times, drumming his fingers frenetically on the surface of the island, but after a few exchanges, he finally looks at her and responds with a hint of a smile.

Leila and I observe them talking more easily and decide not to interrupt, giving them space to find each other again.

"How are you? I mean, what's the situation with your father right now? Was he able to ask for your forgiveness before he was hospitalized?" As I talk, I carefully fold the napkins and tuck them under the cutlery.

"When I got here, Dad was in a bad way. Acute bronchopneumonia is hard on a body, but that didn't stop him from treating me like shit." Leila lets out a self-deprecating laugh, surprising me. "You know, when our uncle called to tell me about his illness and said he wanted to bring the family back together and redeem himself...I almost bought it. I really should've known better," she says, reaching around me to put the plates down next to the napkins. "It was only later, once I got here, that I realized it wasn't my father who asked us here; it was my mother. She was the one who wanted us to come. She was the one who was hoping to reunite us in some way, and when I really think about it, it's for the best that Thomas decided to stay in Corvallis. I don't know what would have happened otherwise."

"Why did you stay? You could have called us anytime, and we would have come and gotten you."

She shrugs, tucking her bobbed black hair behind her ears. "I know, but I didn't want to leave my mother alone with him. It hasn't been easy this last year and a half, turning my back on her. I always had a good relationship with her, and deciding to leave was painful. But I couldn't leave Thomas by himself, not after what he'd gone through in the past few years. And the few times I've heard from her since we left, she assured me that Dad had stopped hurting her. But now more than ever, I'm betting she was lying to me."

"What makes you think that?" I ask, instantly alarmed.

"When I got here, she had bruises on her arms. I asked her how she'd gotten them, and she obviously made something up about her shopping bags being too heavy a few days earlier."

My eyes go wide with fear. "I can't believe it, even now at the end of his life…"

Leila gestures for me to speak softly, putting her index finger against her lips and glancing at the kitchen.

"Do you really think he did it?" I ask finally.

"I can spot my mother's lies. I've been doing everything that I can to get her to tell the truth ever since Dad was hospitalized. But years and years of living under threat has warped her. She was terrified to talk to even me about it."

Instinctively I turn to look from Lauren to Thomas, who seems to have found some harmony with her. I wonder what would happen if Thomas found out. "We should do something; he can't—"

"Vanessa," she interrupts me, her eyebrows drawing together. For an almost imperceptible moment, it seems that I can see Thomas's cold stare in his sister's eyes. "You have to face reality. My mother wouldn't admit what's happening to her even under torture. But suppose that she did; what would it do? Do you really think he'd be sent to prison to live out his final days behind bars?"

"Yes!" I answer with even more conviction. This man needs to pay for all the evil he's done and continues to do. He can't just get away with it all.

"No, he wouldn't. My father has the entire Portland police department behind him. They worship him, and after"—she heaves a sigh, rubbing her face—"after we lost my brother, it just made everything worse. Everyone sees him as this poor man who lost his son and then watched his life crumble in his hands. He turned to the bottle, then he got sick, and his good little wifey never stopped taking care of him, not even for a moment. *She must love him so much*…that's what everyone in this city thinks. They have no idea who my father really is. Do you think any of them would be willing to believe the truth?

"But there's proof!" I manage, beside myself with rage. "There were marks, and your brother told me that his friend Ryan knows everything; he could testify—"

"Ryan has a criminal record, Vanessa. His family is so screwed up that, in the eyes of the law, his testimony would be less than worthless. As for my mother, sure, she had bruises. But in all these years, she's never filed any charges. She stayed with him. So many women stay with their abusers because they get so annihilated by fear that they end up unable to leave. I'm sorry to disillusion you here, but where I come from, you learn pretty quick that the bad guys don't always get what's coming to them."

I lapse into a furious silence. Furious at the resignation I feel from her. Furious because this is one of the biggest injustices I've ever personally witnessed. But above all else, I'm furious because I know that she's telling me the truth.

Our conversation ends when Thomas and his mother join us in the dining room. Lauren's carrying a large pot that produces the delicious aroma of meat, carrots, and potatoes while Thomas has a basket of rye toast. It's a shame that my appetite has completely vanished after the conversation with Leila. I try not to look too unsettled as Lauren invites me to sit. I'm doing my best not to arouse suspicion, but Thomas knows me too well for that, and he immediately realizes something is wrong. When I sit down next to him, he puts a hand on my thigh and leans close to my ear, whispering, "Is everything okay?"

For a moment, I have no idea what to say.

Leila, sitting across from us next to her mother, begs me with her eyes to keep quiet. So I swallow hard, and putting on a polite smile, I nod.

He frowns, unconvinced. "You sure?"

I put hand over his and murmur, "Very sure. Are you okay?"

He nods, still looking doubtfully at me. Then he pulls back to take a sip of his water.

Dinner proceeds to go off without a hitch, mostly thanks to Leila's chatter. We talk about school and about what we'd like to do in the future. Lauren asks about my family, but the answers I give are terse and dry.

"Vanessa, do you like sweets? Leila and I made an apple pie this afternoon," Lauren tells me as she clears the table with her daughter's help.

I dab the corners of my mouth with a napkin and nod. "I love pie. When I was little my grandmother used to make this gingerbread crust that went with all kinds of pie."

"I've never tried a gingerbread crust, but it sounds appealing," she replies with a sweet voice and genuine smile.

"Oh, you absolutely have to try it; it's probably the best thing on the face of the earth!" I answer with an enthusiasm that makes Thomas chuckle.

"Maybe next time we could all make one together?" his mother offers, looking at her son and me with hope in her eyes, the same hope that is shining in Leila's face.

"Of course, I'd love to," I answer, looking to my boyfriend and waiting for his response. When Thomas realizes that all the attention is on him, he shrugs and sits up straighter in his chair. "I don't make pies." His mother bows her head slightly, but then he adds in a more conciliatory tone, "At most, I'll eat them."

"Great!" Lauren exclaims, trying to contain the enthusiasm that beams from her face. Leila silently thanks her brother with a smile.

After taking all the dirty dishes to the kitchen, Thomas's mother returns to the dining room and places a glass cake stand with the pie on top in the center of the table.

"It looks marvelous," I exclaim sincerely.

Leila cuts slices and plates them while Lauren hands them to us. As she stretches out her arm to pass me a plate, the sleeve of her shirt rises a few inches and reveals a bruise just above her wrist. Confronted by the angry purple mark, I feel my stomach clench, and I freeze as I realize that I'm not the only one who has noticed. Thomas's gaze is also fastened on that area. His expression shifts radically in the space of a second. Before Lauren can pull her arm back, he's grabbing it abruptly. The plate he was holding slams down on the table, and with a jerk, Thomas lifts Lauren's sleeve up to her elbow. I put a hand over my mouth, horrified by the bruising not just on her wrist but up her entire forearm. Lauren pales with the expression of someone who knows that a catastrophe is about to unfold. Leila instinctively gets to her feet while I remain paralyzed in my seat.

"What are those?" Thomas asks in a chill-inducing voice.

His mother tugs her sleeve back down with shaky fingers. "I–It's nothing... It's j-just..."

"It's *nothing*?" Thomas pounds his fist against the table, knocking over some glasses. I spring back, pushing away from him. My heart is pumping in my throat at light speed. My legs are trembling. Leila appears by my side and takes my arm, just as scared as I am.

Suddenly, Thomas starts tearing around the room from one side to the other, throwing open all the cabinets, apparently looking for something. I realize what he's searching for only after he gets to the kitchen and pulls several liquor bottles out from the under-sink cupboard. Some are full, some half empty and hidden away under there.

"Christ, I can't believe this. Not a fucking thing has changed; it's business as usual!" he yells, hurling one of the glass bottles at the floor. Immediately, he shatters another one against the table in front of him. Then a third on the wall to his right, making a deafening sound. And then another and another and another and another until his mother is begging him to stop with tears in her eyes. Leila tightens her grip on my arm and buries her face in my shoulder. I can feel her flinch every time Thomas smashes another bottle. I squeeze my eyes shut, as though this small gesture will somehow be enough to stop this madness. But of course it doesn't work. Thomas is a loose cannon.

"Stop, please," his sister begs. "You're scaring me." Her voice breaks into convulsive sobs. I squeeze her tighter, trying to offer her some reassurance, but I'm just as frightened as she is.

When he's finished smashing every bottle to smithereens, he looks around, panting. The veins in his neck are throbbing, and his eyes are alight with rage. He wipes his mouth with the back of his hand and, with a menacing look on his face, advances on his mother. "Tell me where he is."

She shakes her head, clasping her hands to her chest. Her lower lip is quivering. "I'm not going to let you ruin your life this way."

"Either you tell me where he is, or I will search every fucking hospital in this city until I find him and kill him with my bare hands." Fury contorts his face, making him almost unrecognizable. His mother is shaking her head vehemently, sobs wracking her entire body as tears pour down her cheeks.

"Okay, then. I'll find him myself." Thomas stalks away angrily, not caring at all about us. He grabs his jacket off the back of the sofa and leaves, slamming the door loudly.

For a moment, we all just stand there frozen, staring in shock at the glass scattered all over the floor. Then Lauren slumps to the ground and starts picking up pieces, unable to control the tremor in her hands.

"I–I'm so sorry, Vanessa. This is humiliating," she says, her voice shaking as she wipes away her tears.

"Don't…don't worry…" I'm about to get down and start picking up the shards of glass along with her, but Leila begs to me to go after Thomas and stop him. I feel stupefied, like I'm trapped in a nightmare. Everything feels surreal to me. One moment, we were all talking peacefully, and the next, all hell was breaking loose. It doesn't take much to bring me to my senses, though, just the thought of Thomas driving off with the express purpose of finding his father. I leap up and run out the door.

"Thomas, wait!" He's just a few steps away from the car. If he gets there before I get to him, it's all over. I run as fast as I can, and panting heavily with my heart racing, I throw myself between him and door, putting my palms on his chest just before he reaches the handle.

"Get out of the way," he hisses through clenched teeth.

"No. You're about to make a huge mistake!"

"A mistake? A mistake?" he shouts even louder. "Even when he is dying, he can't help but put his fucking hands on her!" He slams his hand down on the roof a few inches from my face, making a dull thud. I jolt, intimidated. He must have noticed my reaction because I can see the shame in his eyes, but he can't control himself right now. "I'm not going to tell you again: Get out of the way."

I remain immovable. He gives me a hard look.

"Don't look at me like that. You don't scare me," I lie, pretending to be much bolder than I am. Because the truth is, while a large part of me knows that Thomas would never hurt me, I cannot deny the existence of another smaller part that is, right at this moment, feeling a little afraid.

Thomas narrows his eyes to slits, bringing his face close to mine. "There are a million different ways I could hurt you without ever laying a finger on you. So, for your own sake, go away."

"Sorry, Thomas, but I'm not going to let you do it this time. I'm not going to let you push me away again…get rid of me. I will not allow you to get in this car and go do something that will cost you your life. So you can just forget about that. You brought me all the way here. You wanted me with you because, deep down, you were afraid that you were going to need someone's help. So insult me if you want. Try to scare me. Punch the car, yell, and curse all you like; I can handle it. I can handle the worst of you. But know that I'm not moving from this spot, and neither are you." I take a deep breath and loosen the fists I didn't even realize I had clenched at my sides. I watch his chest rise and fall in agitated pants. We stare at each other in a silence heavy with tension. It's like we're in a competition to see who can be the most ballsy and immovable. First one to give in loses. But we are stubborn and proud in the exact same way. And there won't be a winner or a loser in this competition. Just two broken people trying, in their own ways, to fix each other.

After a few seconds that nonetheless feel endless, Thomas grinds his teeth. He slowly draws closer to my face, saying, "You're a fool."

I blink several times, surprised not by the insult but rather by the tone of his voice, which isn't dripping with venom the way it usually does when he gets angry. Instead, what I'm actually hearing is a hidden well of gratitude. I lift my chin and square my shoulders proudly. "If my foolishness keeps you from getting into this car, then I'm happy to be a fool."

Thomas gives up in the face of my determination. He shuts his eyes and places his hands down on the car on either side of my head, trapping me between him and the metal. Then he hangs his head in exhaustion. "I thought…I thought that getting out of here would appease some of his anger. That me being gone might help him calm down in some way. Instead, all I did was give him the freedom to do it without anyone getting in the way. Because I wasn't there to defend her, to keep him from hurting her again. I ran away and left her here alone to face a beast that couldn't be tamed."

"It's not your fault, Thomas." My voice is just a whisper.

He breathes deeply, and I can see that he's slowly coming back to himself. "I screwed up in there."

"Doesn't matter."

"I lost control and put you in the position of having to suffer this part of me again."

"It doesn't matter," I murmur again under my breath, holding his face in my hands to reassure him. "You can make it right. Let's go back inside and talk to her…"

He shakes his head and then rests his forehead against mine. "I don't want to go back in there. I want to go find him."

"Thomas, please…"

He backs away from me and sits down on the ground, leaning back against the wheel of the car with one leg extended out before him, the other bent up. He takes the pack of Marlboros out of his jacket and puts one in his mouth. He allows himself a few drags before speaking again.

"Maybe my uncle wasn't completely wrong. Maybe, if I talked to him, if I faced him once and for all, I could get out from under this weight that is pressing down on my chest, constantly crushing me…"

"You really want to talk to him?" I take a seat next to him, skeptical.

He nods and keeps his eyes fixed on the house as he exhales cigarette smoke. "I want to tell him what a giant piece of shit he is and has always been, and shout in his fucking face what a complete and total failure he was. I want to do it now when he can't fight back, when he can't escape."

I consider this for a few seconds. "If that will give you some peace, I can let you do it, but only on one condition: I'm coming with you."

"No."

"Yes."

He gives a frustrated sigh as he runs a hand through his hair. "I don't need a babysitter, Ness."

"I don't trust the person you become when you're angry, Thomas. And that man always seems to bring out the worst in you. There's no way I'm letting you go alone."

We stare fixedly at one another for a moment until, with a wave of his hand, he surrenders. "Whatever you want."

While Thomas calls his uncle to get the name of the hospital, I text Leila to tell her everything that happened and try to reassure her.

As soon as we arrive at the hospital, the sterile, chemical smell overwhelms me, leaving behind an oppressive sensation. I rub my arms, trying to get rid of the gooseflesh.

Thomas heads straight for reception, where we find a nurse occupied on the phone. "I'm looking for Joe Collins. I know he was admitted here a few days ago," Thomas says as soon as the woman hangs up.

"And you are?" she asks, pushing her circular glasses down to the tip of her nose.

"His son," he answers through gritted teeth.

"Just a minute." The nurse starts typing something on her keyboard, glancing over at the monitor, and after a few seconds, she informs us, "Mr. Collins is in the ICU, in the east wing. Continue along corridor B, and then take a right."

We follow the nurse's directions until we reach a large waiting room with muted green walls, lit by irritating fluorescent lights. Some doctors in scrubs enter and exit through a sliding door. A nurse carrying some medical records asks us what we're doing there. Thomas explains that he came to see his father, and she tells us that only immediate family members can go inside and for no longer than ten minutes because visiting hours ended an hour ago.

Thomas nods, but when she leaves, he just stands still, unsettled, watching the doors as they open and close. All the boldness that has driven him this far now appears to be faltering. I take his hand, entwining our fingers, and with my free hand, I touch his cheek. "Are you sure this is what you want to do?"

He turns to look at me. He bites his lip and then brings my hand to his mouth, kissing the knuckles. His eyes catch on the bracelet I'm still wearing around my wrist. He threads his fingers into my hair and pulls me to him, kissing me for a long moment. With my hand on his chest, I can feel his heart beating as rapidly as mine. He caresses my cheek slowly, and the cold steel of his rings makes me shiver. "I'm sure."

He goes to the sliding door, where a nurse helps him dress from top to bottom in sterile protective gear. Then he pushes a red button to the side of the door, which lets him inside. I wait, a strange feeling of disorientation descending upon me the moment the doors close.

Everything's going to be okay, Vanessa. It'll all be okay.

I pace the room, my heart beating faster and faster as I take deep breaths to calm myself down. I jump at every noise and go on alert every time the doctors and nurses enter or exit the ICU. Each time, I try to peer through the doors. I obsessively check my watch; the promised ten minutes have already passed. I wonder what's going on in there, what Thomas is feeling in the face of this dying monster who took away all his faith in humanity. I'd like to be there in that room with him. To lend him strength, to make him feel like he's not alone. I'd like to talk to his father myself, tell him that his violence nearly destroyed his son, but underneath all the rubble, Thomas's heart is still good, and it beats for the people he loves.

It's been twelve minutes now, and my palms are sweating when the doors of the ICU open to allow two large machines to go through. I take the opportunity to look, and I spot Thomas and his father in the room beyond. My view is restricted by a blue curtain, which covers his father's body entirely. But I can see that Thomas is leaning over. It seems to me that he's listening carefully to something his father is whispering in his ear. Whatever it is, it can't be good because Thomas's eyes cut to me with a violence that freezes me in place. He stares at me. And then the fury that I saw on his face just a moment ago gives way to an expression of disorientation. Like he's just been hit with the weight of a realization that he's going to have to cope with for the rest of his life.

What is happening? I suddenly feel short of breath, and I don't know why. The doors close, leaving me without information once again. But it isn't much longer before Thomas emerges from the doors with heavy steps and a shadow darkening his eyes. He tears his protective gear off furiously and throws it at a receptacle on his right, not caring if it goes in or not. Then, he walks past me without a glance, as though I'm not even there.

"Hey, what happened?" I run to him in a panic, never taking my eyes off of him.

"I have to get out of here; I need a smoke," he says urgently.

"Thomas, wait! What happened in there? What did you two say to each other?" I grab his shoulders, forcing him to stop and give me his attention, but this just seems to irritate him more. My heart is pounding frantically in my chest, and my breaths are getting shorter and shorter.

"You shouldn't be here." His voice is so harsh that I immediately freeze up.

My face falls and I blink, taking a step back. "W-what are you saying? Of course I should be here, I'm here with you, *for* you." I put a hand on his arm, but he pulls away as though repulsed by me.

The muscles in his jaw contract and his face hardens. "That is exactly the point. This is all wrong."

All wrong?

My hands are shaking and my legs feel suddenly leaden; it feels like I'm not breathing anymore. "What are you talking about?" I answer a few moments later, my voice cracking.

But Thomas doesn't have time to say anything else because a high-pitched sound from the direction of his father's room makes both of us whirl around. In less than a second, a whole cadre of doctors carrying a defibrillator and oxygen mask rushes in, snapping out orders. Thomas instinctively approaches the doors, but a nurse stops him.

"You can't be here right now."

"It's my father in there," he answers, without a single emotion coloring his voice. He isn't sad or relieved. Neither upset nor calm. He's just…empty.

The nurse rests a hand on his shoulder and gives him a compassionate look. "I'm sorry. I guarantee that will do everything we can to save your father's life, but you have to leave the ward right now."

Thomas throws the nurse's hand off his shoulder furiously and spits at her, "I don't give a shit what you do or don't do; I just want to know what's happening."

"Your father is suffering from acute bronchopneumonia. As soon as you left the room, he went into respiratory crisis—" The nurse stops when she's called away to join the rest of the team.

Thomas and I stand there, paralyzed, our eyes glued to the closed door. But we can hear the beeps from the monitors out here, and they are becoming more insistent and closer together, mingling with the voices of the doctors. Until, finally, the beep turns into a steady tone.

And then everything stops.

PART TWO

Twenty-Three

ON THE DAY OF THOMAS'S father's funeral, my stomach is in knots, and I can't stop chewing on my lip. I want to ask Thomas how he's doing, but it's obvious that he's not okay. I want to ask him if he needs something, anything, but I'm afraid he won't answer me. Ever since he walked out of that hospital room, he's been cold toward me.

"This is all wrong," he told me, and the words haven't stopped echoing in my head ever since. He never brought it up again. I tried, but Thomas wouldn't allow it. He barely acknowledges me now. And sometimes, I even get the feeling that he's irritated by my presence. I spent the last two days with Leila and Lauren, while Thomas was always out who knows where and doing who knows what.

I talked with his mother and sister, and did my best to help them with the arrangements. Lauren also finally confided in Leila and me. She told me that, after her children left, she contacted them as seldom as possible to make sure that they didn't try to return to their hellish home. She always tried to soothe Leila with lies, saying that her husband had stopped raising his hand to her in the hopes of giving her daughter the chance to start a new life in Corvallis. To let her be free the way that Lauren had never been.

It was only when her husband got sick that she gave in to her desperate desire to see her children again. She asked Robert to intercede and convince them to come back with yet another lie. But I can't find it in my heart to condemn her; the suffering she's experienced is too vast, too horrendous. She did what she thought was right. She told me about her depressive episodes and about having found the strength to heal in the love she had for her children. And I know that she and Leila are going to do a lot of rebuilding now. Because they both care.

Although none of us particularly felt like going, Lauren asked us to attend the funeral. She doesn't want to attract attention and cause weird rumors to spread. Leila and I agreed to the charade because now Lauren really does have a chance to start over, free from that monster.

When we arrive in front of the church, Thomas refuses to go inside. I don't press him about it. I don't know where he hides out during the service, but I get a pretty good idea when he comes to the burial in the cemetery. He shows up dead drunk, face twisted into an angry expression and a bottle of Jack Daniel's in one hand. His misery has transmuted into rage, and anyone can see in his eyes that it's hurting him.

I break away from Leila and her mother before they spot Thomas and go over to him. "What are you doing here? I thought you decided not to come," I whisper once I'm standing in front of him.

Thomas runs a hand through his disheveled hair, swallowing. "Before they put him in that hole next to his son, thought I ought to give him a noteworthy send-off... You know, for the last time," he says sarcastically, raising his chin and swaying.

He tries to get past me, but I block him, putting my hands against his chest. He gives me a spiteful look.

"You can't even stand up straight... I don't think this is a good idea."

He emits a defiant snort. "You think you can stop me?" He uncorks the bottle with slow, clumsy movements, attracting the attention of some of the other people present.

"*How rude.*"

"*He showed up drunk to his father's funeral?*"

"*So disrespectful.*"

"He's always been a lowlife."

I can hear them whispering behind us. I try to stay calm because it seems like the only sensible thing to do. "There are a lot of people here, okay? Your mother and your sister are here...and it is still a funeral, Thomas. You don't want to embarrass them in front of everyone like this. I know you don't want that. I get what you're feeling, trust me; I'm not trying to belittle it. I'm just trying to keep you from making a mistake."

He sneers derisively at me again and takes another drink. "You should really stop."

"Stop what?" I ask, confused.

He gives me a scornful stare as he wipes his mouth with the back of his hand. "Stop thinking that I'm going to listen to what you say just because you're the one saying it." He grabs the neck of the bottle and pushes it into my chest, forcing me to fall back. "Your words don't mean shit to me."

He shoulders past me carelessly, leaving me staring speechless into the distance at the cars parked around the entrance to the cemetery. I am hurt, of course, but what's even sadder is that I'm learning to get used to this feeling. Because this is the version of Thomas that I've been dealing with ever since the night his father died.

When I turn, I see him heading right for the circle of people around the closed coffin. I immediately spot alarm in his mother's and sister's eyes when they see that he's arrived. They both attempt to hold him back, but he dodges them. I run to help them, but all that does is inflame Thomas's anger further. Thomas, under the indignant eyes of all those present, launches into a rant, dredging up every horrible thing his father inflicted upon him and the rest of his family. He vents his fury at how his father had the pure dumb luck to leave this earth without ever paying for a single one of his sins.

I helplessly watch him pour what remains of the bottle onto the coffin, amidst the shouts and protests of the assembled mourners. It's only then that his uncle Robert grabs him, trapping his arms against his body and physically dragging him away, though not without considerable effort. He takes him all the way back to the car, and I follow in total silence, Leila and Lauren sobbing behind us. I'm so incredibly ashamed of what he's just done, but I also feel deeply sorry for Thomas.

Rob manages to wrestle the car keys away from Thomas. "I think it's time for you to go home," he suggests after shutting his nephew into the passenger seat. I nod, red in the face, my eyes still glittering as I grab the door handle of the SUV with a trembling hand.

"I–I'm so s-sorry…"

"Don't be sorry. He's going through a hard time… And we're in no position to judge him." He tugs on the knot of his tie, loosening it. "Now more than ever, he needs someone to be with him. I'm sure that once he gets back home, away from this place, he'll get better." He shoots a sympathetic look through the window at Thomas, who has closed his eyes and is resting his head against the glass. I can see the anguish on Robert's face, but I need to believe that he's right. I need to believe that everything will be back to normal soon. And that Thomas will turn back into *my* Thomas. Moody and irascible, yes, but also caring and sweet in his own way, and then this version of him will just be a distant bad memory.

I drive south for almost two hours in total silence, with Thomas collapsed in the seat next to me. It's late by the time we get to campus, so after cutting the engine and taking the keys out of the ignition, I jingle them slightly. "Do you…do you want to stay at my place?" I venture as his eyelids slowly open. I would imagine that after a day like this, it would be better for him to have someone by his side. Someone to hold him, to fall asleep with, someone who can take care of him. And I don't care about what happened at the funeral or that he hasn't spoken to me. The only thing I care about is him. I don't want to leave him alone right now.

Thomas, apparently, does not feel the same way because he hisses an emphatic, "No." He gets out of the car with difficulty, clinging to the door. He wobbles, and as he attempts to get his cigarettes out of the back pocket of his jeans, the pack falls to the ground. He bends over to pick it up but almost tumbles over onto the asphalt.

Feeling bitter, I immediately get out of the car and pick it up for him. "Here, take it." I put the pack in the palm of his hand. "Lean on me; I'll get you home. Where would you rather go? The dorm or the frat house?" I ask him softly, looping an arm around his waist to support him.

But he jerks away from me, irritated. "Go home. You've got better things to do; don't waste your time with this bullshit."

Disappointment makes my voice break as I mutter, "You...you're not bullshit." How can he even think that?

"Well, that says a lot about your judgment." I can hear the thread of mockery in his voice. In fact, I'm sure that's exactly what he intends. He wants to taunt me. Ridicule my concern for him to make me feel stupid.

"Don't do that. Don't talk to me like I'm dumb. You're in pain... and I...I just want to be near you. There's nothing wrong with that."

He shakes his head as if trying to belittle my words, as if they mean less than nothing to him. And then, without saying anything, he waves me away and leaves me standing there watching him swaying as he goes.

I don't hear from him the next day. I call him in the morning when I don't see him in class. No answer. At lunch, he isn't in the cafeteria. By afternoon, his prolonged absence is really starting to worry me. But, in the end, I tell myself that he just needs more time. He needs time alone to digest all the horrific things that have happened.

Then that very same night, two hours before the end of my shift at the Marsy, he walks through the doors. It only takes me a second to spot that he is already drunk. Rubbing his temples, he sits down at the bar and orders a glass of Jack Daniel's. I categorically refuses to serve him. Maggie, although reluctant, can't do the same. After all, serving customers is our job. We have to do it.

In the end, Thomas stays right there in the same damn spot drinking until he can't stand up anymore. I have to call Vince to take him home because, even working together, Maggie and I can't get him to get up from the stool.

The last five days have all passed in the same scummy fashion. He doesn't show up for any of his classes; the basketball team has to look for a temporary replacement for him; I can't even find him at the frat house. Yet, I see him every single night at the bar and have to put up with his surliness there.

I'm wiping down the counter, trying to ignore his presence at a nearby table and thinking about finally giving him an ultimatum, when I see Leila come in. She just got back to Corvallis today, but I've kept her up to speed on what's been happening these past few days. Sure enough, she doesn't seem surprised, just disappointed, when she comes face-to-face with this drunken version of her brother.

I watch as she sits down next to him at the table and starts what begins as a civil conversation but soon escalates into a loud fight in the Marsy's parking lot. Since I can't leave with them, I pretend I need a short break. I lock myself in the staff bathroom and give in to the urge to eavesdrop through the small window overlooking the parking lot.

"Is this how you're gonna be from now on?" Leila's sharp voice reverberates around the lot.

"Spare me the lecture, JC," he answers.

"The lecture?" Leila echoes indignantly. After a brief tense silence, I hear her add, "We finally have a chance to start over. Start over for real this time! Dad is gone. Mom welcomed you back home; you've found someone who makes you happy. Why do you want to ruin everything?"

My heart batters my rib cage as I await his response. But he doesn't open up. Lump in my throat, I imagine him drinking the dregs of the Jack Daniel's he took out there with him.

"Do you hear what I'm saying?" she continues angrily. "If you decide to fuck everything up again, I'm out. I'm done, Thomas. I'm done with all this shit. I sacrificed everything for you, for Mom, to try to fix some of the damage this sick, cursed family of ours has done.

And now that I'm so close to finally feeling free...I'm not going to just let everything fall apart! You are my brother, and I love you more than my own life, but I didn't bury Dad just to watch you turn into him!" From the sound of her footsteps fading into the distance, I gather that she's leaving.

I put my palms against the cold tile. My mouth hangs open. My heart pounds. *Stop her, Thomas. Don't let her go. Please, don't let her go.* But I hear only the metallic click of a lighter, the crash of glass shattering and a low muttered curse from Thomas. Maggie knocks on the bathroom door, making me jump.

"Hey, you alive in there? You've been gone awhile, and the room's filled up. I need you."

"Y-yeah, I'm all good. I'll be right out," I whisper, pressing myself against the door. I try to gather myself, taking a deep breath. I adjust my pleated skirt and go back to work.

After a few minutes, I see Thomas return as well, looking exhausted. He flops down on what has now become "his" stool at the bar, and when I hear him ask Maggie for another Jack, the disappointment I feel is so overwhelming it makes me want to cry. Trapped inside that tiny bathroom, I hoped with all my heart that his sister's words would have some effect on him.

He spends the next few minutes drinking and ordering more drinks. Drink and order, just like that. Until, furious and so tired of this, I decide that the time has come to intervene.

"That's enough," I say, staring determinedly at him. "That's the sixth drink you've had in less than an hour." I snatch the bottle out of Maggie's hands and put it back on the liquor shelf behind me.

He cocks his head and narrows his eyes at me. "You get paid to serve, not to talk. So why don't you do your fucking job and shut your mouth?"

The lack of respect both chills and disgusts me. I want to be able to get angry and answer him in kind, but I'm at work, and he's wasted. If there's one thing I've learned in these last few days, it's that facing off with the drunk version of Thomas is never a good idea. He gets so angry and just rips into me. But that doesn't mean I have to obey him either.

Feigning courage that I don't feel, I snatch his glass and lean forward until I'm face-to-face with him. The ends of my pigtails brush against the dark wood of the bar. "If you want to wreck yourself like this, go ahead. But don't think for a minute that I'm going to let you do it right in front of me."

His jaw stiffens, and he clenches his fist so hard on the bar that his knuckles go white. We stare at each other in silence: me, determined not to give in; him, blind with rage. It makes it almost impossible to recognize him anymore and almost makes me fear his reaction. Finally, he pulls a few bills out of his jeans pocket and slams them down hard on the bar. "You aren't saving anybody with your ridiculous fucking morals; you're just making it all worse."

He gets shakily off the stool and goes outside without taking a single look back. I find myself staring at the bar's door and swallowing thickly. I'm so tired. And hurt. And I know it's the liquor talking, that it's making him behave like this. And I also know that alcohol can turn even the best person into a heartless monster. But I don't know how much longer I can take this.

A few seconds later, Maggie puts a comforting hand on my shoulder. "Everything okay?"

I just shake my head, not needing to say anything else. I feel helpless and disheartened.

"You can take a break if you want, I'll cover you."

I sniffle, and with a deep breath, I roll my eyes upward and blink my tears away, trying to compose myself. "No, I've got it, thanks."

"Really, though, if you feel the need to take five minutes and get some air, cry, kick the wall, or maybe your boyfriend's shitty twin there"—she lifts one corner of her mouth—"feel free. I've got your back, coworker."

I grab her hand on my shoulder and squeeze it gratefully. "It's just...it's just a rough patch... It'll pass." If I keep repeating it to myself, then maybe someday it really will pass. Because it has to, right? That day has to come?

She gives me a smile full of compassion, but there is something darker lurking behind the expression. Like what she really wants to tell me is, *No, it's not going to pass. You need to understand that this is the way things are now.*

I'm sitting at a table in the school cafeteria with a steaming cup of coffee in my hands, but I can't bring myself to swallow any of it. I have a lump in my throat and a hollowness in my gut that has kept me up all night.

"It just keeps getting worse and worse," I tell my two best friends, who look sadly at me. "I just don't get it; he hated his father. How can the man's death have destabilized him this much?"

Tiffany reaches her hand out to squeeze mine. "I imagine that, when Thomas's father died, a big part of Thomas's life went with him. It was a toxic existence that he got trapped in like a loop. But I think that, even though that existence was poisonous, he feels lost without it."

Alex nods. "Maybe he just needs more time to grieve."

I shake my head, looking down. "No, it's not just that; I'm sure of it. There's something else...something he's not telling me. Something that's torturing him. Something happened the night he went to see his father in the hospital; he changed so drastically after that. And the more days that pass, the further I feel him slipping away from me. I don't know how to stop it from happening. I feel stupid for thinking it, but part of me was hoping that my being there would be enough for him. That just knowing that I was with him, by his side, would have kept him from completely falling apart. But that didn't happen. I'm losing him anyway."

"Hey, you're not losing him," Tiffany says immediately.

I nod, and I can feel my eyes filling up with tears. I know she's wrong.

"No, honey, you can't think that way. It's just that, unfortunately, our love isn't always enough to save someone. And you don't have to see it as a flaw or a failure; it's just the truth."

"You can't make him your responsibility; he has to find the will to pull out of this on his own," Alex adds. "Or he runs the risk of dragging you down with him."

"And what am I supposed to do in the meantime? Just watch as he destroys himself? I can't. It's too painful."

Neither Tiffany nor Alex respond. They don't have to; sometimes words aren't unnecessary. I hang my head miserably, and we just sit there, surrounded by a silence freighted with meaning. I can't listen to their advice; anything I try would be useless. But I also can't just sit back and wait for time to heal this wound.

When we finish our coffee, I trudge listlessly to my philosophy classroom. Thomas's usual seat is vacant again. I find myself tapping my pencil on my notebook through the whole lecture, staring robotically at the blank sheet before me while Professor Scott reviews some of Nietzsche's works.

"Vanessa... Psst! Vanessa!"

I snap out of my thoughts with a jolt. I turn to the right and see Logan. "What is it?" I ask, confused. His eyes widen, darting between me and the professor, who is also staring at me.

"We're waiting on you," Professor Scott says, pushing his glasses further up on the bridge of his nose.

I straighten up in my chair, tuck my hair behind my ears, and clear my throat. "I...um...well, I got distracted. I'm sorry," I admit, not bothering to beat around the bush.

"Yes, we noticed. I was asking you about your thoughts on fragility as a component of the human condition."

I blink, discombobulated. Is that the topic of this class? God, I've missed everything. "Fragility as a component of the human condition? I–I don't know."

"Think about it. In fact, I invite all of you to do the same." This last bit is addressed to all the students in the classroom. "Develop a thought on the topic, and the next time you are called upon to discuss it, we might get to hear some interesting, diverse points of view. That's it for today."

I sigh, tucking my books and notes into my bag and leaving the classroom.

"Hey!" Logan says, falling into step beside me.

"Oh, hey, hi," I answer, not even looking at him. I'm too busy checking my phone to see if Thomas has called. But of course, he hasn't.

"I haven't heard from you since you canceled our meetup. And lately, it seems like you've always got your head in the clouds; is everything okay?"

"I'm sorry for blowing you off at the last minute and never following up," I say, typing out a quick text to Thomas, just to ask how he's doing. "Some things came up that I had to prioritize. But I'm still willing to help you study." Resigned to the fact that I'm definitely not going to get a reply, I stick the phone back in my bag. "Actually, what am I saying? I don't work Thursdays, and I only have two classes in the morning. We could mee—" I'm interrupted by a shoulder check that makes me stumble back a few steps.

"Oh, so sorry, I didn't see you there." Shana snickers mockingly, flanked by a group of her friends. She also throws Logan a dirty look as she passes.

"Why is she so mad at you?" asks Logan, who watches her go by with a troubled look.

I stare at him for a few seconds, not saying a word. "I could ask you the same question," I say finally.

"Huh?"

"The looks you two give each other..." I answer, adjusting my bag to sit better on my shoulder.

His face twists into a grimace. "What looks are you talking about?"

"Well, the one she gave you just now, for instance. But also that time in the cafeteria, right before she poured that stupid smoothie on me." I shudder a bit at the memory.

"I've only noticed how much she seems to dislike you. She doesn't seem like a very nice person," he says, rubbing the back of his neck.

"Well, you're right about that. Not nice at all. But are you sure that's all there is to it?"

He gives me a serious look. "Of course I am. People like her don't pay attention to people like me," he answers. But something behind me seems to have caught his attention. I start to turn, but then he speaks again: "Anyway, I have to go. I'll be waiting for your call about Thursday."

"Oh, yeah, okay...see you—"

He leaves abruptly before I even have the chance to finish saying goodbye. What's going on with him? Confused, I'm still watching him walk away when two large hands grasp my shoulders, startling me.

"Little Gem, weren't you told to stay away from that guy?"

I sigh, rolling my eyes and turn to face Vince. "Are you still on about that? Until I get a valid reason to end a relationship, I'm not going to do it. Do you know something I don't? If so, I'm all ears. But if not, let's just leave it alone."

"Let's just leave it alone," Vince grumbles, his mouth twisting.

Just like I thought.

Huffing, I start walking down the hallway, heading outside, and he follows along behind me. "Did you get any sleep last night? You look worn out," he asks me.

I glance at him and shake my head. "I finally shut my eyes about twenty minutes before my alarm went off. I have a splitting headache."

"How is he?" he asks, sadness in his voice, as he holds the door open so I can exit.

"Not good," I answer with a sigh. "He doesn't go to practice anymore; he's always drunk and out of control. I never hear from him, and he doesn't want to be found."

"He did just lose his father. I'd fall apart too. We should give him some time. I'm sure he'll get better."

"Do you really believe that?" My voice reflects my mood: low, defeated, disillusioned.

"Do you not?" he answers, sounding sorry. But it's clear that Vince doesn't know much about Thomas's past; he can't imagine how complicated the situation really is. If he could, maybe he would understand my beaten-down attitude.

I shrug, but our conversation is interrupted by my phone, and my heart nearly leaps out of my chest. When I see my mother's name of the screen, however, I deflate like a balloon. I gesture to Vince that I need to go and take the call.

"Hi, Mom."

"Hello to you too. Don't sound so excited; I'm just your mother for goodness' sake." She's trying to be funny, but right now, a Jim Carrey marathon couldn't make me smile.

"Sorry, this isn't a great time," I explain, walking toward my dorm.

"Why? Did something happen?" she asks, her voice going shrill—a sure sign that she's getting agitated.

"No, Mom, everything's fine. Don't worry." I am once again forced to lie to my mother. "What did you want to tell me?"

"I was just calling to let you know that I got a reservation at Maple Garden for this Friday at eight."

I stop in the middle of the sidewalk. "Sorry, didn't we agree that I would call you when I decided on a date?"

"Yes, sweetheart, that's what we agreed. But then I never heard from you...again. And you know, if the mountain won't come to Esther White, Esther White will go to the mountain. Don't be mad; it's just dinner."

God, my mother and her pathological need for control. She couldn't have chosen a worse time for this.

"Okay, but know that there's a good chance Thomas won't be there. But I guess that won't be much of a problem for you anyway."

"Why wouldn't he be there?"

Well, let's see...because he trashed his mother's house, showered his father's coffin with whiskey during the man's funeral, got into a huge fight with his sister, and has been perpetually drunk for the past five days.

Obviously, I can't say any of that, because my mother would literally lose her mind, and within five seconds, she'd have called every rehab facility in the city to get him immediately committed. And, honestly I kinda wonder if I shouldn't actually let her do it. Thomas is sinking into a spiral of self-destruction that is seriously starting to worry me.

"Because..." I narrow my eyes, pressing my fingers into my forehead as I try to come up with a plausible excuse to give her. Knowing her, the instant she finds out what kind of man his father was, she'll start passing judgment on the whole Collins family, sticking her nose in where it doesn't belong. And so, once again, I have to lie.

"The game is on Friday; it could go long..."

"That's not a problem. The table was booked for eight, but we can wait for him. I would really like it if he could be there. If I want to start over on the right foot, I suppose I should at least apologize to him."

I raise my eyebrows in disbelief. "You want to apologize to him?"

"Do you find that so strange?"

"Yeah, Mom. You...you never apologize to anyone."

"Well, I don't have an excuse this time. I treated the boy poorly before I even knew him. I'm not going to guarantee that this dinner will change my mind about him, because a mother senses things sometimes before she sees them happen, but I can at least give him the benefit of the doubt."

"Wow..." I manage in a shocked whisper. I find it just a bit surreal that she's decided to give Thomas a second chance when he's at his absolute worst.

"So I'll see you Friday, then?"

"Okay. See you on Friday," I answer, having no other ways to deflect her.

As I end the call, my thoughts inevitably go to him. As much as he's hurting and enraging me, my only real desire is to be close to him. I can't just abandon him without first trying as hard as I can. And that's why I decide to change direction and head for his dorm.

Larry lets me in, but when I ask him if Thomas is in his room, his only response is a shrug. I decide to give it a shot anyway. Before opening his door, I take a deep breath, preparing myself for the worst.

Carefully, I put my hand on the doorknob and slowly turn it. Inside, the room is shrouded in darkness. All the lights are off, the blinds are shut, and the smell of alcohol mixed with smoke is overwhelming. My face contorts into a queasy grimace.

I shut the door behind me and blink repeatedly, trying to adjust my eyes to the darkness. There's nothing to suggest that he's here, except that I can hear heavy breathing. I get my phone out of my jeans and turn on the flashlight app. Clumsy as I am, I'd end up on the floor in less than two seconds without it.

I point the light in the direction of the bed and see him stretched out there, unkempt, one leg dangling off the mattress.

"What the fuck, Larry? Get out of here, you dick!" Thomas sputters, throwing his hand over his face.

"Relax, it's just me," I say cautiously, turning the light away so it won't bother him.

He raises his head a little, brushing hair out of his eyes, and gives me a confused look. "What do you want?" he asks in a drowsy voice. But he's not as hostile as I feared. This encourages me to get closer. I sit on the side of the bed and give him a concerned look.

"I came to see how you are."

He tries to sit up but then collapses back down, emitting an angry grunt. "Awesome."

The flashlight's dim glow gives me a peek at the conditions he's been living in. There's light enough for me to see the empty bottle of Jack Daniel's on the nightstand next to the bed and some cigarette butts.

"Don't start," he snaps, short and biting.

"Thomas, all this..." I'm about to tell him that it's wrong, that he's only hurting himself, and that he's never going to find peace this way, but I stop myself because I realize that none of it would be any use. Because Thomas never confronts his pain, nor does he allow himself the luxury of sharing it with anyone else. He anesthetizes himself instead. He himself admitted that he abuses anything that'll give him some fleeting feeling of relief: alcohol, drugs, sex. It's the only way he knows to cope. And I can choose to walk out that door and leave him forever, or I can stay and try to pull him out of the chaos his head has become.

I stare silently at him, unable to tear my eyes away from this defenseless figure who kindles a feeling of infinite sadness in me. And still, all I can think is that I love him. I love him unconditionally. And even though I also hate him for what he's doing to himself, to me, and to our relationship, I still don't want to be anywhere but here. Next to him. Because it is precisely when we're falling into darkness, succumbing to our weaknesses, that we most need someone to hold out their hand and keep us from slipping away. And I want to be that someone for him, now more than ever.

I push off my shoes, lift up the covers, and lie down next to him.

"What the hell are you doing?" he blurts, half irritated, half surprised.

My back is pressed against his warm chest, which moves erratically. It's the first time we've been this close in too long. Even in Portland, he chose to sleep alone on the couch.

"Shut up. I'm going to take care of you whether you like it or not." I grab his hand and pull his arm over my stomach, interweaving our fingers. "I don't know what's going on with you or why you're suddenly doing everything you can to put me at arm's length. But I do know that I'm not going to let you do it. I already told you once, I can handle your worst. And if that's all you can be right now, okay, I accept that. But I'm not leaving."

I feel his body go rigid, rejecting contact with me. For a moment, I wonder if he has been expecting me to give up the moment things got difficult. Maybe he hasn't taken my stubbornness into account, or maybe he has even been hoping I'd just stop hanging around.

But eventually, I feel him sigh against the nape of my neck. He lets his face drop into the hollow of my shoulder and presses his body against mine. "You always choose wrong," he grumbles before slipping into a deep sleep. I just keep staring at the closed blinds in front of me, a flicker of hope lighting up my heart and making me think that maybe Tiffany and Alex were wrong. Maybe, with a little time and patience, we can leave all this behind us and start fresh.

Gently rocked by his deep breathing, I end up falling asleep as well. I don't get out of his bed until it's time to start my shift at the Marsy.

Thomas doesn't show up at the bar tonight for the first time since we got back to Corvallis. On one hand, I'm relieved, but on the other, I spend my whole shift wondering where he is and what he's doing.

When I finish up late at night, I immediately head for my dorm to take a quick shower, intending to go back to Thomas's room. He doesn't give me the chance, though, because he shows up at my door without warning.

"Hey," I say, standing in the doorway, observing him. His cheekbones are slightly reddened, and his eyes are tired. But he seems sober for the first time in over a week now. "Is everything okay?"

He nods, rubbing the soft bit of hair that always falls over his forehead. "They're having a party at the frat, but I'm not in the mood. And Larry's blasting an anime marathon in the dorm."

"Oh, I understand." Is that why he's here? Because he didn't know where else to go?

He must be able to read my mind because he steps forward, taking my chin between his thumb and index finger, and brushes my lower lip. "I wanted to see you."

These words are enough to coax a little smile from me. It feels like I can finally breathe again after days of struggling for air.

"Little warm in here, isn't it? What's the heat set to?" he asks when he gets inside, peeling off his jacket.

I glance as the thermostat mounted on the wall next to me. "Seventy-seven."

"You're nuts." He chuckles a little, and it feels like an eternity since I last heard him do that.

"I just run cold...you know." I smile hesitantly at him, pulling down my shirtsleeves. He smiles back at me, quirking one corner of his mouth. I haven't missed the gloom that still hangs in the air between us, and I realize that now is not a good time to start a conversation. "Do you want to watch TV?" I suggest instead, getting a packet of microwavable popcorn from the kitchen cupboard. "This has been waiting to get devoured since my first grocery run. Alex and I were going to have a movie night." What I don't tell him is that it never happened, because although Alex did his best to cheer me up, I wasn't in any mood for company or entertainment.

"Sure, whatever you want," he answers without enthusiasm, slumping onto the sofa with his legs spread. He pulls his phone from the pocket of his black sweatpants and types out a message.

"Okay," I murmur, trying to ignore the odd feeling of awkwardness between us. I unfold the bag of popcorn and put it in the microwave. "So my mother called today."

"What did she want?"

"Um, the usual stuff. She wanted to know how I was, to point out once again that I don't call her..." I stall a little as I set the timer. "And to tell me that she's booked a table for the four of us this Friday evening." I don't look at him. I don't have the guts. And his silence only adds to my nerves. Finally, I turn uncertainly toward him. His forehead is creased into a frown.

"I don't think that's a good idea," he says, staring straight ahead at nothing in particular. Then he tucks his phone away. His answer doesn't surprise me, but I still feel a little disappointed. This wasn't how I hoped it would go. I wanted him to go with me to the family dinner, and I wanted my mother to change her mind about him. And he promised me that he'd be there. But that was before everything went downhill.

I paste on a smile to hide my sorrow. "Don't worry. I already told her you probably wouldn't be able to make it." I turn my back to him and shut my eyes, focusing on the sound of the popcorn popping, which is now filling the room. I hear him let out a sigh and approach me. I feel his chest brushing against my back and his hands resting on my shoulders.

"Look, I'm saying this for your sake... If I said or did something that—"

"Don't worry about it," I interrupt him, sounding colder than I'd like. "I get it."

He leans against the kitchen cabinet, folding his arms over his chest and looking at me. "You sure?"

I nod, trying to look convincing.

But I can feel the weight of his stare on me. He knows I'm lying. He rubs his face in frustration before saying, "Eh, never mind. I'll be there."

I look up at him; he doesn't seem at all happy with the decision he's just made. "You don't have to. I mean, it's just dinner."

The popping sound is subsiding. And I need to do something—anything—to get rid of the nervous energy that his presence is causing. I grab the bag out of the microwave and pull it open immediately, almost burning my fingers.

"I said I'll be there," he answers with an air of finality, plucking the bag from my hands. "Tell me where and when."

I get a bowl out of the cupboard and hand it to him. "At Maple Garden, eight o'clock."

"Maple Garden? Fancy-ass place, isn't it?" He pours the hot popcorn into the bowl. Then he goes over the sofa and turns the TV on. I don't answer because I don't know what else to say; he's right.

We both watch TV in near silence. I also spend a lot of time watching him. I can't tell if he notices; he seems focused on the screen. He's so captivated by this banal TV show that I can't help but wonder what he's finding so fascinating about it. Why doesn't he talk to me instead? He hasn't even kissed me. Doesn't he even want to know how my day went?

I remove the bowl of popcorn between us and, a little bit uncertainly, scooch closer to him. "Hey, do you want to talk?"

"About?" he asks absently, barely glancing at me.

"You seem distant…" As I wait for an answer, I decide to turn off the TV and take some control over the situation. I settle myself on his lap and take his face in my hands, forcing him to look at me. "Thomas, what is it?"

"What do you mean?" His hands draw lazy circles on my backside. And for a moment, I find myself sighing internally over the fact that he doesn't take his hands off me. Nor does he remove me from his lap.

Despite the gulf between us these days, Thomas still has the same effect on me that he's always had. For a moment, I wonder if it's just the same for him, but I force myself not to dwell on that right now. The important thing is figuring out what is going on inside his head.

"You know you can talk to me. You can tell me anything, everything." I take a breath and press my forehead against his, slowly tracing his cheekbones with my thumbs. "We can make it through this rough patch, I know we can, just so long as you don't leave me behind."

"What if it's not just a rough patch?" His eyes lock on my lips while his fingers creep under my shirt to stroke my side.

"Is it about your father? About what he said to you that night in the hospital?"

He briefly stops stroking but then starts again.

"That's it, isn't it? What did he say to you, Thomas?"

He puffs up his cheeks with air and then blows it out in resignation. "Nothing I didn't already know."

"What did you know?" I push, concerned.

He sighs and shuts his eyes. "I don't feel like talking about it. Not now."

"Sooner or later, we're going to have to—" I can't finish the sentence because suddenly his lips are on mine and his fingers are sinking into my hair.

"We will. But not now." He lays me down on the sofa, underneath him. The bowl of popcorn topples to the floor, scattering kernels everywhere. His hands slip under my shirt, and the effect that his touch has on me is so powerful that I can't find the will to fight it, even if a part of me does want to because I know very well what switch has been flipped in his mind. Losing himself in my body will allow him to briefly get out from under the feelings that are crushing him. To free himself from his thoughts, from the voices inside his head, and make way for silence. The silence he's used to taking refuge in. The silence that he used to look for in other people, trying to find comfort.

He gets up, gathers me in his arms, and carries me to the bedroom, all without breaking the kiss. When we get to the bed, his sighs are not ones of pleasure but of frustration. His touch is not sweet; it's desperate. It's the same desperation that I can see when I look into his eyes, and it kindles such an urgent need in me to reassure him. I don't even know exactly what's wrong, but I feel the need to tell him that it's all going to be okay. That one way or another, we are going to heal. So I raise a hand to touch his cheek, but he doesn't let me. He pushes my hand away from his face and pins it firmly above my head. Before I can whisper his name, he covers my mouth with a rough kiss.

"Don't. Don't talk," he says against my mouth. He doesn't want to hear anything from me. He doesn't want to give me a chance to even try to say something that might ease his mind. And that's when I finally get it. I realize that, whatever idea he's convinced himself of, he's not going to let me change his mind. Not this time.

I wake up the next morning with a lump in my throat that makes my eyes sting when I realize he isn't there.

Twenty-Four

LEANING ONE HAND ON THE rim of the sink, I bring the glass of water to my lips and swallow my birth control pill. I take a deep breath and stare at my listless reflection in the mirror. There's been a weight bearing down on my stomach ever since I woke up and found Thomas gone. Knowing that I've allowed the man I love to use me, to use my body as an escape hatch, as an outlet. To treat me like a one-night stand and then leave me alone the next morning.

This feels like rock bottom. And I hate myself for it. But I don't regret it. I wanted him; I wanted all of him. Even though I knew what he was doing, I gave him what he wanted because of the need I saw in him. It made me willing to risk everything. Maybe I chose wrong, but I'm human; I have my weaknesses. And he is one of them.

I look down, and my eyes land on the bracelet I wear on my right wrist, which I never take off. My last happy memory with Thomas is tied up in this bracelet. The moment when he looked into my eyes and told me that I was the only thing that felt right in a sea of wrong. I touch the textured leather, thinking back on that moment. Thomas told me to remember it if I ever doubted how much my being there meant to him. And lately, I've been doubting that. A lot.

Still, I'm not going to call him today. Nor will I try to find him. He has to be the one to do it. I put the blister pack back in my makeup case and brush my teeth. I pull my hair out of its tangled bun. I'm wearing a long fuzzy white sweater that leaves one shoulder bare, some basic skinny jeans, and my Converse. I keep my wavy hair loose, just pulling it back on one side with a bow-tie hair clip that matches my sweater. Then, without bothering with breakfast, I go to the newspaper office to give Leila the article I've been working on for the last week.

At lunchtime, I go to the cafeteria, and walking past the snack bar, I almost have a heart attack when I see Thomas sitting on a sofa with Shana by his side. They're intent on carefully going over some papers that Thomas is holding. She, with her legs crossed and her upper body leaning into him, giggles at something Thomas says without taking his eyes off the papers. I feel like I'm collapsing in on myself.

I have to scrounge up all my self-control to avoid losing my temper and jumping to the wrong conclusion, like I did last time. After all, they're just talking, I tell myself. And in a public place too. They both realize they could be spotted by yours truly at any moment. But it's really goddamned hard to stay calm in front of a scene like this. Is it really possible that, after we just spent the night together, he can find time for her but not for me?

My instinct is to rush over there and crumple those fucking papers right in his face, reminding him that if there's anyone he should be spending his time with, it's me. Me, his girlfriend, dammit. But I don't. Because my pride tells me that I can't look weak, jealous, and insecure in front of Shana, who, I know perfectly well, would love that. And I don't particularly want to hear Thomas call me stupid for misinterpreting things again.

I could leave. Out of respect for my poor heart, maybe I *should* leave. But as has now been well established, I am a first-class masochist. So I stay in the doorway, half of my body hidden by the wall, and watch them surreptitiously while Thomas's words echo in my head: "At least when I was fucking her, things were easy!" Just watching them sitting there on the sofa, I can see how everything really was simpler with her. Shana doesn't require commitment, responsibility, or involvement...

unlike me. And I wonder if that isn't exactly what Thomas needs right now. Someone who doesn't make him feel trapped or burdened.

"People like them will never be right for people like us." Logan's voice resounds in my ear, making me jump.

"W-what?" I spin around, embarrassed to have been caught spying on my boyfriend.

He backs up a few inches, increasing the distance between us. He crosses his arms over his chest, looks at Thomas and Shana, and shakes his head. "Sorry, I was thinking out loud. I shouldn't have."

"There's no *them*. They're just talking, just like us," I clarify, hoping that I sound more convinced than I feel.

"Is that what you tell yourself to feel better?" he asks, raising an eyebrow. "Come on, you wouldn't be standing here spying on them if you weren't thinking the same thing I am."

I glare at him. "That's my boyfriend you're talking about. I trust him. And for your information, I'm not spying on them. I don't need to do that," I lie.

"Look, you can say I'm rude and tell me go to hell all you want, but you need to open up your eyes. You and he are like night and day. You're too different not to combust. Those two, however, they're on the same page. They understand each other. Look for yourself." He takes my shoulders and turns me around, forcing me to look at Thomas and Shana.

They're still there. She has a cup of coffee in her hands. He writes down something on a piece of paper and immediately gives it to her. Then he stands up, and for a second, it looks like he's about to touch her cheek. Immediately, my blood starts to boil, but at the last second, his hand changes trajectory and merely grabs a cigarette from where it was stuck behind her ear. Shana tries to get it back, stretching out her arm in a flirtatious way that makes me sick. Then, Thomas heads for the exit, Shana following along behind him.

"Trust me," Logan continues, whispering in my ear. "Those two are acting shady."

I'd like to be unmoved. I wish I could say that Logan's words didn't affect me, but that would be my second lie of the day. When I turn to answer him, my reply dies in my mouth. In the face of my silence, he just gives me a knowing look.

"Thomas would never do something like that to me," I say without much conviction. It feels like a thousand needles are stuck in my throat. Logan sticks his hands in his pockets and glances at the sofa, where, until recently, Thomas and Shana were sitting.

"Seems to me that he already has." He backs away without another word, walking off and leaving me with nothing but question marks and burning jealousy.

In a couple minutes, I see Thomas return with Shana, who is now talking on the phone. His cheeks are a little red from the cold. He shakes out his forelock and unzips his leather jacket. They are both about to return to the sofa, but then, for the briefest moment, Thomas's eyes meet mine. I see him startle a little and move toward me. I jump like an idiot; then all too suddenly, I come back to myself. I turn around and melt into the crowd. I don't want to talk to him; I don't want to face him. I'm too anxious and too hurt.

I speed up until I get to the ladies' room. I take refuge inside, knowing he won't follow me in. I swear, in this moment, I hate him. I hate him for using me. For leaving me alone. I hate him, because after days of being gone, the first person he shows up with on campus is her. Damn it, knowing how she treated me, he shouldn't even want to be in the same room with her.

I splash my face with cold water and take a deep breath, trying to banish some of the negative thoughts that plague me. After a few minutes, I leave, hoping that Thomas isn't around. But as soon as I step out of the door, I see him leaning against the opposite wall with his arms and ankles crossed. Waiting for me. He anxiously toys with the ball of his tongue piercing. His green eyes study my face intently, trying to decipher my mood.

"What do you want?" I ask, detached. I start to walk away from him, and he pushes off the wall, falling into step beside me.

"Are you okay?"

I give a contemptuous snort. "Do you care?"

He grabs my shoulder and pins me against the wall. He looks like he's about to tell me something, and I pray to God that he does. Let him tell me that, yes, he cares more than anything. Instead, he remains silent.

I shake my head. Yet another disappointment. "Let me go." I slip out of his hold and keep walking straight ahead, but he grabs my wrist again.

"Why did you run away?"

"Because I saw something that made me sick."

"We weren't doing anything."

"Yeah, that's what you always say."

"It's the truth. She wanted me to help her fix a problem, and I did. That's all."

"Oh…" I click my tongue against the roof of my mouth, stopping in front of him and folding my arms over my chest. "How sweet, you've suddenly become charitable. What's next? Going to help some Girl Scouts deliver cookies? You're out of your mind if you think I'm going to believe that. And let me tell you, you have some nerve talking to me like nothing happened." I stab a finger angrily into his chest. "I woke up alone and naked this morning. You left me there like a piece of trash—that's how you made me feel. And all this was after you gave me nothing but indifference and nastiness for days. A real asshole move, but I'm betting you already know that. And now here you come, asking me how I'm doing only because I caught you with her. You know what? Fuck you, Thomas. Fuck you," I enunciate each word with all the resentment that I can muster, while he just absorbs the anger that I'm blasting at him with a frustrated look and his hands clenched into fists at his sides.

"I thought it would be better that way."

"'Better that way'?" I echo, disturbed. "Okay, so why did you think that?"

He sighs and rubs his eyes with the heels of his hands. "Look, I don't know. I don't know what's going on in my head. Maybe it's better if—"

I raise a hand to stop him. I can't bear to hear him say the thing I fear most in the world, that he has to break up with me. "I don't want to hear it," I say, like a coward. "I'm leaving now. And until you are at least willing to apologize to me, don't try to find me." I walk away, secretly hoping that he'll follow me and take me in his arms, but he doesn't. It's the final blow after days of anxiety.

Angry and with a pounding headache, I head for the campus lawn. This whole situation is going to drive me insane. At first, I thought his breakdown was about losing his father. But now I'm starting to think that I'm the issue. He's done everything he can to avoid me for days now, and I have no idea why.

I walk toward the redbrick building where Alex's photography workshop is being held. He should be finishing up in a few minutes, and I really need to talk to someone. Now more than ever.

As soon as I see him emerge from the building, I grab him by the arm. "Hey, wanna go for a walk?"

"Hey, I didn't see you there. What are you doing? Were you lying in wait for me?" he asks with a grin. I wish I had even a fragment of his good mood. "Where were you thinking about going?"

"Oh, nowhere in particular. We can just walk around here on campus. There's that rain smell in the air; you know how much it chills me out," I answer with a sad smile.

"Things with Thomas still going poorly, huh?" he asks me with his familiar sweetness.

I nod. "Yeah, but I'm not here to talk about him. It's all I do lately, and I've realized I don't know anything about your life anymore," I say, desperate for a distraction. "Talk to me; how are things with Stella?"

"Good. She's coming down next week for Thanksgiving, and after finals I'm going to her place in Vancouver so we can slip in a trip to New York as well."

"Right, the trip! How long are you planning to stay?"

"If all goes well, I'll come back right before the start of next semester in January."

"What!?" I stop in my tracks and give him a shocked look. "That's so long!"

"Not really, it'll be a little over three weeks..." he says, downplaying it.

"Three weeks is decidedly too long!"

Alex chuckles. "What's up with you? Are you afraid you'll miss me?"

"Pfft, I can live without you. I've been doing it every summer for the last thirteen years, remember?"

"Sure, but you had time to prepare for that kind of separation. This is coming on you like a bolt from the blue. But never fear; my whole life is here, and I don't plan to leave it for at least the next three years. I want to give this thing with Stella a real shot, though. I feel like we could work out."

I let out another lungful of air, realizing that I have no right to act like this. It's just that, for a split second there, the idea of losing Alex too knocked me off balance.

"I'm sorry, you're right. I'm actually really happy Stella's coming here next week. You two seem great together."

We sit down on a bench and chat through the lunch break. Finally, in a fit of despondency, I tell him all the latest news. I confide in him about the events of last night, saying that at least knowing that Thomas chose to lose himself in me this time rather than in a bottle gives me some sense of relief. Alex listens to me without judgment and offers a few sage pieces of advice. And I think it's going to be really hard to face the holidays without him.

"...Nietzsche calls into question a human being's faith, thus revolutionizing Western philosophical thought."

It's Thursday afternoon, and I'm in the library for my first tutoring session with Logan. Last night, after my talk with Alex, I texted Logan and asked him if we could put our argument aside and just focus on studying. We agreed on a few rules to start: I would help him, but anything about Thomas and me would remain out of bounds. For the moment, he seems committed to keeping his word.

"Why did he question faith?" Logan asks.

"Because he sees Christianity as a conspiracy against the human being to inhibit his basic impulses. And in order to move on, to progress and become a population of Übermensch—or, rather, free people without chains or restrictions—we need to destroy the certainties derived from religion, which holds men captive."

"Destroy to create again?"

"Exactly. His philosophy is somewhat based on that concept: Destroy a house and build a palace. Destroy a wreath, make a crown, et cetera," I explain, nervously brushing my hair over one shoulder. Nervous. That's how I feel all the time now. Perpetually nervous. I haven't heard from Thomas since yesterday. But this time, unlike all the others, I didn't chase him. I was trying to follow Alex's advice and take a step back from the whole situation. But I would be lying if I said I didn't miss him and didn't constantly hope for a phone call or even a visit in the middle of the night. And I know that, if he showed up, I'd give in despite all my best intentions. Just like I always do when it comes to him. The good news is that he didn't come to the Marsy yesterday to get drunk either. I can only hope he wasn't just doing it somewhere else.

My phone vibrates in my pocket while Logan uses his laptop to take notes on everything I've just explained to him. It's a text from Matt. I'm a little weirded out because we never text each other.

Did you hear your boyfriend started coming back to practice again?

This knocks me for a loop. I had no idea. But the news does make me unaccountably joyful: He's back on campus; he's playing again. Maybe the worst really is almost over?

Me: I didn't hear anything about it. But that's a good thing, right?

Matt: Not exactly. Look, I don't think I should be the one to tell you this, but I'm worried the person who should worry won't. Recently, the coach decided to give the entire team a surprise drug test before practice. Thomas popped hot for cocaine and got kicked off the team.

My eyes fly open, and my heart begins to beat so hard that I can feel it reverberating through my entire body. It can't…it can't be true. I gulp air, swamped by nausea and a sudden wave of heat. I'm struggling to breathe, like some supernatural force is bearing down on my lungs. My palms are sweating, and I see that I'm starting to tremble.

"Are you okay? You look…" Logan's voice comes to me like an echo from far away. My mind blurry with anxiety, I leap to my feet.

"Sorry, Logan, but I have to go."

"What, now?"

"I–I'm sorry, I promise I'll make it up to you," I babble, stuffing textbooks and notebooks into my bag as he stares at me, bewildered.

"Hold on, you're scaring me." He grasps my hand. "What happened?"

I fervently shake my head. "D-don't ask me, please, I don't know what to say." I pull free and run away, swerving around students as I pass. I run with no idea where I'm headed, only that I need to get off campus right away. Rolling my eyes skyward, I clutch my phone to my chest and take a series of deep breaths, trying to calm my racing heart.

Breathe, Vanessa. Breathe. You have to breathe.

But I can't. Why can't I breathe?

All around me I hear confused murmuring, see blurry images. Cold shivers pass through my body. I have never felt like this before in my entire life. What is happening to me? Am I having a heart attack? Am I dying? I need to do something. I think I need an ambulance.

"Vanessa…"

I recognize Logan's voice behind me, and I want to turn around but I really…really can't. I feel trapped, petrified, like my feet have been glued to the concrete. All I can hear is the beating of my heart against my rib cage and my breaths getting shorter and shorter.

"Vanessa, give me your hand, come with me," he says softly, now by my side.

I shake my head no, unable to manage a single word. I don't want to go anywhere. I just want this to stop, but it only gets worse. My ears are tingling, and my head feels like it's about to explode.

"I'm afraid you're having a panic attack. And being here, surrounded by all these people, isn't good for you. Come with me. I'll take you inside, into the lobby, and you'll feel calmer there, I promise." He takes my hand, and I, incapable of thought, let him pull me back into the entranceway.

"Here, sit down." He eases me into a soft chair. He unzips his sweatshirt, takes it off, and wraps it around my shoulders, rubbing my arms as he does. "Now, listen carefully to me. I need you to take some deep breaths, okay?"

I shake my head. I can't do what he's asking me to do.

Fortunately, he seems to understand. He kneels down so he can look into my eyes and takes my hands in his. "You can control this; I promise you that you can. It is all in your head."

I close my eyes and try to make myself to do as he says. I force air into my lungs over and over again.

"Good job; keep going. I'll go get you some water."

By the time he comes back, my heartbeat has almost returned to its regular rhythm. I drink all the water and hand him back the empty bottle, taking one last deep breath. "Feeling better?" he asks.

I nod. "I...I don't know what happened to me." I press my fingers into my temples, bowing my head. I feel embarrassed and stupid.

"You had a panic attack," he says again.

I raise my head, still in shock. "That's the first time it's ever happened to me, and I'm not exaggerating when I tell you that it felt like I was dying."

He nods. "The feelings are more or less the same, yeah. It happens during especially stressful times. The hardest part is learning to control them."

"You seem to know a lot about the subject."

He lowers his eyes, focusing on the floor. "I've been living with them for years." Then he adds, almost shamefacedly, "For a little while, I went to therapy for it, but it didn't help me that much."

I wince. "I'm sorry...I didn't know."

"Don't worry about it," he reassures me. "Instead, do you maybe feel like telling me what happened? My therapist always told me that it's easier to control your fears if you know what's triggering them."

That oppressive feeling starts brewing in my chest again. "I really don't feel like talking about it right now," I admit after another deep breath.

"Of course. I understand." He stands up and holds out a hand to help me do the same. "Are you sure you feel okay? Should I go get you some more water?"

"No, I'm fine." I shrug off his sweatshirt and hand it back to him. "I'm sorry I screwed up the tutoring session."

"No worries," he exclaims, with an accompanying wave of his hand. "We'll make it up." He pulls his sweatshirt back on and cracks a smile. "Were you headed home? I can go with you if you want?"

The only thing I want right now is Thomas. I want to see him. I need to. I've got to look him in the eye and get his side of the story. Because I refuse to believe that this is real.

"That's sweet, Logan, but I think I need some alone time right now. But thank you, thank you for all of this." I smile gratefully at him, and despite the clear disappointment on his face, he promises to get in touch in the next few days. Though my hands are shaking, I manage to get my phone out and ask Matt where I can find Thomas right now.

I run all the way to the men's locker room, and I'm so out of my head that I just rush right in without even knocking. Luckily for me, it's almost empty. There's only Thomas, sitting on a bench with a white towel wrapped around his waist and another hanging around his neck. His hair is dripping over his forehead, and elbows resting on his thighs, he's cradling his head in his hands. But the moment he senses my presence, his eyes snap to me, and the coldness that flares in them stops me in my tracks.

Twenty-Five

I CLOSE THE DOOR BEHIND me, my stomach clenching. "Please tell me it's not true," I beg, advancing on him.

Thomas stands up, irritated, and goes to his locker. "How'd you find out?"

"That's not important."

"It is to me. So give me the name of the motherfucker who talked." He yanks the towel off his neck, briskly rubbing his hair before throwing it wrathfully into the hamper.

I completely lose my patience with his nonchalant attitude. I grab his face in both hands and force him to look me in the eye. "Look at me. I'm here freaking out, and your only concern is getting the name of the person who told me? What is wrong with you?"

"More than you can imagine," he answers through gritted teeth, shaking off my hands.

I move aside, and blinking in confusion, I murmur, "What does that mean?"

"Nothing. Leave me alone."

I rub my hands over my face, trying to sort out my thoughts, because sorting out his thoughts is impossible for me. "I thought that part of your life was over." My voice lowers to a hiss, and I give him a regretful stare. "How long, Thomas? How long has this been going on?"

He gives an exhausted sigh. "It only happened once, twice at the most," he explains with a vague wave of his hand, like we're talking about binging on candy or chocolate. He opens his locker and starts emptying his personal effects out of it. "The other night at the frat party, there was some stuff floating around—" he continues, but I suddenly interrupt him because a realization has just torn my heart from my chest.

"Hold on a second..." I step back, my eyes full of horror. "The frat party? The one you left right before coming to see me?"

His eyes widen at me, but not so much as a breath comes out of his mouth. Silence. A damning and deafening silence.

"So that means that, when you came to me...you...you were high?" My voice is trembling and swallowing is a struggle.

He continues to stare unblinkingly at me, the lines of his face all tight and his jaw clenched. Like he's just realized that he's let out a secret he wanted to keep, and now there's no going back. He closes his eyes for a moment, pushing his forehead against the locker.

"Fuck, Ness. This doesn't change anything."

I goggle at him, shocked. I cannot believe him. He was high. He was like that the *whole time*. How in the hell did I not see it? How? Who was I even with that night? Who was I kissing? Who was I touching? God, it feels like I'm losing my mind.

"It doesn't change anything?" I shriek in anguish. "It changes everything, actually. Everything has changed!" I turn my back on him. I can't take another minute shut up in this room with him while he looks at me like his admission doesn't mean anything!

I run for the exit and grab the door handle. But the moment I start to leave, Thomas slams his palm against the door, closing it on me. He chest presses up against my back, trapping me between him and the wood of the door.

"Don't," he growls, only a breath away from my ear. There's a pleading tone hidden in his voice, and against my will, it makes me weak.

"Don't touch me," I manage finally, my voice cracking with tears.

He takes me by the shoulders and turns me to face him. I don't fight him. "I'm not expecting you to understand. But…fuck, I just needed to put an end to all the shit that was constantly going through my head."

I shake my head, wiping my tears on my shirtsleeve. "It's worse than I thought, if we're already at the point where you're making excuses for yourself."

He doesn't answer, he just gives me a look filled with resentment. He might as well have stuck a knife right into my chest. It's difficult for me, because my throat is burning with rage and sorrow, but I sniff, and like the true masochist that I am, I push the blade in deeper. "It was all bullshit, wasn't it? You didn't come over the other night because you wanted to see me or because you missed me. You came because you needed a body to use."

He shuts his eyes, guilty. "Ness."

"Admit it."

"What do you want me to say? That I needed to turn off my brain more than I needed you? Yeah, I did. You wanna hate me for that? Get in line. But I wasn't looking for a fucking body to use; I was looking for you. I wanted you. I needed to lose myself, and like a dumbass, I did, but you were the person I needed to do it with."

"Is that supposed to be comforting? Make me feel, I don't know, special because you were able to use me as an escape hatch? Do you realize how humiliating that is? I should hate you for this. I should hate your guts for everything you're doing to me!" I pound on his bare chest with my closed fists.

"Do you think I don't know that? Why do you think I skipped out the next morning? I felt like a piece of shit!" He slaps the wood of the door next to my temples, making it vibrate. For a long moment, we just stare silently at each other, breathing heavily.

Finally, I speak. "You've handled everything poorly, Thomas. All of it. Ever since your father's death, it's just gotten steadily worse. A succession of bad choices and actions designed to hurt me, to get me as far away from you as possible. You've locked me out and put up your walls again. Still, despite all of that, I've tried to understand. I've tried to take care of you, easing your pain, riding out your bad moods, watching you drink yourself into oblivion, swallowing bitterness after bitterness for days, waiting for being with you to feel good again," I say, all in one breath. "And I don't regret it. I did it because I really believed that was what you needed, someone to be there for you even in your lowest moments. Someone who accepted the worst of you. I did it because I wanted to do it, because I promised you." *Because I love you*, I scream internally. "I promised you that I wouldn't leave you alone and that I'd be here for you, no matter what. But this…" I stop and suck in a deep breath. "This is beyond my limits. I'm sorry."

With an angry jerk, he brings his face closer to mine, staring furiously at me. "What are you trying to say?"

"That I can't keep running after you if all you're going to do is push me away."

I watch a flash of pain cross his face but, in a second, it's gone. Thomas drops his arms to his sides and steps back, as though my words have produced a shock wave forcing him away. "Do you want to end it?"

The question makes me freeze up. No, that's not what I want at all. I don't want to leave him; I struggle to breathe just at the thought of it. But last night really was the straw that broke the camel's back. It is devastating to find out that he was on drugs when he was with me. I feel like I don't even recognize this person standing in front of me.

"N-no, that's not what I'm saying. But it would be better if you stayed away from me for a while. I need to figure this all out, and I can't do that when you're around. You confuse me. You fog up my mind, and I can't afford that anymore."

He watches me intently, and it's only a matter of moments before the disorientation on his face gives way to a contemptuous sneer. "Those fucking games won't work on me," he pronounces, running a hand through his damp hair in frustration. He walks away from me to a bench in the center of the room.

"What games are you talking about?" I ask him, bewildered.

"Asking me for time to think just because you don't have the guts to tell me that you want to end it," he answers icily, tossing his uniform into his bag. Then he turns his green eyes on me, full of anger. "I don't do half measures. Either you're in or you're out."

My throat tightens. "Excuse me? You, the guy who wanted me in his bed but not in his life, are telling me that you don't do half measures?" I realize that this is not the point, but I find it ridiculous that he thinks he's in a position to give me an ultimatum.

He shrugs his shoulders arrogantly, zipping up the bag. "Things change."

"Oh, go to hell, Thomas! After everything you've put me through in the last few weeks, you have zero right to try to back me into a corner!" I scream with an outrage that I can no longer contain. "If we've reached that point, you are the one to blame. You chose alcohol over me. You chose drugs over me. Yet I'm still here, and all I'm asking for is time! But if it's easier for you to break up with me than to respect my decision, then you know what? Do it."

I don't give him any time to answer before I'm already out the door. He tries to catch my arm, but I wriggle free. He calls my name, but it's not enough. The last thing I hear before I turn the corner is the locker room door slamming with a thud.

I run all the way home. I throw my bag on the floor and fall into bed. I burst into tears, sobs wracking my body. I cry all afternoon, all night, until I have no more tears left. The next day, I call in sick to work and skip my classes. I don't want to do anything. I tell Alex and Tiffany that I'm too busy studying; I don't want to talk to them either. I just want to lie here in bed, surrounded by wet, crumpled tissues, and stare up at the ceiling.

And I know it's contradictory because I was the one who wanted it, but Thomas's silence hurts me. I really didn't want to break up with him. I didn't want him to break up with me. I just wanted it to go back to how it was before his father. Before everything collapsed.

By evening, I find the strength to get out of bed and take a shower. I have to at least try to make myself presentable for dinner with my mother. I don't want to make her suspicious. So I use concealer to hide the dark circles under my eyes, and give myself a light dusting of blush and a transparent coat of lip gloss. Then I pull on a pair of sheer black tights and a black skirt that falls just above my knees followed by a white turtleneck. I wear my black boots and a long coat. Before I leave, I look into the mirror and try to produce the fake smile that will be my faithful companion throughout the evening. But I don't look at all convincing. I try a couple more times, but I end up just looking like I'm having mouth spasms. I give up.

Half an hour later, I'm sitting with my legs crossed and my foot jiggling nervously under the table. I stare out the enormous windows overlooking the garden outside, all refined furnishings, warm tones, and soft lighting. It's one of those places where they check a book for your reservation, pull back the chair when you sit down, and try to pass off a small appetizer as a full first course. Crooks. The drinks alone are going to cost an arm and a leg. My mother seems perfectly at ease though, and Victor, dressed to the nines, studies the menu with all the intensity he'd use to plot his next chess move against some imaginary opponent.

My mother's bright blue eyes, on the other hand, scrutinize me relentlessly as I stare into the middle distance and swallow the last sip of the sparkling wine that they offered us on the house. She knows that something is bothering me, and I'm sure she's just racking her brain trying to figure out what it is.

I already told her during the car ride to the restaurant that Thomas was too busy with the team to come. At first, it seemed like she bought it. Yet she's still giving me suspicious looks.

"You're very quiet this evening," she observes. "More so than usual, I mean."

I gulp down the last bit of wine and clear my throat. "I'm fine," I answer, improvising one of those smiles I practiced earlier, hoping that I sound convincing. "Just a little tired, that's all."

"You shouldn't work so many hours. It's counterproductive to your mental and physical health and, most importantly, to your studies, which I hope you aren't neglecting."

"Esther," Victor chides her.

"Work isn't a problem," I explain calmly, fiddling with the corners of my napkin. It's true; it's everything else in my life that's a mess…

"And how are things with that boy?" she asks, sounding as though she doesn't really care about the answer. "It's too bad he wasn't able to come; I was counting on it," she finishes, giving the slim watch around her wrist a gentle shake.

"Things are fine with him too," I answer, trying not to let my voice tremble.

"You don't sound very sure of that," she says, her mouth twisting slightly.

Fortunately, we are interrupted by the server, who comes to take our orders. As soon as she leaves, I change the subject to ease some of the tension. "This is a lovely place."

"It's very lovely," my mother adds. "This is where Victor took me to celebrate our second-month anniversary." Elated, she intertwines her fingers with those of the silver-haired man sitting next to her. They exchange such knowing looks that I want to vomit. The look that I secretly give my mother is anything but conspiratorial, however. It's a mixture of discomfort and confusion. At their age, they shouldn't care about "monthiversaries." What the hell? My mother was a married woman, and now she's acting like a teenage girl with her first crush?

But maybe that's just me becoming cynical about love. It's tough to admit, but I think that some part of me is feeling kind of envious of my mother. Which, I suppose, makes me a bad person. But she just looks so happy. Satisfied and carefree. There is a glow to her that I've never seen before and I certainly don't have. Not anymore at least. She has such a full life now, and I feel so empty and…oh my God.

I almost leap out of my chair.

Oh my God, that's Thomas's car.

My heart pounds violently in my chest, sending a lightning bolt through my body. I watch through the windows as a black BMW parks in front of the entrance. But he doesn't emerge from the driver's side like I'm expecting; instead, he gets out of the passenger side. As I watch him with my heart in my throat, I see that he's staggering. My heart palpitations increase, as does the sheer horror in my eyes. He can't be doing this. He can't be showing up here to dinner with my mother while *drunk*. He can't!

The moment I see him head for the front door, I jump up.

"What is wrong with you?" my mother exclaims, concerned, while Victor looks at me with a dumbfounded expression.

"Nothing," I manage, praying to God that neither of them turns around and sees what's going on. "S-sorry, I just remembered that I left something in the car. I'll be right back."

I hear them muttering something, but I can't make out what because I've already left. I move furiously to the front door. Thomas and I put our hands on the doorknob at the same time, me trying to exit, him to enter. But I'm the one who pulls it back first. He stumbles back with a faint gasp. "Hey, baby."

"Baby"?

I grab him by the arm and drag him behind the granite gazebo in the garden, far from prying eyes. Before I start talking, I pause to glare at the person in the driver's seat of Thomas's car, only to find that it's Vince. I keep glaring at him, but he raises his hands and shakes his head, as if trying to exonerate himself.

"I didn't have a choice; he would have gone by himself otherwise, and that didn't seem like a good idea to me," he says in a voice loud enough to be heard.

"Are you out of your mind?" I scream through gritted teeth before turning my attention back to Thomas. "What are you doing here?"

"Are you mad? Why do you look mad? It's your mom's fault, right? Did she already make you regret coming?" he slurs, attempting to touch my cheek or maybe to kiss me, but I dodge him. That seems to make him feel bad, which hurts me as well.

I try to calm some of the rage that is circulating throughout my body because I have learned the hard way that when he's in this kind of condition, it's no use trying to take it out on him. "No, Thomas, I'm not angry," I lie. "I'm just trying to figure out why you're here."

"You asked me to come."

My forehead wrinkles in a frown. "What? When would I have done that?"

"The other night, in your room. You're convinced I don't remember, but I do, I do remember."

I shut my eyes as it begins to dawn on me. "God, I don't believe this..." I whisper. I pinch the bridge of my nose and sigh. "I said I wanted you here with me, Thomas. But not this way, not when you're like this. And have you already forgotten what I told you yesterday? That I need some time away from you? I haven't changed my mind one day later. And I'm not going to change it if you keep doing this to yourself. You're drunk again."

"I'm not drunk," he manages. "I maybe had a few drinks before coming, but I'm solid."

I huff and cross my arms over my chest. "Please, there isn't a single solid thing about you right now."

"Shit, you're right," he says in an exhausted sort of way. Then suddenly, his expression darkens. "I've haven't done anything but let you down. How is that possible?" His words and the way he looks at me, so lost and helpless, make my heart hurt. He seems so broken, and it is destroying me. I keep telling myself not to give in to this, but for the first time since his father's death, it's like I can see something in his eyes other than anger and contempt. A glimmer of real, sincere emotion. He really is suffering. And trying to remain unmoved by that is really damn hard for me.

He presses his forehead against mine, waiting for a response that he doesn't receive. I can't tell him he's wrong. I'd like to, but I can't.

"Not answering, huh?"

"I don't know what to tell you."

"Tell me you're still my girlfriend."

"Thomas..."

"Say it, Ness," he begs.

"This isn't the time to talk about it. My mother is in there waiting for me, and if she saw you like this, she'd have a meltdown—"

He kisses me.

Instinctively, I try to push him away with my hands against his chest, nauseated by the taste of alcohol that pervades his mouth, but it's useless. "I need to hear you say it," he says against my lips in a deep rumble. "Because the idea that you might not be any more is fucking with my head." He grabs my hips with both hands and pushes me flat against the gazebo. It's demanding and desperate, this kiss of his. And when his tongue finds its way into my mouth, it becomes harder to resist it. "I didn't sleep at all last night." He pulls back, resting his forehead against mine again. "I forced myself to stay away from you because that's what you asked me to do, but I need to know that you're still with me, that I haven't lost you for good." The anguish that I can hear in his voice disarms me.

"You know that I'm with you," I reassure him. "I just want some time to think about it, about how to better deal with this whole situation. For both of our sakes."

"Think about it..." he echoes in low tones. "I knew we'd get here someday. To the point when you'd smack into harsh reality and then you'd leave."

Remembering the things Thomas said to me that night when he opened up completely for me, I feel sorrow tightening my throat until it's hard to breathe. *"You'd never look at me the same again. You'd see me for what I am. And what I am, Ness? You wouldn't like it at all."*

And I promised him that wouldn't happen. I promised him that I would stay. I let out a miserable sigh and hold his face in my hands, but before I can tell him anything, a voice interrupts us.

"Vanessa, darling, where have you been? You didn't even take the car keys..."

Oh, no.

No, no, no, no.

"Shit," Thomas whispers, squeezing his eyes shut.

"M-Mom." I emerge from behind the gazebo and watch her expression shift when she realizes that Thomas is there with me.

"Oh. You're here," she says, with no enthusiasm but, strangely enough, without too much hostility either.

"Actually, he was just leaving," I say quickly, rubbing my hands on my skirt.

"He's leaving? Did he come all this way just to leave? Don't be silly, Vanessa. Come on, let's go inside. The plates have arrived, and the three of us have things to discuss." A wave of panic washes over me, but then, suddenly, the noise of a car horn rings out in the plaza. We all turn to look at the BMW, which is producing the noise, and Vince gestures for Thomas to come with him. *Thank you, Vince, for jumping in at the right moment.*

"Something came up unexpectedly and I can't stay any longer," Thomas explains to my mother.

"I hope it's nothing serious."

"No, nothing serious," he answers immediately, running a hand through his hair and tilting his face downward.

She frowns and, looking almost worried, asks, "You look awful; are you feeling all right?"

"Um, yeah," Thomas says, trying to disguise his slurring voice as much as possible. "Just a little nausea. I get carsick."

I hold my breath, hoping with every fiber of my being that my mother believes this and lets him go as quickly as possible. But, from the way she's eyeing him, I can tell that she isn't even kind of buying Thomas's lie.

My mother advances upon us with an eerie calm. The closer she gets, the more furiously her eyes burn and the faster my heart beats. She examines Thomas from top to bottom before saying, disgust clear in her voice, "Since when does motion sickness smell like liquor?"

"Mom!"

But she shuts me up with the point of a finger. "Quiet!" she hisses venomously. "I asked you a question, boy," she continues, positioning herself just a few inches from his face. The dizzying stilettos she wears allow her to almost match Thomas's height.

He doesn't answer; he just stares icily back at her.

"I can't believe this!" my mother explodes, turning purple. "I was right about you from the start. You're just a pathetic delinquent!" Her voice is sharp, each syllable a cruel strike.

"Now you're going overboard!" I move in front of Thomas, facing my mother firmly. "You have no right to talk to him like that!" I realize that finding her daughter's boyfriend—whom she already hated on sight—drunk isn't great. But I'm not going to let her disrespect him right in front of me.

"Enough, Ness," Thomas scolds me sharply while my mother looks at me like I've lost my mind.

"Are you defending him? I'm so disappointed in you, Vanessa. This"—she looks him up and down in repudiation—"this societal reject that you insist upon associating with has completely brainwashed you! It seems like you can't even tell right from wrong anymore. Travis never would have acted like this! He would never, ever embarrass you like—"

"Are you still talking about him?" I interrupt, digging my hands into my hair. "Are you ever going to be able to accept that he was a jerk?"

"You cannot tell me that this is what you want for yourself! Spending your life with a drunk who can barely stand up? Having to make up lies to explain his tardiness when he's too drunk to show up on time for a simple dinner with your mother? That is not how I raised you! That is not what I taught you!" I see her hand fly into the air, but with quicker reflexes than I was expecting, Thomas grabs my mother's arm just before her palm collides violently with my face for a second time.

"Don't you dare," he says clearly and angrily.

I observe this scene in shock, my heart beating wildly.

"My daughter made a huge mistake with you. The biggest mistake of her life!" she spews at him. "She gave up everything she had for you, and this is how you repay her? You should be ashamed of yourself!"

"I don't even know what you're talking about," he says, surly even as he releases his grip on her wrist.

She gives him a shocked look, eyebrows raised. "Are you kidding?"

"Mom, please just *stop*!" My legs are trembling at the idea of Thomas learning the truth.

But she ignores my pleading, unleashing all her anger instead. "What do you think is the reason for our estrangement? It's you, of course. When I gave her a choice, she picked you and threw everything else away!"

Silence descends.

"I didn't know that," he admits, troubled. "Is that true?" he adds, turning to look at me, disappointment plain on his face.

My heart pounds faster and faster; I can feel my cheeks burning. "Thomas…" I murmur, my voice trembling.

"Oh, don't pretend you were in the dark about this," she continues furiously as Thomas and I just keep staring at each other as if we are the only two people in existence.

The words are stuck in my throat. My eyes beg him tearfully not to let her get in his head. He gives me nothing but dismay in return.

Meanwhile, in the background, my mother just continues her rant. "My daughter left home to be with an animal like you. You've wrecked her life, deluded her into thinking you could offer her things you'll never really be able to give her! My daughter was happy before you. Carefree! Look at her now! Do you see what you've done to her?" She waves her arms like a madwoman.

Hearing these words, Thomas visibly surrenders. As if they have affected him more than he wants to let on. As if, in reality, all my mother has done is give voice to his own darkest thoughts. So he turns and leaves.

I don't think twice before I run after him.

"Vanessa, come back here!" my mother yells, in the midst of a nervous breakdown.

"Shut up!" I answer, not even bothering to turn around. And before Thomas can get the car door open, I grab him by the back of his shirt and block his way. "Let me explain!"

"There's nothing to explain. I shouldn't have come here. I shouldn't have done a lot of the things that I did." He sighs and looks back at my mother, chewing on the corner of his lip. "Go back to her. Your mother is right; you've deluded yourself, and it's my fault for letting you."

"What? No...no, she's not right. She said all those nasty things just because she hates you! Don't fall for it!"

He moves his hand over his mouth and then his jaw, sighing. "Is what she said true? Am I the reason you left home? That you put your education at risk?"

I don't understand anything anymore. Panic strangles me. This is all happening too fast. "I–It wasn't just about you. She wanted to control my life. All my choices, Thomas."

"And was I one of them?"

I put my hands in my hair and then pull them out again. "Not in the way you're thinking!"

"Yeah, but still! I don't want to be the reason you end up homeless or without a mother or unable to fucking study!"

"What was I supposed to do?"

Thomas goggles at me. "You were supposed to listen to her! We're not in one of your fucking romance novels, where you can blow up your whole life for a fucking crush! If you have to give up everything to be with me, I don't want you!" He shouts it into my face with an intensity that paralyzes me. Then he turns his back on me and climbs back into the car. A moment later, Vince, visibly embarrassed, starts the car, and they drive away.

I stand there, watching the car disappear as Thomas's words echo in my ears. Behind me, I also hear that Victor's come out of the restaurant. He asks my mother what's going on, and I hear her rambling. I blink and break out of the catatonic state I've been in. The anger I feel toward my mother dominates all my other emotions—enough to make me fight back. I turn my stare on the woman who gave life to me and now seems to take a ghoulish pleasure in trying to ruin it for me. Then, I rush over to her.

"Are you happy?" My voice is shaking with fury.

She raises her chin proudly and shrugs her shoulders. The same shoulders that Victor rests his hands upon. "I would be much happier if I thought I opened your eyes once and for all. That boy is no good for you. Even he knows it."

I exhale with an expression of disgust. This is pointless. It's all pointless with her. "You're always going to see him as the villain of the situation, aren't you, Mom?"

"Not a villain. Just wrong. Wrong for you. It's so obvious that I wonder how you don't realize it yourself!"

"Why don't we all try to calm down now?" Victor says, trying to de-escalate things, but I ignore him.

"Maybe you're right. Maybe he's wrong for me. Or maybe I'm the one who's wrong for him," I say, turning to my mother. "But just know that when you put me out on the street, he welcomed me into his home, ensuring I had a roof over my head when you had taken mine away from me! Just know that the only reason I am here tonight is because he convinced me to accept the stupid invitation. Because he wanted me to have a civil relationship with my mother again. Him, not me. He's not perfect, I acknowledge that. But neither am I. Neither are you. And you have no idea what he's going through right now. So don't you dare talk about him like that ever again," I warn her angrily as she stares at me in discomfort. "My evening ends here."

I walk away with brisk strides, ignoring my mother's insistent calls. And just when I think she's about to come after me, I realize that Victor is holding her back. "Let her go; this isn't where she wants to be right now," I hear him say. I thank him mentally for stopping her.

I pull my phone out of my clutch and frantically call an Uber. While I wait, I try to call Thomas. But it goes to voicemail on the second ring. I call him again, but this time it goes straight to voicemail. That's not good. That's not good at all. I'm shaking, both from the cold and the anxiety. I left my coat at the restaurant, but there's no way I'm going back for it. I just want to find Thomas and explain the situation, try to salvage what I can. Because there is still something to be saved, I tell myself. There has to be. Because he took a step tonight, coming back to me. And I'm not going to let this second chance slip through my fingers because of my mother.

    I call Vince, who, fortunately, answers immediately. There's a giant racket in the background. Music, yelling. He's at a party. He confirms it, telling me that he's at Matt's. And that's exactly where I have the Uber driver take me.

Twenty-Six

WHEN I GET OUT OF the Uber, I'm surprised by the number of people both inside and outside the frat house. Many more than usual. I guess today's game went well, even without Thomas. I walk down the sidewalk, ignoring the chaos around me, from the empty cups scattered on the grass to the small group of shirtless boys who, despite it being the end of November, are running around throwing cups full of beer on each other.

Shana's here too, of course. She leans on the doorjamb, grinning at me as she nibbles on the rim of the plastic cup she's holding. I try to look indifferent, pretending she doesn't even exist. But, as I pass her, she exclaims, "Uh-oh! Trouble in paradise?" I don't pay attention to her. I shoulder past her hard, now that I have the chance to return the favor.

I walk into the house and look around for Thomas, but all the people crammed together make it hard to see. I spot the figure of Vince in the distance. He's in the kitchen with some girls who are sitting on the table while he pours drinks directly into their mouths. I take a step toward them, but my path is blocked by a tall muscular guy. He's wearing light-wash jeans with rips in the knees and a completely unbuttoned plaid shirt. His eyes are red, and like everyone else here, he seems to have had at least one too many. He smiles at me. But the way he does it, I don't like at all.

"Sorry, I need to get through," I say, glancing nervously at the surrounding crowd, hoping to spot Thomas there.

"There's nothing interesting over there." He smirks, head cocked to one side, and takes a few steps closer to me. "You here alone?"

"No."

Ignoring my answer, he gets even closer to me, and I feel a lump beginning to form in my throat. "My boyfriend is somewhere in here," I iterate. "So if you'll excuse me..." I raise both eyebrows, gesturing for him to make room and get out of my way. But he doesn't.

"Why don't you tell me your name? You're gorgeous," he continues lewdly, trying to grab me by the hips. I push out my hands to stop him from getting any closer and step aside, bumping into someone else's back. Suddenly, another boy emerges and joins the first, playfully wrapping an arm around his neck and pulling him away from me.

"Dude, what are you doing?" the second guy shouts in the first's ear, trying to be heard over the music.

"I'm having a good time; isn't that what we're here for?" the asshole replies, staring hungrily at my legs.

His friend raises a red cup to his lips, looks carefully at me, and shakes his head. "Not with her, trust me. Let's get some air."

I narrow my eyes to slits. I'm not sure what that was about, but I feel a sickly sensation growing inside me at the thought of that guy going on to harass someone less fortunate than I am.

The perv protests a little bit but eventually allows himself to be pulled away. Only then do I start breathing again. I shut my eyes and try to remind myself why I'm here again. When I open them, I walk into the kitchen and touch Vince's shoulder to get his attention. Luckily he, at least, isn't drunk. I ask him where Thomas is, and he tells me that as soon as they got here, Thomas went upstairs. I thank him hurriedly and rush up to Thomas's room.

I push open the door and find him at the foot of his bed, his back pressed into the mattress and both feet planted on the floor. His eyes are glued to the ceiling, and he has what appears to be a joint between his fingers. "If I wanted to see you, I'd have answered your call, don't you think?"

I close the door and approach him. "You left before I had a chance to explain."

"I don't wanna hear your explanations," he replies, sitting up and taking a hit off the joint. "Look where they got you."

I shake my head. "I don't regret the choice I made or where it's gotten me. I'd do it again, a thousand times, because it was what I wanted. You can't blame me for that."

"I absolutely can. Is it possible that you actually don't see it? What, do you enjoy ruining your life, or are you just too stupid to understand when you've got a problem right in front of your face? I mean, what more do you need before you finally get that I'm not good for you?"

My brow furrows. "Are you the same guy who showed up drunk to dinner with my mother just now? The one who begged me to tell him that I was still his girlfriend?"

He glances quickly at me. His eyes are cold and foggy. "That was bullshit, actually. Never listen to a drunk." He pauses. He stubs out the joint at the bottom of an ashtray next to him on the mattress and then continues: "I should have let you go, just like you asked. In fact, that's what I should've done at the beginning, but instead I got myself trapped in this *thing*, and now everything is fucked."

"Why, Thomas? Why are you saying this?"

"Because it's the truth. I'm a problem. I always have been, and I'm not going to stop being one just because you're in my life. You have to understand that—I mean really understand it."

I kneel down on the floor, resting my hands on his thighs. "Is that what has been torturing you? Awareness of what you are and fear of how it could affect the people around you?"

"I'm not afraid of what I am. I'm afraid that you aren't. It scares me that you're so delusional that you actually believe that you can change me, that this thing between you and me could possibly end well! It scares me that whatever it is that makes you want to be with me also makes you accept all my bullshit, all my disrespect, all my freak-outs. But what scares me most of all is that every single time, you're ready to rationalize my behavior. To defend me and forgive all my screwups. To choose me even over your own family. That scares the shit out of me. Because I am a time bomb, and you just keep holding on to me like a lunatic, waiting to blow yourself up. Do you want to end up like my fucking mother? Because if that's your plan, I'm telling you, you're on the right track!"

The cruelty of his words twists my stomach. But I force myself to take it. "Don't be absurd, Thomas. You would never do to me what your father did to her; how can you even think that?"

"Do you think that when she met him, she had any idea the kind of man he would turn into? No. No woman ever does. Do you know how she ended up trapped in a marriage with a man who beat her? By rationalizing. Forgiving him. And then before she knew it, she opened her eyes one day and it was too late. A person's nature doesn't change, and I refuse to change for you."

I shake my head, rubbing my temples. "Thomas…you can't…you can't seriously believe that. Don't you see that the mere fact of you recognizing the risk of the situation repeating itself makes you different from your father? You are going through a hard time right now, and yes, on more than a few occasions, you have been at your worst. You do things that I don't agree with, and that does hurt me, but it doesn't make you a monster."

He snorts, lowering his gaze. And as he turns the joint over in his hands, he whispers, "You're still doing it. Still rationalizing what I do."

"You're wrong. I'm not rationalizing. But I won't let your brain trick you into believing something that isn't true. Your father's death has clearly thrown you off-balance, but—"

"My father's death is not the problem! The problem is us! I was selfish with you. Petty. A total bastard. I took out my frustrations on you, forced you watch the 'Thomas is a failure' show every fucking day for the last two weeks. I kept you with me even when I knew it wasn't the right thing to do. And despite all my shit, the drinking, the drugs… you stick with me. Why? Why are you doing this?"

"Because you're my boyfriend, Thomas. I can't just turn my back on you when you're having trouble. That's not in my nature."

"Is it in your nature to just accept it all?"

"No. You know it isn't."

"Then why the fuck do you keep doing it?" He throws his arms out wide in frustration.

"Because I love you!" It escapes from me like some kind of release, and I'm the first to be shocked by it.

Thomas's face contorts into a mixture of upset and denial. Silence reigns for a handful of seconds before he demands, "What did you say?"

Not without hesitation, I reach for his face in the hopes of touching his cheek, and I repeat stubbornly, "I love you."

It's the last bit of fuse before everything explodes in our faces. Thomas grabs both my wrists and tosses them away. The enraged look he gives me tears a chasm in my chest. "You've fallen in love with me?" he hisses, his mouth twisting into a disgusted sneer. "What the fuck is wrong with you?" he bursts out, leaping to his feet while I stay kneeling on the floor, staring into the void ahead of me with a lost look. "I just finished telling you how dangerous I am to you, and this is what you say to me?"

I don't answer him; I can't. I'm too stupefied by his reaction to say anything at all.

"No one said anything about love," he continues, almost to himself. "I started all this by fucking you every now and then because I felt like it. Because you were there and easy. Then I let myself get drawn into this ridiculous relationship that is constantly foundering, all because you kept throwing tantrums like a spoiled little girl. But no one ever said anything about love or any of that shit! It's honestly pathetic that you could even think that."

I'm completely speechless. Unmoored. Shattered. *He's drunk*, I remind myself. *And angry. He doesn't mean what he's saying. This is not him. This is not who you fell in love with. You fell in love with the good parts. The sweet, sensitive, and caring person that he allowed you to slowly unearth. Don't let him ruin everything. Don't let him treat you this way. Fight back.* I say the words over and over in my head, like a mantra. I feel about an inch tall and more humiliated than I've ever been in my life.

"When you're with someone…it's normal to develop feelings," I whisper in a broken voice. "Some things are just beyond our control…" My eyes are watering, and with extreme difficultly, I turn in his direction.

"Bullshit. Everything can be controlled! You spent years being treated like shit by a guy who'd rather fuck other girls than be with you, and now you're going to tell me that you've fallen in love with someone like me? So let's hear it, then: When did I make you fall in love with me? Was it when I fucked you and used your body like the bastard I am? Or maybe it was when I started coming inside you? Maybe that was the moment when you fooled yourself into thinking that it meant something to me? Or was it because I took you to my parents' house? Fuck, you're acting like a child." His words hit me like a slap, taking my breath away.

"Enough," I say, in a barely audible murmur. "Please, stop it." I pick myself up off the ground with slow movements. It feels like the room has started spinning, and I look around for something to hold on to. But the only things I find are my own arms, which I hug tightly to my chest.

With one step, Thomas closes the distance between us. A gust of alcohol and weed hits me right in the face, making me feel nauseous. Or maybe it's just him that makes me want to puke. He looms over me, looking menacingly down at me. He grabs me by the shoulders and brings his face down close to mine. Still in shock, I let myself be manipulated like a marionette.

"I don't love you," he spits cruelly at me. "And I never will."

I am breathless. "Why…why are you doing this to me? What did I do to you to deserve this?" My voice has been reduced to a strangled sob. I can feel the pressure of his fingers slacken.

He's looking at me. His chest rises and falls like he's out of breath. I remain chained to his stare. And I don't know how, but I feel like the look on his face is telling me—screaming at me—*I will never be able to get the memory of your face right now out of my head.* My face. A blank face. Ripped apart by suffering. Ripped apart by the man I love.

"You can do better," he growls through gritted teeth. "You deserve better." He releases me with a shove that makes me stagger back. "Now get the fuck out of this room; I want to be alone," he finishes, turning his back to me and grabbing the bottle of whiskey from the desk.

I just stand there helplessly, staring at his broad back with my legs trembling. I want to vent all my suffering at him. But I can't so much as utter a word. It's like a part of my brain has been paralyzed. I have no idea how, but I do somehow get out of the room. The room that, until a few weeks ago, I shared with him. The room that still contains some of my books, some of my clothes. A piece of me. I leave it there. I leave it with him, and then I disappear with my broken heart.

I got it all so wrong. I confessed my feelings to the man I love, and he, without even a shred of respect for me, obliterated them right before my eyes. Ridiculed them. I shouldn't have done it, not like this. I made a mistake, a serious one. But I can't believe that I just made up a love that never really existed. All those times he defended me, supported me, encouraged me, and protected me. He took care of me; he gave me everything he had to give. The night my mother kicked me out, he took me by the hand and brought me to an ice-skating rink because he knew how happy it would make me. He took me stargazing so I could relive a piece of my childhood. And he indulged me when I asked to stay in the rain with him, just because it would bring me joy.

That is the guy I fell in love with. The boy whose arms became my favorite place in the world, and didn't he promise that I could stay there as long as I wanted? The boy who, after making love, drew his face close to mine and whispered that he'd never be able to be without me again. Who got me a bracelet just because he saw how much I liked it. Who took me to his home, to the places where he grew up, and showed me the most important parts of his life: his mother, his brother. I wasn't building castles in the air. I refuse to believe that. I fell in love with him because he was lovable.

But his words, so full of contempt, keep running through my head.

And I swear I'd rip my brain out of my skull rather than continue to hear them. Just like I'd rip my heart from my chest rather than feel all this pain.

I spend the night sobbing in my bed, occasionally falling asleep and startling awake several times. I feel like I've been tossed into some nightmare, and for a few moments in the thick darkness of my room, I can even fool myself into believing that is what's happening.

The first rays of dawn come slowly. When you're suffering, time seems to stop. But the pain remains. It's all there, inside of you. And it kills you; it sucks out your life force. It tears at your soul. I'm about to slip into another muzzy half sleep, but then I feel my phone vibrate with a new text. I gasp slightly when I see his name come up on the display.

That's not possible. He couldn't possibly have the guts to text me now. I stay there with my phone clutched in my hands for a few seconds while I consider whether to read the text or just delete it.

I decide to read it.

I need you to come here. I'm begging you.

I stare at the message in consternation for a long time, trying to make some sense of it. He has completely lost his mind. Where does he get the audacity to ask me for something like that? After the way he treated me, I shouldn't even be thinking about it, but damn it, the wound is too fresh, and thinking is all that I can do. Love makes us stupid. Exploitable. Dependent. Screwed up and weak. And I'm all of that. Right now, I'm every one of those things. Which is why, for a second, I actually consider going over there. Even if it's just to shout in his face how cowardly and disgusting he was toward me and claw back a modicum of the dignity that he shredded.

Then, another text: It's urgent.

Panic takes the wheel. With one hand pressed against my chest, I leap out of bed. What if something actually happened to him? The worry is enough to get me rushing over there.

I walk to the frat house with my stomach in knots and a nauseous feeling that intensifies with each step I take. I'm even momentarily afraid that I'm going to have to stop and vomit. The front door isn't locked, and the interior is full of sleeping guys and girls, even though it's already almost noon. There are empty bottles scattered everywhere. The smell of weed and sweat permeates everything. On the floor, I spot three Spanish lit books, carelessly abandoned. I pick them up, because the thought of leaving them in the midst of all the chaos hurts my heart.

I climb the stairs, trying to soothe the agitation that's turned my knees to water. I grab the door handle, and a terrible kind of premonition comes over me. It's like an alarm bell going off in my head, a voice whispering that I should run away. But I don't pay it any heed; instead I turn the handle and go in.

My blood runs cold. I see clothes scattered across the floor. An empty whiskey bottle on the desk. Thomas's belt at the foot of the bed. His shirt dangling half off the mattress. White powder on the bedside table. And him on his stomach, wrapped in a sheet, *asleep*.

But none of that is what steals my breath. What freezes my heart are the glacier-colored eyes that stare mockingly at me. The barely there grin that slowly appears on a mouth smeared with lipstick. The shock of tousled red hair falling over bare breasts, the rest of her covered by the same sheet that surrounds my boyfriend's naked body.

No.

Not my boyfriend.

Not anymore.

I feel the ground shaking beneath my feet. My ears are ringing. That retching feeling is crawling back up my throat again.

"Oops," Shana says maliciously, sitting up straight. "Surprise."

The books I'm holding fall to the floor with a dull clatter that wakes Thomas up. Instinctively, he throws his arm out toward the part of the mattress that, until recently, I occupied. His hand lands on Shana's belly, and I feel a stabbing sensation in my chest.

This is not possible.

This is not really happening.

But then Thomas raises his head and turns to look at her. "What the fuck are you doing in my bed?" he growls, leaping to his feet. My eyes land on his boxers—he's still wearing them—but that doesn't mean anything.

It's only then that Thomas notices I'm in the room. And the expression on his face shifts dramatically. He's no longer surprised; instead he seems terrified. He pales, and I'm sure that he knows it too; he knows that this is our point of no return.

"Fuck, no," he says, moving to me and taking me by the shoulders. "It's not what it looks like, I promise you."

My eyes fill with tears.

"Do you hear me, Ness?" He shakes me slightly, trying to get me to say something, but I can't.

I'm paralyzed. All I can do is look at him with disgust.

"I have no idea what she's doing here or how she wound up in my bed!"

"You're the one who wanted it; don't you remember?" Shana interrupts in a honeyed voice. She rises from the bed, utterly unashamed in her nakedness. She plucks her bra and panties off the floor and puts them on.

"What the fuck are you talking about?" Thomas snaps.

"After she left, you came downstairs. You were tense, mad. So I asked how you were doing, and you started telling me that you were so fucking done. You said she was making your life impossible. And that you couldn't take it anymore."

I'm making *his* life impossible.

He can't take it anymore.

"So we had a few drinks, and you took me upstairs because you didn't want to be in the middle of all the chaos down there. We did a few lines, and when I was about to leave, you stopped me." She approaches the two of us. "I tried to reason with you, tell you that you weren't doing the right thing, but you didn't give me a chance to talk. You grabbed me and fucked me on that desk...and then on that sofa... and finally in the bed..."

He interrupts her. "Bullshit! I don't remember any of that."

She giggles. "Well, with all the shit swimming around in your system, I'm surprised you still remember your name." She picks up her dress from the floor, buried amongst Thomas's clothes, and then, with a malicious grin, she informs me, "Not a smart move, telling him you love him."

It feels like I'm dying. I can't even swallow for the lump in my throat.

"Get the fuck out of here!" Thomas shouts at Shana, his fingers still gripping my shoulders. He holds me like he's trying to keep me there with him for as long as possible, like he's afraid that the moment he lets go, he'll never get me back again.

And it's true.

He's lost me. He's lost me forever.

I won't be able to look at him again without seeing Shana and him together. Talking together, getting drunk together, kissing and touching each other. Her, naked in that bed. The same bed where he said he had brought only me. Him taking her there. While I was shattered into pieces. Alone, wounded, and ashamed because of him.

Now, even his scent disgusts me. I'm disgusted that he's still touching me. Everything about him disgusts me. I thought I had experienced the apex of suffering last night. I thought that was the worst nightmare I'd have to live through. But I was so wrong. This is the real nightmare.

I jerk away from him, and without having the slightest idea where I'm going, I run away. My mind is hazy with hurt. With rage. I want to disappear. Get as far away from him as I possibly can. Far away from this place that can only bring back crushing memories.

"Ness! Fuck, stop!" he shouts from the room, but I'm already down the stairs.

I see Thomas's keys hanging on the hook by the front door, and in a fit of madness, I grab them and run out the door. I start the car and hit the gas, peeling out at top speed. I don't want to be caught. I don't want to be touched. I don't want to be seen. I don't want anything anymore.

I drive for endless, aimless miles. My phone rings constantly, and all I do is cry. I cry bitter tears that I can't hold back. The image of Shana naked in our bed materializes in front of me. Thomas's clothes tossed around the room. Cocaine on the bedside table. He told her. He told her about our fight, about the problems we had. He even told her that I love him. Then they got high together, and then they had sex. He… my Thomas…in our bed with someone else. I'm crying so hard that my vision blurs, and without realizing it, I'm veering into the other lane. A car honks and almost hits me. I steer hard to the right. The tires screech, and for a second, I think I'm screwed, but then, fortunately, the wheels get a grip back on the asphalt, and I emerge unscathed. The other car too. The panic that seizes me afterwards is so intense that it forces me out of the car immediately.

I press my hands to my chest in an attempt to calm my breathing. I'm wheezing so hard that it feels like my lungs might burst at any moment. Some passersby stop their cars and ask if I'm okay, if I need to call someone for help. With my legs and arms shaking, I tell them that I'm fine. "It's all right," I tell them and myself. At least I can stand upright. It was just a big scare. Just a huge lapse on my part that could have had much worse consequences. I could slap myself. I lean back against the car door and breathe deep as I run my hands through my hair, pulling it back. I look up toward the sky, which is blanketed in grayish clouds. The first drops of rain start falling, bathing my face and hair.

I glance around, trying to get a bead on where I am. When I figure it out, I nearly burst out laughing. It's a nervous laugh. Hysterical. Despairing. I ran away from the frat house because I wanted to get as far away as possible from Thomas and anything that might remind me of him. And then my subconscious or whatever the hell else had me driving in circles until it brought me right to a place that is more him than anywhere else. I'm just outside of Chip Ross Park, at the trailhead that leads into the woods. The woods where his tree house is hidden.

When I'm able to breathe regularly again, I get back in the car and decide to park it in a lot not too far away. Then I step out. I lock the car with the remote and start off on the trail. I don't know why I'm doing it, but I am doing it.

I walk on, undaunted, arms wrapped around myself, rain seeping into my clothes, until I reach the tree. Our tree. Drops of rain run down my cheeks along with the tears as I lift my head up to the look at the little house above me. I'm not going up. I'll stay down. I sit down on the ground, pressing my back against the tree's trunk and pulling my knees up close to my chest as cold shivers wrack my body. And it's here that I allow myself to be overwhelmed by despair. By the pain that bursts forth with all its strength. Memories run through my mind like stills from a movie. And they hurt. They hurt so bad that the only thing I can think is that I wish I never met him. I wish I never talked to him. I hate him. I hate him terribly. He promised me that he'd never do that to me. He promised. And like a moron, I believed him.

I don't know exactly how long I stay at the foot of the tree, but when I see the sun going down, I realize that it's getting late. Part of me doesn't want to leave. There are so many memories tied up in this place, and I'm not ready to leave them behind me. But I have to. Everything I experienced with Thomas—good and bad—has been blown apart in the worst way. I gave him everything I had. I tried to save him in every possible way, to get close to him, to know him. Right up until the end, I hoped that despite the challenges and the differences between us, we would eventually be able to find a way make it work.

But some things simply aren't meant to be. The two of us are one of those things.

I pull my phone out of my pocket, seeing about ten missed calls from Thomas. I trash them all, feeling a sense of déjà vu. I broke up with Travis because I found out he cheated on me. I ran away from him and ignored his calls, just like I'm doing now with Thomas. Is this what I am condemned to do? To relive all of my life's mistakes like I'm in a damn time loop?

It's pathetic. My whole life is.

My fingers scroll through my contacts, looking for a number as if they have a mind of their own. There's no reason to do this. I'm messed up. That's the only reason I have.

"Vanessa?"

"Hi." My voice is low. Without emotion. I almost don't recognize it anymore. "I need you to come get me."

"Did something happen?"

"Yes."

"Where do I go?"

"Lester Avenue."

"I'll be there."

"Thank you. Thank you so much, Logan."

Twenty-Seven

MY HEAD LEANS AGAINST THE window. My sodden clothes cling to my skin. Every now and then, my body is shaken by a sob. The soft light of the streetlamps passes me by as I stare up at the sky. It's black. Starless.

"Tell me what happened."

I keep looking outside and don't answer. I touch the leather of my bracelet with my fingertips. His bracelet. The more I touch it, the more nausea fills my belly.

"If you don't want to tell me, that's okay. You'll do it when you're ready. Should I take you home?"

No. That's the last place I want to go, because Thomas will be looking for me there. And I don't want to be found. Maybe that's why I called Logan of all people. He's the last person Thomas would think of. I shake my head almost imperceptibly, aware that Logan is looking to me for an answer.

"Okay," he says, confused. "Where to, then?"

"Wherever you want. It doesn't matter," I say apathetically, watching raindrops smash into the glass and then slide away.

Silence falls inside the car. We meander around for a few hours with no specific destination, moving deeper through the dark and deserted streets of the city. Exhausted, I close my eyes, but all I can see is the two of them, naked in bed together. I can hear the words he spat at me last night. The cold way he dismissed me.

"I don't love you. And I never will."

Logan stops the car, and the change in motion wakes me up.

I lift my head. "We're on campus," I note in an expressionless voice. I asked him not to take me home, but that's exactly what he did. Why doesn't anyone ever listen to me?

"Look." Logan takes his hands off the steering wheel. He puts one on my thigh with a level of intimacy that I didn't grant him. But I don't push it away. I don't have the strength. Instead, I just stare at his hand as he continues to talk. "We've been around and around in the last three hours. I'm nearly out of gas. And you seem really shaken up. Your clothes are soaked, and you're pale. You need to take a hot bath and get under the covers, because you're shivering. I don't know how long you've been like this, but you're going to get sick."

I don't argue because he's right. I've been shivering since I got into the car. I've been shivering for a long time, actually.

"So I'm taking you home now, whether you like it or not."

"Okay, fine," I answer, nodding slightly.

Logan stops near my building and tells me to go inside while he goes to look for parking. I pray I don't find Thomas lurking somewhere waiting for me, but my prayers are in vain. There he is, sitting on the floor with his back against the door to my suite. It's almost eight in the evening; how long has he been here? He looks horrible. Anguished. And I shouldn't even care even a little bit. I'm the injured party.

He sighs in relief the moment he looks up and sees me. He leaps to his feet and, in two strides, comes to me and grabs my arms. But I back up, slipping out of his grasp.

"Jesus Christ, where have you been? I've been looking for you all day! I used GPS to find the car in a parking lot a few miles from here; some people at the gas station told me they saw the car go off the road!"

I pull the keys out of my pants pocket and throw them at him. He catches them on the fly automatically. "Your car's fine."

"I don't give a fuck about the car. I just want to know what happened. Are you hurt?" He tries to take my face in his hands, but I dodge him.

"You can't touch me. You can't do it ever again," I demand, making him stumble back. The elevator doors open behind me. I can tell that Logan is here by the way Thomas's face goes hard. He lunges for him immediately, but I manage to get in between them and push Thomas back. Thomas returns to the fray, towering over me, though he is careful not to actually touch me. I'm not his target; Logan is.

"Fuck off," he warns Logan through gritted teeth.

"I'm here because she wanted me here," Logan answers from behind me.

Thomas stares down at me. I can read a mixture of incredulity and anger in his expression. "Get rid of him. We need to talk."

Where does he get the balls to give me orders after everything he's done?

"No. We don't have to do anything anymore. You told me everything you needed to last night. And after this morning, if there's anyone who needs to fuck off, it's you." I turn my back to him and take Logan's elbow, gesturing for him to follow me. I know perfectly well that this is going to enrage Thomas, but I don't care.

I don't even have time to get my key in the lock before Thomas is grabbing my wrist to stop me. Then, everything happens too fast. I see Logan moving closer to me, as if intending to free me from Thomas's grasp, and I see Thomas grab Logan by the collar of his shirt and slam him ferociously against the wall. It's a horrible bit of déjà vu.

"Touch her again, and you're finished," Thomas tells him, an inch away from his face. The veins in his neck are throbbing. His voice is so low. Rough. So devoid of emotion that he doesn't even sound human.

Logan, however, remains unintimidated and merely gives him a mocking smirk. He knows that things between Thomas and me have changed, and now he wants to provoke him. Under different circumstances, I'd get angry and tell him to leave. But I hate Thomas so much right now that I have no intention of stopping Logan. In fact, his brazenness inspires my own. I jerk Thomas back with all the strength that I have and jab a finger at him.

"You have no right to treat him like that! You have no right to show up here and pretend you want to talk to me, and you no longer have any right to make a scene like this. So just leave and get out of my life!" This time, I open the door without any interference. I take Logan by the arm, and before Thomas's confused and impotent eyes, I slam the door right in his face.

Thomas yells my name as he pounds his fist repeatedly on the door. His blows are so hard that I'm afraid he's going to break the wood at any moment. Fortunately, we hear a campus security officer intervene and, with no small amount of effort, force Thomas to leave the dorm, shouting threats and curses as he goes.

I close my eyes, let out a sigh, and, with a voice full of shame, I turn to Logan. "I'm sorry you got mixed up in all of this. For the umpteenth time. You always end up getting hurt."

Mortified, I look at the wrinkled collar of his navy-blue sweater, which brings out the color of his eyes.

"It's okay, don't worry about it. I'm fine." He smiles reassuringly at me. But I feel anything but calm or reassured. My pulse is racing, my breathing is labored. I hurt. I hurt like hell.

"If you don't mind, I'm going to go take a shower. I really need it."

"Sure, go for it. I'll stay here."

After showering and putting on the thickest pajamas that I have, I sit down with Logan on the sofa. He's waiting for me with a mug of hot tea in his hands. He gives it to me as soon as I sit down. "I took the liberty of using the kettle I found in the kitchen. It'll be good for you to drink something warm. Are you feeling a little better?"

I shake my head, clasping my hands around the hot mug. I take a sip of tea before looking at Logan with tear-filled eyes and answering, "It's going to be a while before I feel better."

He lays his arm along the back of the sofa and moves closer to me. "What happened? Would you like to tell me about it now?"

"What happened is that I keep falling in love with the wrong guys. All wrong..." I take a long breath, doing my best not to fully burst into tears again. "I fall in love with them, and they destroy me." From the regretful face he gives me, I can tell that there's no need for me to add anything else. I put the mug on the coffee table in front of us, closing my eyes and brushing back my hair. I see the same scene I've been watching on loop since this morning. I'll never be able to scrub it from my mind again. And then his eyes... Thomas's eyes, so full of desperation, begging me to believe him. The same eyes, the same desperation that I just saw in the hall before Logan arrived. Before I yelled at him to go and kicked him out as harshly as I could.

"I knew he was going to hurt you sooner or later," Logan murmurs, troubled.

"I never thought he'd be able to hurt me this much," I admit, my gaze locked on the floor.

"Hey." Logan touches my cheek, brushing a tear away with his thumb. "You don't deserve this. These tears..." He rubs another one away, bringing his face closer to mine. "With me, you wouldn't have cried."

"Logan..." I whisper, my vision blurry. Then I put my hand over his and move it away from my face.

"It's okay. I'm not asking for anything. It's just that sometimes I regret not trying harder." With one finger, he strokes the back of my hand. We stare at one another in silence as the thoughts spin uncontrollably inside my head. I've been pushing Logan away all this time because I was afraid of undermining my relationship with Thomas. A relationship that has just been as undermined as it's possible to be. And now Logan is right here, and he's being so sweet and considerate that I wonder how I ever could have treated him so poorly before.

"Is there anything else I can do for you?" he asks, bringing me back to my senses.

I shake my head. "You mean on top of everything you've already done? No, but thank you. Thank you for not even hesitating to come get me. And for driving me around town and making sure I got home. I'm sorry I called you out of the blue like that. I'm guessing you had your own things going on, and I—"

He interrupts me. "You don't need to be sorry or even thank me. I did it because I wanted to."

I give him a grimace that I hope can pass for a smile. Then I stand up, preparing to walk him to the door, and he follows me.

"Call me if you need anything, okay?" he advises me. I nod but I'm not very sure it was a convincing one. He tucks a strand of hair back behind my ear. "I mean it," he insists, looking closely at me.

"Don't worry, I'll be okay." I stand up on my tiptoes to hug him. I keep on holding him, for perhaps a few seconds longer than necessary. With my chin pressed into his neck, I can smell cedar. My fingers interlace around the back of his neck, caressing his honey-colored hair. And I'm aware of the mixed signals that I'm sending him, but I don't stop. The truth is, I want to prove something to myself. That I can feel anything, even the slightest bit of emotion, through all the pain. I want to so badly. But I can't.

I feel his hands slide down my back and grip my hips. Then his lips are brushing my earlobe. "Do you want me to stay?" he whispers into my ear. I understand immediately what his question means. I don't say yes. But I don't say no either. I slowly back away from him, lowering myself down on to my heels.

We just keep staring at each other for a few moments, until Logan cups my face in his hands and kisses me on the lips. I remain perfectly still. And he must have noticed that his kiss isn't being returned because he takes a half step back. "S-sorry, I shouldn't have done that." He rubs his eyes with his right index finger. "It's just that—"

I don't let him finish the sentence. Instead, I grab his face with my hands and pull him into me. I kiss him in a way that hurts me, that makes me feel soiled. Like my whole body has been covered in slime. But I pretend that isn't how it feels. I close my eyes, hoping to banish the feeling of repulsion that is taking over my body. Repulsion at the knowledge that the lips I'm kissing don't belong to the man I love. The tongue that entwines with mine is not the tongue of the man I love. And then these hands that push me back against the sofa are not the hands of the man I love. The man I want. The man I feel like I belong to.

But the little voice inside my head reminds me that man doesn't belong to me anymore. He doesn't want me. He doesn't love me. And the pain of it is too much for my heart to hold.

I don't know how, much less when, but I find myself lying down on the sofa with Logan stretched out on top of me, his hands creeping up under my shirt, approaching my bra.

This disgusts me.

Horribly.

But I don't stop him. I keep kissing him. I keep hurting myself. I throw myself into it, hoping that the disgust will overcome the hurt. Or maybe I'll just get to the point where I can't feel anything at all anymore, and then the pain will vanish too. That's what I want—what I need.

A tear dribbles down my face, and my stomach twists as Logan undoes his belt, whispering against my lips, "You want to do this?" Even now, I don't stop kissing him. I don't answer him. And he apparently reads my silence as an invitation to keep going, because he unzips his pants and pushes them down his thighs. Then he begins to pull mine down as well.

His groin, covered only by the thin fabric of his boxers, presses against me, and I feel my gorge rising. In an instant, that small flicker of lucidity that I have been trying to extinguish roars back to life and forces a reaction. I don't want to do this. I don't want him. I want him to go away. Right now.

"Logan, wait, stop it," I murmur, but he doesn't seem to hear me. He continues to kiss and bite at my neck forcefully.

"L-Logan, stop, I don't want to."

He moves to kiss me again, but I turn my face away. I try to push him away, pressing my palms against his chest, but it doesn't work. Panic seizes me as he tries to stick his hand inside my panties. I summon all my strength and shove him as hard as I can, making him tumble off the sofa. I stand up immediately, pulling up my pants, adjusting my shirt, and hugging myself protectively, as though the clothes I'm wearing aren't enough to cover everything he was about to take. And which I was about to give him.

"What is wrong with you?" He gets to his feet, hair disheveled, cheekbones reddened, and lips swollen from kissing.

Another retch prevents me from answering and forces me to rush to the bathroom, where I vomit. Logan comes after me, trying to pull back my hair, but I push him away roughly. I want to yell at him that he shouldn't have gotten so close to me, he shouldn't have touched me like that on the sofa. The sofa where, just a few days ago, I was lying with Thomas. But I know that I let him. I let him because I wanted to feel empty inside. So empty that I no longer felt anything else.

"Please go away," I sob.

"Vanessa, I'm sorry, I didn't mean to... I thought that... I mean... you..." He gestures vaguely, out of breath.

"I said get out!" I scream, and I don't care right now if I hurt him or used him or made him mad. I don't care about anyone anymore. Not even about myself. Especially about myself.

I sit on the bathroom floor with my back against the wall until I feel an urgent need to get under the boiling jet of the showerhead and scrub every trace of his touch from my body, as though the water could somehow wash away the memory of what just happened. I lather up my bath puff and scrub every inch of skin in an almost obsessive fashion until it hurts. Then I crouch down, hugging my knees to my chest, resting my cheek on top of them, and letting the water pound down on me.

Was I really about to make that kind of mistake? Having sex with Logan in a futile attempt to stop thinking about Thomas, if only for a second? To forget...? I shake my head, disappointed in myself, because apparently this is just what I do. Throw myself into the arms of the first man who comes along every time I get my heart broken. Though even as I think it, I know. I know that it was different with Thomas. Because I wanted him; I wanted him more than I've ever wanted anything. It's always been like this with us, and that's exactly why I can't pick up the pieces of my shattered heart now.

When I wake up, I have no idea what time it is or what the weather is like outside. My blinds are shut, and darkness swallows me. I just lie there with my hands on my stomach, unmoving, staring up at the ceiling. Although I have lost the will to do just about anything, I do feel that one more step has to be taken before I can put a definitive end to this whole story.

I get out of bed with a certain reluctance. I take out my phone, and the lock screen informs me that that it's three o'clock on Sunday afternoon. I call Matt, and after a few rings, he answers with a concerned tone. "Tell me you're okay!"

I walk to the kitchen, where I turn on the tap and fill a glass to the brim with water. "I've been better," I answer in a monotone. "But that's not why I called you. I want to know if Thomas is at the frat house or not."

"Right now?"

"Yeah, now. Some of my things are still there. I need to come get them, but I don't want to see him."

I hear him let out a long sigh, and I imagine him scrubbing a hand over his face. "No, he's not. But you two need to—" I hang up on him because I don't want to hear anything else.

I drain the glass of water and get dressed, throwing on the first wrinkled sweat suit I can find in my closet. Then I grab one of the boxes left over from my last move. I put on my shoes, pull up the hood of my sweatshirt, and decide to also slip on a pair of sunglasses to hide my swollen red eyes from the world.

When I get to the frat house, Matt opens the door and lets me in. I don't miss the worried look he gives me when I take off my sunglasses and lower my hood.

"You look terrible."

I glare at him. "Don't worry, you won't have to look at me for long. I'll be out of here in a hurry. This place makes me sick."

"I didn't mean to offend you, sorry. I just…I don't like seeing you this way."

"Yeah, well, me neither. Did you tell Thomas I was coming?"

"No."

"Good. Just to be clear, if you do that, I swear to God I will slash all your tires." I'm more serious than I've ever been, and without giving him a chance to respond, I brush past him and go upstairs. The moment I step into Thomas's room, I can feel a squeezing sensation in my chest. Memories of yesterday come crashing down on me with all the intensity of a gut punch, while the smell of Thomas lingers in the air. I can feel it clinging to my clothes, which makes me want to tear them all off and burn them.

I take a few seconds to look around the room, which is just as I left it. It looks like he didn't step foot back in here again. The empty whiskey bottle is still on the desk. Remains of white powder still dust the bedside table. And the bed is unmade. That bed…God, I can't look at it. I close my eyes, take a deep breath, and steel myself. The sooner I get started, the sooner I can leave.

I set the box on the desk and start filling it up with the few things I left here. A few clothes still folded in the drawer, some books on the bookcase, including the philosophy textbook that I let Thomas borrow in the hopes that it would be useful for him. A bottle of perfume from the bathroom cabinet. I stare at it before bringing the atomizer to my nose and sniffing. It brings back the memory of when we went to the mall together for the first time, the same day I moved into the frat house. He resisted at first, surly as always, but then I gave him my best pleading doe-eyed look and managed to convince him to go with me. And in the end, we left with Thomas loaded down with bags and me triumphant, with a pistachio ice cream cone in hand. He picked out this perfume. I had been torn between a cherry-scented one and a vanilla one. But Thomas, tired of my constant indecision, grabbed one with notes of raspberries. That was the right one for him because, he said, it reminded him of my freshly washed hair. So not even waiting for my approval, he went up to the checkout and bought it. He even had the cashier gift wrap it and tie a ribbon around it. That made me smile. What kind of gift could it be if I already knew what it was?

Thomas, laughing, told me that I ought to appreciate it because he wasn't going to do anything else like that for the next hundred years. It was a beautiful moment. And this perfume will always remind me of it. Maybe I shouldn't put it in the box. The fewer things I have to remind me of him, the better off I will be.

I leave it on the desk, next to the small wooden box where Thomas keeps his steel rings. I open it instinctively. I touch the rings, scattered around haphazardly, and press them between my fingers before bringing my hand to my chest. It's as though by doing this, I can hold on to a part of him one last time. Say a final goodbye to him, in my own way. And what a paradox it is that this is where our story ends, right here in this room where it all began. In this room...

I shut the box, and eyes blurred by tears, I notice the leather bracelet tied around my wrist. Another gift from Thomas. I get goose bumps when I think about the things he said to me when he tied it on my wrist, the weight that gesture seemed to carry, the importance he seemed to have settled on me. I'm just about to untie it, when the door behind me swings open suddenly and then closes again with a thud that makes me jump.

When I turn around, Thomas is looking me up and down with bloodshot eyes, breathing heavily, his face weary and waxen. Then he spots the cardboard box and demands, "What...what are you doing?"

"What does it look like? I came to get my stuff." I grab the box and try to lift it, but he holds my wrists and guides it back down to the desk. The anguish in his eyes is palpable.

"You're not taking anything." He shoves his hand through his hair. "Are you trying to drive me crazy? I didn't sleep a wink last night knowing you were with him! And now you show up here with no notice and grab your stuff. What next? Are you going to go off the grid and end things without giving me a chance to explain?"

"Explain?" I laugh in a hysterical way. "There's nothing to explain! It's all too clear!"

He grabs my arms, and I hate how warm and comfortable my body feels at his touch. This is the kind of comfort I needed last night. The kind I still need today, because it represents a cure for all that ails me, but at the same time, it's the source of all those ills. Joy and damnation. Roses and thorns. How do I overcome that kind of conflict? How do I *want to* overcome it?

"I didn't sleep with her, Ness; you have to believe me! I don't remember touching her or letting her in; I don't remember any of what she told you!"

"Only because you had too many drugs in your system to remember anything!" Anger vibrates in my chest as I pull roughly away from him.

"Christ, how could you ever think that I would do that to you? Look at me, for fuck's sake; I'm destroyed!"

"You?" I exclaim indignantly. "You are destroyed?" I yell, shoving him back. "I" Another shove. "Am." Another. "Destroyed!" I continue to rain blows on him, but he does nothing to stop me. "I trusted you! I trusted you! I put my heart in your hands, and you...you crushed it! Do you think that's my only problem? Whether or not you slept with her? You told her about the two of us, damn you! You made me feel stupid for having feelings. You looked me right in the eye and told me that you would never reciprocate those feelings! You hurt me, humiliated me, and mocked me! Do you seriously have the gall to come to me and tell me that you're the one who is destroyed?" I'm crying again and breathing hard. I didn't want to cry. I didn't want to be weak in front of him. But I can't control the pain—it controls me.

I turn my back to him and grasp the edge of the desk. "I was prepared to be everything you needed, Thomas. All of it. Your shoulder to cry on, your heart, your voice. But you threw it all away instead." I sniffle, wiping away tears. "But that doesn't matter because I made mistakes of my own."

"It's not your fault..." Thomas's voice is broken, and his eyes are glistening. Seeing him like this throws me off balance, but I can't let it affect me.

"Of course it is, partially." My throat gets tight as I try my best to hold back more tears. "You told me over and over again in every way you could that you aren't made for that kind of thing. You never were.

But I didn't want to hear you. And now look where my stubbornness has gotten us."

Thomas falls down on the foot of the bed in defeat. "It's not your fault. It's my fault, only mine. I never wanted any of this for you."

I heave a sigh and answer. "It doesn't matter anymore."

"Yes, it does," he growls, getting to his feet. "It fucking matters to me."

A bitter laugh floats out of my throat. "So did it matter when you called me a delusional idiot for hoping for something more with you? Did it matter when you were an inch away from my face telling me that you'd never love me and calling me pathetic for even thinking of it? Or when you told me that the only reason you got with me was because I kept throwing tantrums? Did it matter when you kicked me out of this room like a stray dog? Or when you found yourself in bed with someone else the next morning?" My shouts hang in the air between us, leaving us both momentarily speechless.

"You said our relationship is constantly foundering, and you know what? You were right. I realized that over the last month, I've put so much energy into trying to save this, but in the end, I was destroying it all along. I never should have let it get this far. You and I are poisonous to one another."

"Don't say that."

"It's the truth. This was a mistake. The night you asked me to come with you to the frat house, I should have said no."

"Stop," he begs me, but I keep going.

"I should never have kissed you. Asked you to stay with me. Tried to ease your pain. Fooled myself into thinking I could be enough for you. Because it's clear to me that no one will ever be enough for you."

"You were enough for me from the first moment I saw you," he confesses in a weak whisper.

"That's not what you said!"

"I know what I said!" In a fit of rage, he hurls all the objects off the desk onto the floor. The empty bottle shatters into a thousand pieces with an awful sound. "You were never the problem!"

"Right. You're the problem. You always are, aren't you? Because life has been unfair to you. Because you grew up without any guidance. Without love. You lost your brother. Your mother. Your father. And the only way you know how to deal with the catastrophe inside your head is to destroy everything around you. Because in your insane way of seeing the world, if you have someone by your side, then you have something to lose. Something to ruin. If you don't have anyone...well then, you aren't risking anything. And that's why the idea of being loved scares you so much. Love is the ultimate self-destruction as far as you're concerned. And you'd rather destroy the feeling than risk being destroyed by it. You're really just a coward. And I pity you for that, Thomas. I feel a deep pity for your constant need to shame people who don't fear happiness and aren't afraid to show themselves as they are!"

As good as he is at hiding emotions, I spot something new in his eyes this time. Something different, fragile and vulnerable, which tells me that my words have hurt him like they never have before. But he doesn't flinch. In fact, he stays right there, ready to absorb the next blow, fully aware that he deserves it. And none of this calms me down because hurting him gives me only a momentary sense of well-being.

Fingers trembling, I slide the leather bracelet off my wrist and put in on the desk. "Do whatever you want with this. Throw it away or burn it if you like. It doesn't mean anything anymore." I try again to take the box and leave, but he stops me once more, holding my shoulders and pressing my back against the wall.

"Please don't go."

"Move," I order harshly, glaring at him. Because the despairing way he says those three words is making me waver. And I can't. I don't want to falter.

"No."

"Thomas," I chide him.

He presses his forehead against mine. "I can't, Ness. I can't just let you go like this. I...I need you."

I can feel my heartbeat thundering deep in my throat. My certainty is slipping away. And that's when I decide to do the one thing that will free me of him. It's the only way I'll be able to stay away from him. Otherwise, I know that I'll give in—I know it. But I won't let it happen again.

"I slept with Logan."

I say it just like that, straight out, shooting the lie at him like a bullet from a gun. For a second, everything stops. Neither of us is breathing. A flame ignites in his green eyes, spreading to me. "What the fuck did you just say?" he breathes out, moving his head back a few inches.

"You heard me."

He stares blankly at me for endless seconds. "No. I don't believe you. You're only saying that because you're angry. You wouldn't do that."

"Are you sure?" I raise my chin, challenging him. "I did it with you the night I broke up with Travis, remember? What makes you think I wouldn't do the same thing with him?"

He pulls away as though touching me is suddenly repulsive. His chest rises and falls rhythmically. His jaw muscles tense. "Tell me it's not true." He's standing there, waiting for my reply. But I don't say anything. Not a thing. I want him to suffer like I'm suffering and to hate me the way I hate him.

And then, all of a sudden, Thomas's fist crashes into the wall next to my face. I squeeze my eyes shut, holding in a gasp. When I open them back up, his fist is still there, surrounded by cracked plaster, stained with blood along his knuckles. Thomas's head is bowed, and his eyes are closed.

"Why?" he murmurs, looking up at me. "Why?" he shouts, just inches from my face.

I shrug my shoulders with false unconcern while I die inside. "Because I felt like it. Because he was there and easy," I hiss venomously.

Thomas stares at me, knowing full well it was no coincidence that I chose those particular words. "Take your stuff, and don't come here again," he demands. Then he leaves, slamming the door so hard that the walls shake.

Twenty-Eight

SEVEN DAYS.

Seven days have gone by since that morning. Since the moment time stopped. Seven days without any news of him. Seven days that I haven't gone to class. That I haven't answered any of the phone calls I've gotten. That I haven't opened the door to anyone who comes knocking. Seven days where I've struggled to sleep because waking up is always the same: anguish and tears.

As luck would have it, the Marsy's plumbing broke down, and the bar has been closed until further notice. All I do is lie curled up in my bed. In my darkened room. Wallowing in pain. Letting myself fall into the immense void that Thomas has carved out inside of me. I managed to email Professor Scott and tell him that I had to cancel my tutoring lessons because of the flu. Thank goodness Logan didn't show up anyway.

Tiffany came looking for me every day, but I didn't let her in. The same went for Alex. He bombarded me with messages and calls, asked me if I wanted to spend Thanksgiving with him and Stella, who was visiting. I told him no. I don't want to be around anyone. Not even the people I love. Because I know myself, and I know that I would feel obligated to show them that I'm having the right sort of reaction and not just feeling sorry for myself the way I actually am. I would feel obligated to pretend that I am fine. But I'm not fine. I feel worse with every day that passes.

I know I sound pathetic. After all, it was just a relationship and not even one that lasted very long... Yet, despite all of that, I feel lost without him. And I hate him; I hate him for what he did to me. I hate myself for letting him make me feel this way. Like an automaton drained of any spark of life.

On the eighth day of my confinement, a knock on the door pulls me out of the restless sleep I fell into.

"Nessy, open the door!" It's Tiffany.

I pretend I can't hear her. I roll back over in my bed and close my eyes. If I just don't answer her, eventually she'll leave.

"Just so you know, I brought reinforcements this time!" I hear her yell after a few seconds of silence. "So if you don't open the door, I'm going to have these big strong dudes do it. They're out here cracking their knuckles, ready. Choice is yours."

She wouldn't, I think, staring through the darkness of the room at the wall in front of me. *Or maybe she would?* I huff. The last thing I need right now is a broken door that I have to pay for. I walk over and open the it, only to discover Tiffany and...no one. She played me.

"Finally," she says, with her hand on her hip, before pushing past me and walking inside. "Oh my God." She holds her nose with a disgusted grimace on her face. "Honey, it smells horrible in here."

She puts her bag down on the table, shrugs off her coat, and immediately heads for the window, pulling up the blinds. Then she repeats the same operation with all the other windows in the suite.

"Now you've let the light in," I whimper, covering my eyes with my forearm.

"That's the plan, darling. We're going to bring you back to the land of the living."

"The land of the living sucks," I grumble, rolling over in my bed and pulling the comforter over my head.

"The land of the dead sucks even more, sweetness. The afterlife's got Hitler, Stalin, Josef Mengele..." She grabs the edge of the comforter and yanks it off of me, peering down at me from above. "Makes the living world look pretty good in comparison," she concludes with one of her cunning little smiles. She sits down on the mattress next to me and strokes my hair, the way a mother might with her daughter. Then, with a hesitant little sigh, she says, "If he's the reason you're not coming to class anymore, you should know that he dropped all the courses you two shared."

I am seized by a stabbing pain in my chest so strong that I almost stop breathing, but I pretend I don't feel a thing. I pretend that this news doesn't devastate me at all.

"Well," I swallow hard, lowering my gaze. "At least he did one thing right."

Determined not to keep talking about this subject, I get out of bed and pretend I need to go to the bathroom, leaving Tiffany alone. After I lock myself in, I lower the toilet seat lid and sit down on it. I let out all the air in my lungs and cradle my head in my hands. My heart is beating rapidly, and my stomach is clenched like a vise. He dropped all the classes we had in common. The same classes he had once chosen specifically to be with me. As much as I want to pretend it's not hurting me the way it is, I have an uncontrollable urge to weep. I have to splash my face with cold water several times to keep that from happening. I lean my palms on the rim of the sink, bowing my head and closing my eyes.

Nothing matters anymore.

Nothing matters anymore.

Nothing matters anymore.

I walk out of the bathroom repeating this mantra to myself and find Tiffany intent on changing my sheets. I notice that she's already gotten rid of the crumpled pile of tissues I left on my bedside table. My heart squeezes at the sight of her caring for me like this when I've done nothing but push her away.

"You don't have to do that, Tiff."

"You've locked yourself inside this room for a week, you have a rat's nest on your head, and I don't dare ask when you last took a shower. But you are still my best friend, and picking up a few tissues soaked in snot and misery is hardly the end of the world. Provided you tell me everything that happened, right now."

"It's over. Now you know," I answer apathetically, moving into the kitchen to make coffee.

She follows me. "I know things have been bad since his father died, but how did you two go from that to...this?" she asks, looking meaningfully at my unkempt appearance.

"How...?" I echo feebly. "I don't know how any better than you do. It was a lot of things all at the same time..." I sigh, passing a hand over my face. "One night, shortly after we got back from Portland, Thomas found out from my mother that he was the reason I got kicked out of the house. All hell broke loose. But the worst part was when, like an idiot, I tried to reassure him. I told him I loved him."

"You what?" Tiffany exclaims, her eyes bugging out slightly.

I grab two mugs from the cabinet. "You can't imagine the way he looked at me. He was disturbed, or maybe disgusted. He started saying all these horrible things. Really horrible." My voice falters at the memory.

"I can't believe it... What is wrong with that boy?" Tiff blurts out, furious on my behalf.

I shake my head and add sugar to Tiffany's cup. "Whatever it is, it's no longer my concern. He stopped being my problem when I found him in bed with Shana."

"What?" she says in a menacing growl. "No way, that is not possible."

I stare at her, more serious than ever. "It is though. I saw them with my own two eyes."

She stands there just staring at me with her mouth open. "You caught them?"

I nod. "The morning after we fought, I got a text from Thomas. He asked me to come to the frat house because he needed to see me. He said it was urgent, and I got scared and ran over there like a dummy."

"Hold on a sec," Tiffany interrupts. "He asked you to come see him? That feels like a setup."

"Exactly. I was too shocked at the time to really think about it, but now that it's been a few days and my head is clearer, I've come to the conclusion that Shana had to be the one who sent the message from Thomas's phone." I pour every last drop of coffee into the two mugs. Then I take a sip and continue: "When I got there, he was still asleep. And when he woke up and saw me, he was truly surprised. He didn't seem to have any clue why I was there. She, on the other hand, was awake and had the triumphant look of someone who has finally won."

"It was that bitch! She ambushed you!"

I stare down at the mug in my hands. "I should have known those texts weren't from Thomas. But either way, he *was* there with her. I can't absolve him of that. And then there's the other thing: He's started using hard drugs again."

For a moment, we're both silent, staring into space. Then Tiffany says, "I can hardly believe it; this feels like some surreal story."

"I know, but it's the awful truth."

"So Logan had nothing to do with it?"

My head snaps up. "Logan? Why do you ask about him?"

"Because last week I saw him leaving the cafeteria and he was in a bad way. He had a black eye. I thought…"

I freeze. "W-what?"

Tiff nods her head, which tells me everything I need to know. I feel my legs give out, and I grab on to the kitchen counter with both hands.

"Honey, are you okay?" she asks, putting a hand on my shoulder.

Oh God, what have I done? "N-no…I…I think I've screwed up big time."

"What does that mean?"

Breathing heavily, I begin to pace and fan myself. "I told Thomas that I slept with Logan."

"You slept with Logan?" she shrieks. "What the hell is wrong with your brain?"

"No! I mean, we did kiss, and then he…" I pause, thinking back on that moment, and I feel the same nauseous feeling rising again. "But then I stopped him," I confess, without going into too much detail. I think I hear her whisper something that sounds like, "Thank God!"

"So you just told him that out of spite?"

"I told him that because I was suffering! I was angry, and I wanted to hurt him! It was stupid, I realize that, and I regretted it the moment I did it, but I didn't think…" I can't get air. "I–I didn't even think for a second about the consequences my words could have for Logan. I should have anticipated it; I should have protected him, and instead…"

"Okay, okay, calm down. It's not your fault."

"Of course it is! If I hadn't lied, Logan wouldn't have a black eye right now."

"Thomas shouldn't have gone and hit him, no matter what! Especially not after the things he did himself."

"I have to call him; I need to know if he's okay." I grab my phone out of the drawer in the bedside table. I call him but, after the sixth unanswered ring, I hang up in frustration. "He's not picking up!"

"Maybe he's busy?"

"He's going to hate me, Tiff. He'll hate me forever," I rave desperately.

"Okay, that's enough." She pulls the cell phone out of my hands and puts it on the bed. She takes me by the shoulders and looks me right in the eye. "You don't need to worry about him right now, okay? In fact, you don't need to worry about anyone except yourself."

"I'm fine," I answer in a small voice, unable to meet her eyes.

"Oh, you're fine? Is that why you haven't been coming to class and you've lost weight?" she notes with a hint of reproach, folding her arms over her chest.

"I'm getting notes for my classes and keeping up with the studying. There's no need to worry about my weight, because I assure you I'm eating just fine."

"Rice cakes don't count." She looks pointedly at a half-empty bag of them left open on my desk. "Listen, you're broken, and I get it. You put your heart and soul into the relationship, it went tits up, and that sucks. It really, truly sucks. But you can't wither away like this. I won't let you. So we're getting out of here."

"I don't want to go anywhere," I tell her, more brusquely than I want to.

"Well, too bad. That's exactly what we're going to do. Even if I have to drag you out of here by your hair, which I will absolutely do. Considering that, I suggest you go take a shower, because God knows you need it. And then we're going out."

Reluctantly, I admit defeat and do as she tells me. Because I know my friend, and she is possibly the most determined person in the world. If she's decided that she's going to get me out of this room today, then nothing is going to get in her way.

After washing my hair and putting it into a low ponytail, I put on a baggy sweat suit that, judging from the look she gives me, Tiffany does not approve of. For once, though, she lets it go, just pursing her lips and shrugging. "You ready?" she asks me, pulling her coat back on and swinging her purse over her shoulder.

"Where are we going?" I ask listlessly.

"To the spa." She smiles at me. "I'm about to give you the most relaxing day of your life."

"It's eleven in the morning; don't you have classes?"

"Not today. Today, I'm all yours." Grinning broadly, she grabs me by the hand and pulls me out of my apartment.

During the car ride, Tiffany tries to make conversation, and to keep her from feeling awkward, I fake a smile as she tells me about a bizarre incident that happened in one of her classes. Then I pretend to be interested as she lists all the things we're going to do once we get to the spa. I pretend like I don't feel like there's a knife stuck in my chest. Like I'm not alone. Or empty.

"Hey, hon, we're here." Tiff jostles my arm slightly, bringing me out of my thoughts.

I unbuckle my seat belt, and when I step out of the car, I find myself in front of a luxurious edifice that I've never seen before. "What is this place?"

"It's one of the hotels my dad uses for business. By which I mean when he's fighting with Mom and needs a place to spend the night, he comes here instead. He bought shares in this chain and is also a member of the golf club. I know all of this because he's been forcing me to learn this stuff for a month, so we'll charge today to his account. Consider it a fair compensation for my apprenticeship." She smirks.

I look around, shrugging my shoulders—what can I do but agree?

The receptionist, who is dressed to the nines, welcomes us with a wide smile. She has a quick chat with Tiffany before handing us two bags full of everything we'll need for the spa, including maps of the place and menus with a description of all the services on offer. We spend the rest of the day in the thermal baths and saunas in between getting hot stone massages and manicures. After some initial resistance, I agree to wrap the day up with a visit to the in-house hair salon.

Tiffany decides to touch up her hair color, while I fall back on a simple revitalizing hair mask. And while Tiff focuses on reading a fashion magazine, I just stare blankly at myself in the mirror. I can't deny that today was pleasant, and I love Tiffany for trying to cheer me up. For a while there, she even succeeded. Too bad all it took was a young couple walking by, beaming at one another as they cuddled, for the memory of Thomas to hit me and the pain to overwhelm me, somehow even stronger this time.

Everything starts to feel flat again. Colorless. Thin. I wonder if this feeling will ever go away, or if this is just what awaits me now, a bland world, devoid of hue and texture.

"Hey, Billy," I say suddenly, turning to my hairdresser. He's been bustling around with creams and colors while my mask is setting. He comes to me and puts a hand on my shoulder.

"What's up, hon?" he asks with a warm smile.

"I want a cut."

He goes still, looking at me in the giant mirror in front of us. He chuckles, but when he sees that I'm serious, he falls silent.

Tiffany closes her magazine with a snap. "A cut?"

I nod. And repeat firmly, "Yeah, a cut. And color." They both keep staring at me, but I don't give up. I stretch out my arm to point at the reflected image of a poster behind us. "I want that. Like what that model has."

I watch as a crease appears on Billy's forehead as he looks at the reflection. Then, still bemused, he replies, "Okay. I can do that."

I breathe a sigh of relief, pleased and nervous at the same time. The last time I cut my hair, I was ten years old. I went with my father to the barbershop, and Alex, who always tagged along with us, convinced me to get a bob. I listened to him only to bitterly regret it and sob like a maniac because I wanted my hair back. Ever since then, I've only trimmed it once in a while. As for the color, that doesn't bother me. I've been dyeing my hair for years.

Once the job is done, the result is more satisfying than I imagined. It's a layered and slightly choppy style that hits right at my clavicle. My hair remains jet black at the roots, but from about midway down, it fades into a light gray that matches and highlights the color of my eyes. I walk out of the salon proud of my decision. Tiffany might be even more thrilled than I am because she can't stop telling me how great this new carefree look is.

It's already evening by the time we get back to campus. Tiffany invites herself to dinner by ordering McDonald's for the both of us. I don't object because I realize she doesn't want to leave me alone. It's the same reason she arranges our dinner on the coffee table in front of the sofa and puts on an episode of *Shameless*. The moment it ends, she turns to look at me and asks softly, "Hey, how are you feeling?"

I give a long sigh as I clean the salt and oil off my fingers with a napkin. "If you want the truth, not good."

"I know." She takes my hand and squeezes it affectionately. "I can tell."

"But it was nice to spend the day with you at the spa; it really was," I offer sadly. "I wish...I just wish I was handling this whole situation better. That's what I really want."

"There's no one right way to handle pain, honey. And you don't have to do it all alone; we can do it together. And I promise you that this is going to pass. I promise that you are going to laugh again and feel good again, like you did before him. Before my brother, even before your father." Her voice is full of sincere hope. But I have lost all my hope.

With my eyes downcast and my heart broken, I murmur, "I'm going to end up like her."

"Her?"

"My mother."

"Oh, please. No, no way." She chuckles.

I look up at my friend. "Yes, actually, I will end up exactly like her. Disappointed and cynical."

"What are you talking about? You're not going to be like her at all. You're going to find someone who will love you and make you happy the way you deserve. Or maybe you won't find someone. I mean, whoever said you need a man by your side to be happy? You'll find your true happiness here"—she presses her hand against my heart—"on the inside."

I feel a lump in my throat. "But that's my point; I'm not sure I can do that anymore. The problem isn't just Thomas; it's me. Everything has been bad for too long now. I may be a good student, but I don't have any plans for the future, while everyone around me has a clear path they're on. Look at you; you're continuing your criminology studies while you work with your father. My entire family has turned their backs on me. With men, I do nothing but screw up... I feel like I've lost myself, and I don't know exactly when it happened, but it did happen, and now I don't know how to find myself again."

"You do know. Your head knows; it's your heart that's refusing to see. Stop everything for a minute. Focus on that moment, the moment when you lost the most important thing. The moment when you felt the earth go out from under your feet. Focus on that, and then go from there. Reconstruct your life from the pieces left behind, and you'll find yourself again, you'll see."

Her words touch something deep inside me. I ruminate over them for the rest of the night, while Tiffany gives me a warm hug goodbye, when before leaving she suggests that I come back to class this week, our last week before the holidays. I think on her words in the shower and when I lie in bed. I think about them for hours, until I watch the first streaks of dawn appear. Finally, it's clear to me. It is perfectly clear to me where I need to go to start over.

The next morning, I wake up with a determination and motivation that I thought I'd lost forever. I have a goal in mind, but I plan to go after it only once I've discharged all of my responsibilities. Specifically, passing the exams required to move on to the next semester.

I force myself to go to every class all week, and I realize with no small amount of pain that what Tiffany told me about Thomas is true. He's withdrawn from all our shared courses. Alex, on the other hand, is always waiting for me on campus, and he does everything he can to make sure I'm okay. We don't have much time to spend together, however, because he finishes his exams two days before me and leaves immediately for New York to celebrate Stella's birthday.

On Saturday morning, after having taken my last exam (philosophy), I decide I'm not going to waste any more time, and spring into action. I jump out of bed. I put on jeans, a sweatshirt, my Converse, and a heavy jacket. On autopilot, I grab an elastic band to tie up my hair, but feeling it between my fingers, I remember that I've cut my hair, and I feel almost sorry. For the first time, I get the slightest twinge of nostalgia for my very thick, very long hair.

I get my largest duffel bag out of the closet and start haphazardly stuffing clothes into it. I zip it shut. Then I get out my wallet and check that I have enough cash. I also take a quick look at my ID and travel documents, making sure nothing's expired. Then I put on my woolen hat and walk out of my apartment.

I move hastily through the halls of the student dorm, fully aware that I look like I'm on the run. Fortunately, it's seven forty-five in the morning and practically no one else is around. I call an Uber to take me off campus and straight to *his* old house. The one where Mrs. Gorman now lives, an elderly widow famous in the neighborhood for her tasty lemon meringue pies.

When we stop in front of the house, I feel a chill remembering the last time that I was here. I remember feeling unwanted, almost like an intruder.

My stomach is in knots as I ring the doorbell, and a few moments later, Mrs. Gorman opens the door. Her hair, pulled back with a clip, is even whiter than it was the last time I saw her. "Hi, Mrs. Gorman, do you remember me?"

When Mrs. Gorman bought this house three years ago, I visited her every now and then. She doesn't have any children, and her husband's dead, so I felt bad that she spent so much time alone. But after I started college, my visits unfortunately got fewer and farther between. I feel a little guilty showing up here after a year and a half just to pry some information out of her.

"Oh, do I remember!" she says enthusiastically, peering at me through the glasses balanced on the tip of her nose. "How could I forget those big gray eyes? Come in, dear, come in." She waves me inside and forces me to sit down at a kitchen table laden down with cookies and breakfast sweets. I must have interrupted her.

"I know it's really early. I hope I didn't disturb you, Mrs. Gorman," I say, taking off my hat.

"Of course you didn't! And, for goodness' sake, call me by my first name." She grabs the coffee pot and pours its contents into a mug before handing it to me. "Black, no sugar, am I remembering right?"

"You remember perfectly, Dorothy. Thanks, I really needed this." I smile at her before taking a long sip.

She sits down next to me and grabs some shortbread cookies, putting them on a napkin and sliding it under my nose. My stomach is locked up tight, but I know she'd feel bad if I don't at least try one. So I force myself to take a bite.

"It's been a while since I've seen you. You've become a young lady." She tenderly touches my cheek with the back of her wrinkled hand. "Are you doing well?"

"Yes, thanks," I lie, chewing on my lip. If I recounted some of the recent events of my life...poor woman, she'd probably have a heart attack.

She gives me a careful once-over; then her eyes land on my bag, and her forehead creases in a frown. "Are you going somewhere?"

I lower my gaze to the bag as well. "Sort of."

"Aren't you in school? You're not going to tell me you've dropped out, are you?"

"Oh, no. Don't worry, Dorothy. I took my last exam yesterday, and today is the first day of winter break."

"Oh, that's wonderful. And where are you headed?"

It takes me a moment to answer because a lump is blocking my throat. I swallow the last bit of cookie, dab the corners of my mouth, and say, "To Montana." I swallow before adding: "I want to find my dad."

The first few times I came to visit Dorothy, I'd told her about the separation, about Bethany and my father's baby. I explained how Bethany hated me so much that she didn't want my father to have anything to do with me. I only found out they were moving by pure chance. My father and I hadn't talked for a while—little by little, he stopped calling and quit taking my calls. But sometimes, on my way home, I would walk past their driveway, just to feel a little closer to him. One afternoon when I was doing just that, I saw a sign on their lawn with the words For Sale printed on it. I remember feeling completely devastated. I ran to the door, howling like a maniac, looking for my father.

But it was Bethany who opened the door and told me about their imminent move to Montana. I was so shocked and angry that I just stormed away. I didn't understand how my father could possibly have made such a huge decision without even telling me. Sometime later, I went back to ring the doorbell again, hoping that I was wrong. But it was Dorothy who appeared in the doorway, and my father really was gone. He left me alone with my mother, to live a life without him. He, who had always been my fixed point, my anchor, was abandoning me with an ease that completely felled me. Did I really matter so little? I burst into tears on the porch, and Dorothy invited me into her home for the first time.

Grateful to her, I came back to visit frequently in the following days. During one of those visits, Dorothy confessed to me that she'd found my father's new address. It happened by accident when she'd gotten a letter for my father and contacted him to have it forwarded to his new house. I refused to write it down, though. I was too angry. I didn't want to know anything about him anymore.

But now things are different. After hearing Tiffany's advice, I feel like I have to face all of my demons if I ever want to feel good again.

Dorothy is surprised for a moment. Then, without batting an eye, she gets up from the table with slow, weary movements and heads for the entryway. I track her with my eyes and watch as she pulls a crumpled piece of paper from a chest of drawers. "I knew this moment would come, sooner or later." She returns to me and, smiling sweetly, presses the note into my hands. "The address is right here."

Twenty minutes later, I'm at the airport. The panic that grips me as I stare at the flight information boards is directly proportional to the size of this place. It's the first time I've ever set foot in an airport in my life. And I'm doing it alone. Without the slightest idea of what is waiting for me. My throat is dry and my breathing is labored as I fan myself with a one-way ticket to Billings, Montana.

Part of me can't help but think that I'd feel better if Thomas were here. More secure. More protected. Ready to face what comes. But he's not here. And that's not what I really want. I can be enough. I want to—and I have to—learn how to be enough.

When my phone rings, I answer without even checking who it is, because I can't tear my eyes away from the boards.

"Hello?"

"You finished all your exams and I'm proud of you, but don't think you're going to get away from me that easily. We're going Christmas shopping this afternoon!"

"Tiff..." I murmur, unable to add anything else.

"I'll swing by after lunch, so be ready. I don't want to hear any excuses."

"Uh, I...I can't."

"Why not? Don't tell me you're back in bed!"

"No, I'm...I'm at the airport."

Silence falls for a few moments while I imagine her blinking in surprise.

"I'm sorry, what?"

"In ten minutes, I'm getting on a flight to Montana."

Again, there is a very long, very anxious silence. "Did you by chance hit your head recently?"

"I know it sounds crazy. But I've thought a lot about what you said to me the other night. About needing to reconstruct my life, remember?"

"Sure, but what does that have to do with Montana?" she asks, unsettled.

"It has to do with Montana because that's where my father lives."

"Oh..." she says loudly, as if everything has suddenly become clear to her. "I forgot about that."

"Yeah."

"Wow, I get it. And what are you going to do when you get there?"

"I don't know." I sit down in a flimsy chair, letting out all the air from my lungs. "Honestly, I haven't the faintest. I don't have a plan. I just want to talk to him. I want to ask him why he left, why he stopped reaching out to me."

"Montana isn't exactly next door, though. It's kinda wild to go by yourself, especially at the last minute like this."

"I'll be careful. I'm sorry I'm telling you this over the phone, but I didn't want to talk about my plan before it came together. And then everything happened so fast this morning, and before I knew it, I was standing here with a one-way ticket in my hand."

"Why a one-way? Nessy, just how long are you intending to be gone?"

I take a deep breath. "I'll be back by the start of next semester. After winter break."

"Three weeks?"

"I know it's a long time, but I feel like I really have to do this. I feel like I need to take some time for myself, no matter how it goes with my dad. I need to get away from all the turmoil here in Corvallis."

"Aha!" I hear her swear under her breath. "I knew he was behind this insanity somehow. Goddamned Collins. I swear, I'm gonna kill him. I'm actually going to kill him this time! Yes, you dick, I'm talking to you! You're a dead man, you hear?" I can hear her yelling from far away, like she's pulled the phone away from her face for the moment. And then my heart stops at the idea that she might actually be addressing Thomas. That he's right there, a few feet away from her.

"Hey, Tiff. Listen, I don't want you to be mad at him. He hurt me, not you. And please believe me when I say that he's not the only reason I feel like I need to do this. It's a combination of everything. You were right, I need to find a way to start myself over again. And I can't do that if I'm standing still in the same place while everything goes to hell around me. If I don't do it now when it's vacation and school is closed, I don't know when I'm going to get another chance."

Tiff answers after a few seconds of silence. "Please just tell me you know what you're doing."

"I do."

"Are you truly, truly sure about this, Nessy?"

"I am. It's not just a whim, I promise. I want to do this. I need to."

Another prolonged silence. So prolonged that, at a certain point, I start to wonder if she's still on the phone. "You there?"

"You have to call me every day. I want to know every move you make, understand? If you go to the grocery store, you tell me. If you hit up the pharmacy, you tell me that too, got it?"

I tuck some hair behind my ear, chuckling softly. "Got it."

"Okay, then. Leave, go to Montana. Put the pieces of your life back together, and then you come back here. To your home. Because I can deal with that hair-gelled blond dolt Alex being gone, but not you. I love you, and remember, keep me updated on everything."

I smile. "I promise I will. And I love you too."

Twenty-Nine

THE FLIGHT WAS ALMOST TWO hours. I was tired as hell, but I still didn't get a wink of sleep—too much adrenaline in my body. When we landed, I grabbed my bag and got into a taxi, giving the driver the address from the note that Dorothy had given me. Now I'm here, sitting on these worn taxi seats. The roads we're traveling on are windy, and the car bounces over potholes while I look out the window at the snow-covered Montana countryside and the white hills in the distance. It must have snowed last night.

I find myself jiggling my feet and chewing my thumbnail, two gestures that I repeat in a nearly mechanical fashion. Neurotic. The taxi driver glances at me several times through the rearview mirror, his forehead wrinkling. He's probably wondering what's wrong with me.

"We'll be there in just a few minutes, miss." He smiles at me, probably thinking to reassure me, but my heart only beats more wildly as he says it. There's a roaring in my head. I haven't seen or heard from my father in more than three years. And he certainly isn't expecting to see me now. I'm insanely afraid of what might happen, and I'm starting to think it wasn't such a good idea to come out here.

The driver stops at the entrance to a private road bordering a series of town houses all decorated for Christmas. He explains to me that the address on the paper is on this street but that, because the area is restricted to residents, he has to leave me here. I pay the fare and get out of the car.

I drop my bag on the ground, raising a puff of snow that settles on my Converse, dampening them immediately. Maybe wearing canvas shoes wasn't my brightest idea. But I don't pay it much mind; I'm too busy staring around in bewilderment.

Despite being the largest city in the state, here on the outskirts of Billings, the air feels clean, and the sun warms my face even if the wind is biting. I look up at the sky, an almost blinding blue that is only accentuated by the blanket of snow on the ground. I shut my eyes for a few seconds and inhale deeply; the air smells like winter and sunshine.

Okay, I'm here. I can do this.

I sling my bag over my shoulder and set off. The street is wide and deserted. I walk along for a few feet, listening to the sound of snow crunching beneath my shoes until I find a mailbox in front of one house with the words *Turner and Clark* written on it. My heart begins to pound in my chest again.

This is the one. This is his house.

There's a little snowman standing in the front yard, with a carrot for a nose, two chestnuts for eyes, a little wool hat on top, and branches for arms with a child's gloves stuck on the ends. I realize, with a pang in my heart, that my father probably made that snowman with his son. The son for whom he shoved me aside.

I've just ginned up my courage and walked toward the house when a disheveled gray cat hurls itself at my feet, purring against the toes of my shoes. A tiny smile escapes me as I crouch down. "Hey little guy, where'd you come from? Aren't you getting cold just hanging around out here?" I scratch him under the chin, and he seems to really appreciate it. He lingers there, his belly bared to the air and his eyes closed, just rubbing his head against my shoe. "Are you lost?" I check to see if there's a collar around his neck, but I don't spot anything. I guess he's a stray. I pet him for a few minutes, just observing the house in front of me.

The porch is decorated with strings of lights, which are already on even though it's broad daylight. There's a back patio that looks immaculate, and a well-tended garden. A child's toys are scattered around in the snow. My head throbs at the idea that this child is my brother. The last memory I have of him is from one afternoon in the late autumn when I was at my father's house. Dad had gone to take a work call, and Bethany and I were left alone in the kitchen. Even though we weren't speaking to each other, I offered to help watch little Liam if she had work to do as well. That particular afternoon, the baby kept tugging on the hem of my jeans to get my attention. I barely had time to pick him up, intending to put him in his high chair, when Bethany shoved me aside and took over, glaring angrily at me.

I got the message loud and clear: I wasn't to touch the baby. Liam stared up at me with big bewildered eyes while he gummed his fingers with the kind of innocence that only children have. I was so hurt by the rejection that I just grabbed my things and ran out so I wouldn't burst into tears right in front of her. I was only fifteen and trying to be accepted, an effort that she always nipped in the bud.

I snap out of those thoughts with a shrug. I look down at the cat and smile again. "I really do have go, you know?" I stand up, and he stretches before jumping up onto a large rock nearby and posing there like he's trying to sunbathe.

I, on the other hand, take a huge breath and approach the door. I hesitate a moment before I ring the doorbell. What if she opens the door? She'll probably chase me off, and my journey here will have all been for nothing.

Anxiety eating away at me, I put my ear to the door in an attempt to try to listen for my father's voice on the other side. There's a bit of confusion, but I think I hear both voices, albeit muffled. Enough of this. Without overthinking it, I reach out and ring the bell. Then I step back immediately, like the doorbell has shocked me.

The wait lasts a couple of minutes, and I feel like I'm dying the entire time.

I rub my palms on my jeans, chewing aggressively on the corners of my lips. Then, I hear the sound of heavy footsteps drawing closer and closer, and there's suddenly a part of me that feels a strong urge to flee. The other parts, however, are practically imploding with the need to see who it is.

Then the door opens, and my father appears in the doorway. For a second, I can't breathe. He seems bewildered. I know I've changed since he saw me last. I was smaller; my hair was still my natural color and a lot longer than it is now. Plus, I'm sure that of all the people in the world, I'm the last one he expected to find on his doorstep. The moment he registers that the face in front of him belongs to his daughter, he grabs onto the doorjamb like he's about to faint.

"Vanessa..." he whispers, his voice barely audible.

"In the flesh," I breathe.

"What...what are you doing here?" I watch him swallow hard.

"It's been a while since we've seen each other," I babble through an arid throat, wringing my hands. "I thought it was time that I pay you a visit."

The shock on his face slowly turns into a frown. He sticks his head out the door, checking down one side of the street and then the other. "You're alone?"

I nod.

"How did you get this address?" he asks, even more shocked.

"Mrs. Gorman. The woman who lives in your old house," I stammer, wondering why he didn't invite me inside. He didn't ask how I was either. Or any one of the many goddamned things you should ask your daughter who you haven't seen in three and half years.

"Aren't you going to let me in?" I prod him hesitantly.

He rubs his forehead, and I can tell from the look on his face that he's struggling. Maybe he's even embarrassed.

"Look, this isn't a good time," he whispers, casting several glances over his shoulder. Probably worried that Bethany's going to spot me. "If you had called or told me you were coming, I could have—"

I interrupt him, scowling. "How?"

He looks at me like butter wouldn't melt in his mouth. "What?"

"How could I have possibly told you? I haven't heard from you in years. And your old phone number hasn't worked since you left."

He rubs his thumb along his eyebrow, thicker and whiter now. Just like his hair, which is thinning a bit at the temples. In all other respects, he looks like the man I remember, the one who was my hero. Maybe with a few more wrinkles at the corners of his mouth. Broad shoulders, a bit of a belly, and his usual casual clothes: a flannel shirt and worn, baggy jeans. Yet, I can't feel that bond that once tied us together—that made us inseparable.

My father opens his mouth to answer me, but Bethany gets there first, her disembodied voice making him jump. "Peter, who's at the door?"

He turns suddenly and, breathing rapidly, answers, "Uh, um, no one, sweetie. Just the neighborhood kids asking me to help shovel." Then he steps out, quickly shutting the door behind him.

"The neighborhood kids?" I repeat to myself, disturbed. I'm his daughter. The daughter who he abandoned without looking back. The daughter he seems to have forgotten about entirely. I came hundreds of miles to see him, and he's hiding me from her like I'm some kind of monster.

I can't believe it. It feels like I've traveled back in time. Back to when he walked out and picked that woman over me. And even though I'm older now, it hurts just like it did the first time.

I stare down at my snow-sodden Converse, feeling like a fool for hoping that this encounter would go any other way. For hoping that he might welcome me with open arms. Or that he might be even a little happy to see me again after all this time. For a moment, I even stupidly deluded myself into imagining that he was behind the anonymous check sent to pay for my tuition. I let myself be tricked by the fantasy that, despite all this time and distance, he still wanted to be around me.

"I pictured this differently." Now my voice is a barely audible murmur.

"I'm sorry, what was that?"

I raise my head. "I don't know what I was thinking, convincing myself that coming to see you was the right thing to do." The bitterness in my voice is palpable. "Pretend I didn't do this. Pretend I was never here." I turn my back to him and start to walk away without another word.

"No, no, hold on. Please," he begs, wrapping his big hand around my forearm. "I'm sorry. I'm terribly sorry, but I need time to process this. I'm not asking you to leave, but right now, I can't give you the time I would like to. But tomorrow I can, any time you want; you can pick. But you have to give me a chance to prepare my family for your arrival first."

His family.

Another punch to the gut.

I give him a look full of resentment. "I am also your family."

He's struck speechless. "Of course you are. But Bethany…she, well, I'm not sure she would understand. Not right away, at least."

Before I knocked on his door, I felt uncertain and afraid; now, I just feel blood-boiling rage. "What is there to understand? I'm your daughter. It's not up to her to decide whether or not I can see you. I didn't come all this way for Bethany; I came here to see my dad. Instead, I've found a person without an iota of backbone or human empathy!" I pull out of his grasp and head down the driveway.

"I'm begging you." He runs to catch up with me, blocking my way again. "I do want to talk with you, hear how you are, how your life is going…"

I snort. "Funny that you want to know all about my life now when you haven't bothered to take an interest in the last three years." My father freezes in place, not saying a word. "Not a single text. Not a single visit. Not even a phone call, Dad. Why? Didn't you ever think about what that was like for me? How hard it was for me to start over all alone? How much it hurt knowing that you moved so far away from me?" The hurt I've been repressing for years breaks its bonds, flooding both of us.

He sighs, rubbing the back of his neck. "It's…it's complicated."

My eyes go wide. "Complicated? You find it complicated to explain why you abandoned me?"

"It's complicated to explain to you right now, under these circumstances," he stammers, spreading his arms wide. Then he allows his head to droop helplessly. "Please come back tomorrow. I will spend every second of my day with you; I will answer all the questions you have."

"If Bethany lets you," I grumble.

"I'll do it, but promise me you'll come back tomorrow," he replies seriously.

I look anywhere but at him, focusing on a fir tree, its luxuriant branches illuminated by the sunlight. I grasp the shoulder strap of my bag while I think about how to answer him.

I'm angry. Extremely angry. And hurt. But the truth is, I traveled all these miles just to talk to him. To understand. If I leave now, I'll be right back where I started. So, swallowing the lump of bitterness in my throat, I answer, "Okay, tomorrow."

The lines on his face relax instantly, and I don't miss the faint sigh of relief he makes. "Thank you." He pauses for a moment, then asks me, "When did you land?"

"Forty minutes ago," I say, checking my wristwatch.

"Do you have a place to stay?"

I shake my head no. He stares thoughtfully at me for a moment before reaching into the back pocket of his jeans and taking out his cell phone. He calls some guy named Ralph and paces back and forth in the street as he talks, eventually wandering away. It's a quirk I recognize. In the past, he would pick up a phone call in the kitchen, and by the time it ended, he would inexplicably find himself in the living room. I have so many memories of my father, and sometimes I wonder if the same is true for him. Does he still keep them locked up safely inside his head? And when he thinks about them, does a melancholy feeling take over until his eyes get teary like me?

After he ends the call, he comes back to me. "I talked to a friend of mine. He runs a ranch about ten-minute walk from here. He has some rooms available, and he assured me that you're welcome to stay as long as you need."

"That wasn't necessary; I could have found a place to stay on my own." It irritates me to see him being so considerate of me now, when, a minute ago, he wouldn't even let me into his house.

He smiles tightly at me. "I'd rather know you're somewhere safe."

"Okay, then," I say, chewing on the inside of my cheek. "See you tomorrow."

He starts to take a step toward me, albeit uncertainly. Maybe with the intention of hugging me? But I don't let him. I leave before he can.

After ten minutes of following the directions on my phone, I find myself at the ranch. There's a girl with slicked-back dark hair wearing muddy jeans and a jacket a few sizes too big for her. She's feeding some goats in the warmth of a stable.

"H-hi, I'm…" I start, trying to get her attention. But then I just leave the sentence hanging there because I realize that I don't actually know how to describe myself. Given the way my father greeted me, I doubt the neighbors know about his past. Even if they do, I don't know how much they know.

"Clark's daughter," she finishes for me, impatient. So he didn't keep me a total secret. That's a small consolation at least.

I sigh. "Yeah, that's me. Vanessa."

She scatters one last handful of goat feed and comes over to me. "Nice to meet you. I'm Beth, Ralph's niece. Huh…" She looks me up and down, tilting her head slightly. "I pictured you differently."

I shake her hand and give her a puzzled look. "Differently?"

"Yeah. More like him, I guess. Daughters usually look like their dads. At least, that's what my grandma always said. But you probably take after your mother."

I nod to appease her as she leads me deeper into the ranch. The only things I got from my mother are my pale complexion and my all-consuming need to control everything. And that's plenty.

"Is Ralph here? I'd like to introduce myself and thank him for his hospitality," I say, walking behind her up a set of stairs.

"He's not here right now, but you'll see him tonight. He should be back in time for dinner."

When we stop at a room on the top floor, Beth explains that the ranch has five rooms in total. Three are occupied at the moment, mostly by families. Still, the mood is pretty quiet. When she leaves me on my own, I lie down on the mattress and stare up at the ceiling. I still feel shaken and troubled by my interaction with Dad. I didn't have many expectations for it, yet I was still disappointed. And that was what I'd been most afraid of.

I send a text to Tiffany telling her everything that's happened, and I update Alex while I'm at it. Then I pull out one of my favorite paperbacks and spend the afternoon reading. Later in the evening, Ralph appears and invites me to have dinner with everyone and get to know them better. I don't say much during dinner. It's all a bit foreign to me, very foreign. I just listen to them talk, and when we're done, I thank them once again for their hospitality.

Before I crawl under the covers, I take a hot shower in the hopes of loosening up some of my accumulated tension. Since I know I'm going to have trouble sleeping, I try to listen to some playlists. But it doesn't help much. My head is just too full of stuff. With a sigh of resignation, I roll over and look out the window.

It's a full moon, and it's so beautiful outside that I can't help but get up out of bed and approach the window to get a closer look at the landscape. The white blanket of snow gleams in the moonlight, even the trees are still snow-clad. The colorful lights on the nearby buildings give off a familiar magical Christmas-y feeling, and in the background, the dark sky is punctuated by millions of stars.

I wonder if my father is looking up at them right now as well. Or if, when he left Corvallis, he left everything to do with me in Corvallis. I close my eyes, feeling a pang in my heart.

Thomas.

The last time I stargazed was with Thomas.

I shouldn't be thinking about him. I shouldn't even allow my brain to veer in that direction. I was doing so good today; I managed to keep him out of my head almost all day.

But apparently all I need to do is realize that I haven't thought about him for memories of him to roar back from my subconscious. The more I try to force myself to banish him, the more he insists upon lingering. It's a vicious cycle that brings me—and has brought me—only more pain.

I breathe out through my nose before grabbing the curtains and pulling them closed. I don't have to let him sneak into my head anymore. And if those damned stars make me think about him, then no more stars for me. No more moon. No more anything.

I go back to bed, and finally, exhausted from fighting him from my thoughts, I fall asleep.

It's half past eleven, and I've been pacing the room for about forty-five minutes now, staring at my phone the whole time. We don't have a precise appointment, but I think this is a more than reasonable time to go knocking on my father's door again. So I gather my courage as well as my coat and head out.

Soon, I find myself walking down his street and ringing his doorbell again. When he answers the door this time, he invites me to come in and sit down, but I tell him that I'd rather go somewhere else.

"Sure, whatever you like," he says, after some initial surprise. "I'll just get my keys and wallet and let Bethany know."

I nod, biting my lip. I've been thinking about it a lot this morning, and while it is true that I really wish he invited me in yesterday, I don't know how comfortable I could have been with Bethany there.

"Where do you want to go?" he asks, shutting the door behind him. From the somewhat stilted way he moves, I can tell he's still quite nervous.

"Anywhere'll do."

"A coffee shop?" he suggests, sticking his hands in his pants pockets.

I nod.

We get into his new pickup and drive to the city center in silence.

Thirty

"SO..." HE SAYS, SOUNDING TENSE, as we take a seat at a table inside the coffee shop.

"So..." I echo, looking around to check out the surroundings. It's a quiet place, not very busy. The smells of coffee, cookies, freshly baked cake, and homemade jams fill the air.

"Your hair looks very nice like that," he begins, in a tone of voice that I suspect he thinks is casual and relaxed. I get the feeling he wants to break the ice, but it's going to take a whole lot more to do that, considering that what's between us is really more of a giant iceberg.

"It's new," I answer impassively, touching the choppy gray ends.

"When you were little, you wouldn't let anyone touch your hair. We had to bend over backward every time just to convince you to let us trim a few inches," he says with a smile.

"Yeah, I remember." I also remember that I loved it when he brushed my hair.

My father flags down a waitress, and we order drinks. He insists on also getting something to eat, and we hand back the laminated menus.

"How was your night?" he asks me.

"Fine."

"And now...?" He sighs. "Are you okay now?"

I nod my head.

He squints at me. "You sure?"

"I've been better."

"Would you…I don't know…maybe like to talk about it?" he asks, looking uncertain and apprehensive.

"No. It's just stupid matters of the heart."

"Oh." He sits up straighter. "I…I didn't know that you…I mean, that you had a boyfriend."

"There's a lot you don't know," I tell him sharply.

He falls silent, looking at me like I just slapped him.

"Touché." He stares down at his clasped hands on the table. I can almost see them trembling. "Listen, I want to apologize to you again. I know I handled your arrival in the worst possible way, but you have to believe me, I was completely caught off guard."

I nod. "Yes, I can understand that."

We are momentarily interrupted by the waitress, who sets our coffees down on the table. Then we're alone again.

He takes a deep breath before making another attempt: "Vanessa, please don't get me wrong, but…why are you here? Did something happen at home? Is your mother okay?"

"Nothing happened, and Mom is good. Or…how she always is, at least," I manage, unable to suppress an annoyed grimace. I take a drink of my coffee, and after dabbing my lips with a napkin, I continue: "Is it really so weird that after you completely disappeared for three years, I felt the need to come looking for you?"

"No, of course not. I'm sorry, I didn't mean to make you think that." He fidgets in his chair as though it's suddenly gotten too small to contain him. "Everything's so difficult…"

"Yes, I actually find it very difficult to understand your choices," I snap. I have no desire to be conciliatory. In fact, I don't think I'm capable of it anymore.

"I must have looked like such a coward to you," he says, almost ashamed. "But I want you to know that things are not always as they seem."

I wrap my hands around my cup. "And what does that mean?"

We stare into each other's eyes for a silent moment. "I never wanted to leave like that."

Although I feel a pang in my heart, I am determined not to feel sorry for him. "But you did. And you never looked back. Which means, all things considered, it must have gone pretty well for you."

He wrings his hands and says, almost breathlessly, "I had no choice."

I stare at him, astounded. "You had no choice but to basically disown Mom and me, abandoning us like garbage on a curb?"

His eyes widen resentfully. Then he shakes his head and averts his eyes, focusing on stirring his coffee. "I wanted to call you, I wanted to come and see you, I wanted you to come see me, spend some time with Liam…but it wasn't possible."

"If you really wanted me, I would have gone with you. I don't think you had a gun to your head."

He bites his lip hesitantly. When he finally breaks the silence, he sounds like each word takes extreme effort. "It was your mother. She stopped me." He says it through gritted teeth.

I leap to my feet, the legs of my chair screeching on the floor. "I'm not going to let you say that about Mom! She's got a lot of flaws, and sure, she was angry and hurt at the time, but she knew how much I suffered because you weren't there! She never would have kept me from you! She never did! You're the one who left; you're the one who chose another family. Trying to shift the blame onto her just makes you a miserable, petty liar!"

"Please believe me," he begs, lowering his voice, probably in the hopes that I'll do the same. "I'm not trying to shift the blame. I just want to be honest with you."

I stare at him, my mouth fallen open. "And why on earth would she do that?"

"Because there are things…things you don't know."

"What don't I know? What are you talking about?" I ask him, sitting back down.

He shakes his head. "You should ask your mother about it."

"Well, as you can see, she isn't here. But I am. So whatever it is, I want to know. And I want to know now. You owe me that much."

"No, Vanessa. I'm sorry, but I promised your mother I wouldn't—"

"I don't care about what you promised her. You're keeping something from me, and don't you think I have a right to know what it is? I'm not a little girl anymore, and I don't need to be protected from the world. I've grown up; I'm an adult now, and I demand to be treated like one."

He doesn't say a word. He faithfully keeps the silence he promised to my mother.

Drained, I make one last-ditch effort. "Dad, please. I'm so tired of dealing with these half-truths. I can't stand it anymore. You're always trying to protect me by keeping me in the dark, and all it does is hurt me even more. I'm saying please; I'm begging you…"

He closes his eyes, heartbroken. "I can't do that to you…"

"Tell me," I demand, grasping the arms of the chair tightly in my hands.

"I don't…" My father loosens his shirt collar, undoing the first two buttons. "I wouldn't even know where to start…"

"You can start wherever you want."

"Before I tell you anything, I want you to know that everything I have done for you and with you, I have done out of love. And that love hasn't changed over time, and it never will. I put everything I had into our family. I tried my best to coparent you with Esther, passing on our values, giving you a good education. I did whatever I could to be everything you could need: a father, a friend, a confidant. All I wanted was to make you happy."

I can feel my saliva drying up and my heart beginning to race. Why does he feel the need to tell me this? I already know all this; I was there with him the whole time. "Where is this going?" I ask, bewildered.

"Have you ever wondered why I chose to pack my bags and disappear from your life like that?"

"Every day."

"Did you ever find an answer?"

"Not one that made sense," I say in a whisper, feeling increasingly uneasy.

"I would never have left you, Vanessa. I was ready to fight; I was prepared for a legal battle. I was determined to request joint custody, anything so I wouldn't lose you. I had a good lawyer, but Esther...she had pictures of Bethany and me. Proof of my adultery. With that kind of evidence, my case would have been DOA. She swore to me that if I didn't disappear from your lives, she was going to ruin me. She would have asked for damages. We're talking about a lot of money here, Vanessa, a whole lot. And with the evidence she had, she could have gotten it. But she wouldn't have stopped there. She would have taken the house, the car, and demanded not just child support for you but alimony for herself as well. She promised me that, so long as I stayed in Corvallis, she wouldn't work to force me to fund her life. She was furious, she felt humiliated, and she didn't want to see me ever again. She didn't want Bethany and me in the same city. She was very clear with me; she was going to bankrupt me if I didn't do what she wanted me to do. Which was to go away forever and, above all else, to cut you off."

I stare at him in disbelief. It feels like someone launched me into another dimension. This cannot be true. It's just a pack of lies on his part. My mother is manipulative, yes, but she'd never go that far. This is pure evil.

"What...? Why force you to leave the city? Why keep you from seeing me? Or even talking to me? She was mad at you, and she wanted to make you pay, but what did that have to do with me? That makes no sense. Despite the evidence of your affair and her all her threats, you still had the same rights as her when it came to me. You could have asked for sole custody. That way, the house would have stayed with you. I could have stayed with you. I would have done it, Dad. I've always been closer to you than to Mom, you know that."

"I couldn't take you away from her," he answered, his voice subdued. "No matter how dirty she played, I never would have done something like to her. It wouldn't have been right."

"It wouldn't have been right to let me live with you? Why not?"

He lowers his head, absolutely wrecked. "Because she's your mother."

"And you're my father."

"No, I'm not."

I am motionless, staring at him, unable to muster even a single word. I'm gripping my coffee cup so tightly that I'm afraid I'm going to break it in my hands. The low murmur around us no longer exists. I don't even know where we are anymore as I try to make sense of what he's just said. Then, stupefied, I loosen my grip on the ceramic mug and look directly into his eyes.

"Funny," I scoff, trying to keep my fingers from trembling. "True, in recent years you haven't exactly lived up to the title, but that doesn't mean that you—"

"Vanessa," he interrupts me, reaching across the table to take my hands in his and giving me a look full of compassion and...dread. "I'm not...not the man you think I am."

My brain is spinning so rapidly that I can't even remember my own name. It's as though I'm just waking up from a nightmare, unable to distinguish reality from fantasy. There's only emptiness. A sense of emptiness that presses in on me until I can't breathe.

"I–I don't think I get it," I swallow, struggling to form coherent thoughts.

"When I met your mother, she had just moved back to Corvallis." He takes a deep breath before continuing. "You had just turned one, and Esther and I made the decision that I would legally recognize you as my daughter."

That confused feeling is back, even stronger than before. Like a flashback in a TV show, I go through every single memory I have of him. I analyze his moves, actions, words. Looking for a single moment in all those years we lived together when I should have figured it out.

But there's nothing.

Not even one moment.

I toss my head. Maybe I'm dreaming. Maybe I never even got on a plane to Montana. We never came to this café. We didn't start talking about the past. I have to be dreaming, because otherwise, it would mean that I've been living a lie all these years. My entire life...it was a lie. His words circle around in my head, chasing each other like an echo. He... he...isn't my father... I can feel my body freezing up, and I force myself to blink several times in an attempt to focus my eyes.

"That's why you've been able to keep away from me all this time, isn't it? You could do it because, deep down...you knew the bond we had wasn't...that it was built on a lie. That's why you chose Liam, because he..." I gasp for breath. "He's actually your son, while I...I..."

"No, Vanessa, don't ever think that. I may not be your biological father, but I raised you and loved you as if I were. And I suffered just like you suffered. But I was forced to go along with your mother's decision, or she would have destroyed my life. She was so afraid that sooner or later, I was going to tell you the truth, and that fear brought out the worst in her. She was trying to push me away because she was hurt and didn't want to see me anymore. She would have done whatever she had to."

"And you'd rather leave me, lie to me, and make me hate you than just tell me the truth!" I shout.

"I stupidly thought it would be easier for you to deal with my abandoning you than to learn such an upsetting truth. And it wasn't just about me either. I had people I needed to protect."

This is all too much for me.

I jump up uncontrollably, looking around in a bewildered way. Then I do what I always do when the world comes crashing down around me: I run away as fast as I can.

"Vanessa!" he calls, following me out of the café.

I stop and whirl around, raising a hand to stop him. "Don't come any closer," I breathe, my voice broken with pain. "Don't." I feel like everything I knew has been stripped away from me. My life, my certainties, my identity. And the worst part is that the person who did it is the same person I loved with all my heart.

"Please, let me help you deal with this. Don't run away," he whispers hoarsely, his eyes bright and imploring.

"Don't run away?" I repeat indignantly. "You and Mom betrayed me. You kept me in the dark for years, about everything! And who knows how much longer you would have continued if I hadn't convinced you to talk to me? Maybe forever," I add angrily. "How am I supposed to continue living my life knowing that there's some man out there in the world who probably looks like me, who has my same blood running in his veins, and he's a stranger to me?"

The way he looks at me, he somehow seems even more disturbed than I am. "This is why I didn't want to tell you."

"Yeah, well, I should have listened to you!"

"Vanessa, please calm down."

Calm down? How am I supposed to calm down?"

"You...you know who he is? What his name is?"

He gives me a heartbroken look. "I never knew a thing about the man. Esther didn't want to talk about him, and I didn't want to pry."

I'm finding it increasingly difficult to breathe as I realize that my life is nothing but a succession of men abandoning me as if I am worthless. And for a moment, I find myself thinking maybe they're right.

Taking advantage of this moment of hesitation, Peter—the man who, until a minute ago, I called Dad—puts his hand on my arm.

"Don't you dare touch me. Don't come after me. Just keep on ignoring me and never contacting me like you've done so far." It's the last thing I say before turning my back on him.

I run until my legs give out. Gasping, I try to pull air into my lungs. I prop myself up on a bench that I cling to as if it's a lifeline while I try to wrestle back control over my rudderless body and mind.

This is just like last time. My hands are sweating, I'm trembling, and I can't breathe. I'm having another panic attack. And once again, I can't control it. I squeeze my eyes shut, trying to concentrate on my agitated breathing. I remember what Logan said, how he told me it was all in my head. That I could control it.

And I try, I really try to control it, but it's stronger than I am. I need someone who is stronger than it.

So in the midst of my panic, I pull my cell phone out of my pocket. After a few seconds, I hear Thomas's voice on the other end.

"Hello?"

My heart skips a beat, and my pulse, instead of calming down, pounds even faster than before. I open my mouth and try to say something, but nothing comes out.

"Hello?" he says, getting irritated. I try to speak again, and I fail, again. My lips are sealed. I close my eyes and rest a hand on my chest. I realize that only now is my breathing finally evening out. It's as though just hearing the sound of his voice, even at an incredible distance like the one between us, is enough to give my body the strength it needs to calm down.

"Ness..." he whispers hesitantly after a few seconds. "Are you there?"

I'm chastened by the sound of my name. My eyes fly open, and I realize immediately that I've made yet another stupid mistake. I hang up, furious with myself. How is it possible that, after everything he's done to me, he's still the first person I look to when I have a moment of weakness?

I slump down on the bench, absurdly hoping that, at any moment, someone will pinch me and tell me this is all just a bad dream. That none of what I was just told is the truth. But the only person who can do that is my mother. Running my fingers through my hair, I decide to give her a call.

"Vanessa?" She answers after a few rings, sounding skeptical.

"Yes, it's me, Mom."

"Vanessa," she says, stunned to hear from me again after weeks of radio silence. "Oh, thank God. I knew you'd call sooner or later."

"I didn't just call for a chat," I press the palm of my hand to my temple because my head is spinning. "I have a specific reason."

"Tell me."

"Do you know where I am?"

"I don't know... At school, I presume?" she says uncertainly, like she struggling to understand. Then she asks me, "Wait, where are you calling from?"

"I'm in Montana."

I hear her dry swallow. "W-what?"

"Billings, specifically."

It's a few seconds before she responds. "If this is a joke, Vanessa, it is in very poor taste."

"Oh, I wish I were joking, but I assure you I'm not."

"Why…why did you go to Billings?"

A few minutes ago, I was still in a state of shock, but now I can feel my anger mounting. She's still pretending, she's still messing with me. "You really can't think of a reason?"

"I don't know what you're talking about."

"I talked to Dad," I declare, deciding to put an end to this farce. "Or at least, to the person I thought was my father."

"Come home right now," she orders a few seconds later. "Do you hear me, Vanessa? Come home," she repeats decisively.

I stare stiffly out into space, my fingers tightly grasping the phone. It's true. It's all true. She's been guilty all along. She's been screwing with me all these years. She let me build up all this hatred for my father; she led me to believe a completely incorrect version of the situation. She talked badly about him and took advantage of his absence right up until the end. She manipulated all of us like puppets for her own ends.

A wave of anger swamps me. I spit in a low voice, "You and I are done." I pause before adding, "Forever."

"Vanes—" she begins, but it's too late. I'm hanging up. I call an Uber instead and hurry over to the ranch to get my bag. I'm so blind with rage that I don't care about anyone anymore: my mother, who keeps blowing up my phone, my father, who comes to Ralph's and begs me desperately to let him drive me instead of taking another Uber. I *shoo* him away aggressively.

I don't know how to deal with a single word of what I've been told. But I know that I'm going to have to. I'll have to find the strength.

He's not my father.

So who is my father?

Where is he?

Why didn't he acknowledge me as his daughter?

Did he ever try to find me?

Is he...alive?

I feel like I'm losing my mind. I put my bag over my shoulder and leave a note on the bedside table thanking Ralph for the hospitality. Shortly thereafter, I'm back at the airport. Yesterday, I was so afraid and uncertain about the idea of seeing my father again, and today I just feel...lost.

I don't know what to do or where to go. Staying here doesn't make sense anymore. Going home is out of the question. I was serious when I told Tiffany that I needed to get away from Corvallis for a little while. Now, after what I've learned, it's the last place I want to be.

I read the departing flights board and see a number of exotic destinations where it would be easy to leave it all behind. I see the names of several other U.S. cities and then... Of course, Vancouver! Alex and Stella must be back in Vancouver by now after their trip to New York. There's no direct flight, but with a short layover in Seattle, I could be there in five hours. Before we parted, Alex promised me that I could reach out to him whenever I wanted. And, right now, Alex seems like the closest thing to family that I've got.

I call him and tell him somewhat confusedly that the meeting with my father went badly and that I really don't want to go back to Corvallis. Before I even have a chance to ask, he's booking a last-minute plane ticket for me. Not to Vancouver, like I was expecting, but to Phoenix, Arizona, where Stella's grandparents live.

When the loudspeakers announce that my gate is open, I get in line with my stomach still roiling, my heart torn into pieces, and the sad realization that I've finally found the answers that I've been looking for all these years.

Time's up here in Phoenix after three weeks. Tomorrow, Alex and I are taking a flight back to school. I don't know if I'm really ready. The first few days here were a parade of depression, pain, new anxiety attacks, and sheer confusion. I suddenly felt like I no longer belonged to anyone.

Like the family that raised me had been snatched right out of my hands, forever. I felt alone, truly alone.

My thoughts often returned to Thomas. The most self-destructive part of me kept insisting that, despite everything, he was the only person I really wanted to be with at this moment. But I stayed strong. I resisted the urge to call him again. I forced myself to remember that, if I was making a list of people who have disappointed, wounded, and betrayed me, he would be right at the top, and for that exact reason, he can never come back into my life again.

Alex, Stella, and her entire family have been so wonderful to me. I probably wouldn't have made it without them. They stood by me, welcoming me unreservedly, but they also knew how to accommodate my need to be alone when I chose to stay up in my room. Even Tiffany did everything she could to help me through this hard time via phone calls and video chats. Maybe it was their love, the knowledge that I wasn't really as alone as I feared, or maybe it was the approaching new year and all that comes with it. Either way, after those first days when I felt drained of all feeling, I started to realize that I had to take my life back. It wouldn't be easy, but I owed it to myself.

So I steeled myself and began to fight a little more each day until, eventually, I found myself watching a movie with Alex and Stella, laughing and joking in what was a real moment of lightheartedness. It was the same lightheartedness that I felt during a family Christmas dinner at Stella's grandparents' house, or when Stella and I spent a whole afternoon working out with a punching bag. I was shocked at just how much built-up tension I was able to release. It was exactly what I needed.

Today, for our last day in Phoenix, we've decided to walk around the downtown area, which is full of stands offering just about everything: food, clothing, antique furniture, even a body-painting station. But it's the stand set up for tattoos that catches my eye.

I stop, charmed by the designs with thin elegant lines as well as the ones in the old-school style. Enthralled, I say instinctively, "I want one."

"You want what?" Alex asks, giving me the same gobsmacked expression as he did when he first saw my new haircut.

"A tattoo," I say again, more decisively. Seeing his uncertain face, however, I begin to question my choice. "Is that crazy?"

"Not at all," Stella answers for her boyfriend. "You know what they say, don't you? 'A little nonsense now and then is relished by the wisest men.'"

"Oh God," Alex says, rolling his eyes. "Ever since we watched *Willy Wonka and the Chocolate Factory*, she's been obsessed with Willy Wonka."

"He's a marvelous character!" I exclaim.

"He's a crazy person," Alex says.

"Still marvelous, though," I answer him with a smirk.

"So a tattoo?" Alex says, getting back on topic.

I nod.

"And what if you regret it?"

"That's not going to happen. Listen, this is our last day of break, and I know when we go back to Corvallis tomorrow, I'm going to have deal with everything I left behind because all my problems are still there. But right now I feel so good, and I want to remember this feeling forever."

"Come on, don't be a wet blanket, Alex!" Stella echoes, grabbing his arm and shaking it a little bit.

"Okay, okay, I'm done," he says, raising his hands in surrender. "After all, you have to screw up sooner or later." He claps his hand on my head, messing up my hair in the way he always does, then nudges me toward the stand.

We examine the drawings on display. I ask about their meanings, but in the end, I let my instinct guide me to a drawing of a rose with all its thorns. It's the mixture of passion and torment, the tattoo artist explains to me, because, sooner or later, lovers always suffer.

"Where do you want it?" the tattoo artist asks me, after letting me into the chamber next to the stand, where there's a bed covered in sterile paper and all the necessary supplies. Alex and Stella have to wait outside for reasons of hygiene.

"Honestly, I haven't thought about it yet. Any advice?" I take off my coat and lay it on a chair while he arranges everything he needs on a tray next to the bed and slightly personalizes the design. The tattoo artist examines me closely. I don't see any leering, just professionalism.

"You've got a good body. We could really do it anywhere. A lot of people have been getting them between their breasts lately, but it's pretty painful. Since this is your first time, I don't recommend that."

"That's where I want it," I say decisively. Pain doesn't scare me anymore.

"All right, then. Come on up." He pulls on his sterile gloves, inserts ink into the gun, and sets it on the steel tray.

In the meantime, I take off my shirt and then, with some hesitation, my bra. I make certain to cover my breasts with my hands, and I admit I'm feeling a little uncomfortable. But he doesn't even look at me, too busy arranging his tools. This calms me down.

I lie down on the bed, and we decide together exactly how high to put the tattoo. Once we've made a decision, the artist wipes the area with some disinfectant and goes over it with a disposable razor in preparation. I just stare up at the ceiling until the only thing I can hear is the hum of the gun as it approaches my chest.

Once the tattoo is done, I admire myself in the mirror, feeling something I've never felt before. He was right, it did hurt, but to my enormous surprise, I got through it. And it was worth the pain because it's beautiful.

The slender stem of the rose, covered in thorns, trails down my sternum while the petals are nestled in my cleavage, just high enough for them to peek out from my neckline. Good grief, I can't believe I just did it. Even just a few months ago, this would have been impossible to imagine. And now I have a tattoo. I smile at myself in the mirror like an idiot.

"Satisfied?" the tattoo artist breaks in.

"Absolutely!"

"Good, would have been a problem otherwise." He grins, proud of his work. Before he lets me go, he gives me some salve, the same kind he applied to the tattoo a little while ago, covering it immediately after with a clear film. Then he tells me how to take care of it in the next few days. I take note of everything, pay him, and tell him again how much I like it. I walk out of the little chamber with a toothy grin on my face. I immediately give Alex and Stella a peek, careful not to move the film around too much. Seeing the looks of surprise and approval they give me, I'm even happier with my choice.

"Your new era has begun, girl!" Stella says conspiratorially.

When I wake up the next morning, the magic spell is over. Alex and I are back home, both of our morales low but each for different reasons. He's already missing Stella while I'm longing for the rare peace I managed to find far away from Corvallis. Far away from my mother. But more than anything else, far away from him...

Thomas.

Winter break is over. Classes start back up tomorrow. And I'm going to see him again. I know I have to stay strong, though. Thoughts of Thomas have haunted me these past few weeks, it's true. But the more days went by, the more I've learned to manage it. I've learned how to keep him out of my head and out of my heart. And I've been working on myself. On my weaknesses, my insecurities. I started atoning for all my mistakes. Because I was well aware that I made a lot of them. I've learned to welcome the hurt, to accept it, and, finally, to get past it.

Now that my whole life has been called into question and everything I thought I knew has crumbled like a sandcastle, I actually feel stronger. More secure. So yeah, I can do this. If I can give up the idea of my father, if I can cut off my mother, then I can also share spaces with Thomas. Walk down the same hallways. This time, I won't be affected. I won't be moved. He no longer has any power over me.

I said these words to myself over and over again on the plane and then in the Uber on my way back to Howell Hall. I spent the evening mentally preparing myself, organizing my books and notebooks, choosing just the right outfit. I continued to tell myself that he has no power over me even as I was lying in bed. I let the mantra lull me to sleep.

And I've continued to repeat it to myself for about a quarter of an hour as I stare petrified at the open expanse of the university campus, surrounded by a horde of students all over the lawns.

But then I feel it, right behind my back.

The roar of a motorcycle drowns out all the other noise and raises goose bumps on my skin.

I can feel it vibrating all the way down to my bones. Like it's calling out for me.

And I know, I know exactly who that roar belongs to.

I know because, suddenly, every inch of earth under my feet starts to tremble. Every form of thought flees my mind. My heart bursts in my chest, and my throat is as dry as the Sahara desert.

It's a reckoning; it's a damnation. Thomas is here.

And I can't keep running away.

PLAYLIST

RECOMMENDED LISTENING WHILE READING

1. "HEATHER" — CONAN GRAY
2. "I NEVER KNEW" — WRB FEAT. MIKAYLA JOSEPH
3. "THE NIGHT WE MET" — LORD HURON
4. "SOMEWHERE ONLY WE KNOW" (COVER) — GUSTIXA AND RHIANNE
5. "IT'LL BE OKAY" — SHAWN MENDES
6. "IMAGINATION" — SHAWN MENDES
7. "LIKE THAT" — BEA MILLER
8. "LOSING MY RELIGION" — BELLSAINT
9. "GANGSTA" — KEHLANI
10. "ONLY LOVE CAN HURT LIKE THIS" — PALOMA FAITH
11. "LIGHT ME UP" — INGRID MICHAELSON
12. "TRAIN WRECK" — JAMES ARTHUR
13. "YOU AND ME" — LIFEHOUSE
14. "FAMILY LINE" — CONAN GRAY
15. "PLAY WITH FIRE" — SAM TINNESZ FEAT. YACHT MONEY
16. "I WANT IT ALL" — CAMERON GREY
17. "BAD LIFE" — SIGRID AND BRING ME THE HORIZON
18. "STREETS" — DOJA CAT
19. "BEFORE YOU GO" — LEWIS CAPALDI
20. "LOVE ME OR LEAVE ME" — LITTLE MIX

KEEP READING FOR AN EXCERPT FROM BOOK ONE IN CARRIE LEIGHTON'S BETTER SERIES

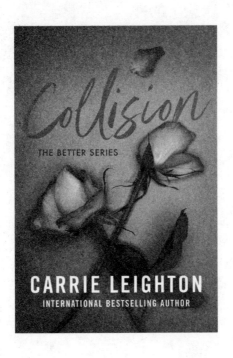

One

CORVALLIS IN THE FALL HAS a special charm. With its little houses, parks, and dense forests all around, it looks like one of those enchanted snow globe landscapes that I used to collect when I was a little girl. The arrival of the first storms makes everything even more magical. Just like now, with the rain pounding violently on the asphalt, the rustling of the leaves in the wind, and the smell of the wet streets. There's no better awakening in the world, to me.

The peace doesn't last long, though, because the blaring sound of the alarm clock reminds me that today is the first day of my sophomore year at Oregon State University. Needless to say, I wish I could keep curled up under the covers a little longer, but after the third beep, Nirvana's "Breed" comes on at full blast, practically giving me a heart attack. I reach over to the nightstand next to the bed, groping for the phone, as Kurt Cobain's voice fills the room. When I finally get ahold of it, I turn off the alarm, pull up my green frog sleep mask, and force myself to open my eyes.

Clutching the phone in my hands, I give in to the urge to check for a message or call from Travis. Nothing. I should be used to it, but it's still a disappointment every time. That's how it always is with him: after every quarrel he goes off the radar for entire days, demonstrating time and time again how little he cares about salvaging our relationship, now on its last legs.

Is it possible to be exhausted before your day even begins?

Reluctantly, I pull myself out of bed and step into my fuzzy unicorn slippers. I gather my messy hair into a loose bun, throw on my fleece robe and inhale the intoxicating perfume of fresh laundry, and walk over to the window in front of the bed. I pull back the curtain, rest my head on the cold glass, and let my gaze wander over the garden path wet with rain.

Travis takes it for granted that I'll be the one to make the first move. But this time I have no intention of breaking the silence, not after what he did. Seeing an Instagram story with my own boyfriend falling-down drunk, dancing and grinding on a bar with two random girls, while I was at home all by myself in bed with the flu, is a kind of pain I wouldn't wish on anyone. When I called him, furious and looking for an explanation, he dismissed me with his usual "Vanessa, you're overreacting," and wisely decided to hang up and not call back again. I spent the entire weekend holed up at home, depressed, drinking ginger tea to soothe my sore throat, reading and organizing books and notebooks to get ready for the first day back at college. But not even FaceTiming with Tiffany and Alex, my best friends in the world, was able to completely erase the memory of that video and the humiliation of being disrespected like that by Travis for the umpteenth time.

The situation has become so consuming that I don't even have the strength to cry anymore. Which is strange, because for as long as I can remember, the only thing I can manage to do when I'm overwhelmed by emotion is cry. In a burst of frustration, I hurl the phone on the bed, massage my face, and compel myself to think of something, anything else, because the alternative is giving me a headache. I'd better start getting ready, I have a long day ahead of me.

After a quick shower, I go back to my bedroom to get dressed, and even though I know it's stupid, I take another little peek at the phone. But once again, no calls and no messages. An unhealthy desire to call him and shower him with insults starts welling up inside of me.

"Nessy, are you up?" My mother's shrill voice snaps me out of those thoughts, along with the smell of hot coffee wafting through the house. It's a little like walking a tightrope between hell and heaven.

"Yeah, I'm up," I respond hoarsely, lifting a hand to my aching throat. The cold from the last few days totally wiped me out.

"Come down, breakfast is ready!"

I let out a big sigh, and still wrapped in my robe and with my hair wet, I head downstairs, hoping I'll be able to camouflage my awful mood. The last thing I need is to be subjected to one of Mom's never-ending lectures where she repeats that I've got to hold on to this one because he's from a good family. Who cares about his mistakes and my suffering—the love my mother harbors for Travis's family fortune is even bigger than the love she has for her daughter. When, two years ago, she found out that I was in a relationship with the scion of an oil company executive, to her it was like winning the lottery.

When I arrive in the kitchen, I find her already ready for the day: a perfectly arranged blond chignon, elegant white palazzo pants, a Tiffany blue button-down, and impeccable makeup, with mascara emphasizing her blue eyes and a light layer of red lipstick on her thin lips. Her innate class always manages to undermine my already scarce self-esteem.

Before I can even say "good morning," she comes at me with a barrage of unsolicited information.

"I left some bills and the checkbook on the entry table; it would be great if you could take care of them today." A little frenetic, she darts over to the coffee maker and pours two cups without interrupting my to-do list. "You have to pick up the dry cleaning, grab something for dinner, and, oh, before I forget," she says, handing me a mug—I listen to her go on, trusting in the coffee's increasing effect—"Mrs. Williams went out of town and asked me to take care of her chihuahua. I told her you would be happy to."

All these orders first thing in the morning put me even more on edge than I already am.

"Need me to do anything else? Maybe mow the lawn? Go see if any of the neighbors need help? Organize a get-together for the homeowners' association?" I look at her sideways, set my phone on the counter, and sit down at the table.

"You know Mrs. Williams doesn't have anyone else she can count on. I couldn't say no to her—how would that look?" She brings her mug to her lips, and after taking a sip, goes on: "And I thought you'd be happy to take care of that little mutt. You love animals."

"Yeah, but that doesn't mean I have the time or desire to do it right now."

"Neither do I," she retorts, oblivious. "When I took this legal secretary job, I didn't know it was going to suck the life out of me. But someone's got to bring home the bacon."

I look at her, suddenly mortified. I'm well aware that since Dad left three years ago, Mom has had to cover all our expenses. I admire her for it, but she forgets that I have a life too, and I can't live it as a division of hers.

"You're right, I'm sorry." I get up and take a box of granola cereal from the pantry and pour some into a bowl. "Taking care of Mrs. Williams's dog won't be a problem. I can take him on a walk before I leave for campus and when I get back. I'll take care of everything, don't worry," I reassure her conciliatorily.

"That's what I like to hear." She pats me on the shoulder, her fingernails perfectly manicured, pale pink. "And please, at least for the first day, try to look a little bit put together."

She drains her mug and waves goodbye unceremoniously with a promise to be back for dinner. I stay in the kitchen to have a little breakfast. I pour some milk over the granola and go sit at the table. After a moment, the phone lights up on the counter: a new message notification. Dropping my spoon into my bowl, I leap up like an idiot to see who it is, tripping on the kitchen mat with granola stuck to my lip.

I'm so pathetic, I deserve to fall face down on the floor. Maybe a good knock on the head is just what I need.

When I realize that the sender is Tiffany, my best friend and my boyfriend's twin sister, I sink into disappointment once again.

I was really hoping to see Travis's name on the screen, but evidently the end of the world is a likelier event.

Hey nerd. Your life's purpose resumes today.

Yeah, I was so excited I didn't get a wink of sleep, I reply wryly.

I'm sure. Listen, I wanted to ask you, practice starts tonight, do you want to come with me?

My eyebrows furrow as I read and reread the message, not understanding. Since when does Tiffany care about sports? Her only interests are the latest trends in fashion and makeup, her weekly salon appointment, and her beloved true crime podcasts. She would never want to waste her time watching some dumb practice basketball game.

Then I realize it's not Tiffany asking me, but Travis, in a despicable attempt to extort information via his sister. What a coward! First, he falls off the face of the earth for two days, abandoning me to total self-pity without even claiming some far-fetched excuse that in all likelihood I would have bought or pretended to. Then he uses my best friend to get to me.

Annoyed, I reply: Tell your brother if he wants to ask me something, he'll have to make the effort to do it in person.

Her reply came immediately: He made me, I didn't want to. You know I'm on your side. I'm coming to get you; we can head to campus together. Be outside at 8. Love you.

I knew it was him. Infuriating! I throw the phone on the table. He made me lose my appetite. I rinse out my mug and bowl and go up to my room. I open my closet, and for a second, I entertain the idea of listening to my mother and wearing something cuter than my usual jeans and monochrome hoodie. I try on a white peasant top with lace trim. It's nice, but looking at myself in the mirror, I notice it reveals too much of my abundant chest. If I wear this, everyone's eyes will be on me, which is precisely what I try to avoid.

I hang the top back up in my closet, concluding that my usual anonymous look isn't so bad after all. I pull on dark blue jeans, slim fitting and high-waisted, and a white sweatshirt that hangs past my bottom—that's more like it. After drying my hair and putting it up in a high ponytail to tame the frizz, I grab my bag and slide in *Sense and Sensibility*, one of my favorite books; reading it between classes will help distract me.

Before leaving the house, however, I glance at myself in the mirror and instantly regret it. The image I see reflected is not pleasant: I'm pale, two violet bags weigh down my bloodshot gray eyes, and my raven-black hair is begging for mercy. I let it down and smooth it a little, but the situation doesn't improve. I throw in the towel and, armed with my umbrella, go out before I lose my mind.

ACKNOWLEDGMENTS

Thank you.

Thank you for giving Thomas and Vanessa another chance. Thank you for waiting for them and for going along with them on their journey thus far. A thorny, chaotic, undoubtedly painful journey, but one full of emotion that I hope has made your hearts pound, coaxed smiles out of you, and—why not?—even caused you to shed a few tears.

Their journey doesn't end here. There is yet one last turbulent, agonizing volume awaiting you.

Yes, you read that right: agonizing.

Because, trust me, everything you've read so far is nothing compared to what is about to happen.

But until that moment, I'm waiting right here for you, in the hopes that you might return to the pages of this story and the lives of these two crazy kids.

See you soon, strangers.

ABOUT THE AUTHOR

Carrie Leighton is the pen name of a young Italian writer who prefers to remain anonymous. An avid reader of romance fiction, she debuted on the Wattpad platform, gaining great popularity in a very large community. When not writing, she enjoys watching TV series. She's author of the Better trilogy: *Collisione* (*Collision*, 2022, Better #1). *Dannazione* (*Damnation*, 2023, Better #2) and *Ossessione* (*Obsession*, 2023, Better #3).

Instagram: @carrie_leighton_
Tiktok: @carrie_leighton